SWEPT UP IN THE TURMOIL OF A NEW ERA, BOUND BY FATE TO FORCES BEYOND THEIR CONTROL . . .

LIEUTENANT MICHAEL DEAN—Once a highwayman, he'd forged a new identity, only to be trapped in the living hell of a convict settlement run by a sadistic tyrant.

ALICE FAIRWEATHER—Betrayed in love, haunted by a terrible secret, she built a bold new life, then risked it to embrace justice's cause.

ROBERT WILLOUGHBY—Exiled from England by his aristocratic father, he used women and discarded them callously—until he met the one woman whose cruelty surpassed his own.

LUCY TEMPEST VAN BUREN—Born with an insatiable hunger for wealth, without a conscience, she'd stop at nothing—even murder—to get what she wanted.

WILLIAM BROOME—Out of the blackened ruins of shattering tragedy, he was determined to carve a new life in the uncharted wilderness—and to share it with the one woman he loved.

THEY WERE THE GLORIOUS AND THE DAMNED,

Other books in **THE AUSTRALIANS** *series*
by William Stuart Long

VOLUME I	The Exiles
VOLUME II	The Settlers
VOLUME III	The Traitors
VOLUME IV	The Explorers
VOLUME V	The Adventurers
VOLUME VII	The Gold Seekers
VOLUME VIII	The Gallant
VOLUME IX	The Empire Builders
VOLUME X	The Seafarers

THE COLONISTS

VOLUME VI OF THE AUSTRALIANS

William Stuart Long

A DELL BOOK

Created by the producers of **Wagons West, Yankee,** and **The Kent Family Chronicles.**

Chairman of the Board: Lyle Kenyon Engel

Published by
Dell Publishing
a division of
The Bantam Doubleday Dell Publishing Group, Inc.
666 Fifth Avenue
New York, New York 10103

Produced by Book Creations, Inc.
Chairman of the Board: Lyle Kenyon Engel

ISBN: 0-440-11342-3

Printed in the United States of America

July 1984

10 9 8 7 6 5

KRI

This book is for Bill Mann, as a token of my gratitude for his many years of patient and almost uncomplaining help and encouragement.

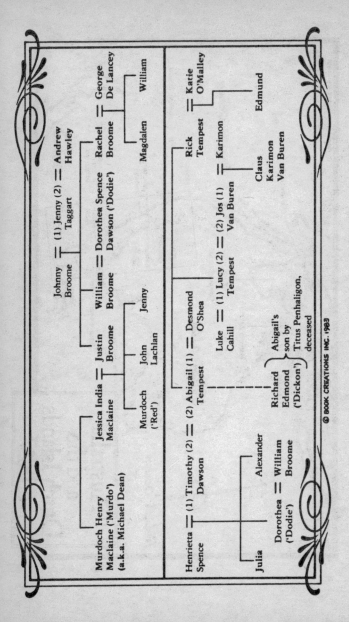

© BOOK CREATIONS INC. 1983

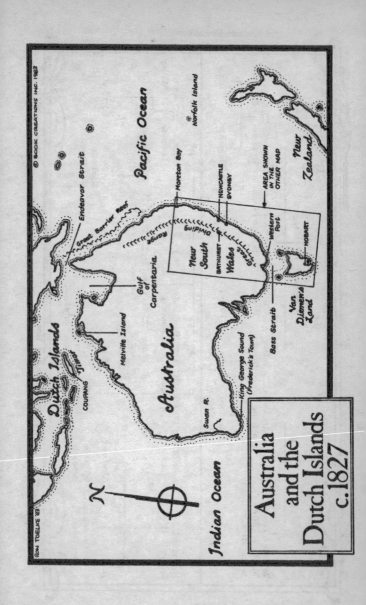

Australia and the Dutch Islands c.1827

RON TOELKE '82 · © BOOK CREATIONS INC. 1982

Dutch Islands

COUPANG TIMOR

Indian Ocean

N

Swan R.

King George Sound (Frederick's Town)

Melville Island

Australia

Gulf of Carpentaria

Endeavor Strait

Pacific Ocean

Norfolk Island

Great Barrier Reef

Dividing Range

Moreton Bay

NEWCASTLE
SYDNEY

New South Wales

BATHURST

Western Port

Bass Straits

Van Diemen's Land

HOBART

AREA SHOWN IN THE OTHER MAP

New Zealand

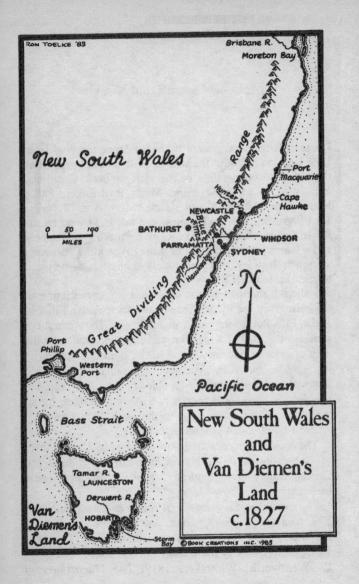

RON TOELKE '83

Brisbane R.
Moreton Bay

New South Wales

Range

Port Macquarie

Cape Hawke

Hunter R.

NEWCASTLE

BATHURST

Blue Mts.

PARRAMATTA

WINDSOR

SYDNEY

Hawkesbury R.

Great Dividing

N

0 50 100
MILES

Port Phillip

Western Port

Pacific Ocean

Bass Strait

New South Wales and Van Diemen's Land c.1827

Van Diemen's Land

Tamar R.
LAUNCESTON

Derwent R.

HOBART

Storm Bay

© BOOK CREATIONS INC. 1983

Acknowledgments and Notes

I acknowledge very gratefully the guidance received from Lyle Kenyon Engel in the writing of this book, as well as the help and cooperation of the staff at Book Creations, Inc., of Canaan, New York: Marla Ray Engel, Philip Rich, Glenn Novak, Carol Krach, Mary Ann McNally, Jean Sepanski, Pamela Lappies, and last but by no means least, George Engel. All have given me encouragement and a warm friendship that has made my work as an author so much happier and less lonely than it was before I teamed up with BCI.

I should also like to put on record my appreciation of the help given me by my British publisher, Aidan Ellis, of Aidan Ellis Publishing, Ltd., in publicizing The Australians series in the United Kingdom, and my appreciation of the help always so patiently given in the domestic sphere by my spouse and Ada Broadley. My thanks also to the editorial and sales staff of Doubleday Pty. Australia and the many relatives and friends in Sydney who made me so welcome on my recent visit to the land "down under," where I lived so happily for eight years.

The main books consulted were supplied by E. G. Glover of Sutton-in-Ashfield, Nottinghamshire, England, and Conrad Bailey of Melbourne, Victoria, Australia. These included:

The Australian Encyclopaedia: Angus & Robertson, 1927; *The Convict Ships:* Charles Bateson, Brown Son & Ferguson, 1959; *History of Tasmania:* J. West, Dowling, 1852; *Description of the Colony of New South Wales:* W. C. Wentworth, Whittaker, 1819; *The Macarthurs of*

Camden: S. M. Onslow, reprinted by Rigby, 1973 (1914 edition); *Australian Explorers:* Kathleen Fitzpatrick, Oxford University Press, 1958; *History of Australia:* Marjorie Barnard, Angus & Robertson, 1962 (copy kindly supplied by Bay Books); *Australian Historical Monographs,* various titles, edited by George Mackaness, Ford, Sydney, 1956; *Port Arthur:* M. Weidenhofer, Oxford University Press, 1981; *National Portraits:* Vance Palmer, Melbourne University Press, 1940; *In Step with Sturt:* Swan and Carnegie, National Library of Australia, 1979; *For the Term of His Natural Life:* Marcus Clarke, Lloyd O'Neil (reprinted 1970); *The Beginning:* Appleyard and Manford, University of Western Australia Press, 1979.

Other books were kindly lent by Ian Cottam, and research in Sydney was undertaken by Vera Koenigswarter—my other invaluable Sydney researcher, May Scullion, having sadly died last year.

This book, like the others in the series, is written as a novel, with fictional characters superimposed on the narrative. Their adventures and misadventures are based on fact and, at times, may seem to the reader more credible than those of the real-life characters with whom their stories are interwoven. Nevertheless, I have not embroidered or exaggerated the actions of any of them, save where it was expedient to dramatize these a little in order to avoid writing "dull" history.

Part One

THE DISINHERITED

CHAPTER I

"They are here, Papa," Emily Willoughby announced nervously. "Robert and James. They await your pleasure."

Rear Admiral Sir Francis Willoughby looked up from the book he was reading to eye his daughter with stern disapproval. "Have I not bidden you to knock before you enter my study?" he demanded with asperity.

In awe of him, as she always was, and fearing his temper, Emily apologized. It was of no use, she knew, to tell him that she had knocked; he would not admit that it was his increasing deafness that had prevented him from hearing her. His disapproval, she also knew, was of her brothers, not herself, and although she could only guess at the reason for it, she supposed it was Robert's conduct that had, once again, aroused their father's ire.

Since his court-martial two years ago and his dismissal from the King's service, Robert had been in such constant trouble that, for some time past, he had been forbidden the house, his name never mentioned in the admiral's presence. For this reason, Emily had been surprised to learn—only the previous day—that he had been sent for, and poor young Jamie with him. Though what Jamie could have done to warrant the peremptory demand for his attendance passed her comprehension.

She sighed. Her younger brother was thirteen, a cadet at the Royal Naval College in Portsmouth and nearing the end of his first year of study there. The excellence of his reports had hitherto afforded their father great satisfaction, and she could not help wondering why—in the middle of term—the boy had been required to make the long journey to Plymouth at what had evidently been very short notice.

"Shall I bid them come in, Papa?" she inquired, anxious to make her own escape. She would be sent out of the room, of course, once the boys presented themselves. Whatever their father had to say to them would not be for her ears, but she was accustomed to her exclusion, as a female, from purely masculine affairs and, in particular, from matters pertaining to the naval service.

Since her mother's death eight years ago, she had kept house and supervised the upbringing of her two younger sisters, but, Emily reflected, conscious of a faint twinge of resentment, her duties and responsibilities had been purely domestic and largely taken for granted. She had never enjoyed her father's confidence or merited the interest he had shown in his sons . . . until, that was to say, poor Robert's fall from grace.

When news of the findings of the court-martial had reached him, her father had wept, and, for the first and only time that she could remember, he had permitted her to witness his grief and to offer him consolation. Since that moment, however, he had held more aloof from her than ever, as if ashamed that he had allowed her to sense a weakness in him that she had never previously imagined he possessed.

"Shall I," Emily began, since he remained pensively silent, "shall I serve coffee for you and the boys, Papa? Or a bottle of your madeira? They have had no time to break their fast, and Jamie has traveled all night. He—"

"No!" The admiral cut her short. "You will serve nothing."

The book he had been reading was flung down with such force that it slithered across the polished surface of his desk, to fall with a dull thud at her feet. It was a legal treatise, Emily observed with surprise as she bent to pick it up and replace it carefully within his reach.

Her father's beetling white brows met in a forbidding

frown. Offering no explanation, he gestured impatiently to
the door. "Summon your brothers, if you please. And . . .
I wish you to be present when I talk to them, since what I
have to say concerns you also, if indirectly. I must warn
you, however, that it may well come as a shock to you."

Emily hesitated for a moment; then, her heart suddenly
heavy with foreboding, she hastened to obey him.

Her brothers were waiting in the pleasant, sunny room
that had been their mother's boudoir and was now termed
the morning room. Robert, tall and in the civilian dress
that made him seem a stranger, had, she saw, anticipated
their father's refusal to offer him refreshment, for there was
a decanter of brandy on the table beside him, and he had a
half-empty glass in his hand.

Jamie, looking ill at ease, cut an oddly contrasting
figure in his cadet's brass-buttoned uniform, his cap tucked
correctly beneath his arm and his hands empty, although
Hawkins—the admiral's onetime coxswain and now employed as butler and coachman—had set out a glass for
him.

Robert spun round at his sister's approach, quickly draining the contents of his glass before asking aggressively,
"What does the Old Man want, Emmy, for God's sake?
Why have we been sent for in such an almighty hurry, do
you know?"

Emily shook her head. "I don't know, Rob. Papa hasn't
told me anything, except that he wishes me to be present
when he talks to you. He—that is, he says the matter is of
some concern to me also."

Robert swore under his breath. "No," he objected.
"Plague take it—no! I do *not* want you there when he
takes me to task for my failure to live up to his damned
outmoded standards. Please, Emmy, stay away if you care
for me at all."

Emily flushed. "You know I care for you deeply, Rob.
But I cannot disobey Papa. What he has to say is to all
three of us."

Her glance at her elder brother was uneasy. His cravat

was stained and badly ironed, his shirt cuffs frayed, his jacket worn and in need of repair. Wherever he was now lodging, it was obvious that little care was given to his wardrobe, and . . . Assailed by a sudden suspicion, she asked apprehensively, "Rob, are you still in employment? Are you still at the bank in—where was it? In Exeter Street?"

Robert laughed shortly. "Oh, Lord, no—Old Moneybags dispensed with my services two months ago. And be damned to him—I wasn't sorry! It was abysmally boring work, and I could never have taken to it. Besides, he's a tightfisted old swine, and he reported everything I did—or didn't do—to Papa."

Jamie started to speak and then thought better of it, reddening awkwardly. As she had often done when he was a child, Emily made to put her arm round him, but he evaded her embrace and stammered, eyeing his brother uncertainly, "We should not keep Papa waiting, R-Rob."

"No, indeed," Robert agreed, with mock humility. "The Lord High Admiral must *never* be kept waiting. They teach you that at the college, do they not? Respect for your betters—hats off and three cheers for the commandant or take a dozen of the best from your cadet captain! And I bet you cheer your head off, you yellow-livered little prig!"

Jamie's color deepened and spread. He said in a hoarse whisper to Emily, "He's drunk, Emmy. He—"

Robert glared at him. "Just you get under way, little brother. Spin the Old Man a yarn about how you're aiming for the term prize or the dirk of honor or whatever they give the cadet who never answers back. I'll be with you as soon as I've had another glass of brandy."

His hand, as he splashed liquor into his glass, was shaking visibly, and Emily's anxiety grew as she watched him. Their father disapproved strongly of heavy drinking, but, as if determined to flout his authority, Robert indulged in the habit as openly as he could whenever he came to the house. On more than one occasion he had arrived in a state of insobriety, as, it seemed, he had this morning. . . . She took the barely tasted brandy from him, set down the glass, and linked her arm with his, wishing that there were time to serve the coffee her father had forbidden.

"Come," she urged persuasively. "Truly we should not keep Papa waiting—Jamie is right; it will only anger him. Try to control yourself, Rob."

"I'm not drunk," Robert asserted. "I just need a little Dutch courage, that's all."

He gave her a thin smile and permitted her to lead him across the long, stone-flagged hall. It was a thousand pities, Emily thought sadly, that he still persisted in defying their father. He had done so for almost as long as she could remember, even as a boy, and throughout their mother's lifetime. Robert had been Mama's favorite, and looking back now, she found herself wondering whether this fact had soured his relationship with his father. Certainly Mama had indulged him, in every way she could devise. She had insisted on employing a tutor for him, instead of allowing him to go to school, and that had led—after a bitter family quarrel—to his being sent to sea at the tender age of eleven.

"It will make a man of him," their father had said. "Instead of a spoilt milksop. . . ." And, for all poor Mama's tearful pleas, he had refused to alter his decision. Robert had spent his first three years as a so-called volunteer on board the seventy-four-gun *Monarch* in the Mediterranean, under their father's command. Robert had never talked to her of those years, Emily remembered, but they had changed him. He had grown to manhood in the King's service, seeing action against the French and the Americans in other ships and under other commanders, culminating in the great fleet action at Algiers, when he had been commended for his gallantry by the commander in chief, Lord Exmouth.

His father had been proud of him then, but . . . She drew in her breath sharply. All that had changed with his court-martial and the fact that Their Lordships of the Admiralty had declined to confirm his commission twice in the ensuing years. He had been twenty before he had gained lieutenant's rank, and then . . . Robert's fingers tightened about her arm.

"How is your romance with Dr. Simon Yates progressing, Emmy?" he asked, taking her by surprise and grinning at her discomfiture when the embarrassed color leaped to her cheeks. "Or perhaps," he added unkindly, "there is no need to ask? Has Papa found a way to put an end to that, too?"

They were at the study door. Jamie knocked on it and stood back, to allow Emily to precede him, and there was no time to make even a brief reply to Robert's cynical question. In any event, he knew the answer, she thought bitterly . . . the handsome young doctor, who was assistant to the family's physician in the village of Murton, had been forbidden the house a long while ago. Their meetings were now infrequent and clandestine, save on those occasions that took place in the public gaze, or when she attended the local church for matins or evensong, accompanied by her father or sisters.

An ill-bred young fortune hunter—that was what the admiral had called Simon Yates, and . . . Lips close to her ear, Robert whispered maliciously, "Papa will permit you no suitors, you know, whilst he needs you to keep house for him."

Emily put a hand to her mouth to stifle the indignant denial she had been about to utter, wishing that Robert would not so often and so deliberately seek to wound Jamie and her and set them against their father. And his claim was not true: Papa was not like that, she told herself. While he might show her little affection, he was always generous. He gave her everything she needed for herself and for the household expenses, willingly and without question, and they lived well. Murton Chase was a large and beautiful manor house, standing in its own extensive grounds just outside Plymouth, more than adequately staffed, and . . .

"Emily . . . James—" The admiral indicated two chairs
on the far side of the room. "Be seated, both of you, and
you'll oblige me by listening in silence to what I have to
say to your brother. Robert—" An imperious wave of the
hand directed Robert to stand in front of him, as if, Emily
thought pitifully, he were a criminal, already judged and
condemned.

And indeed, in their father's eyes, it seemed, he was.
She listened in numb dismay to the catalog of Robert's
misdeeds, from his court-martial for incompetence and
insubordination, which had led to the loss of his ship, to
his dismissal from the merchant bank in London for, it
appeared, much the same reasons.

In cold and censorious words, he was reminded that he
had publicly insulted his former captain and, contrary to
the law of the land and service custom, had challenged his
superior officer to a duel.

"You have brought disgrace on our family name," the
admiral accused him. "Four generations of Willoughbys
have been your predecessors in the King's service. You
have had the example of a long line of brave men, not one
of whom ever left that service, save on his death or his
honorable retirement. I named you Robert Horatio, believing that you would, in your turn, do honor to one of
England's greatest admirals . . . but you have caused me
bitterly to regret having done so."

Robert attempted to protest, but he was brusquely silenced.
"There is no excuse for you, sirrah! None to which I can
listen any longer. Until now, God knows, I have tried to
give you the benefit of any doubt that existed, but I have
stood enough."

"Captain Neville's charges against me were malicious
and without foundation, Father. I swear they were brought
for the sole purpose of covering up *his* incompetence, not
mine. That was why I challenged him, sir—and why he
refused to face me!" Robert's voice shook with the intensity of his feelings, but once again he was harshly bidden
to hold his tongue.

"You have run up debts and I have settled them," his father asserted wrathfully. "I have used my influence to procure you employment, but you have spurned all my attempts to help you. And now—now I have been informed by a Mr. George Barton—who is, it would appear, an attorney you engaged—that charges of the most sordid and unpleasant nature have been brought against you. *Criminal* charges, Robert! Damme, boy, do you deny it? Do you deny that you are at present released on bail, pending prosecution at the next county assizes?"

Emily's heart plummeted as she saw the color drain from Robert's flushed face. His expression told her that this time he had no answer to the accusation, which, it was evident, had taken him by surprise. Had he, she wondered unhappily, supposed his father to be unaware of the impending charges against him—had he perhaps hoped to keep him from finding out?

"I put up bail for you," the admiral said bleakly.

"I did not ask you to," Robert retorted, tight-lipped.

"No—Mr. Barton did. You had persuaded him to bail you, and he doubted he would ever see his money again. Had I not acceded to his request, you would, he informed me, have been held in custody to await your trial. And, the devil take it, if the charges are proven, you will be liable to a seven-year sentence—most probably of deportation to New South Wales! It is even possible that you could incur a life sentence, if Barton is to be believed . . . and I take it he is."

Beside her, Emily felt Jamie stiffen. Her young brother was deeply affected and close to tears as, indeed, she was herself. Robert had been his hero, the object of his unstinting admiration since childhood, and this revelation had clearly shocked him almost beyond bearing. But, also like herself, he was too much in awe of his father to find the courage to interrupt, and the admiral continued with barely controlled anger, heaping accusation upon accusation.

"You are charged with having violated the person and besmirched the reputation of a virtuous young woman, the daughter of a tavern keeper in Plymouth . . . here on my very doorstep, you unmitigated rogue! And the father of that poor, unfortunate girl is a man well known, both to you and to myself . . . Daniel Raven, who served under my command as warrant gunner of the *Monarch*. And''—as Robert again attempted to speak—''do not try to pull the wool over my eyes by claiming that you did not know who Raven is. Or, come to that, damn your soul, seek to tell me that you were not aware of the appalling scandal it will cause if the case comes to trial. My good name would be sullied with yours, since it is my name you bear!''

''Sir, I beg you to listen to me,'' Robert pleaded. ''I give you my word that I—''

''Your word!'' the admiral thundered. ''Of what value is your word? I have borne enough and I have reached a decision. It is for that reason that I have sent for you—and James, since my decision will affect his future as well as yours.''

He controlled his rising temper and, to Emily's relief, spoke with measured calm. ''You will forfeit your bail, Robert, and place yourself beyond the court's jurisdiction. There is a convict transport, the *Mary Anne*, due to sail for Port Jackson from this port within forty-eight hours. You are to repair on board at once, do you understand? Your passage has been booked for you, and you will travel in the name of Roberts. I will arrange for the sum of two thousand pounds to be made available to you when you reach your destination—that will suffice to set you up as a farmer in the colony.''

Robert gave vent to a smothered exclamation, but the admiral ignored the interruption. He went on crisply, ''I have made inquiries. The Colonial Secretary, Lord Bathurst, is seeking settlers with capital behind them, with a view to developing the colony's wool trade and agriculture. Land grants are to be made in newly explored territory, opened recently for settlement and suitable for the raising of sheep and cattle. You will apply for a grant to the government surveyor in Sydney on your arrival there, and I will see to it that you are provided with suitable introductions.''

His father paused, and Robert eyed him in stunned dismay. "But, sir, I'm not cut out for a farmer. I've no experience of the land, no hankering for it. I—"

"For what else," the admiral countered contemptuously, "have you any aptitude? Do you prefer to go out to New South Wales in chains, as a convicted felon?" Without waiting for Robert's reply, he exclaimed forcefully, "By heaven, boy, I'd let you go thus were it not for the scandal your trial would cause and the damage it would do to my good name! Because of that, I am willing to offer you a last chance to make something of yourself. But it will be your last chance."

The sight of her elder brother's stricken face was too much for Emily. She rose to her feet, intending to range herself beside him, but a thunderous command from her father brought her trembling to a halt.

"Resume your seat, miss," he ordered. "I have not done." Turning again to Robert, he pointed to a rolled document on the desk before him, tied, like a legal brief, with pink tape. "This is my will. In it, I have disinherited you and made your brother James my heir. Apart from bequests to my daughters, James will, on my death, inherit everything I possess save, alas, for my baronetcy, which the law ordains must go to you . . . although I hope that you will not claim it. You will have the two thousand pounds I intend to make over to you—but only on the condition that you leave this country at once. And if you should see fit to refuse this offer, I shall cut you off without a penny, and, for all the shame it will bring, I'll let the law take its course." He paused, eyeing Robert with thinly veiled scorn. "Well? Do you accept my terms?"

Robert drew himself up. He was deathly pale, Emily saw, feeling sick with pity, but he managed to answer with a show of spirit.

"You leave me with no alternative, sir. I can only accept . . . but with reluctance. The last thing I want to do is to leave England."

Jamie found his tongue at last. With an eloquence of

which Emily had not supposed him capable, he besought his father to change his mind.

"I have no desire to be made your heir, Papa," he insisted. "I beg you not to do anything of the kind. Please, sir, will you not permit Robert to stay here and accord him another chance?"

"If he stays, he will have to face trial, James," the admiral reminded him. "And I have accorded him chance after chance. When he was in the service, I gave him my patronage. I did all in my power to obtain seagoing appointments for him and to advance him in rank . . . and how has he repaid me? By bringing his service career to a disgraceful end! I am ashamed to call him my son. But you, boy—" His tone softened. "You, I know, are of a different caliber. Your reports from the Naval College are admirable, and you will in the fullness of time, I feel sure, make me proud of you—which your brother has failed to do. So do not waste your breath in pleading for him. My mind is made up. Robert will sail at once for New South Wales, as I have arranged. You heard him—he has accepted my terms, and there is no more to be said."

But Jamie would not give in. "Then, Papa," he requested earnestly, "will you permit me to quit the Naval College and go with him? I'm keen on farming, and I'm not all that keen on the service, sir, honestly—"

Wrathfully, his father cut him short. "I'll not hear of it, boy! You are, perhaps, too young to understand the sordid nature of this latest affair in which your brother has contrived to involve himself . . . and, damme, I don't intend to explain it to you! But understand this—if Robert does not leave this country immediately, he will face charges in a civil court against which he has no defense." Leaning forward, he gestured with a bony hand to the door. "You may leave, James, and Emily with you. See to it, Emily, that James catches the afternoon stage. Hawkins can drive him into Plymouth in the trap, and he will return to the college tomorrow."

James hesitated, his thin young face contorted in a brave

attempt to hide his distress. "Rob," he whispered wretchedly, "I want no part of your inheritance. Believe me, I
truly did not know what Papa intended."

"Be thankful, little brother," Robert called after him
derisively, "that you are so favored! It's no more than you
deserve."

Emily, biting back her tears, closed the study door behind them. This time Jamie did not try to evade her when
she put her arm about his shoulders. When they reached
the hall, he said miserably, "The Exeter stage leaves in an
hour, Emmy, and it's always punctual. If I'm to catch it,
I'll have to go now. Anyway, perhaps it will be best if I
do. Rob won't want me here now, will he? Not after . . .
after all this. And I cannot face Papa again."

Emily's arm tightened about him in wordless understanding. "I'll tell Hawkins to bring the trap round," she
answered. "But you haven't eaten, Jamie. Shall I pack you
up some bread and cheese? Or some fruit, at least?"

He shook his head. "I feel too sickened to eat," he
confessed. "But perhaps a couple of apples to sustain me
on the journey."

Emily watched him drive away ten minutes later, a
feeling of desolation sweeping over her, and this became
still more acute when Robert finally emerged from their
father's study, grim-faced and seething with resentment.

"The Lord High Admiral's orders are that I'm never to
darken his doors again, for as long as he lives, Emmy,"
he announced wryly. "And I'm not to see the little girls,
even to bid them farewell. I'm permitted to take leave of
you, but that's all. As soon as Hawkins gets back with the
trap, he's to take me, collect my gear from my lodgings,
and then he's to wait and confirm that I've boarded the
infernal *Mary Anne*. I pointed out that he'd need a glass to
do that, if she's finished loading and is lying out in the
sound, and—" He smiled mirthlessly and gestured to a
breast pocket of his shabby cutaway coat. "Papa gave me
his own Dollond, which I'm to hand over to Hawkins, for
the aforesaid purpose . . . but no other."

"Oh, Rob!" Emily managed, her throat tight. "Dear Rob, I'm so sorry. But you—"

"But I've asked for it, I suppose?" he finished for her.

"I did not mean that."

His expression relaxed. "No, I know you did not. You're a darling, Emmy—the best of sisters, and I shall miss you more than I can say. But dear God in heaven, what a prospect lies before me! New South Wales, a savage land, turned into a penal colony and peopled by the scourings of our jails! And I'm to become a scurvy farmer at the back of beyond."

"It might have been worse for you," Emily began thoughtlessly. "If you had been forced to go out there as a—" She broke off, reddening, and as he had before, Robert completed what she had intended to leave unsaid.

"As a convicted felon, in irons—true, that would be infinitely worse. I must learn to thank God for small mercies, must I not? And for my father's grudging generosity." He took a folded square of stiff paper from his pocket and offered it for Emily's inspection. "This is a draft on his agent in Cape Town, with which I'm to purchase livestock there. It seems that is the thing to do—cattle and sheep are cheaper there than in the colony. One makes a profit, provided the infernal creatures survive the passage to Port Jackson."

Robert moved away, making for the morning room. The decanter and glasses were still there, and he helped himself to what was left of the brandy, gulping it down thirstily. Emily watched him but offered no reproof, and he said, an edge to his voice, "I'd have jumped my bail in any case, Emmy—I would not have let them bring me to trial, you know . . . for *his* sake, as well as my own. I had planned to go to Ireland as soon as I could raise the necessary funds."

Conscious of an unreasoning hope, Emily asked eagerly, "Then why not go to Ireland now? Oh, Rob, surely you still could, could you not?"

Glumly he shook his head. "I have exactly twenty

pounds, which our parent has given me for my shipboard
expenses, and about five of my own. I'd not last long on
that, even in Ireland. And I stand to gain two thousand,
you know, if I do as he wants."

"Yes, but—"

"Emmy dear, as I told *him* just now, he's left me with
no alternative. I'll go to his blasted New South Wales,
but—" His smile returned. "I don't have to stay there for
the rest of my days. Like the proverbial bad penny, little
sister, I shall turn up here again."

"Oh, Rob, I'll pray that you will!" Emily looked up at
him, seeing his face through a mist of unshed tears. She
wanted to ask him about the charges that had been laid
against him, but hesitated, fearing to hurt him anew. As
their father had described them, the charges appeared to
concern a young woman, the daughter of one of the town's
tavern keepers, with whom, it seemed, Robert had become
amorously involved. Papa had spoken of her as a virtuous
young woman, Emily recalled, and had accused Robert of
having violated her person, which meant that he . . .

As if she had spoken her thoughts aloud, Robert said
flatly, "I was to be charged with rape, Emmy."

The ugly word, with all its implications, hung between
them like a dark shadow, blotting out the warm spring
sunshine streaming in from the garden outside, and Emily
caught her breath on a sob.

"Oh, Rob . . . oh, surely you—"

"It was a ploy," Robert told her, with bitterness. "Daniel
Raven, the girl's father, is a scheming rogue. He served as
warrant gunner under Papa's command in the *Monarch*
and before that in the West Indies, under Sir Samuel Hood
and Sir Francis Laforey . . . and he made a small fortune
in prize money. Enough to buy the Crown and Anchor
tavern on North Quay and set himself up in a tidy way of
business. I used to drink there when I was in town. It's not
a place that is usually frequented by officers, and . . . I
knew Dan Raven well. The junior mids and the young
volunteers were in his charge on board the *Monarch*. We

messed with the warrant officers, you see, and he was the senior. I had a high regard for him in those days. He was good to me, and I trusted him.''

In those days, Emily thought pityingly, Robert had been a lonely little eleven-year-old, dragged unwillingly from the bosom of his family and forced to endure the harsh discipline of the navy. It would be natural for him to trust anyone who was—as he had put it—good to him.

''Go on, Rob,'' she invited gently.

Robert shrugged. ''Oh, very well, if you truly want to hear the wretched story. But—'' He broke off and held out the empty decanter. ''Can you get me some more of this brandy, little sister? I really need it, and . . . talking's thirsty work, you know.''

''I'm sorry,'' Emily apologized, with genuine regret. ''But Hawkins keeps all Papa's liquor under lock and key. And he's not here. I could bring you some ale from the kitchen, if that would do, and something to eat, perhaps? You could have it here.''

''What about Papa? I don't want him to see me.'' Robert's tone was again fraught with bitterness. ''It might be regarded as an abuse of his hospitality.''

''Papa never comes in here,'' Emily told him. ''Do you not remember—this was always Mama's room.''

She sped off to the kitchen and returned with a laden tray. ''There was some cider, and I thought you would prefer that. They are busy with the preparations for Papa's luncheon, but Cook gave me cold meat, with cheese and pickles and a fresh loaf . . . will that do, Rob? Oh, and there's an apple pie.''

''That will do admirably,'' her brother assured her. Seating himself, he fell hungrily upon the simple fare, his lips twisting into an odd little smile as he ate. ''Old Moneybags never fed his miserable clerks like this,'' he observed. ''Do you wonder that I was thankful to quit his employ?''

''No,'' Emily conceded. She waited in silence until he pushed his plate aside with a satisfied sigh and reached for the jug of cider. Then, curiosity getting the better of her, she asked shyly, "Rob, what is she like, the—the young woman who has made that terrible charge against you?"

"Rebecca Raven—Becky?" Robert sighed audibly. "Oh, she's comely enough, but a child, barely sixteen. Unlettered, brought up in a low tavern, with a slatternly mother and a horde of brothers and sisters . . . she's what you'd expect after such an upbringing, I suppose. I've sunk pretty low since Their Lordships threw me out of the service, but . . . I could not have married her, Emmy."

"You could not have *married* her?" Emily echoed, startled. "But I thought—" She stared at him in bewilderment, wondering whether she had misunderstood him.

"Dan Raven bears a monumental grudge against Papa," Robert said gravely. "I never fathomed out precisely why, but I know that his warrant was withdrawn when the *Monarch* paid off, and he never went to sea again. I played into his hands when I started going to his tavern, only I was too big a fool to spot what the fellow was after. He threw that girl of his at me. I'd go to his taproom, and he would see to it that I was plied with liquor, and then he'd send her to me. Devil take it, I'm only human, and Becky was willing enough, or she seemed to be! I swear I did not rape her, Emmy. But Raven accused me of it, and so did she, and I'd no defense—it was his word and hers against mine, with a bunch of riffraff ready to back him up. He offered to withdraw the charge if I undertook to wed her . . . but I could not. I simply could not saddle myself with such a wife. And," he added wryly, "I feared that Papa would cut me off if I were to do so."

"Did you imagine that Papa would not find out that you had been charged?" Emily asked.

"I hoped I could prevent it," Robert admitted. "If that greedy crook Barton had not demanded the bail money, I might have succeeded. But he guessed that I was planning to skip bail before the case came to court and went to Papa with his damned hard-luck story . . . and without telling me what he'd done. Truly, Emmy, you could have knocked me down with a feather when Papa taxed me with it."

He sounded aggrieved, and Emily began, for the first time, to doubt her elder brother's veracity. How could he possibly have hoped to keep their father in ignorance of his impending trial when—as Papa himself had reminded him—it was due to take place on his very doorstep? Plymouth was only three miles away; the circuit judges numbered among his friends and acquaintances, and, since his last appointment had been that of port admiral, the name of Sir Francis Willoughby was widely known throughout the length and breadth of the town.

Even if Lawyer Barton had not informed him of his son's arrest, would not someone else, surely, have done so, sooner or later? Emily's teeth closed over her lower lip, in a vain attempt to still its trembling. Her brother Robert, she thought regretfully, was about to go out of her life, to embark on a twelve-thousand-mile voyage to the other side of the world; she could not, she *would* not let him go with even a suspicion that she doubted him.

"Rob," she began, in a strained whisper. "Rob, I am truly sorry. If there is anything you need—"

"Money," Robert said, avoiding her gaze. "I'll have to square up for my lodgings, unfortunately. If you could spare me a few pounds, Emmy, I'd be grateful."

She had only a few pounds of her own, Emily knew— five or six, perhaps, left over from her dress allowance, which had to last her until the end of the quarter, but . . . She went to the bureau that had been her mother's. There was the month's housekeeping money, virtually untouched. If she economized, if she let some of the tradesmen wait until next month to be paid, she could give her brother half of that, and their father need never know what she had done. She seated herself in front of the desk and recklessly counted out five gold coins of her own and another ten from the leather bag containing the housekeeping money.

"It's not much, Rob, but—" The sound of horse's hooves on the gravel outside told her that Hawkins had returned with the trap, and she rose to her feet, mindful of her father's instructions. "I—I'd better tell Hawkins that he's to drive you into town. I'll tell him to wait until . . . until you are ready."

But Robert, too, was on his feet with unexpected alacrity. "No point in prolonging the agony, Emmy dear. I might as well be on my way and have done." He pocketed the coins and, smiling, reached for her hand. "Thanks! Er— you'll bid Charlotte and little Biddy farewell for me, won't you?"

Looking up at him with swimming eyes, Emily nodded her assent. Robert bent and planted a kiss on her cheek. "You might do a lot worse than marry your Dr. Yates, you know—whatever Papa says! Yates is always talking about becoming a missionary and taking modern medicine and Christianity to the Maoris of New Zealand, is he not? At least then we'd be neighbors, if not exactly next door to each other, so think about it, will you? Good-bye and God bless you, Emmy, and may He have you ever in His keeping!"

"And you, Rob dearest." Now that the moment of parting had come, Emily's doubts faded and she was conscious only of her impending loss, willing to forgive him for his teasing reference to Simon Yates, which, she told herself, had not been intentionally unkind. Although in the circumstances . . . She stifled a sob. "I pray that you will have a safe passage and that you—that you will be able to make a new life in Sydney, and new friends."

"Undoubtedly I shall," Robert retorted, with bitter sarcasm. "Plague take it, it's a penal colony, is it not? I shall feel quite at home there."

He led the way into the hall, picked up his hat and cloak, and reaching the front door, flung it open with a flourish, calling out to Hawkins to pull up and wait for him.

The man did so, showing no surprise. Robert held Emily to him briefly, then he strode across the gravel driveway and climbed into the small, two-wheeled carriage, to seat himself at the coachman's side.

"You—Rob, you will write?" Emily pleaded.

Robert shrugged and pointed toward the house. Guessing that their father had come to stand at the study window, in order to witness his elder son's departure, Emily turned to glance behind her.

The admiral's face was grimly set, she saw. He gave no sign of his feelings and did not offer even a token gesture of farewell.

Robert, smiling mirthlessly, put two fingers to his hat but did not bare his head.

To Emily he said, lowering his voice, "I'll address no letters to *this* house—they would be unwelcome. But I'll write in the care of Dr. Simon Yates at Murton, when I've anything worth writing about . . . that will give him an excuse to seek you out. Take care of yourself, Emmy, and don't let the Lord High Admiral ruin your life, as well as mine." He clapped a hand on Hawkins's broad, livery-clad shoulder and ordered, with conscious mockery, "Put your helm up, cox'un, and set course for my lodgings in Breton Street. You know where we're headed, I imagine?"

"Aye, sir, I do," Hawkins answered woodenly. "To the *Mary Anne* transport, out in the sound. And I'm to see that you board her, sir." He whipped up his horse, and the trap went bowling down the long drive. To Emily's chagrin, Robert did not look back.

"The bird's flown the coop, Martha," Daniel Raven announced, with a satisfaction he did not try to disguise. Motioning his wife aside, he drew himself a tankard of ale and drank deeply before continuing. "You kept on saying 'twas a waste o' money having his lodgings watched—but it's paid off, woman! Come back with that toady Mick Hawkins in a trap, he did, less'n an hour since, packed up all his gear and lit out. Charlie followed him. Says he took a wherry out to that convict transport, the *Mary Anne*, with a load o' bags and boxes. Didn't I tell you as Admiral sodding Willoughby was planning something o' the kind, when he went on board whilst she was loading at Guy's Wharf last week? I knew I was right!''

His wife regarded him with lackluster dark eyes. "Do you mean," she questioned, pushing back a lock of graying hair that had fallen over her face as she worked at swabbing the bar counter, "do you mean young Mr. Willoughby's skipping his bail?''

"He was always going to," Raven told her with conviction. "The admiral would never have let him stand trial. But Botany Bay—that's where the *Mary Anne*'s bound—I'd not expected him to send the young swine there, I grant you. Not until I seen him hanging round Guy's Wharf, that's to say. It came to me then. Best place for him, of course, only he ought to be going out there chained up on the orlop, 'stead o' having his passage paid for him.''

Martha Raven regarded him uncertainly. Wise in her husband's ways after seventeen years of marriage, she had not supposed that he would give in easily. The treatment that Admiral Sir Francis Willoughby had meted out to him, when their ship, the *Monarch*, paid off, still rankled as deeply as it had then, and Daniel was not a man to forget—much less forgive—such an injury to his reputation and his pride.

She had not held with the methods he had resorted to in order to avenge the injury. Becky was her daughter, as well as his, and granted the girl's virtue had been in danger of corruption long before Robert Willoughby had made his drunken assault on it, the effect on them all had been little short of disastrous. Becky had become sullen and rebellious; she had believed her father when he had promised that young Willoughby would wed her and, imagining herself in love with him, had refused initially to support the charge of rape. Dan had been obliged to beat her into submission, and . . . Martha expelled her breath in an unhappy sigh. She and Dan had quarreled bitterly on that account, and then the discovery that the girl was pregnant had widened the rift between them.

Becky, poor little wench, had threatened to put an end to it by taking her own life. She had even made an abortive attempt to do so and had now to be watched, lest she try again. . . .

"Dan, is it over, this mad scheming of yours? Are you going to let young Willoughby go to Botany Bay?" Martha's tone was pleading. "You can't put the law on him now, can you? Surely it's too late for that."

Her husband took another long swig from his tankard. He wiped the froth from his bearded lips with the back of his hand and flashed her an oddly furtive smile. "It's not too late for that, no—the *Mary Anne*'s still in British waters. But I've a better notion." He leaned forward to grasp her arm, forcing her to look up at him. "Martha, I'm going to take Becky out to the ship. Old Parson Crickley's agreed to come with us and—"

"Parson Crickley!" Martha exclaimed, her voice shrill with alarm. "That crazy old man? Oh, Dan, you can't—he's never sober!"

"He's still a parson, ain't he? He can still perform the marriage service." Dan Raven's strong, blunt fingers bit into the flesh of his wife's arm. "Robert Willoughby shall marry my daughter and take her with him to sodding Botany Bay as his wife. He shamed her, didn't he? He got her with child, so he's a right to wed her. If he refuses, then, by God, I *will* put the law on him! But I've a hunch that this time he won't refuse. He'd have the admiral to reckon with, if I had him brought back."

"And Becky?" Martha asked bitterly. "What has she to say about it? Or didn't you tell her what you're aiming to do?"

Raven's smile widened. "She's over the moon, the silly wench. I told her young Willoughby had sent for her. She's packing up her glad rags, ready to go, and she wouldn't care where the plaguey ship was taking her, just so long as she's going with him." He shrugged. "Best take your leave of her now, wife. Old Crickley won't be long. I sent Charlie to dig him out."

Martha felt her heart sink. Becky had always exasperated her, and never more than during the past couple of months, when her noisy grief had driven them all almost to distraction, but . . . the lass was her daughter, her own flesh and blood. And the good Lord knew that Dan had used her very ill, with his scheming and plotting, his single-minded quest for vengeance.

"All right." The bar till was beside her, and Martha opened it and, under her husband's disapproving eye, extracted all the coins it contained. There were not many; they amounted, in all, to about five pounds, but at least Becky should not be penniless.

The coins jingling in the pocket of her apron, Martha sought out her daughter and found her, as Dan had claimed, brimming over with happiness. She had rolled her few possessions into a bulky bundle and had changed into her Sunday best, a pretty sprigged muslin, which—already a trifle tight for her—revealed all too plainly the telltale signs of her pregnancy in the swelling curves of her breasts and abdomen. But her small, pinched face was aglow, lending her a beauty so unexpected that it tore at her mother's heartstrings.

"Did Pa tell you?" she asked excitedly. "Did he tell you that Rob Willoughby's taking ship to someplace they call Botany Bay and wants me to go with him? Oh, Ma, ain't it wonderful? It was all lies about him not being willing to wed me! Old Parson Crickley's coming with us so's we can be wed before the ship sails . . . did Pa tell you that?"

Aware that Dan had not told her the truth concerning Robert Willoughby's sudden departure, Martha gazed at her daughter with conscience-stricken pity. Unable to bring herself to shatter the girl's illusions, she thrust the money she had taken from the till into her hands and hugged her. Dan's scheming, daft though it sounded, might achieve the result he wanted, she told herself—Rob Willoughby might fall in with his wishes. He would not want to be shamed in front of the *Mary Anne*'s passengers and crew, and the old priest's presence, coupled with the threat of putting the law on him, might break down his resistance, stubborn though it had been. And besides, he was going out to a convict colony, where a wife like Becky would not be the social stigma it would be here in England. Even the military officers married convict girls out there, and the soldiers and civil officials certainly did, so that . . . Martha stifled the prompting of her conscience and managed to smile through her tears.

"You must take good care of yourself, Becky love," she urged. "Wrap up warm when you go on deck—you've packed a shawl, haven't you? And you'll need clothes for the baby—I'll see what I can find. You—" An impatient summons from her husband cut short the flow of good advice she had intended to offer.

Becky kissed her hurriedly and broke away from her clinging arms. "I'll have to go, Ma," she exclaimed. "Pa says the ship's due to sail very soon. But Rob won't let them sail until I'm on board. Good-bye, Ma, and thanks for the cash. It'll come in handy—per'aps I'll be able to buy clothes for the baby with it."

Martha had time only to take off her own shawl and wrap it round her daughter's thinly clad shoulders, and then she was gone, clutching her bundle and rushing down the narrow wooden staircase as if the devil himself were after her.

In the taproom below, Dan Raven waited, a big hand grasping Parson Crickley by the elbow. The damned old reprobate had been half seas over when he had made his appearance, grumbling mightily at the intrusion Charlie had made into his afternoon's drinking. But the promise of a sovereign and a bottle of the best French brandy for his services had ended the grumbling, and a mug of black coffee and a session under the pump in the backyard had sufficed to restore him to a semblance of sobriety.

When Becky joined them, Dan relieved her of her bundle and sent Charlie scurrying ahead of them to engage a wherry to take them out to the *Mary Anne*. She was lying

half a mile offshore the last time he had seen her, and a
hasty inspection with a glass had shown him a bunch of
female convicts being exercised, under guard, on deck
. . . a sign, he had reassured himself, that she was not yet
ready to get under way. The breeze was nor'easterly,
though, and blowing strongly—her master might decide to
take advantage of it, instead of waiting till next morning.

Impatiently he urged his charges onward. Becky was not
unwilling; chattering like a magpie, she skipped along at
his side, asking eager questions about Botany Bay that he
had neither the will nor the knowledge to answer. His
service had been in the West Indies, the North Sea and the
Baltic, and finally in the Med; praise be to God, they had
never sent him to the Indian Ocean or the Pacific, and he
had only once been to Rio and the Cape. Dan frowned.

"Save your breath, lass," he bade his daughter repres-
sively. He shifted her heavy bundle from one shoulder to
the other, and paying no heed to the old parson's queru-
lous protests and faltering steps, guided him at a brisk pace
down the cobbled street.

The wherry was waiting when they reached the quay,
the ragged, sharp-featured street arab Charlie seated on a
bollard a few yards away. Dan delved into his pockets and
found a couple of shillings with which to reward him, and
the boy, grinning, assisted Becky and Parson Crickley to
ensconce themselves in the passengers' seats.

"I'll pull an oar," Dan offered. "We're in a hurry."

The boatman eyed him sourly and, sensing a ruse to
trick him out of his full fare, shook his head, motioning
Dan to a seat in the stern.

"I'll get you where you be goin', Mr. Raven," he
asserted, in a thick Devon burr. "The *Mary Anne* transport,
ain't it, out in the sound?"

He plied his oars with commendable vigor, and the
unwieldy boat, expertly handled, skimmed over the surface of the dark harbor water at heartening speed. Once
they were out in the sound, however, the wind took a
hand, whipping up choppy waves and sapping the oarsman's

energy as he strove to keep on course. Finally, sweating freely, he moved along his thwart and said gruffly, over his shoulder, "Take an oar now, Mr. Raven, if you'm minded to. This 'ere old wind's makin' powerful 'eavy goin' of it an' no mistake."

It was Becky who sounded the first note of alarm. Crouched in the bow, she suddenly gave vent to an agonized cry. "Pa! Oh, Pa, look—the *Mary Anne*'s setting sail! Pa, she's going—she's going without me!"

Dan swiveled round, cursing angrily. The ship, he saw, was indeed getting under way. Her lee anchor had been hove up and catted, the weather cable brought to a short stay, and he could hear, across the intervening distance, the clank of her capstan and the sound of men's voices, mingled with the steady tramp of bare feet on her deck planking. Her headsails were loosed, the topmen aloft, laying out along the yards, letting fall topsails and courses as the weather anchor came up. Slowly, majestically, the big, bluff-bowed vessel gathered headway and her sails filled.

Aware of the futility of trying to make himself heard, Dan cupped both hands about his mouth and yelled. There was no response. He had known there could not be, but . . .

"Gawd!" the wherryman exclaimed, in shocked tones. "Watch out, miss! You'll be in the water else!"

Becky, Dan realized, was standing up, teetering unsteadily on the bow thwart, the wind tearing at her flimsy dress and whipping her hair into wild disorder.

"Pa, Rob Willoughby never sent for me, did he?" she flung at him bitterly. "He never did mean to wed me, not ever. You—Pa, you lied to me. It wasn't true—none of it was true!"

All the happiness had vanished from her face; his daughter's gaze, as it met his, was accusing, the big, dark eyes brimming with tears. Dan lurched toward her on his knees and, suddenly, sickeningly certain of what she intended to do, reached out in an attempt to grasp her ankles. But Becky eluded him, still poised precariously on the thwart, yards beyond his reach.

"Don't try to save me, Pa," she warned, her voice a shrill whimper of sound, just audible above the wind's increasing bluster. "I want to die, I . . . ain't got nothing to live for anymore."

She let herself fall into the cold gray water, and the boat rocked dangerously as Dan desperately grabbed at her flying skirt, to measure his length on the bottom boards, a scrap of torn muslin grasped in one hand.

"You'll have us over!" the wherryman bawled. "For Gawd's sake, mister, take an oar an' help me bring 'er about!"

Dan obeyed him, his stomach churning. Like most British seamen, he had never learned to swim, and stunned though he was, he knew that their best—perhaps their only—chance of saving Becky was to remain in the boat. Two other boats, one an excise launch manned by a crew of six, joined in the search, but it was Parson Crickley who was the first to see her.

"There she is!" he croaked, and displaying a reckless courage of which Dan had never supposed him capable, the frail old man splashed in an awkward belly-dive into the water. He reached the sodden white object that was Becky and trod water, gasping for breath and contriving, somehow, to keep her afloat. The wherryman maneuvered his boat alongside them, and Dan, exerting all his strength, hauled both of them inboard.

His daughter lay inert on the bottom boards, her eyes open and sightless, gazing up at him in mute reproach. Frantically he sought to revive her, knowing in his heart that it was too late.

Old Parson Crickley, soaked to the skin, his lined face blue with cold and his teeth chattering, grasped his arm. "The poor young lass is dead, Mr. Raven," he said gently. "May God have mercy on her soul!"

Dan Raven sat back on his heels. Through misted eyes he watched the *Mary Anne*, under a press of sail, head for the open sea, a glistening, churned-up wilderness of water in her wake. She was gone, he thought dully, and the thrice-damned Admiral Willoughby's son with her.

The chances were that, in the bustle of getting their ship under way, none of her people had seen his daughter's drowning, or if they had, they had attached little importance to it. Accidents happened in the sound. The men laying out along the *Mary Anne*'s upper yards would have deemed it no business of theirs, whatever they had seen, but . . . bile rose in Dan's throat, almost choking him.

He shook his fist at the distant ship, calling down curses on her and everyone aboard her.

"You would do better to pray, Mr. Raven," Parson Crickley admonished him sadly. "Rebecca is in the arms of her Heavenly Father now, and there is nothing you can do to bring her back."

It was true, Dan Raven was forced to concede, looking down at Becky's still, white face. His daughter was dead, but her seducer—*her murderer*—should be made to pay for it. If there was a God to whom he could pray, and if that God was a just God, Rob Willoughby should not be permitted to escape unscathed.

For a moment or two, he considered the possibility of making the long voyage to Port Jackson in pursuit of him, and then dismissed the thought. He had a wife and family to think of, and the Crown and Anchor was a gold mine . . . besides, had not Rob Willoughby's infernal despot of a father, Admiral Sir Francis sodding Willoughby, gone out of his way to ensure that he would never be permitted to set foot on board a King's ship again? Anything else was unthinkable for a man like himself, who had served in the Royal Navy for the greater part of his life and who had risen to warrant rank. As for taking passage in a scurvy convict transport like the *Mary Anne* . . . Dan's mouth hardened.

But Becky should not go unavenged. *The mills of God grind slowly*, he reminded himself, *but they grind exceeding small*. He closed his eyes and, under the benevolent

gaze of old Parson Crickley, prayed silently and blasphe-
mously, ending his prayer by declaiming aloud, "God rest
my poor Becky's soul, but may *his* soul rot in hell!"

In his cabin on board the *Mary Anne*, Robert lay, fully
clothed, on his bunk. He had not gone on deck when the
ship was preparing to weigh anchor, having no desire to
look his last on Plymouth.

Earlier, however, in the congenial company of two other
young gentlemen—whose destination and purpose appeared
similar to his own—he had enjoyed a drinking session in
the cuddy. The elder of his two new acquaintances, Henry
Daniels, had told him, with much hilarity, that he was
escaping from his creditors and, apparently well supplied
with funds in spite of this, had advised him solemnly that
judicious tipping would ensure relief from the tedium of
the long voyage.

"A few well-greased palms, Willoughby . . . you'll see
will work wonders for us. So spread your largesse, my
dear fellow, where it will do most good. The steward, for
example, and of course the first mate—only don't let the
master see you doling it out. He's a damned old Puritan."

Emmy's gold coins had been expended in accordance
with Daniels's advice. Robert smiled to himself. A stock
of liquor had been set aside for him by the steward, and
before going on watch, the mate had promised to send a
young woman from the convicts' quarters in the orlop so
that, as he had put it with a leer, "You gentlemen may
have your washing and mending done properly by a female
and your cabins kept to rights."

Asked what manner of woman he would fancy, he had
replied flippantly, Robert recalled—his flippancy induced
by his fifth or sixth brandy and Henry Daniels's witty
comments.

"A young virgin, if you can find one, Mr. Mate," he
had said, and Daniels had laughed his head off at what he
deemed a tall order. He . . . A soft knock on the cabin

door caused him to sit up, resting on one elbow. "Come in," he responded, his voice slurred.

A small, frightened figure stood framed in the aperture—a girl of perhaps fifteen or sixteen, with blue eyes and a mass of chestnut curls, who, absurdly, might have been Becky Raven. Or her twin. Robert stared at her, bereft of words and fearing, for a moment, that by some mischance Becky had found him.

The girl dropped him a clumsy curtsy. She whispered nervously, "My name's Alice, sir—Alice Fairweather from Honiton. The officer said as you would give me protection, sir. He said you'd want laundry done and mending and your cabin kept clean and tidy. I—" She drew a quick, anxious breath. "I'd be better off with you, sir, he told me, than I'd be on the prison deck, with the other women. Some of them are . . . well, they're pretty rough, and they talk as if . . . oh, I don't know. They called out after me, when the officer took me away. They called me a . . . a whore, sir. But I'm not, believe me I'm not."

Robert said thickly, "Are you not?"

He was seeing her face indistinctly, through an alcoholic haze, but the illusion was fading. The girl shook her head and, gaining courage, added pleadingly, "No, sir, truly. My folks were God-fearing people, and I had a good Christian upbringing."

"But you are a convict? You are being deported to New South Wales?"

Alice Fairweather hung her head. "I took a few yards of lace from my employer, that was all, sir. And I'd have returned it, but she wouldn't let me. Sir, if you—" Her head came up. "If what you want is a—a woman to bed with, then please, I beg you, send me back to the prison, because I—"

Robert reached for her, cutting short her plea, and, with his mouth on hers, silenced her cries as he took her brutally and without compassion.

CHAPTER II

The government sloop *Elizabeth Henrietta,* on passage from Port Jackson to Norfolk Island, buried her sharply raked bow into the depths of a towering, white-capped roller and then rose shuddering to its summit, shipping water as her stern fell into the trough.

Her commander, the tall, fair-haired Lieutenant Justin Broome, shouted a warning to the man at the wheel. "Meet her as she 'scends, quartermaster! And keep her full!"

The *Elizabeth,* built in Sydney from materials shipped out from England, was an unweatherly vessel in even a moderately heavy sea, prone to pitch violently and even to yaw before a following wind. She had capsized at her moorings soon after her launching, but Justin Broome had commanded her now for almost two years and had become accustomed to her vagaries, if never quite resigned to them. And with this wind . . . Frowning, he glanced aloft to check the trim of her sails, the dismal clanking of her overworked pumps sounding in his ears. She was sailing close-hauled on what he had calculated should be the last leg on the larboard tack before sighting the island. He snapped open his glass and had started to move across the narrow quarterdeck to the lee side when the masthead lookout hailed.

"Deck there! Land-ho, sir, fine on the larboard bow!"

From halfway up the mainmast shrouds, glass to his eye, Justin was able to make out the dark smudge of land that was their destination. Norfolk, he was aware from previous visits, was not a large island. Discovered by Captain Cook in 1774, it had been claimed and settled in February 1788 by the late Governor King, then a young lieutenant in the colony's First Fleet. A mere seven miles long and four broad, it was a wild and beautiful place, chiefly remarkable for its fertile soil and for the magnificent pine trees, which reared their stately heads a hundred feet above the surrounding forest.

Under King's benevolent governorship, Norfolk Island had prospered, with convict labor to raise crops, cut timber, and breed livestock in quantities out of all proportion to its size. Since King's day, however, Norfolk had been transformed into a prison for the worst of Sydney's malefactors and, under a succession of less benevolent rulers, had been likened to hell on earth by the wretched felons who were banished there, to toil in chains with no hope of escape from its rocky fastness.

Justin shivered involuntarily, remembering previous calls with mail and fresh consignments of exiled prisoners, when Colonel Joseph Foveaux had been commandant. The onetime Rum Corps officer, on the pretext of tightening up discipline, had instituted a four-year reign of terror, marked by the almost daily use of the floggers' wooden triangles and the fearsome punishment cells for the most trivial offenses. Although only a boy then and serving under his father's command in the ill-fated *Norfolk*, he recalled that women had been sentenced to the lash in those days. Men had taken their own lives rather than endure Foveaux's tyranny, and the tyrant himself had lived in constant fear of an attempt to murder him . . . or of mutiny.

In February 1814—ten years ago—the island had been abandoned on orders from the British Colonial Office, its convicts and its free settlers evacuated to Van Diemen's Land. For the convicts, this had meant exchanging one harsh prison for another, and they had accepted the transfer with sullen indifference. But the handful of free settlers, many of them former soldiers and seamen, had been heartbroken, for they had built up flourishing small farms on the land they had cleared, and all were loath to leave their snug homesteads in order to start life anew in virgin territory, where the native blacks constituted a dangerous and growing menace.

Justin snapped his glass shut and descended to the deck as the memories came flooding back. With his small trading vessel, the *Flinders*, he had assisted in the evacuation and had listened, with helpless pity, to the pleas and protests of those he had been instructed to convey to Hobart—the women in particular. They had watched their homes set on fire and burned to the ground, together with the prison buildings and the hitherto carefully guarded granaries and storehouses. They had seen their livestock slaughtered and their vines and fruit trees left to rot, and many had been in tears as they stood on the *Flinders*'s deck, looking their last on the island that they had made their home.

But now, in its wisdom, the Colonial Office had sent instructions to Sir Thomas Brisbane, the present Governor of New South Wales, for the prison to be rebuilt and Norfolk Island to become, once again, a place of exile for the scourings of the main colony's convict establishment. The so-called capital respites—men condemned to death for crimes committed within the colony, and subsequently reprieved—the absconders and escapers, those who ranged the wild, unsettled bush country, stealing at will and terrorizing the settlers whose properties they raided, the recalcitrant and the rebellious . . . these were to be the new population of Norfolk Island, together with the guards and overseers and jailers who would accompany them to the Island of No Escape.

His own instructions, Justin reflected wryly, were to land and make a report to the Governor as to which, if any, facilities were still left standing, and to assess what would be required in the way of labor and building materials, in order to prepare the place for the resumption of its old role. It was not a task he relished, but . . . He had brought

James Meehan, from the government surveyor's office, and his own brother-in-law, George De Lancey, as passengers, both of whom had volunteered their assistance. George, who had never seen a penal establishment at first hand, had come more out of a desire for knowledge than in the belief that he could offer practical help or advice. As assistant judge advocate and Sydney's senior magistrate, he had all too frequently been obliged to prosecute men for crimes committed within the colony, and, with typical conscientiousness, he had insisted that it was his duty to see for himself the conditions in which the guilty would be confined. And, Justin thought, he had probably heard rumors. He . . . Eight bells of the morning watch struck, and as the watch below came on deck, he turned to find his second-in-command, Master's Mate Rufus Harding, at his elbow.

Harding was thirty-five—two years older than himself—an experienced seaman and a reliable navigator, promoted from the lower deck, and Justin had been pleased when he had been appointed to the *Elizabeth*, since her two junior officers were young midshipmen, as yet unable to stand a watch without supervision.

"I checked the chart, sir," Harding said, bracing his short, muscular body against the ship's violent pitching. "I reckon we should be off Sydney Bay in about two hours."

Justin nodded. Sydney Bay, and the landing place opposite the old settlement at Kingston, was his destination, and he gave his orders with crisp precision.

"Come about in half an hour, Mr. Harding," he finished. "And keep the land abeam. We'll have to beat in, and with this wind, it's not an easy approach. Sydney Bay is not the best of anchorages, either. Too exposed for my liking, when the wind's sou'easterly."

"Were you thinking of the *Sirius*, sir?" Harding asked curiously.

"Yes, that's so," Justin admitted. "The old hands still talk of her loss. I wasn't born at the time, but my mother used to tell me how near Sydney came to starvation when the *Sirius* was driven onto the Norfolk reefs. Governor King wanted the passage enlarged, to enable ships of her size to cross the bar. But it was never done, and it's still a somewhat difficult landing by oared boat—as you'll find out in due course! Needless to tell you, Mr. Harding, I intend to anchor well off the landing place and lay out both bowers and our stern hook. We'll take no chances." He smiled, meeting Harding's concerned gaze. "Well, I'll go below and break my fast. Call me when you have Nepean and Phillip islands in sight."

In the cramped stern cabin that served as the *Elizabeth*'s gunroom, he found George De Lancey eating a meal of porridge and cold, smoke-cured mutton—the latter evidently not greatly to his taste.

"This vessel of yours is uncommonly lively, Justin," he observed, a rueful expression on his lean, good-looking face. "I had supposed myself immune to *mal de mer,* but now—" He pushed his plate away. "I'm not so sure. And poor Meehan's flat on his back."

Justin took the chair on the opposite side of the table, eyeing hungrily the plate his steward put before him. "It's blowing pretty hard," he defended. "I grant you the *Elizabeth*'s inclined to slam—she always has, due to what, I fear, is a fault in her design. Not broad enough in the beam for her overall length. But you get used to her."

"God forbid!" George retorted, with mock dismay. "Damme, I'm a landsman, not a seaman, and I can't wait to get back on dry land. When do you anticipate that we shall arrive at our destination?"

Justin laughed. "Oh, within a couple of hours. And, with any luck, we'll be able to shoot some of the Norfolk Island pigs when we go ashore, and enjoy a change of diet. They're rumored to have bred very freely since the settlement was abandoned."

He thought, as he ate, how much he liked George De Lancey and how fortunate his sister, Rachel, had been in her choice of a husband. Now practicing successfully as a member of the legal profession in Sydney, George—for all he had been born an American—had served with distinction in the British Army during the Peninsular campaign and in the great battle of Waterloo, which had finally seen the defeat of the Emperor Napoleon and the end of the war with France.

His elder brother, Colonel Sir William De Lancey, had been the Duke of Wellington's chief of staff, an officer of immense courage and ability who had been mortally wounded when the battle was all but over and the enemy in retreat. But George himself, despite his family connections and the fact that he was unquestionably a gentleman, had never allied himself, as he might well have done, with the elitist faction in Sydney society. Indeed, by marrying Rachel, who was the daughter of an emancipist, he had placed himself in the other camp and had displayed no hesitation in doing so. The Governor, Sir Thomas Brisbane—much less liberal in his views than his predecessor, Governor Macquarie, had been—had indicated no disapproval of the match, and both George and Rachel had been received at Government House functions with every appearance of pleasure.

True, such functions were now few and far between. Sir Thomas, who was an enthusiastic astronomer, had set up an observatory and a powerful telescope in his official residence at Parramatta and by choice spent most of his time there, working with two German assistants whom he had brought out from England with him. He ruled with an advisory council and, it was said, left even major decisions to them. George had been appointed to the council, and that had set elitist tongues wagging, but— Justin glanced across at his brother-in-law. For no reason that he had ever fully understood, George De Lancey had been the butt of malicious gossip since his arrival in the colony—partly, no doubt, because he was an American—but George took it all with unruffled equanimity, refusing to be provoked.

He looked up now, meeting Justin's gaze with a smile. "Did you know," he asked, an odd note in his deep, pleasant voice, "that an uncle of mine—my father's elder brother, James De Lancey—wanted to set up a colony in New South Wales forty years ago? Before it was decided to make it a penal colony and before the First Fleet set sail . . . Uncle James wanted it for the American Loyalists, after the War of Independence."

Justin shook his head. "No, I was not aware of that, George. What happened and why did the notion fall through?"

"British jails were dangerously overcrowded, and the Colonial Office gave first priority to the need to relieve their congestion and rid the country of its rogues and ne'er-do-wells." George shrugged. His tone was flat as he went on, "Rewarding the American colonists who had fought for the King—and lost their homes in consequence— took second place. Sir Evan Nepean held the view that, since most of them had been resettled in Nova Scotia, they were best left there. In view of your present mission, though—it is interesting, is it not, to speculate as to what a different colony New South Wales might have been had my uncle's Loyalists been entrusted with its settlement. Indeed, Justin, I take leave to doubt whether it would have been necessary to reopen Norfolk Island—or to consider the establishment of a secondary place of punishment at Moreton Bay for the colony's incorrigibles."

Justin helped himself to tea. "True enough," he agreed. "Yet if the home government were to take more care in selecting the type of people they sentence to deportation, there would be little need for either. But they never have, and we're compelled to accept any riffraff they choose to send us. The old, the sick, and the evil—prostitutes and townsfolk, without the skills to fit them for life here. And Irish rebels, of course."

"The most incorrigible of all," George said dryly.

"Yet there are plenty of decent, hardworking folk, too, convicted of quite minor crimes. Professional men, like the architect Francis Greenway, artisans and farm workers, teachers and even lawyers, who are worth their weight in gold out here. The vast majority of *them* make good, if they are given a chance to put the past behind them and hold a stake in the land . . . even if it's only a few acres that they can call their own." Warming to his theme, Justin spoke feelingly. "Governor Macquarie gave them that chance and encouraged them, as you know . . . but Sir Thomas Brisbane's policy is to keep them in landless servitude, without regard for merit. He grants the newly opened lands to rich adventurers and speculators, whose only desire is to make money."

"That's the policy of the British Colonial Office, Justin," George amended. "Brisbane is duty bound to carry it out. He has no choice, and as a good soldier, he obeys orders. I served on his staff for a couple of months in the Peninsular campaign, and I was with him at Toulouse. He's a brave man and an honest one—a mite lacking in imagination, perhaps, but straight as a die."

"All the same," Justin objected, with some heat, "he needn't listen quite so attentively to John Macarthur. The wealthy settler policy was Macarthur's idea, and he persuaded Commissioner Bigge to recommend it to Lord Bathurst, when he went back to London. The Colonial Office jumped at it! But I'll warrant the new free settlers are selected with no more care than the convicts . . . and Macarthur will add to his fortune by selling them his pure merinos. Just as he used to sell his rum, at a hundred percent profit, devil take him!"

"You hold no brief for Mr. Macarthur?" George suggested mildly.

"No, by heaven I don't!"

"Might one inquire why?"

"For a start," Justin returned, "because he's an unmitigated rogue. It was he who plotted the Rum Corps' rebellion and the deposition of Governor Bligh . . . and then left the unfortunate George Johnston to take the blame for it. You should hear my stepfather, Andrew Hawley, on the subject. Andrew was on Governor Bligh's staff and in the thick of it." He started to go into details, but George cut him short.

"Give Macarthur his due—he has played a considerable part in establishing the colony's wool trade, has he not?"

"For his own profit, George. His wife built up his pedigreed flocks and his Arab stud, whilst he was compelled to remain in England. If he had come back here without Colonial Office sanction, he would have faced an indictment for treason. Rather than risk that, he stayed away for nine years . . . and left his wife to manage his stock and his property. She did so most admirably." Justin set down his cup. It was, he knew, difficult—if not impossible—to explain to comparative newcomers like George De Lancey the destructive part John Macarthur had played in the colony's early days. He himself had been barely seventeen at the time of the rebellion against the late Admiral Bligh, but he had been almost as close to what he had termed the thick of it as had his stepfather, Andrew Hawley.

He had watched the scarlet-clad ranks of the Rum Corps marching on Government House, in order to seize, by force of arms, the person of their lawfully appointed Governor. And he had seen John Macarthur carried shoulder-high in triumph through the crowd, which had shouted, "Death to the tyrant Bligh!" That was a memory, Justin thought grimly, that had etched itself indelibly on his mind. Most vividly of all, he remembered waiting on board his small sloop *Flinders,* in the darkness of Sydney Cove, for Andrew to bring the Governor to the wharf, so that together they could convey him to the safety of the Hawkesbury settlements. But Governor Bligh had not been willing to flee, and—

George said thoughtfully, "Your sister Rachel professes the most warm admiration for Mrs. Macarthur."

"Which is a sentiment I share," Justin responded. "In truth, I know of few who do not—she is a remarkably charming and courageous lady."

"I've met her only once or twice," George admitted.

"But I *have* heard your stepfather discourse on the subject of Macarthur himself. I—" He broke off, smothering an exclamation. The ship gave a sickening lurch, the deck beneath his feet seemed suddenly to vanish as she heeled over at an acute angle, and he had to grasp the edge of the table with both hands to keep himself from falling as plates and cutlery slithered across it toward him. "God Almighty, Justin! What's going on?"

"Nothing unusual—we're going about," Justin told him. "Changing to the starboard tack." He paused, listening intently. "But she does seem to have missed stays. Don't worry—Rufus Harding knows how to handle her. There . . ." A succession of shouted orders and the thud of bare feet on the deck planking heralded the *Elizabeth*'s return to an even keel and then to her accustomed pitching. "She's notoriously slack in stays, among her other defects, and the wind's backing. No cause for alarm, George."

"Nevertheless, Captain Broome," George said, rising to his feet a trifle unsteadily, "I'll thank you to excuse me. I feel decidedly queasy—probably because I've been a landlubber for so long. I shall join James Meehan and assume a recumbent position, as he has wisely done. Perhaps you will be so good as to have me called when we come to anchor."

He appeared on deck, however, accompanied by James Meehan, as the *Elizabeth* passed between the two rocky islets of Phillip and Nepean and brought-to on the south side of Sydney Bay. In the lee of the mountainous island, the wind's savage assault had abated, and under head and topsails, the sloop came smoothly into the deserted bay.

Justin supervised the lowering of both bower anchors with extreme care and then hurried aft, to make sure that Harding had been equally careful in laying out a third anchor astern. The bay was exposed, but there was no safer anchorage close to the old landing place and the Kingston prison settlement, of which the inspection had to be made. The passage through the reef was, as he had warned Harding, a hazardous one. Justin took out his glass, training it on the reef.

On all his previous visits, Norfolk Island had been inhabited, and there had almost always been parties of convicts standing by on the jetty, with cork floats and other rescue gear, in case of a mishap in the heavy surf, in which it was all too easy for even a sturdy oared boat to capsize. Now, with the island abandoned, there would be no help available, and he ordered both the longboat and his gig lowered. To Midshipman Bowles, in charge of the larger craft, he gave precise instructions.

"I shall take the gig in with our passengers, Mr. Bowles. I want you to keep the longboat handy but well clear of the bar and come to our aid if we fail to make it in the gig. Once you've seen us through, you can go back to the ship, but keep your boat in the water and watch for my signal from the shore, in . . ." He squinted skyward, estimating the hours of daylight left to them. "In approximately six hours."

"Aye, aye, sir," Bowles acknowledged. "I understand, sir."

"Then carry on, lad." Justin watched the longboat pull away, and then, as the gig tied up to the lee chains, he descended the accommodation ladder and took a place in the bow, in order to get a clear view of the reef ahead. George De Lancey and James Meehan clambered in, and he called to the coxswain to cast off. They approached the bar cautiously. The surf, as always, was smashing violently across the half-submerged length of reef, a cauldron of white, hissing water. But crouched in the gig's bow, Justin had no difficulty in finding the narrow channel between the vicious fangs of weed-grown rock, and obeying his shouted orders, the coxswain steered them safely through and into the calmer water beyond. A series of sun-dappled rollers carried the gig into the shallows and toward the steps of the jetty.

The old, stone-built landing place looked much as he remembered it, Justin saw, despite ten years of neglect. In places the stonework was crumbling, but it was still solid enough. They climbed ashore up steps slippery with slime, and Meehan, his surveyor's instruments and notebooks carried by the young purser's clerk who was to act as his assistant, set off for the prison buildings to begin his task.

Justin, a hunting piece slung from his shoulder, eyed George inquiringly. "A general look round?" he suggested. "And see what fresh meat we can bag for the pot?"

George nodded agreement, and they followed Meehan, at a more leisurely pace, along the rutted, overgrown track leading to what remained of the Kingston penal settlement.

"They left about a dozen dogs here, I was told," Justin observed. "Semiwild creatures which were supposed to kill off any stock that the clearing-up party weren't able to slaughter and salt down before they went back to Sydney. It will be interesting to see if the scheme worked out in practice."

Before long, however, it became evident that it had not. There were no dogs to be seen, but wherever they went among the ruins of the abandoned huts and houses, they encountered pigs and goats running wild, which, at the sound of their approach, scuttled off into the surrounding trees with shrill squeals and bleats of alarm.

The smallholdings, once occupied in ten- and twelve-acre lots and laboriously cleared by emancipist settlers, had degenerated into wilderness, their buildings blackened, roofless shells, the maize and wheat they had sown now long since rotted and overgrown with weeds. The fruit trees, here and on the lower slopes of Mount Pitt, to Justin's surprised delight, were still flourishing, the air heady with the scent of orange and lemon blossoms. In the garden that successive governors of the island had cultivated so assiduously, healthy vines as well as fruit trees grew in abundance, offering promise of a bumper crop when the fruit should ripen. But the fine, two-story house built for Colonel Foveaux and later occupied by those who had followed him was, by contrast, reduced to a crumbling heap of stones, with rats scampering about the ruins, bright-eyed and unafraid of the unexpected human invaders.

Justin shot a well-grown hog that had been rooting in the thick undergrowth, and they returned, carrying the carcass between them, to leave it in the care of the gig's crew, before going to what had been the prison. Meehan was still there, busy with his theodolite and his measuring rods. He said, dabbing at his heated face with a kerchief, "They will have virtually to start from scratch if it is decided to reopen this place as a prison, I fear. The walls are still standing here and there, but the damp salt air has wrought havoc with them. They crumble if you touch them, and there's hardly a roof still in place. If I were the Governor, I'd leave this island to nature . . . or the French!"

"It is much the same everywhere," George told him. He described what he and Justin had seen, and the gray-haired surveyor shrugged despondently.

"But the livestock is breeding and waxing fat," he observed. "My assistant and I have had to drive whole flocks of goats and a sow with a large litter out of the buildings before we could start our work!" He glanced inquiringly at Justin. "I've lost count of the time, but can you give me another couple of hours, Captain Broome? I imagine you will want to negotiate that reef in daylight."

"Indeed yes, Mr. Meehan. But it will still be light in two hours, so take your time. We'll look round here, shall we, George?" Justin gestured to the old prison courtyard and started to move away. "This is what you really want to see, is it not? Prison conditions for those whom it is your duty to sentence for what His Excellency describes as 'the higher class of offenses.' "

George fell into step beside him. "Also quoting the Governor, Justin—'for those felons who will be sent here and who will be forever excluded from all hope of return.' Yes, it is the conditions for such men that I have come to see."

"You will glean some idea, even from these ruins," Justin said, with bleak honesty. "And most of all, I'm afraid, from the burial ground. Conditions are created by the officer appointed as commandant or governor. His powers are absolute. This island, as we see it now, George, could be a productive and far from unhappy place, even for the worst offenders. It has the climate and the fertility to become a small hive of industry, and there's no necessity for the convicts to work in fetters—escape from here is impossible. And''—he waved a hand in the direction from which they had come— "you've seen the smallholdings worked by men who earned emancipation under Governor King and Captain Piper. They're in ruins now, but I can remember the time when they were thriving. I can remember loading my *Flinders* with grain, for export to Sydney . . . aye, and salt meat, too.''

He led the way through the exercise yard and its walls of stone, half obscured now by the invading undergrowth, and George De Lancey frowned, looking keenly about him as Justin pointed out such features as he could recognize. They emerged into the lonely, windswept cemetery, with its mounds of mainly unmarked graves, and he exclaimed, shocked, "God in heaven, Justin, there are hundreds of them! For how long was this a penal establishment? Twenty-five years?''

"The evacuation began in Governor Bligh's day," Justin answered. "But—'' He broke off with a smothered oath. An odd little figure made its appearance, as elusive as a ghost, skipping from grave to grave and watching them intently—ready, it was evident, for instant flight should the need arise. Justin felt his brother-in-law's restraining hand on his arm; he nodded and called out reassuringly. The man came nearer, revealed as a small, stoop-shouldered fellow, with unkempt hair and a flowing white beard. His clothing was so ragged as to leave his body almost naked, and he clutched a rusty ax in both hands, held protectively in front of him.

"Be you from that ship out there?'' he challenged, coming to a halt a few yards away. "Be she British?''

"Yes," Justin confirmed. "And we intend you no harm. Come nearer, so that we may talk to you."

The little man advanced a few cautious paces.

"She's a King's ship, ain't she? And you're a King's officer?"

"That's so. She is the government sloop *Elizabeth*, and I'm her commander. Who are you?"

"I aren't telling, not until I know your business here. Bin rooting around, ain't you? An' there's two others, measuring and poking about down below. I seen 'em— aye, an' I bin watching 'em this hour past, wondering what the devil they was at. 'Tain't often a ship calls here, least of all a King's ship or a Frenchy." The odd little apparition's tone was hoarse and suspicious, but he lowered his ax. "What are you wanting, eh?" He hesitated, regarding them with narrowed eyes, and seeming about to say more, thought better of it and waited expectantly for the answer to his question.

"We are making a survey of the island on behalf of the government of New South Wales," George supplied. He smiled and offered his hand. "My name is De Lancey, George De Lancey. Won't you tell us yours? You are not a convict, are you?"

The proffered hand was ignored, but the old man shuffled closer. "Naw. I were, though—come here when that bloody swine Major Foveaux were in charge. Flogger Foveaux we used to call him . . . an' that were an apt name. He marked my back, did Foveaux. Two hundred lashes, three hundred, it were never less for Foveaux. See for yourselves." He turned, a thin hand drawing aside the torn strips of his filthy shirt to display, to George's shocked gaze, a back that was crisscrossed with hideous scars, showing white and puckered against the tan of his skin. Turning to face his interrogators again, he added with something approaching pride, "But I served me time, sir—three years it were, an' Cap'n Piper made me an overseer an' give me a grant o' twelve acres over yonder." His hand waved vaguely toward Mount Pitt. "He were a

good guv'nor, Cap'n Piper. Married a convict lass, too—
Mary Ann Shears, who were here with her folks. Leastways,
they say he married her. She give him two sons when he
were here.''

He talked on, and George exchanged a rueful glance
with Justin. It seemed likely, Justin thought, that the old
fellow had somehow contrived to remain on the island,
after the clearing-up party under Superintendent Hutchin-
son had departed on board the *Kangaroo,* but . . . good
Lord, that had been over ten years ago, in February or
March of 1814!

He would have been in no danger of starvation, of
course; he had his smallholding, and could have helped
himself at will to the produce of any of the others. There
was fruit for the taking in season, and plenty of water; and
the hogs and goats, which had bred so prolifically over the
years, would have kept him amply supplied with fresh
meat. But with only himself for company, the poor old
devil must have endured a veritable hell of loneliness. An
occasional whaling ship might have called in, for water or
to replenish her supplies, but apart from that, he would
neither have seen nor spoken to another human being since
the *Kangaroo*'s departure.

''Me name's Scaife, sir, Job Scaife.'' Under George's
kindly, quietly voiced questioning, the odd little stranger
was becoming expansive, his bearded lips twitching into a
smile, exposing toothless gums. He set down his ax, his
smile including Justin now. ''I come from Yorkshire—a
reet pretty little village called Mistlethorpe, in t'Dales. You'd
not know it, though—'tis only small. But real pretty.''

The name stirred a chord in Justin's memory. His mother
had often talked of her childhood in the Yorkshire Dales,
and he asked impulsively, ''Is it anywhere near Kirby or
. . .'' The second name came back to him, as if emerging
from the mists of time. ''Milton Overblow?''

''Oh, aye, that it is, sir . . . Cap'n.'' Suddenly there
were tears in the rheumy gray eyes, and a thin, trembling
hand came out to grasp Justin's arm. ''Why, Kirby's

t'next village, an' Milton Overblow ain't above five mile away. Do you come from there, Cap'n?''

Regretfully, Justin shook his head. "No, Job, I don't; I was born out here. But my mother did. Her home was at Long Wrekin Farm, and—''

"Long Wrekin? 'Tis on Lord Braxton's estate; Long Wrekin an' Kirby, too, as I've good reason to know!'' Job Scaife's excited nostalgia gave place to anger. " 'Tis on His bloody Lordship's account that I'm here. Had me up for poachin'—him an' a swine o' a seafarin' man as used to work for him. Gunner, they called him—Gunner O'Keefe. You ever heard your ma talk o' him?''

Justin stared at him, bereft of words. That name, too . . . *those* names, Lord Braxton and Gunner O'Keefe! His mother had spoken of them both, in a voice choked with sobs. He remembered the story she had told him, of a fire . . . the stable at Long Wrekin deliberately set on fire by O'Keefe and another man in Lord Braxton's employ. A fire in which his grandfather had died in a brave attempt to save the horses trapped inside. It had been after that—not long after—that his mother and grandmother had been evicted from the farm and made the long journey to London on foot. Andrew Hawley had gone with them . . . and, Justin now recalled, his mother had been but a child of ten.

"Yes," he confirmed, his throat tight. "My mother talked of them both—Lord Braxton and O'Keefe. But it's a long time ago. My mother was only a child.''

"Aye, sir, an' I were nobbut a lad,'' old Job asserted. The light in his eyes faded, and his voice was flat and tired as he went on, "I bin out here since 'ninety-one. Come out in t'*Atlantic*, sentenced to seven years, thanks to His Lordship. I done three on t'road gang, an' then I run, so they give me another three. I run a couple more times, an' they sent me here . . . to t'Island o' the Damned, that's what they called it in Foveaux's day. An' that's what it were, an' no mistake. But not anymore, not since they closed it down. But . . .'' A sudden suspicion sounded in his voice, and he turned, appealing to George. "They ain't goin' to open it again, are they, sir? Is that why you're here?"

George eyed him pityingly. "Yes, I'm afraid that is why we're here, Job. The chances are that the island is to become a prison settlement again. But you—"

"Then he were right!" Job exclaimed bitterly. "The bloody Dutchman were right! I didn't believe him when he told me, but I should'a known, when I seen you an' them other fellers pokin' around. I should'a guessed!"

Justin tensed. "What Dutchman, Job?" he demanded, his tone sharper than he had intended it to be. "Has anyone else been here recently?"

Job Scaife jumped back in alarm, his faded eyes once again mistrustful and bright with suspicion. "He said I weren't to tell," he began. "He said he'd report me—"

"Why did he come?" Justin asked more gently. "What did he want?"

"Water an' fresh meat," Job admitted sullenly. "I give him what he asked for, an' he give me a keg o' brandy an' some 'baccy. But they was spoilt. Salt water had got into t'baccy, an' t'brandy were rotgut native stuff." He brightened. "Can you give me some that's better, sir? I ain't had a decent smoke nor a drink in years, an' seeing yours is a King's ship, not a trader like the Dutch feller's, I thought maybe—" George took his pipe and a pouch of tobacco from his coat pocket, and the old man seized them eagerly, his gnarled hands trembling as he crammed shreds of tobacco into the bowl of the pipe.

George lit it for him. "Tell us about the Dutchman, Job," he invited, lowering his voice to a conversational tone. With a warning glance at Justin, he gestured to the cemetery wall. "Sit down and enjoy your pipe and tell us what you can, eh? There's no hurry."

Once again under George's patient questioning, the old man talked freely, his narrative rambling and punctuated by frequent coughing, as the unaccustomed tobacco smoke irritated his lungs. But his drift was clear enough, and

Justin said, frowning, "For God's sake—it was Van Buren who called here, and in the *Flinders*! I sold her to Robert Campbell when I was given command of the *Elizabeth*, and Van Buren chartered her, with the old *Dolphin* and a schooner of Simeon Lord's, the *Dorcas*. He's been trading with his fellow countrymen in the Dutch islands, but with hired crews and masters. I'd no idea he intended to take the *Flinders* to sea himself."

"But he's no seaman, surely?" George, too, was puzzled. "I'd always understood that he was commandant of the military garrison at Coupang, and that Lucy Tempest married him after she was saved from a shipwreck. Somewhere off Timor, was it not?"

"Yes," Justin answered, still frowning. "Lucy was the only survivor of an Indiaman, the *Kelso*, which went down in a typhoon in the Sunda Strait, on passage from China. Her owners and her crew were all from Sydney. Jasper Spence and his wife—you'll have heard of them, I'm sure—were the owners."

He remembered, as if it had been yesterday, Lucy Tempest's return to Sydney, with her new Dutch husband, and the warmth of the welcome she had received from her brother, Rick, and her elder sister, Abigail Dawson, who had given her up for dead. The Van Burens had entered Sydney Cove within hours of the colony's sad farewell to Governor and Mrs. Macquarie—indeed, the Dutch vessel and the British transport bearing the Macquaries must have come within hailing distance as the latter cleared Port Jackson Heads.

Abigail, he remembered, had been overjoyed to see her sister again. There had been parties and even a reception at Government House to celebrate the seeming miracle of Lucy's survival, after what had been regarded as an appalling tragedy, affecting many Sydney families. But then, for some reason, the welcome had worn thin.

Major Josef Van Buren—Jos, as he liked to be called— was arrogant and a heavy drinker. He had not made himself popular in Sydney society, even with the elitist

Macarthur set, and there were rumors that he had quarreled with Timothy Dawson, Abigail's husband, over some property to which he had insisted his wife was entitled. He and Lucy had taken up an opulent life, flaunting their wealth in one of Sydney's more exclusive houses, which they had purchased soon after their arrival and staffed with native servants, brought with them from Batavia. In addition they— A sharp exclamation from George broke into Justin's thoughts.

"Good heavens, Justin, did you hear that? Did you hear what Scaife just said?"

Justin shook his head. "No, I wasn't listening. I thought he was rambling, you see. I—"

"Well, he may be rambling, but he seems to have the details pat enough. He says there was a second ship, which came in company with Van Buren's sloop but stood off, outside the bay. And he reckons she was French. That's so, is it not, Job?" George's voice softened. "Tell Captain Broome what you told me."

Job nodded vigorously and repeated his claim.

"A three-master she were, Cap'n, carryin' guns. She kept well offshore, sailin' up an' down, so I never got a real good look at her."

"Then what made you suppose she was French?"

The old man spat. " 'Cause she sent a boat in, wi' half a dozen of 'em. They picked up the Dutchman from his ship and crossed the bar jus' before sunset. Spent the night onshore, they did, an' I kept out o' their way. But I heard 'em talking—jabbering, more like, an' I know frog talk when I hear it."

"What did they do onshore?" Justin asked.

"They roasted one o' my hogs," Job told him aggrievedly. "Them an' the Dutchman. Then they had a look round, jus' like you've bin doing, and made off, back to their ship. Nearly capsized, going over the reef, an' I was hoping they would. The Dutchman stayed till the next day, but the Frenchy set sail, soon as her boat got back, heading nor'west, near as I could make out."

Justin glanced at George and saw his own concern mirrored in his companion's face. Fears of an attempt by the French to establish settlements on Australian soil had long plagued successive British governments, and they both were aware of the probable consequences, should such an attempt succeed. With vast tracts of unclaimed land at risk, the Colonial Office had, for some years past, been urging the establishment of British penal colonies and settlements at strategic points along the coast to the north and west of Sydney to counter the French threat.

Justin questioned Job Scaife minutely as to the actions of the supposed French party and of Van Buren himself, but the old outcast could tell them little more. He indignantly rejected the suggestion that he should leave Norfolk Island and return to Sydney on board the *Elizabeth*.

"I've lived here for ten year past, and I ain't shifting now," he retorted. "If they do reopen t'prison, why, I'll ask 'em for me old job back. But until they do, I'll bide where I am. If you want to do owt for me, then maybe a keg o' decent rum an' a few plugs o' chawin' 'baccy wouldn't come amiss. Aye, an' some clobber from your slop chest, so's I'll be properly clothed for me next callers, if that ain't asking too much."

"You shall have what you need," Justin promised him. "You—" A hail from James Meehan interrupted him, and with a mumbled "Thankee, sir," Job went shambling off, to vault over the crumbling wall of the cemetery and vanish into the surrounding screen of trees.

That evening, back on board the *Elizabeth*, talk was of the visit of the unidentified French warship and its probable purpose, with Meehan loud in his condemnation of Jos Van Buren's apparently secret rendezvous with her officers.

"He never imagined anyone would find out what he's been up to," the surveyor said. "But I've heard talk, as you gentlemen must have done also. A very strange character, Major Van Buren. He's been laboring under a sense of injustice ever since he came to Sydney and the Governor rejected his application for a land grant. Quite rightly, in my opinion, since he's Dutch, not British, and the Dutch were Boney's allies in the war. But I wouldn't trust the man, by heaven I wouldn't! And this proves he's still on the other side. I think the Governor should be told, Captain Broome.''

"Don't worry," Justin assured him gravely. "He'll be fully informed. And no doubt, in the light of all this, His Excellency will want the resettlement of the island put in hand as expeditiously as possible. When do you expect to have finished your survey, Mr. Meehan?"

Meehan considered the question. "Permit me one more day, Captain," he decided. "All being well, I shall have done all that's needful by tomorrow afternoon."

He was as good as his word. Justin put him ashore in the gig soon after first light; by four in the afternoon he announced that his task had been completed and he was ready to leave the island.

Old Job had remained out of sight throughout the day, evidently fearing that attempts might be made to persuade him to leave. Justin, after he and George had searched unavailingly for his hiding place, left the clothing he had asked for by the wall of the cemetery, together with a supply of flour and tobacco and a small keg of rum. All were gone when the shore party made their way to the jetty.

The return to the ship was accomplished without mishap, for all the fury of the surf crashing across the bar and the loss of an oar. The *Elizabeth* weighed anchor and made sail as soon as the boats had been hoisted inboard and secured, clearing the bay and its two guardian islets well before sunset.

Justin stood the first watch, setting course to the southwest, with the wind fresh and northerly and the sea relatively calm. But by the evening of the fourth day of their passage, with the Australian coast in sight, the glass fell ominously and the wind veered from northeast to southerly and rose steadily to gale force. Life on board became, once again, uncomfortable for those below and fraught with danger for the watch on deck.

The *Elizabeth* was well battened down, taking in less water than she normally did, and before the storm struck, Justin had prudently reduced sail to close-reefed topsails and a forestaysail, with the upper yards sent down and two men at the wheel. In spite of this, he passed an anxious night as the sea rose to mountainous heights, with a strong lee set, and the wind, backing easterly a little before midnight, waged a ceaseless assault on the ship's swaying masts and her straining canvas, seeking always to drive her toward the inhospitable shore.

Dawn came at last, faintly tingeing the scudding black clouds with pale gray light, when from the darkness ahead Justin was startled to see the sudden, dazzling glow of an ascending rocket. A distress call, from a ship in trouble, his weary brain registered. Stiff with cold, he peered apprehensively into the spray-obscured dimness and glimpsed the dark outline of a rocky headland, rising over a hundred feet into the air, with surf breaking in a maelstrom of churned-up water at its foot.

"That's Cape Hawke, sir, isn't it?" Rufus Harding questioned, hands cupped about his mouth in order to make himself heard above the roar of the wind. "God help any vessel that's driven ashore there!"

Justin nodded, glass to his eye but unable to make out more than a dark shape, just visible among the tossing breakers, and . . . yes, the slender outline of a mast, unless he was mistaken. Cape Hawke was a rocky promontory situated midway between Port Macquarie and the mouth of the Hunter River. It guarded a small, shallow bay, hemmed in by cliffs, in which, he could only suppose, the ship that had fired the distress flare had attempted to take shelter from the gale.

But her master, due to lack of knowledge of the treacherous coastline or an error of judgment in the darkness, must have failed to weather the point, and . . . A second rocket spluttered skyward, momentarily bathing ship and foreshore in eerie red light.

Justin's half-formed fears became agonizing certainty.

He recognized the ship, despite the surf breaking over her canting deck and foaming about her shattered mainmast—she had been his for too long for him to forget her. He had designed and partly built her; he had been her master before Their Lordships of the Admiralty had seen fit to grant him a commission and appoint him to his present command. . . . He controlled himself with an effort of will, sick with despair at what he knew her fate must be.

"That is the *Flinders*, Mr. Harding," he rasped. "The *Flinders*, with Major Van Buren on board. And God damn his soul, we shall have to try to save him! Turn up the watch below and stand by to go about!"

He saw the alarm in Harding's face and shook his head to the older man's unvoiced question. "A boat would never live in this. Our only chance is to get into the bay and try to reach them from there. Look lively, man! There's no time to be lost. I doubt if the *Flinders* will last more than an hour."

And perhaps not even as long as that, Justin thought bitterly. He crossed to the wheel as the men of the watch below came tumbling up on deck, roused from their hammocks by the call, and cursing as the wind tore at their flapping oilskins.

"Ready about!" Speaking trumpet pressed to his lips, Justin shouted his orders above the shrieking of the wind and the noisy, metallic clanking of the newly manned pumps. Slowly, unwillingly, the *Elizabeth*'s head came round, her lee scuppers awash as she heeled over under the wind's violent pressure. Then, as she righted herself on the new tack, another flare rose from the stricken *Flinders*, and Justin was able to make out quite clearly the jagged rocks of the promontory onto which she had been flung . . . and which his own ship must weather, if she were to reach the sheltered cove beyond.

Even in full daylight it would be a risky maneuver, and he knew that he could not wait for full daylight. It was now or never. He called out to Harding to join him. . . .

CHAPTER III

Soaked to the skin and shivering with a cold that seemed almost to eat into his bones, Major Jos Van Buren dragged himself up into the *Flinders*'s sagging mainmast shrouds. He clung there, straining his eyes into the semidarkness, his stomach churning, as wave after wave of foaming water cascaded across the deck, barely a dozen feet below him. Above him, only the stump of the mainmast remained, and he could go no higher, even had he been able to summon the strength to do so.

Minutes earlier, he had seen his Malay deckhand, Janur, swept overboard as he had attempted to launch their only boat . . . and now the boat was gone and Janur with it, the man's despairing cries borne away by the fury of the wind, yet still ringing in his ears as if they came from beside him.

Van Buren drew a long, shuddering breath. The surf was pounding his small vessel to destruction, he was aware, for even her stout hull would not withstand its relentless assault for much longer, and God knew what damage the rocks had wrought below the waterline. His hopes of rescue, briefly aroused by the glimpse of another ship's riding lights in the offing, were now receding. As nearly as he could make out in the gloom of an overcast dawn, the unknown ship had tacked. She was heading away from the rocky point on which the *Flinders* had foundered, abandoning her to her fate, despite the distress rockets his son, Claus, had contrived, with Janur's aid, to

send up. It was inconceivable that her people could have
failed to observe them, yet . . .

"Claus!" Frantically, at the pitch of his lungs, Van
Buren called on the boy to make one last attempt. "Do
you hear me? Another rocket, in the name of heaven! Send
up another rocket! They are leaving us!"

There was no response, and Van Buren cursed him
savagely for a witless coward. But what else could be
expected of a miserable little half-caste, whose native
mother had resorted to attempted murder when she had
feared that she would be supplanted by Lucy Tempest?
Claus took after her, in both character and appearance; he
had her dark good looks and compliant nature and was
afraid of his own shadow. Doubtless he would be skulking
below with Abdul Wetar, the Malay master, whose want
of navigating skill had brought about the disaster to the
Flinders and who, the previous day, had compounded their
predicament by breaking a leg in a fall from the rigging.

It had been a grave error, Van Buren reflected bitterly,
to take on the two Malays in place of the two emancipist
seamen he had engaged in Sydney . . . although there had
been no help for it. He had been forced to leave the
Englishmen in Batavia when the rendezvous with the French
frigate was arranged, since the risk that they would talk
out of turn was too great to be contemplated. And he had
done well out of the encounter; Capitaine Duperrey had,
indeed, been generous, trading good French brandy for the
Flinders's cargo of Batavian *arrack* in equal measure,
since the fiery native spirit would suffice the Frenchmen
for trade with the Maoris of New Zealand. And his own
profit would have been considerable, if only he had been
able to deliver the brandy to his Sydney warehouse. . . .
Van Buren swore again, with renewed frustration.

Even if he and Claus and the injured Wetar were able to
scramble ashore when the storm abated, the precious kegs
of brandy would go down with the wreckage of the *Flinders*
. . . unless he could manage to attract the attention of the

passing stranger and induce her master to turn back. But perhaps with the coming of daylight . . .

He shouted again, and this time Claus answered him, his small dark head appearing momentarily above the after hatchway coaming. Van Buren did not hear what he said, but after some delay there was a bright flash from the hatchway. A rocket was ignited, but Claus must have handled it carelessly, since instead of rising in a trail of sparks, it flared and exploded, and even above the roar of the wind the boy's shrill shriek of agony was audible.

"Miserable little fool!" his father accused wrathfully. "Do you seek to start a fire? Are we not in sufficient trouble already?"

As before, there was no immediate response. Then, several anxious minutes later, Claus emerged from the hatchway and, choosing his moment, came stumbling unsteadily across the wet, steeply slanting deck. He swung himself onto the ratlines and ascended slowly to Van Buren's side. In the dim light his face looked almost black, and his shirt hung in scorched shreds from his shoulders, flapping wildly in the wind. But, beyond the assurance that there was no fire, he offered no explanation.

"The ship we saw—" he began.

"Is making off, the devil take her!" Van Buren interrupted. "She paid no heed to the flares."

"That is not so, sir," Claus contradicted diffidently. Since coming to Sydney, he had been ordered never to address his father in any other manner, and even in the present circumstances, he was mindful of the fact that their relationship was not to be acknowledged. His color, Lucy had insisted, would give rise to malicious talk; the fact that his English was poor had aided the small deception, and the boy had never complained.

Van Buren eased his cramped arms and glared at him. "What do you mean, idiot? Are you blind, as well as dim-witted? She is tacking, isn't she?"

"In order to enter the bay, sir," Claus said. "With the wind in this quarter, she must steer away from the head-

land and then come about, if she is not to be driven onto
the rocks as we were.''

"What do you know about it?" his father retorted.
"Are you a seaman now, on the strength of two or three
voyages?" His tone was bitingly contemptuous.

"No, sir," the boy conceded. "But I asked Abdul when
I went below for the rocket. And see"—his thin young
arm lifted, pointing excitedly into the gloom to seaward—
"she has come about and . . . yes, she has set more sail.
She's in the lee of the headland, sir, on the larboard tack.
She is coming to our aid."

It seemed that he was right, Van Buren observed with
sick relief. The unknown ship was small—a government
sloop from her appearance, he decided, as she heeled over
onto her new tack and he was able to see the black-and-
white checkered paintwork on her exposed weather quarter.
Not the *Amity*—she was larger—or the *Mermaid,* which
was rigged as a cutter, but undoubtedly a King's ship and
very expertly handled. Straining his eyes, he followed her
progress and expelled his breath in relief as he watched her
bring-to on the far side of the bay.

Claus had also been watching. "She is the *Elizabeth,*
sir!" he exclaimed. "Captain Broome's ship. I have seen
her often in Sydney Cove."

"Broome?" Van Buren echoed. He recalled the disparaging tone in which his wife had, on several occasions,
spoken of Justin Broome.

"He is Australian-born," she had said. "His parents
were both convicts. But the late Governor Macquarie thought
very highly of him and gave the Admiralty Board no peace
until they granted him a commission. He married Mrs.
Macquarie's personal maid."

Odd indeed, the Dutchman reflected, that the man on
whom his rescue depended should be one of the class Lucy
considered socially untouchable. Her sister, Abigail Dawson,
held more liberal views, it was true; she received the
Broomes in her house and even appeared to be on terms of

intimate affection with Broome's wife, the onetime lady's maid.

"Captain Broome," Claus said, "built the *Flinders*, sir. It will grieve him to see her now, I fear."

"It will grieve him no more than it grieves me," his father told him sourly. The ominous sound of creaking, overstrained timbers struck chill into his heart, and fear returned as he felt the ship lurch beneath him. Wind and sea were driving her still farther onto the rocks, and her list became perceptibly steeper as her hull ground against their jagged, unyielding teeth. Only the weight of water she had shipped held her where she was, and Van Buren, looking about him in alarm, thought once again of attempting a panic-stricken dash across the rocks to the cliff that marked the shore. But it was treacherous and steep, the rocks awash, and he knew that such a move offered scant chance for any of them—least of all the wretched Abdul Wetar, with his shattered leg.

They must wait and cling to the hope that Broome and his people would manage to take them off before the *Flinders* finally broke up.

"Have they launched a boat?" he demanded harshly of Claus.

"I cannot see, sir," the boy answered unhappily. "The ship is behind the point." He hesitated and then added more cheerfully, "They will bring her as close as they can, perhaps, and lower a boat when they have shelter from the wind. Sir—" Again he hesitated, and his father grunted irritably.

"Well? What is it? Speak up, boy!"

"I should go below, sir, and help Abdul to reach the deck. I got him to the foot of the hatchway, but the lower deck will be completely flooded now, and he can only drag himself up with his hands."

"Then let him do so," Van Buren ordered. With rescue so near at hand, he was curiously reluctant to let the boy go, though he was poor enough company, heaven knew. And he had sharp eyes—he would see if a boat was approaching. "Abdul can fend for himself—" he began, but broke off as, with a rending crash, the *Flinders*'s foremast went by the board, split off at the cap. A mass of tangled rigging littered the fo'c'sle, and the sloop's bow sank lower into the water beneath its weight. But her stern lifted, and the angle of the list was, he saw, less acute.

"Claus," he shouted again. "Have they launched a boat?"

There was no answer, and looking down, Van Buren glimpsed the boy's slight figure struggling, knee-deep in water, across the deck. Claus hauled open the hatch cover, having to make several attempts to do so, and then vanished from sight without closing it behind him. Evidently Abdul had managed to drag himself at least partly up the ladder, for a few seconds later two dark heads appeared in the aperture, both gasping and spluttering as the surf washed over them. It took their combined efforts to gain the deck, and as he watched in scowling disapproval, Van Buren saw them struggle together to the wheel, which, though awash, would afford a firm refuge. Both clung to it, Claus's thin, bare arm about the Malay master's shoulders to give him additional support.

Then a hail from some distance away distracted Van Buren's attention, and the Dutchman's flagging spirits lifted. They were coming, he thought thankfully—praise be to God, they were coming to his aid at last! He leaned perilously forward and discerned an oared boat approaching the point. It was small—a four-oared gig—but there was a second, larger boat standing off astern. Cupping his numbed hands about his mouth, he acknowledged the hail, his voice hoarse from strain and exhaustion.

"Here—I am here! Van Buren of the sloop *Flinders*! I beg you to make haste—she is breaking up!" In his confused relief he had spoken in his own language, and realizing his mistake, he repeated the words in English.

The answer was a brusque "Aye, aye" as the gig came cautiously nearer. . . .

* * *

In the sternsheets of the gig, Justin lowered his speaking trumpet. Young Bowles, in the longboat, had his orders; as he had done when they landed on Norfolk Island, he would stand off at a safe distance from the rocks and bring his boat in only should the gig get into difficulties. There was a gap in the rocks ahead, wide enough to take the gig and, Justin calculated, measuring it with his eye, deep enough to shelter the small craft from the wind and thus from the pounding of the surf. He steered for it, shouting to the bowman to be ready with his boat hook.

His crew were all volunteers, and they included George De Lancey, who had been the first to volunteer, now belying his landlubberly status by the skill with which he was plying his oar. The gig nosed her way into the rocky cleft, which proved to be wider and steeper than Justin had estimated; the bowman fended her off, and then, with practiced deftness as she lost way, hooked on to rock above his head.

"The sloop's on her beam ends, sir," he yelled. "An' both masts gone. But she's still afloat, an' it looks like there's one o' her people clingin' on for dear life in her weather shrouds. I can't see no one else."

In the old days, Justin thought wryly as he busied himself with the rescue gear he and the coxswain had prepared . . . in the old days, when he had been her master, the *Flinders* had carried a crew of three. Himself, old Cookie Barnes, and a deckhand; Van Buren, who held no master's ticket, would probably have carried four or five, which suggested . . . His mouth tightened. Better not to imagine what that suggested. Certainly, Van Buren himself had survived—it had been he who had answered the hail, no doubt of that.

"Ready when you are, sir," the coxswain said.

Justin tested the line secured about his waist, nodded his satisfaction, and slid the rest of its coils over one shoulder. He had given his orders before the two boats had left the *Elizabeth*'s side, and each man knew what he must do. Aided by two of them, he clambered out of the boat and onto the rocky shore, conscious of a deep sense of sadness when at last, in the growing daylight, he had his first clear view of the wrecked *Flinders*.

That there was no hope for her was immediately and painfully apparent. As the bowman had said, she was lying on her beam ends on the rocks, dismasted, her hull breaking up, and her bow, with its once proud figurehead, all but submerged in the frothing cauldron of water in which she lay. He saw the solitary figure clinging to the remnants of the mainmast shrouds, and then, as the coxswain joined him, secured by a second rope, he saw two others crouching, waist-deep, by the wheel.

Three survivors, then, he decided; the gig could take them off, and there would be no need to risk the longboat. A hand grasped his arm, and he turned to find George beside him, ready to relieve him of the coiled line. There was pity in his friend's eyes as he asked gruffly, "The *Flinders* was your first command, was she not? And she's finished."

"Yes," Justin confirmed. "In another couple of hours there will be nothing left of her." He raised his voice, shouting to make himself heard above the blustering wind, "Ready, cox'un? Right, then follow me. And George— pay out that line slowly, if you please. Don't try to come across until I give the signal."

George nodded, and, bent almost double, Justin set off over the slippery, weed-grown rocks, his coxswain following a few yards behind him, both lines being paid out with meticulous care. They made good progress until they reached a part of the promontory that was periodically flooded under the driving inrush of the surf. It was shallow enough when the waves receded, but unable to keep his feet in the fast-moving torrent of water, Justin was flung against the jagged crests of rock and was bruised and all but spent when he gained the *Flinders*'s lee side.

She was listing so far over that it was a comparatively easy task to haul himself on board, but once there, he found his way impeded by a tangled mass of fallen cordage, brought down by the shattered foremast. There was nothing for it but to wait for the coxswain to rejoin him; when the man did so, gasping and as spent as he was, he took the ax from him and hacked blindly until, miraculously, the whole mass slid over the side. Relieved of the dead-weight of the mast, the *Flinders*'s slender bow rose perceptibly, and, sluggishly now because of the tons of water filling her lower deck and hold, she seemed momentarily to float again, on an almost even keel.

Aware that this might well be the prelude to her sinking, Justin wasted no time. He waved George and the gig's bowman to come to the water's edge, saw them start off, bent under the weight of the hempen ropes they carried, and, pausing only to make sure that the line about his waist was clear of entanglements, made his way aft. The two figures he had seen crouched by the wheel were revealed as a man and a boy, both dark-skinned, and the man clearly injured, for the boy was heroically supporting him.

Justin called out to them, but before either could reply, there was a furious bellow from Van Buren, who came slithering down from the mainmast shrouds to plant his big, dripping body squarely in his rescuer's path.

"Mr. Broome! You are indeed welcome, sir. I am Major Van Buren, and I will thank you to assist me to leave this vessel before she sinks. There is no time to be lost." His tone was peremptory, brooking no dissent, but Justin, drenched and cold and in no mood for argument, motioned him to stand aside.

"I fancy one of your people is hurt, sir. If that is so, he must be taken off first."

The big Dutchman glared at him and started to voice a protest, but Justin ignored it and made for the two by the wheel, slipping the line from about his waist as he did so. It took only a cursory inspection to satisfy him that the Malay seaman's need was urgent. The boy with him, who gave his name simply as Claus, had done the best he could to deal with his companion's fractured limb by securing it to a length of splintered planking, using a belt and strips torn from his shirt to hold it in place. He said anxiously, in halting English, as Justin examined the improvised splint, "Poor Abdul is in much pain, sir. I did try to make him more comfortable, but I fear it is not good for him that I must drag him from below."

"We'll take him off at once," Justin promised. The coxswain—not waiting for orders—was hauling in the lines they had carried, and already one of the thick hempen ropes to which they were attached was on board, paid out by the now unseen shore party at the water's edge. Justin had banked on finding fit men, whom it would have been relatively simple to take off using the ropes alone, but . . . Kneeling on the wet deck, he snatched off his kerchief and used it to augment the strips of linen with which Claus had secured his improvised splint.

Some sort of bo'sun's chair would have to be rigged, he thought, if the injured Abdul were to be spared a great deal more pain . . . and, God willing, if there was time. Rising, he crossed to the sagging lee rail and tested it. The quick-witted coxswain, guessing his intention, held out a hand for the ax.

"I'll do that, sir," he offered. "Looks like you'll have to deal with the Dutch officer."

The warning came an instant too late. Justin turned to find Van Buren advancing on him, swearing angrily. In the dim light his fleshy face was contorted and suffused with indignant color, his dark eyes ablaze.

"In God's name, Broome!" he exclaimed. "Wetar is a damned Malay—a native! I demand that you cease to waste time with him and aid me to leave this ship. She'll go down at any minute, and I don't intend to go with her. I—"

"Stand back!" Justin ordered curtly. "Don't worry, the *Flinders* is good for a while yet—I'll not let you drown. But the injured man goes first."

"No!" Van Buren flung at him. "I do!"

His fist came out, aimed furiously at Justin's face. The

sheer unexpectedness of the blow taking him by surprise, Justin stumbled, lost his footing, and went crashing down onto the deck. Van Buren did not hesitate. Pausing only to test that both ropes were firmly secured, he went over the side, and by the time Justin had scrambled dazedly to his feet, the big Dutchman emerged from the surf to be helped ashore by George De Lancey.

Justin stared after him, keeping a tight rein on his temper. He saw George wave, to indicate that he and his party were ready to receive the next member of the *Flinders*'s crew. Stepping back, he beckoned Claus to his side.

"You can go now, lad," he said crisply. "No reason for you to delay any longer. We'll take good care of your father, never fear."

"You mean Abdul, sir?" the boy asked. He looked up into Justin's bruised face and then lowered his gaze, adding ashamedly, "Abdul is my friend, not my father. It is Major Van Buren who is my father. I am . . . sir, I am most sorry that he hit you. I am sure he—he is not himself. The loss of this ship, you see, and her cargo—has much distressed him."

"All right, lad." Justin clapped a friendly hand on the boy's shoulder. "Be off with you! Your father and I will settle the matter later." And by heaven they would, he thought sourly, and wondered, as Claus moved obediently away, whether the boy's claim was true. It seemed unlikely, but . . . "Cox'un," he called. "The boy's to go now."

"Aye, aye, sir," the coxswain acknowledged, with disciplined woodenness. "Come on, lad. All you got to do is hold fast to these ropes, see, an' the worst you'll get is a ducking."

With his aid, Claus grasped the trailing ropes and went down, hand over hand, with such agility that he was clear of the pounding surf and in the arms of the shore party minutes later.

Abdul Wetar's passage, his body lashed firmly to part of the *Flinders*'s rail, was slower and fraught with some peril, but it was safely accomplished, Justin and his gig's coxswain following the improvised stretcher down and, between them, protecting its occupant from the worst of the buffeting.

George said, when Justin joined him, drenched and shivering with cold, "I sent Van Buren straight to the boat. He was making trouble, so I thought it best to get rid of him."

"What sort of trouble?" Justin questioned.

George gave him a grim smile. "He mistook me for one of your seamen, I think. At all events he offered me a substantial reward if I'd go on board the *Flinders* and try to save some of his cargo. It's French brandy, I gathered— the spoils of his liaison with that French frigate, presumably."

Justin swore. "I'll have a reckoning with Major Van Buren when we're back on board my ship, George. He's not a pleasant fellow. Right, lads—" He waved a hand in the direction of the inlet in which they had left the gig. "Back to the boat, and have a care with the injured man. Cox'un, go ahead, if you please, and call in the longboat— there'll be more space for him in that."

"Aye, aye, sir," the seaman began, and then broke off, with an angry obscenity. "The gig's putting off, sir—look! That sodding Dutch officer . . . begging your pardon, sir, but he's taken one o' the oars, and they're making for the ship!"

He was right, Justin saw. Two men had been left in charge of the gig; there were now three at the oars, and the boat was heading out toward where the *Elizabeth* lay at anchor, plainly visible in the lightening gloom. He had to make an effort to control his indignation . . . devil take Van Buren for a selfish, arrogant swine!

Tight-lipped, he repeated his order to the coxswain to call in the longboat and brushed aside George's attempt to apologize. "You weren't to know what the blasted fellow would do. No doubt he's in a hurry to get into dry clothing and out of this infernal wind. Frankly, so am I, so let's be on our way, shall we? But don't worry, George—I'll add it to his reckoning, and that's beginning to mount up. He has to account to me for losing the *Flinders*, damn his soul!''

But the *Flinders* was still there, on the point, when the longboat came alongside the *Elizabeth*'s black-painted side a little over an hour later. It was as if, brave little ship that she was, she was reluctant to die, even in her extremity, Justin thought sadly.

With a word of thanks to his men, he left Harding and Bowles to deal with the injured Malay seaman, then went to stand alone by the taffrail to watch the *Flinders*'s end, aware that it could not now be long in coming. Yet when it came, he was unprepared for its suddenness. One minute she was there, her stumps of masts seeming to defy the torrents of white-crested water driving her remorselessly against the rocks . . . and the next, she had vanished, slipping silently into her grave as the sea, to which she had been born, closed over and buried all trace of her in its cold, gray depths.

Justin felt tears aching in his throat. He gripped the taffrail, torn between heartbreak and a bitter anger, and tempted to vent that anger on Van Buren, who had caused her loss.

From behind him a shrill young voice hesitantly called his name, and he turned to find the boy Claus standing a few yards away. Still in his sodden duck trousers and the torn and filthy shirt, the boy who had claimed to be Van Buren's son now somehow looked smaller and younger than he had before. Twelve, perhaps, Justin thought, or at the most fourteen—only a few years older than his own son Red—and as thin as a rake, poor little devil. Justin studied him, frowning. The stains on his shirt were scorch marks, and the boy's hands and upper arms were, unless he was mistaken, badly burned.

''What happened to you?'' he demanded. ''How did you get those burns, lad?''

Claus retreated, looking confused. ''One of the rockets,

sir,'' he explained finally. "It—blew up, exploded, you see. But the burns, they are nothing—I am not in pain.''

"All the same,'' Justin told him firmly, "you had better let the cook put some salve on them before they do cause you pain. And change into dry clothes.'' They had hoisted both gig and longboat inboard, he saw, and taken the injured Abdul below. He summoned the midshipman of the watch. "Have this lad taken to the galley, Mr. Cole, and tell the cook to do what he can for him—he's been burned quite severely. Hot gruel and a change of clothing, and then find a hammock for him and let him get his head down, understand?''

"Aye, aye, sir,'' Cole acknowledged. He made to take Claus's arm, but the boy eluded him.

"I will go below, Captain Broome, as you desire,'' Claus promised. "But I was wanting to say to you that I am most truly sorry that your *Flinders* is now lost. My father also will be much grieved.''

"Yes,'' Justin returned dryly. "I am sure he will.'' Van Buren would be even more grieved at the loss of his damned French brandy, no doubt, but . . . The earnest expression on Claus's thin, dark face suddenly evoked Justin's pity, and he summoned a smile. "Thank you,'' he said, with a swift change of tone. "I am grateful for your sympathy, Master Van Buren.''

"Oh, please, sir, do not call me by that name!'' Claus pleaded in swift alarm. "I am known by my mother's name, sir—which is—was Karimon. I—''

"Then, Master Karimon,'' Justin said gently, "accept my gratitude and cut along with Mr. Cole. He'll show you where to go.''

The two youngsters departed, and Justin, conscious of his own need for dry clothing, crossed to where Rufus Harding was supervising the securing of the longboat.

"Weigh and make sail, Mr. Harding, as soon as the boats are secured. I am going to change and take a drink, but I'll be with you before we clear the bay.''

"Aye, aye, sir.'' Harding eyed him questioningly. "Head

and tops'ls, sir? The wind's abated a little—maybe we could shake a reef out of the tops'ls.'' Justin squinted thoughtfully skyward. It was still lowering and overcast, though there was a faint gleam of sunlight to the east. He nodded his acquiescence. Harding said cautiously, "Major Van Buren's a queer customer, is he not, sir? As soon as he came on board, he demanded that I put a cabin at his disposal, and he wasn't satisfied with clothing from the slop chest, to use while his own garments are drying. I had to lend him some of mine."

"*And* your cabin, Mr. Harding?"

"Well, yes, sir. He was most insistent. I had my gear moved into the mids' berth."

Justin's anger flared anew. The Dutchman had the nerve of the devil, he thought resentfully . . . but not nerve enough to acknowledge his half-caste son. Or perhaps his wife, Lucy, was responsible for that. He said, in a clipped voice, "Have your gear moved into my cabin, Mr. Harding. Where is Van Buren now, do you know? Sleeping it off?"

Rufus Harding shook his head, a knowing smile briefly touching his lips. "I fancy he's in the gunroom, breaking his fast. I heard voices coming from there—raised in argument, as you might say, sir. Mr. De Lancey and Mr. Meehan didn't seem too partial to his company, from what I could make out."

"I see," Justin returned briskly. "Well, I'll soon put a stop to that. Carry on if you please, Mr. Harding."

Harding's smile became a wide grin. "Aye, aye, sir," he acknowledged with restraint.

In the gunroom, Jos Van Buren was seated, legs asprawl, an empty plate in front of him and a brimming glass in his big, blunt-fingered hand. George, unusually red of face and clearly annoyed, was in the act of rising from the table when Justin entered, closing the screen door behind him, and James Meehan, he saw, had already gone.

Before Justin could speak, Van Buren raised his glass in mock salute but made no attempt to rise.

"Ah!" he exclaimed. "Our gallant Captain Broome!

Champion of the underprivileged—and seemingly still too concerned for the health of a miserable Malay seaman to have had time to change into dry clothing. Your conshern—'' His voice was slurred, and he corrected himself ponderously. "Your *concern* does you credit, for all it is wasted on one of no account. Permit me to drink to you, Captain!"

George said contemptuously, "The damned fellow is drunk, Justin—drunk and insufferably offensive. He has insulted James Meehan and is endeavoring to provoke me. As the commander of this ship, perhaps you will be so good as to have him removed, for I can endure no more of his arrogance."

"With the greatest of pleasure," Justin agreed. He faced the lolling Dutchman and curtly bade him get to his feet. "Your presence is no longer welcome in my gunroom, Major Van Buren. You have been allocated a cabin, I understand. Go there, if you please, and remain there until we reach Port Jackson. Your meals will be served to you."

Van Buren rose. He stood, swaying a little, fists clenched aggressively in front of him and an ugly expression on his round, sallow face. At his full height, he dwarfed Justin by several inches, and he asked unpleasantly, "Do you propose to make me leave, Mr. Broome?"

"Yes," Justin told him, with icy calm. "By heaven, I do!" He sidestepped the clumsy, anticipated blow the big man aimed at him, and his fist connected perfectly with the point of the fleshy jaw. Van Buren went down as if poleaxed and lay still, breathing stertorously. Justin bent over him and smiled.

"He is out cold! Oblige me with your assistance, George, and we'll remove him to Harding's cabin. I shall post a guard to make sure that he stays there until we drop anchor in Sydney Cove."

George echoed his smile. "With the greatest of pleasure, Captain Broome! And I trust you will not relent—he may be Lucy Tempest's husband, but by the Lord Harry, he's a singularly unpleasant individual.''

Justin did not relent, and when, three days later, the *Elizabeth* came to anchor in the cove, Van Buren was still confined to his cabin, protesting angrily at his treatment, but all his protests ignored.

He went ashore in the gig, taking the boy Claus with him, and—having apparently washed his hands of the injured Abdul Wetar—left in brooding silence, offering no thanks for his rescue but putting on an exaggerated show of dignity, which left Justin unmoved.

"Do you intend to report his rendezvous with the Frenchman?" George asked as they stood together on deck to await the gig's return. "It would cause a great scandal, and—we have no proof, have we, Justin? Just the word of a crazy old man. It might be best to say nothing of it to the Governor."

"If you think so," Justin answered, without conviction.

"I do," George said emphatically. "Van Buren's an odd fellow, and he could be a very dangerous enemy. Let sleeping dogs lie. . . . In any event, what could the Governor do about it? He can hardly send the fellow packing, can he, merely on suspicion."

"No. But—" Justin's expression relaxed. In the garden of his small, white-painted cottage on the south side of the cove, he saw his wife emerge, with their two small sons, and he responded eagerly to their welcoming waves. Perhaps it would be unwise to invoke Van Buren's enmity, he thought—further, that was to say, than he already had. He sighed.

"I shall report the Frenchman's call at Norfolk Island, George—I'm bound to report that."

George inclined his head. "Of course, Justin. And I'll bear you out, if need be." He shaded his eyes with his hand. "Is that not young Lieutenant Dean in the garden with your family?"

"It looks like him," Justin agreed cautiously.

The gig returned, and he gestured to George to precede

him. James Meehan joined them, and they boarded the gig.

"Cast off!" Midshipman Bowles ordered shrilly. "Out oars—put your backs into it, my lads!"

The men, with the prospect of shore leave and the taverns of the Rocks before them, needed no urging. The gig skimmed over the blue, sunlit water of the cove, and Justin saw Jessica running across the road to the landing stage. Her brother, conspicuous in his scarlet uniform, followed more slowly, and the two boys pelted past him with excited cries.

He was home, Justin thought contentedly, at least for a week or two. Forgetful of dignity, he took off his cap and held it high above his head.

CHAPTER IV

In the spacious withdrawing room of Number Six Bridge Street, Lucy Van Buren regarded her husband with thinly disguised disgust. Since his return the previous day, he had been drinking steadily, and he was now asleep on her sofa, his clothing disheveled and his mouth wide open, his heavy breathing punctuated by grunts and snores.

What had she done, Lucy asked herself bitterly, what crime had she committed that God should inflict her with two husbands for whom she could feel only contempt and loathing?

Luke Cahill, of course, had been a weakling, a man of no breeding, lacking in both manners and intelligence, whom she had married on impulse when she had been too young and too naive to see him for what he was. She had not regretted his death, had not mourned him, and in fact had herself been too ill and too shocked by the events that had led to his death to be capable of feeling anything except self-pity.

But with Jos Van Buren it had been different. He was an officer—a Dutch colonial officer, it was true, but a gentleman—handsome and masterful and, she had supposed, well educated and intellectually her equal. She had been attracted to him as keenly as he had been to her, and in the position in which she had found herself following the shipwreck and loss of the *Kelso* on some nameless Dutch island, the attentions of the garrison commandant at Timor had not been unwelcome.

He had treated her with faultless courtesy and respect, Lucy remembered, and although she had quickly sensed his desire for her, he had done no more than kiss her hand. Indeed, for all she had shared his official quarters with him during the weeks it had taken her to recover from the effects of the shipwreck, Jos had never so much as entered her bedroom uninvited.

She had not then been aware that he possessed a native wife, of whose jealousy he was in mortal fear. The woman had been kept in the bungalow, a dark-skinned, beautiful creature she had supposed was a servant, and it was only when the supposed servant had made a murderous attack on her with a knife that she realized the truth.

The attack had been unexpected and had done her little harm, for another servant had intervened just in time. Jos had ordered his wife arrested, and on the return of the Governor from Batavia at the end of the British occupation, she had been tried and condemned to death. After a suitable interval—Lucy frowned, recalling how brief that interval had been—after what *Jos* had deemed a suitable interval, he had proposed to her, and she had accepted him.

They had had a lavish wedding and a lengthy honeymoon in Batavia. Jos had been an ardent and exciting lover, possessing both experience and sophistication, and in the comparatively civilized surroundings of the Dutch colonial capital, she had been ecstatically happy. Indeed, she had believed herself sincerely in love with her new husband. Batavia, freed from the restraints of Stamford Raffles's governorship, had become its old self again; the wealthy Dutch entertained royally and lived in opulent grandeur, and she and Jos were popular and in demand socially, welcome and regular guests at viceregal functions, as well as in the homes of civil and military officials.

Jos had not lacked money, and the velvet-covered box of jewels Jonas Burdock had salvaged from the wreck of the *Kelso* had remained intact, to be used, she had then decided, as her insurance, should that ever be necessary. And it had not been necessary, during the early part of her

marriage. . . . Lucy glanced again, with mingled exasperation and despair, at her sleeping husband.

Jos, she thought bitterly, had destroyed her dream of
happiness. They had stayed in Batavia for over a year, but
then, little as either of them had wanted to, they had been
compelled to return to Timor and the wretched little jungle
village of Coupang. And there, over the succeeding years,
Jos had deteriorated, almost before she had realized what
was happening to him.

He had been stricken with fever and had nearly died.
When he had recovered, he had started to drink heavily.
He had put on weight, lost his zest for life, and started to
neglect his duty. The old Governor, who was a friend, had
tolerated his increasing inefficiency, ignored his peculations,
and turned a blind eye to his illicit trading activities; but
when a new man was appointed, all tolerance had ended,
and Jos had been relieved of his command.

They had gone back to Batavia, and there—finding that
with Jos more often drunk than sober, even Batavia had
lost its magic—Lucy had conceived the notion of returning
to Sydney. The price she had obtained for the jewels had
sufficed to purchase not only a schooner, the *Dirk Wanjon*
of three hundred tons burden, but also a cargo of trade
goods and spirits, which had found a ready and profitable
sale in Sydney. So, too, had the schooner. . . . Lucy
repeated her sigh.

From their profits she had bought a fine two-story
brick-built house in Bridge Street and staffed it with the
native servants—slaves in all but name—whom Jos had
insisted on bringing with them. Certainly they lent an
undeniable cachet to her household, she reflected; her cook
was better than all the convict cooks employed by even
Sydney's wealthiest residents, her dark-skinned majordomo,
Saleh, the envy of their wives. The boy Claus she disliked,
but . . . he had his uses and was humble and self-effacing,
and she tried to forget that he was Jos's son. Since Jos
treated him as one of their servants and showed him no
affection, it was not too hard to erase the knowledge of

their relationship from her mind, and indeed, Lucy thought with satisfaction, the boy never presumed on it.

She had been happy enough, at first, following her return to Sydney. Her brother, Rick, and her sister, Abigail, had given her a heartwarming welcome, and initially Jos had made a considerable effort to pull himself together. The loss of his commission had shaken him, and for the first few months he had drunk very little, with the result that he was fitter and a little thinner, and, still with the remnants of his old charm, he had sought to ingratiate himself with her relatives and those who constituted the respectable members of Sydney society.

But it had not lasted. Jos had been angered by the Governor's refusal to permit him to take up a land grant on the favorable terms offered to new settlers; he might only do so, Sir Thomas Brisbane had decreed, if the grant were made in his wife's name. In addition, the original grant that she had shared with Abigail at Yarramundie had been sold, and Abigail's husband, Timothy Dawson, had—like the Governor—refused to make reparation in kind unless that, too, were in her name.

Lucy rose from her chair and crossed to the window, her dark, delicately penciled brows meeting in a frown. Timothy, it was true, had offered her the excellent farm at Portland Place, near Parramatta, which had once been owned by his late father-in-law and partner, poor Jasper Spence, who had perished with his wife, Frances, when the *Kelso* went down. But Jos, his masculine pride deeply wounded, had rejected the offer as angrily as he had rejected that of the Governor, and this, to her regret, had led to a bitter disagreement between him and Timothy . . . and, inevitably, to a mutual coolness where Abigail was concerned.

She had not wanted Jos to engage in trade, fearing that socially this might damage their prestige, since most who made their living thus were of convict origins. Even Simeon Lord—the first emancipist to be appointed a magistrate—for all his wealth, his woolen factories, and his twenty thousand acres of land, was no longer received at Government House, as, in Governor Macquarie's time, he had always been.

But Jos had been adamant. Without her knowledge or consent, Lucy recalled, with remembered indignation, her husband had entered into negotiation with Simeon Lord for two ancient and ill-found vessels for which the trader had no further use, and a few months later he had chartered the *Flinders*, a small brig-sloop once owned by Justin Broome, from Robert Campbell's yard.

It was typical of him that he had told her nothing of his activities save, somewhat arrogantly, to claim that they were highly profitable, and to hint that the voyage he had then been about to make, in the *Flinders*, was likely to prove the most profitable of all.

Again Lucy turned to look with disgust at the big, slumped figure on the sofa.

Far from making a profit, Jos had lost the *Flinders* in circumstances that—if Claus were to be believed—redounded not at all to his credit and must result in a heavy financial liability. But instead of explaining or attempting to confide in her, he had simply flung himself down onto her beautiful, velvet-covered sofa and shouted to Saleh to bring him brandy.

"Captain Broome's hospitality leaves much to be desired," he had told her wrathfully. "I've scarcely tasted a drink since boarding his damned King's ship, well nigh frozen to death! He had his precious brother-in-law on board—the judge, George De Lancey—and an upstart of a onetime felon from the surveyor's office named Meehan. God knows what they've been up to, but they treated me as if our nations were still at war!"

Perhaps, Lucy thought glumly, that was the reason why Jos Van Buren had made so poor an impression on Sydney's close-knit, elitist society. Perhaps it was not only his drinking and his arrogance that had antagonized Timothy Dawson and . . . yes, even her brother, Rick. Some of the old enmities remained, and Jos was not a man to forget them easily. Unlike the majority of his countrymen during the British occupation of Java, Jos had nourished a keen and lasting hatred for the occupying troops in general and for the British Governor, Stamford Raffles, in particular, despite the fact that he had accepted their hospitality and paid them lip service. He—

"*Mevrouw* . . . madame . . ." The soft, sibilant voice was Saleh's. The Malay houseboy insinuated his slim, white-coated person silently into the room, and Lucy turned, startled out of her reverie.

"What is it?" she demanded sharply.

Saleh's gaze rested for a moment on his master's gross, slumped body and then returned slyly to her face. "Callers, madame," he told her, speaking in the careful Dutch he had been taught as a boy in a Batavian mission school. "I have shown them to the rear veranda, supposing that this was what madame would wish."

The implication was plain, and Lucy did not trouble to deny it. "Who are the callers?" she asked, reluctant, in the circumstances, to receive anyone—least of all her sister, Abigail, who might have taken it into her head to call, in order to offer her condolences, since Jos's loss of the *Flinders* would by now, no doubt, be common knowledge.

"The lady of Captain Broome, madame, with a young boy—*Mijnheer* Broome's son, I think. Is it madame's wish that I serve coffee? Or tea, perhaps?"

"No." Lucy's headshake was impatient. "They will not be staying."

She was at once annoyed and puzzled, at a loss to understand the reason for the unexpected call. True, Justin Broome's ship had brought her husband back to Sydney, and according to Claus, it was thanks to his seamanship that any of them were alive, but . . . Lucy's small mouth hardened. Jessica Broome, she told herself, wouldn't dare presume to pay a social call on her. The young woman had been a Government House servant prior to her marriage, and she was the daughter of a sergeant in Governor Macquarie's regiment and therefore not a lady. Admittedly they had met on one or two occasions at the Dawsons' house, and the fact that Justin Broome now held a commission in the Royal Navy had led to their being received by Sir Thomas and Lady Brisbane on official occasions also. Nevertheless, one had to draw a line, Lucy reflected, and she, at least, had always done so—even if Abigail had not.

She smoothed the skirt of her voluminous silk dress and made her way, without haste, to the cool, shaded veranda overlooking the garden at the rear of the house.

Jessica Broome, slim and dark-haired, rose at her approach, with an apology for the lateness of her call. She was an attractive-looking young woman, Lucy was compelled to concede, neatly if unfashionably dressed in a gown of brown rep, with cuffs and collar of spotless white linen and a small, flower-trimmed straw bonnet framing her face. With her graceful carriage and her glowing pink-and-white complexion, she did not look old enough to be the mother of the sturdy, red-haired boy standing beside her. The boy was tall—only a few inches shorter than his mother—and he smiled with evident amusement when his mother introduced him as Murdoch.

"I'm always called Red, ma'am," he explained politely, and Lucy, despite her reservations, found herself responding to his smile.

"Perhaps," she invited, after shaking his extended hand, "perhaps you would like to go into the garden, Red, whilst I talk to your mama."

The invitation was condescending, as she had intended it to be, but the boy accepted it with unexpected eagerness. "Claus is there, ma'am," he told her. "And I want to hear all about the wreck of the *Flinders*. I'm going to sea very soon with my father. I'd have been with him on his last voyage, only my—er—my mama says I must finish my schooling first."

He flashed an impish glance at his mother, more teasing than reproachful, and made off down the veranda steps, calling shrilly to Claus as he crossed the lawn.

"He's not ten yet," Jessica said ruefully. "But all he can think of is going to sea with his father."

"What a pity," Lucy answered, offering no encouragement to her visitor to enlarge on the subject. She gestured to the chair Jessica had vacated but did not herself sit down, going instead to lean against the veranda rail. "May I," she inquired distantly, "know the reason for your call, Mrs. Broome? Is there something I can do for you?"

"Oh, no, I thank you." Jessica shook her head. "It was your husband I came to see, Mrs. Van Buren. But if it is inconvenient—"

"It is most inconvenient. Major Van Buren was quite exhausted when he returned, and he is sleeping. I cannot disturb him, I am afraid. But surely—" Lucy's brows rose in mute question. She paused and then asked impatiently, "Can I not deal with the matter? Unless, of course, it concerns the loss of the *Flinders*. My husband would have to deal with that." Had the woman come to demand reparation for the loss of the wretched ship, she wondered indignantly, and added, an edge to her voice, "The charter was from Mr. Campbell, you know. I understand that he was the owner of the vessel."

"Yes," Jessica confirmed, with quiet dignity. Two bright spots of color rose to her cheeks, as if she had read Lucy's thought, but she went on, still quietly, "Major Van Buren left some papers in the cabin he occupied on board the *Elizabeth*. My husband was summoned to wait on the Governor, and so he asked me to deliver them for him. He said that they were confidential papers, Mrs. Van Buren."

"Then you may give them to me," Lucy assured her. When Jessica made no move to do so, she spread her hands in a gesture of exasperation. "Come, Mrs. Broome— there are no secrets between me and Major Van Buren."

"No, of course not." Jessica Broome's color deepened. She hesitated for a moment longer, but finally opened the embroidered reticule she carried and extracted a bundle of papers from it. "Justin did say that I should give these to Major Van Buren in person. They are sealed, and he supposed them to be of some value, but if you wish to take them, then—"

"I will take them." Lucy held out her hand. The package was wrapped in oilskin, and she eyed it curiously, noticing that it appeared to be unopened. Clearly its contents must be of some value, if Jos had saved them from the wreck, but in Jessica Broome's presence she could scarcely break the seals, she decided, without giving the lie to her claim to enjoy her husband's confidence. She laid the package on a nearby table with well-feigned indifference and turned to look at her visitor. "Is that all, Mrs. Broome?"

Jessica rose to her feet at once, accepting her dismissal with no hint of rancor. "Yes, that is all, Mrs. Van Buren."

"Then I need detain you no longer. Thank you for your trouble." Lucy picked up the brass bell that would summon Saleh and rang it loudly. Saleh appeared instantly, his dark face expressionless.

"My master wakes," he said. "And he asks for food, madame."

"Then take him food," Lucy bade him. "When you have shown Mrs. Broome out."

"I have a son to retrieve," Jessica reminded her. "If you will permit me to leave by your garden, I will find him."

Her tone was courteous, her manners impeccable, but Lucy sensed a controlled resentment that had not been put into words. Perhaps, she thought, her thanks had been too cursory; the young woman had, after all, done her a service, and in addition, of course, Jos probably owed his life to Jessica's husband . . . a fact that had not been mentioned during their brief conversation. Summoning a smile, Lucy led the way into the garden.

"We will look for him together," she said graciously. "Claus will probably have taken him to the rose garden." They found both boys there, as she had predicted, and when Red was reunited with his mother, Lucy held out her hand. "I thank you again, Mrs. Broome. And I am sure, when he has recovered from his ordeal, Major Van Buren will wish to express his thanks to your husband for all that he has done. Like all his race, Claus is prone to exaggerate, but if even half of what he has told me is true, Mr. Broome performed a very gallant act in going to the rescue of the *Flinders*."

Red started to speak, his blue eyes bright with pride, but Jessica firmly silenced him.

"I give you good day, Mrs. Van Buren," she said gravely, and taking the boy by the arm, led him toward the gate. Claus looked after them longingly, but they did not turn to wave, and he scuttled off, like a whipped puppy, ignoring Lucy's sharply voiced command to wait.

She did not call after him, aware that it would be a waste of breath. Instead, seeking solace, she lingered in the rose garden for a little while, taking comfort from the fragrant scent of the English flowers and the beauty of the blooms that their convict gardener—apart from the two grooms, the only convict servant they had—tended so skillfully.

Then, remembering the bundle of papers, she picked up her skirts and ran back to the house, anxious to peruse them and assuage her curiosity before Jos could claim them.

But Jos, she saw to her dismay, was before her. Unshaven, swaying unsteadily, his clothing in disarray, he was still a formidable figure and, Lucy knew, capable of physical violence were she to attempt to cross him.

She halted, catching her breath, and he asked hoarsely, "How did you come by this?" He held up the package, still unopened. "These are my private papers, *mevrouw*, and not for your eyes, devil take it! What were they doing here? Did you steal them from my person whilst I slept?"

"No, of course I did not." Lucy drew herself up, regarding him with unconcealed scorn. "You were careless— you left them on board Captain Broome's ship. His wife brought them, supposing them to be of value."

"And so they are," her husband told her gloatingly. "They could hang me!"

Before Lucy could utter a word in question or protest,

Jos thrust the package into the open front of his shirt and went stumbling off, shouting for Saleh to bring the food he had ordered.

Claus answered his imperious call. "Your meal is not yet prepared, sir," he began. "Saleh says—"

Jos lifted a big hand and smashed it into the boy's face, sending him sprawling. Lucy bit back a cry but made no move to intervene. Jos's gloating words had alarmed her, and as Claus rose sobbing to his feet, she thrust past him with a derisive, "Run, little *lip-lap!*" and sought the sanctuary of her own bedroom, closing the door behind her.

She must think, she told herself. Think and devise some means of regaining possession of the oilskin-wrapped package. For if her husband had been speaking the truth when he had claimed that the papers it contained could hang him . . . A fugitive smile curved her lips.

Perhaps the time had come to end this marriage, as her first had ended. Certainly it would cause her no more regret, no more grief than Luke Cahill's loss had occasioned. The days were long past when Jos had been infatuated with her and she had been able to twist him round her little finger. Now he seldom sought her bed, seldom attempted to make love to her, and she had long since ceased to welcome his advances. Rather . . . Lucy shuddered.

Rather she dreaded them and went in fear of his violent temper. Besides, he had estranged her from her family, caused a breach between her and Abigail that was not likely to be healed while she remained his wife.

She crossed to the ornate, full-length mirror hanging on the wall opposite her bed and studied her reflection with searching, critical eyes. She was still slender, her reflection told her, still possessed of more than ordinary good looks. And she was young—too young to be chained in a loveless marriage to an uncouth drunkard like Jos Van Buren.

Coming impulsively to a decision, Lucy seated herself at the carved wooden desk she used for her correspondence and, finding quill and writing materials, started to compose an invitation.

Major and Mrs. Josef Van Buren at home . . . No, that was not formal enough. She crumpled up the sheet of paper and began afresh.

Major and Mrs. Josef Van Buren request the pleasure of the company of Their Excellencies Sir Thomas and Lady Brisbane at a Reception, to be held at Number Six Bridge Street on . . .

Lady Brisbane, she reminded herself, had given birth to a child—a son—only a week ago at Parramatta. She must allow time for the Governor's lady to recover from her confinement, so . . . Biting the end of the quill, Lucy considered the question and then wrote: *Thursday, May the sixth, from eight to ten p.m.*

That should suffice. The Brisbanes would surely come to Sydney for their son's christening. She would invite Colonel Erskine, the Lieutenant Governor, and his wife; the officers of the garrison regiment; John and Hannibal Macarthur and their wives; and . . . Archdeacon Scott, the Reverend and Mrs. Samuel Marsden, Mrs. Phillip King, and, of course, Abigail and Timothy.

She would make a list and have the invitations delivered by hand—the coachman could ride to Parramatta with those intended for the Governor and the Macarthurs. And Jos would have to curb his drinking, at least for a few days before the party; she would see to it that he did. . . .

With rekindled hope Lucy compiled her list.

CHAPTER V

The Governor's advisory council, with Sir Thomas Brisbane himself in the chair, had listened attentively to Justin's report of the visit to Norfolk Island. It had been preceded by the surveyor James Meehan's practical assessment of what would be required, in terms of men and materials, to reopen the prison, and the Governor's summing-up seemed to express accurately the feelings of the majority of the council.

He said, with military bluntness, "In my view, gentlemen, it is essential that we should move with all possible speed to reestablish Norfolk Island as a penal settlement. For one thing, I am anxious to rid Sydney and Newcastle of the worst elements of the criminal population. I want to open the Hunter Valley for free settlement, which cannot be done until the penal establishment at Newcastle is shut down. Escape from there is too easy, and as you are all aware, accommodation for the capital respite prisoners here in Sydney is stretched to the limit. In addition, of course, there is the ever-present threat that our late enemies, the French, may attempt to gain possession of areas we leave unoccupied and undefended. You have heard Mr. Broome's account of the French frigate that made a call at Norfolk Island just prior to his arrival."

There was a murmur of assent. The colony's secretary, Major Frederick Goulburn, disassociated himself from it by observing sententiously that Mr. Broome had not witnessed the Frenchman's arrival in person.

"He asks us to take the word of some half-demented fellow who seemingly has lived on the island like a castaway for the past ten years. I, for one, take leave to question its accuracy."

The Governor stiffened, and Justin exchanged a glance with James Meehan, relieved now that he had taken his brother-in-law's advice and made no mention of Van Buren in his report. Frederick Goulburn, he knew, was as unpopular with the present Governor as he had been with Governor Macquarie, owing, no doubt, to his hunger for power and influence. On this occasion, however, Sir Thomas Brisbane chose to ignore rather than to reprove him.

He said crisply, "The home government is well aware of the acquisitive interest the French have always shown in this territory, gentlemen. The Dutch also are making strenuous efforts to exclude us—and, in particular, the British East India Company and Sir Stamford Raffles's recently founded free port of Singapore—from East Indies trade. My instructions from the Colonial Office are, in this respect, clear and unequivocal. New settlements are to be established where and whenever possible along the Australian coastline, and I have the power only to make these penal settlements."

"There is the *Tamar*, sir," Goulburn reminded him. "You—"

Governor Brisbane's firm mouth tightened. "If you will permit me to speak without interruption, Major, we shall, I fancy, conclude our business more speedily." He gestured to a letter lying opened in front of him, but went on, without referring to it, "Captain Gordon Bremner has been dispatched from England in His Majesty's ship *Tamar*, with orders to take formal possession of our northern coast. You will recall, perhaps, that Captain Parker King's survey, six years ago, revealed the suitability of Port Essington, in Raffles Bay, for settlement and the establishment of a trading post."

Once again there was a murmur of assent from the members of the council, but sensing that this was more polite than informed, the Governor turned to John Oxley, the government surveyor. "You have, I think, a map of the area in question, have you not, Mr. Oxley?"

"Indeed I have, sir," Oxley assured him. He searched in the folder of papers on the table before him and brought to light the required map. A lengthy discussion ensued, as members of the council studied the survey map, which, Justin saw, was one that Phillip Parker King had compiled, dated April 1818.

"You have been to the northern coast, I believe, Mr. Broome?" the Governor suggested. He let the discussion continue but, taking no part in it, was tapping with impatient fingers on the edge of the table. Evidently, Justin thought, he had already made up his mind concerning the proposed settlement and neither needed nor wanted the advice of his council.

"Yes, sir," he confirmed. "I have."

"With Captain King?"

Justin smiled. "No, sir—with Captain Flinders. I was with him on his last survey of the coast."

"You must have been remarkably young—that was . . . good Lord, over twenty years ago, surely!"

"I was ten years old, sir. My father was sailing master of the *Investigator*—appointed after Mr. Thistle was drowned. And Captain Flinders kept a promise he made me, when I attempted to stow away on board the *Norfolk* three years earlier. It's a promise—" Justin sighed. "A promise of which my elder son all too frequently reminds me now."

The Governor eyed him thoughtfully. "How old is your son, Mr. Broome?"

"He's nine, sir."

"Ah!" Sir Thomas's lined, somewhat austere face relaxed in a smile of singular warmth. "You are a fortunate man. We lost our firstborn on the passage out here, but, I am happy to say, Lady Brisbane gave birth to a strong and healthy boy ten days ago—when you were on your way to Norfolk Island, so perhaps you have not heard. It means

everything to have a son, Mr. Broome. I intend to name
mine James Australia, and I hope that, like yours, he will
wish to follow his father's calling and—'' He broke off,
his smile abruptly fading when the Chief Justice, Francis
Forbes, asked gravely whether Captain Bremner was bringing his own free settlers with him from England.

"He is bringing a contingent of royal marines for the
garrison, Mr. Forbes. But we are to supply him with a
convict labor force, according to my instructions from the
Colonial Secretary.'' The Governor's tone was firm, brooking no dissent, but Justice Forbes—who, Justin reflected,
had shown himself more sympathetic to the colony's felons than had previous holders of his office—seemed disposed to argue.

"Sir, I must question the legality of such a procedure,''
he insisted. "The new settlement in Raffles Bay must, in
effect, be a place of secondary punishment. The convicts
you dispatch there will be required to perform hard labor,
will they not? Hard labor in irons, no doubt . . . but the
sentences they received in England were specifically for
deportation. Not, sir, for hard labor, and in my view,
Governor, you have no right, under the law, to change
those sentences.''

The Governor drew himself up, an erect, soldierly figure,
sitting stiffly upright in his chair. He answered coldly, "In
my considered view, Mr. Forbes, all dangerous pioneering
work should properly be performed by convicts, whose
lives, in consequence of the crimes they have committed,
are less valuable than the lives of free men. Those sent to
Raffles Bay will be chosen carefully, I assure you, from
prisoners who have incurred secondary sentences since
their arrival here. And they will only be compelled to work
in irons if they attempt escape or prove recalcitrant. That
has always been the policy of my predecessors, and I
intend to follow it.'' He frowned as Forbes attempted to
interrupt him. "Those to be sent to rebuild the prison and
barracks on Norfolk Island will be men in this category,

who will be treated in similar fashion. Good conduct will always be rewarded, Mr. Forbes."

"But, Your Excellency," Justice Forbes began, reddening indignantly, "I was seeking only to safeguard your own position. You—"

The Lieutenant Governor, Colonel Erskine, meeting the Governor's eye, intervened quietly. "I fancy, sir, that His Excellency's position is adequately safeguarded by Lord Bathurst's instructions concerning the allocation of convict labor. Quoting from memory—His Lordship expressed the wish that the situation of the convict must be 'one of laborious employment, tempered with every consideration of proper humanity and with every corrective principle of reformation.' If my memory serves me, he also stated that 'convicts should be distributed throughout the country, out of reach of pleasures which are open to those who reside in towns, and which prevent transportation from being the means of reformation.' No doubt, sir, Major Goulburn will have the relevant correspondence on file, if you should wish to refer to it."

Flustered, Frederick Goulburn agreed that this was so, and Justice Forbes subsided into an offended silence. Goulburn asked, recovering his composure, "Is it necessary for Mr. Broome and Mr. Meehan to remain here any longer, sir? We have heard their report, and Your Excellency has yet to hear from Mr. Oxley in regard to Port Curtis and Moreton Bay."

Justin started to rise, but the Governor motioned him to remain seated. "We need detain Mr. Meehan no longer," he returned crisply. "But I should be appreciative, Mr. Broome, if you would give us the benefit of your experience of the area. You have, I believe, called there many times?"

"Yes, sir, I have," Justin confirmed. "But I—"

"We have another young officer whose opinion I wish to hear on this subject," Sir Thomas Brisbane put in. "One who has taken part in a number of exploratory expeditions, including Mr. Cunningham's recent discovery of an overland route from Bathurst to the Liverpool Plains. Have the goodness to inform Lieutenant Dean that we want him, Mr. Meehan, as you pass through the anteroom, if you please. And I thank you for the excellent work you have done on the Norfolk Island inspection.''

Meehan bowed and took his leave, and Justin waited, a trifle anxiously, for his wife's young brother to make his appearance before the council. Try as he might, he could never forget that Murdo Maclaine had once been a member of a gang of highwaymen led by the notorious Nick Vincent, to whom he owed his escape from jail. Murdo had been sentenced to deportation but, following his escape, had fought at Waterloo under an assumed name and, according to his own account, had been commissioned in that name for gallantry during the battle.

True, he had played the role of Lieutenant Michael Dean with praiseworthy devotion to duty since his arrival in the colony. George De Lancey, with whom he had made the passage out in the transport *Conway*, held Murdo in high esteem, and . . . Justin sighed. His own beloved wife, Jessica, adored her brother and would hear no ill of him. Their son Red had been christened Murdoch in his memory, when Jessica had believed her brother dead, and her joy in their reunion had been heartwarming. It . . . Murdo himself came into the room, trim and slight in his impeccably cut uniform, shako tucked correctly under his arm, the silver medal for Waterloo worn proudly on his chest. He stood to attention and bowed, and the Governor eyed him with a soldier's approval and, greeting him courteously by name, waved him to the chair that James Meehan had vacated, at Justin's side.

"And now, gentlemen," Brisbane said, "let us hear Mr. Oxley's report."

John Oxley, the government surveyor, was, by virtue of his office, a member of the Governor's council, and he spoke with confident authority, affecting not to notice Secretary Goulburn's attempts to hasten him. Although only thirty-eight, he had a long association with the colony, having come out as a midshipman in H.M.S. *Buffalo* twenty years earlier. By training, the onetime naval lieutenant was a maritime surveyor, but in addition to taking part in Phillip King's survey, he had played a leading part in a number of land-based exploratory expeditions and was credited with the discovery of the Castlereagh, Peel, and Hastings rivers, Port Macquarie, and the Liverpool Plains.

His report on the prospective harbor facilities at Moreton Bay was meticulously detailed and enthusiastic, his thin, pale face aglow as he listed the advantages the area offered, initially for penal but eventually for free settlement.

"The land, gentlemen, is excellent, though thickly wooded, and I observed much fine timber, notably cedar, amid the prevailing eucalypts and acacia. The mean elevation of the mountains above the shores of Moreton Bay cannot be less than four thousand feet, and their elevated ridge presents no opening to the interior beyond them. Escape—save by sea—from a prison set up there would, in my view, be impossible. Port Curtis possessed no such advantage, for which reason I decided to use all the time at my disposal to investigate Moreton Bay and its surroundings, since this seemed to me more likely to yield a positive and useful result. The site I selected is well watered, and a large number of convicts could be given profitable employment in tree felling and land clearance. . . ." Oxley searched once more in his folder and offered several sketch maps and two pages of carefully written notes to the assembled council.

"You will observe, sir," he said, placing one of the maps in front of the Governor, "that there is a fine river, beside which I have marked in sites for officers' quarters, a guardhouse and huts, and a jail, the last to be surrounded by a palisade constructed from local timber. And the river, sir, is truly fine. With Mr. Dean and a small party from the ship, I explored it for a distance of some fifty miles, ascending by boat. And, sir, you will see that I have ventured to name it the Brisbane River, in the hope that Your Excellency will permit it to be so designated."

Sir Thomas Brisbane eyed him in surprise and then beamed his pleasure at the implied compliment. "I shall be delighted to give my permission, Mr. Oxley—more than delighted. And I thank you for the suggestion."

Oxley mopped his brow. He looked ill, Justin thought, his pallor accentuated despite the heat of the room. But he went on eagerly, "I believe, sir, that the Brisbane River may be the main outlet for the marshes in which the Macquarie ends. It appears to originate on the eastern side of the dividing range, its chief source being in the elevated lands lying almost on the coastline, between the twenty-sixth and twenty-seventh parallels."

He talked on, basking in the Governor's approval as he described, in careful detail, the botanical specimens he had obtained and the wildlife he had observed. Beside him, Justin felt Murdo stir restlessly, and he glanced at him in mute question.

Murdo said, in a discreet whisper, "The infernal fellow didn't discover his precious river—he was led to it by pure, blind chance!"

"Oxley is a decent enough fellow," Justin cautioned. "Don't rob him of his moment of glory. Besides, I fear he's ill—he's as white as a sheet."

Murdo shrugged. "Oh, very well, if you say so. But there's another side to the story, which H.E. hasn't heard yet—and two poor devils of convicts who might have won themselves a pardon, if Oxley had not seen fit to take all the credit himself."

However, when John Oxley finally, and with evident reluctance, yielded the stage to him, Murdo told his story with praiseworthy impartiality.

"We encountered two white men during our stay, Your Excellency," he said. "John Finnigan and Thomas Pamphlet, who were naked and liberally caked with mud in the aboriginal fashion when they came to meet us. They told me that they had been employed as timber cutters in the Illawarra district and that they had put to sea in a small oared boat, intending to return to Sydney. They were

blown out to sea and, having no compass with them, lost
their bearings. Believing themselves to be south of Sydney
when they closed the coast, they rowed northward and,
after enduring many hardships, landed at Moreton Bay in a
state of great weakness and near starvation. Finnigan told
me, sir,'' Murdo added, pointedly addressing his words to
the Governor, ''that they would have perished, had it not
been for the help they received from the native tribe that
inhabits the area. They had lived with the tribe for close on
two years and were, it seems, accepted into it and well
treated. It was these two men who discovered the river,
sir, and directed us to it. That's so, is it not, Mr. Oxley?''

Thus challenged, Oxley conceded, with a bad grace,
that it was so. ''Our survey would have revealed the river,
of course, sir. Finnigan and Pamphlet saved us time.''

''We brought the men back with us on board the
Mermaid, sir,'' Murdo went on, determined to make his
point. ''They are listed as having run, of course, and they
were afraid they would incur an additional sentence if they
came back to Sydney. I gave them my word, sir, that I
would speak up for them and ask for Your Excellency's
indulgence.''

Sir Thomas Brisbane eyed him pensively and then
glanced, with raised brows, at Oxley.

''Did you believe their story, Mr. Oxley?'' he asked.

Once again, John Oxley was forced to give his assent.
''Yes, sir, I did.'' He smiled unexpectedly. ''It was too
unlikely *not* to be true. And the blackfellows bore them
out . . . that is, according to Dean they did. Dean under-
stands their language—or claims to, don't you, Michael?''

Murdo echoed his smile. ''Yes,'' he asserted. ''I've
mixed with the tribes in the Bathurst region, and these
people seemed to speak in much the same tongue . . . and,
sir, they treated Finnigan and Pamphlet very well, as I
mentioned. I think it was thanks to the trust these two men
inspired that the tribe accepted them and displayed no
hostility to us, when we explored the river and the surrounding land.''

"Very well, Mr. Dean," the Governor agreed. "I shall review their case at the earliest opportunity." He turned to his personal secretary, Major Ovens. "Be so good as to make a note of that, John, if you please. Now . . ." He consulted his own notes. "I fancy we have covered our agenda, gentlemen, save for the matter of the proposed expedition overland to Western Port, which we discussed at our last meeting. You will recall that we feared this proposal would have to be abandoned, since Mr. Hume felt that the money available from government funds was insufficient to equip his party adequately. You don't need me to tell you that Whitehall keeps a tight rein on our expenditure—a damnably tight rein! However, a solution to the problem has been found." The Governor looked from one to the other of them, a steely glint in his eyes, as if challenging objections any of his council might make.

But no one spoke, and he went on, "A gentleman named William Hovell—a retired sea captain who farms seven hundred acres at Narellan and is well known to some of you—is eager to take part in the expedition. He has offered to defray half of Mr. Hume's expenses. Frankly, gentlemen, I see no reason to refuse this offer, since the object of the expedition is, as you are aware, the possibility of opening up more land for settlement."

Justin listened, his interest instantly aroused, but Oxley shook his head. The surveyor said aggressively, "Sir, the country round Western Port is barren wasteland, utterly useless for every purpose of civilized man!"

"I'm aware of that, Mr. Oxley," Brisbane assured him. "But it is the country *between* Lake George and the coast that I am anxious should be examined. Mr. Hume has reported fertile plains south of the Murrumbidgee River, and others have borne out his claim, including Mr. Alexander Berry and, of course, your deputy, Mr. Meehan."

Oxley reddened in annoyance, and Secretary Goulburn started to argue with the Chief Justice, Francis Forbes rashly allowing himself to become heated as a result of the older man's abrasive comments. The Governor brusquely quelled them.

"You are here to advise and not to command me, gentlemen," he reminded them with some asperity.

"The ultimate responsibility rests with me. Try, I beg you, to understand that Colonial Office policy requires me to take all possible steps to settle this vast country in such a manner that French attempts to annex any part of it are discouraged—if they cannot entirely be prevented. We need settlers, and in order to attract them, we must make land available to them wherever it is possible to survey and open it for development. Australia's potential is as vast as the area it covers, but since I'm constrained to keep to a shoestring budget, I can only deploy the means—and the people—available to me. Free men, with capital for investment in livestock and the land, are coming out here all too slowly, alas, but they are coming, and we must offer them every inducement in the form of generous grants and free convict labor." He paused, but no one spoke, and he went on forcefully, "Gentlemen, I am endeavoring to free Sydney of the worst of its criminal elements by banishing the incorrigibles and the capital respites from its streets, and by—" The Governor's gaze went challengingly to Justice Forbes. "By assigning the rest of the deportees to useful toil on the land, outside the towns, where they can best be used—if necessary, in chains."

Heads nodded in concerted agreement, and when Forbes failed to take up the challenge, the Governor shuffled his papers into order, preparatory to closing the meeting.

He said, with finality, "I shall have the Norfolk Island prison establishment reopened as a matter of urgency. That will require two ships and, according to Mr. Meehan, a labor force of about a hundred convicts. The *Mermaid* and the brig *Brutus* should suffice; the *Lady Nelson* must be retained to act as a storeship for Captain Bremner when he arrives. Which leaves me with your vessel, Mr. Broome— the *Elizabeth*."

Justin was instantly alert. "Yes, sir. The *Elizabeth* can be ready for sea in twenty-four hours."

Sir Thomas Brisbane gave him an approving smile. "Then prepare to sail to Moreton Bay, Mr. Broome, if you please, with me as passenger. I am anxious to see the place for myself before coming to a final decision."

"Very good, sir." Justin hid his surprise.

The meeting broke up, but the Governor motioned him to remain. When they were alone, he renewed the congratulations he had offered earlier.

"You did well to rescue Major Van Buren, Mr. Broome. Tell me—what was the purpose of his voyage? He had been to Batavia, had he not?"

"I believe so, sir, yes," Justin admitted cautiously. Despite George De Lancey's advice, he was tempted to mention old Job Scaife's revelation of the Dutchman's call at Norfolk Island, but . . . perhaps it would make trouble. He held no brief for Jos Van Buren—and even less since the rescue—but doubts had been cast on old Job's veracity, and Van Buren himself had never admitted to having arranged a rendezvous with the French frigate. While the Dutchman had been on board the *Elizabeth,* Justin recalled, he had behaved as if he had nothing to hide. The meeting with the French frigate could have been fortuitous and, perhaps, quite innocent, the French brandy he had wanted to save merely a gift. Although . . . Justin hesitated, and the Governor resolved his quandary.

"I do not trust Major Van Buren," he observed, an edge to his voice. "And I don't for a moment imagine that he has our British interests at heart, for all he's married to Mrs. Dawson's sister and has announced that it is his intention to settle here. That is why I've refused to permit him any grant of land, unless it is taken out in his wife's name." His keen eyes searched Justin's face, and he added quietly, "If you have anything to tell me concerning the gentleman, Mr. Broome, rest assured that I shall regard it as confidential. It won't get back to Van Buren."

"Then, sir," Justin responded, "the old man we found

on Norfolk Island, Job Scaife, told me that Van Buren called there at the same time as the French frigate. He did not name him, but he described him as a Dutchman. If Scaife was telling the truth about the French ship, he must also have been telling the truth about Van Buren, sir. And he described the *Flinders* accurately enough for me to know which vessel he saw.''

"I see.'' The Governor's dark brows lowered. He asked a few pertinent questions and then released a long-drawn sigh. "There's little I can do about the matter without positive proof, I'm afraid. Except keep an eye on Van Buren, of course, and perhaps review his trader's license when it comes up for renewal. You said you thought he was carrying liquor in the *Flinders,* did you not?''

"He spoke of it to Mr. De Lancey, sir, but not to me.''

"Well . . .'' Brisbane took his fob watch from his pocket and studied it. "I must get back to Parramatta—my wife will be expecting me, and Mr. Rumker is working with me on a catalogue of stars in the Southern Hemisphere. Believe this or not, Mr. Broome, but we've observed and listed over six thousand from my observatory, and our work is not yet completed!'' He smiled with genuine pleasure and thrust the watch back into his waistcoat pocket. "Let us say I will be ready in ten days' time to join you for the passage to Moreton Bay.''

"Very good, sir.'' Justin rose, taking this as his dismissal. "The *Elizabeth* will be ready to sail whenever it suits Your Excellency. Will you require accommodation for members of your staff, sir?''

"My valet, no one else,'' the Governor decided. "But I think Lieutenant Dean could accompany us with advantage, and possibly one of the two castaways, to serve as guide. Perhaps you'd arrange it with young Dean?''

"Yes, sir, gladly.'' Justin bowed and was at the door when the Governor called after him.

"How about that boy of yours, Mr. Broome? Since we shall not be absent for very long, would you care to give him his first experience of the sea?''

Young Red would jump at the chance, Justin thought—Lord, the little scamp would be over the moon! And Jessica could hardly raise any objection, since, as the Governor had said, they would not be absent for long . . . three weeks, in all probability, or four at the outside, if Sir Thomas should decide to explore the river named after him.

"Thank you very much indeed, sir," he said gratefully. "I should welcome the opportunity."

Murdo was waiting for him, pacing up and down in front of the entrance gates when he emerged from Government House. They fell into step together, and Murdo said, grinning, "So you're to have the honor of taking His Excellency to Moreton Bay, Justin! I suppose it's the Brisbane River he really wants to see."

"Well, you're to have the honor of showing it to him," Justin retorted, echoing his brother-in-law's grin. "He particularly wants you to accompany him—and one of your protégés, Finnigan or . . . what's his name? Pamphlet, to act as guide. We sail in ten days' time."

"And Oxley? And Ovens?"

"They weren't mentioned. But—" Justin's grin widened. "Red is to be given his first taste of life under sail, with H.E.'s express permission. You'll have to aid me in obtaining your sister's, Murdo."

"She won't like it," Murdo said. "But I'll do my best. In ten days, you say? Good!" He fumbled in the pocket of his breeches and brought out a folded card. "At least I'll be excused from attending the Van Burens' reception."

"The Van Burens' *what*?"

"Reception, no less." Murdo read mockingly from the card. " 'Major and Mrs. Josef Van Buren request the pleasure of the company of Lieutenant Michael Dean at a Reception, to be held at Number Six Bridge Street on Thursday, May the sixth, from eight to ten P.M. . . .' A whole batch of these were delivered at the mess this morning. From the colonel downward, we're all invited. Did you not receive one?"

Justin shook his head. "I hardly expect to. Jessica and I
are not on the Van Burens' calling list."

"After you saved the man's life?"

"That does not alter my social standing. You've been
too long in the wilds, my dear Murdo. The inhabitants of
Sydney are firmly divided—the exclusives are precisely
that, in the eyes of Lucy Van Buren."

Murdo started to laugh uproariously. "If she only knew!
Lord alive, Justin, it's hilarious, isn't it? *I'm* invited because I'm supposed to be an officer and a gentleman . . .
yet I've stood in the felons' dock and had the death
sentence pronounced on me because I was caught on the
road, red-handed!" His laughter faded and he put an arm
affectionately about Justin's shoulders. "Sometimes," he
added soberly, "I find myself wishing that Nick Vincent
could see me now. Because it's thanks to him that I came
out here in a scarlet uniform, instead of a magpie suit and
clanking fetters, you know. He made me volunteer for the
army—I'd never have done it if Nick hadn't forced me to.
And I'd never have gone within a hundred miles of Waterloo if I'd had the slightest inkling of what that battle was
going to be like."

Justin shrugged. "But you fought at Waterloo, Murdo.
You acquitted yourself well and earned your commission."

Murdo hesitated for a moment, suddenly tense, and
then, as if making a conscious effort, answered gravely,
"To tell you the truth, Justin, I'd have run if it had been
possible."

"But it wasn't possible—and you didn't run. For God's
sake, I'm sure you weren't the only one who *wanted* to
run! George tells me you carried your regiment's color
until you were wounded, and he said the Fifty-second were
in the thick of it and that they suffered over two hundred
casualties." Justin's tone was warm. "You've nothing to
be ashamed of, Murdo. And since coming here, you've
acquitted yourself damned well. Meehan and Evans and
Cunningham will vouch for the help you've given them on

their exploratory expeditions . . . Oxley, too, if he weren't so anxious to enhance his own reputation.''

''Perhaps,'' Murdo conceded, without conviction. He lapsed into thoughtful silence, and Justin said teasingly, ''Damme, you *deserve* to be invited to the Van Burens' reception, my dear fellow! And I'm grateful that my convict ancestry spares me from having to attend, for if there is one person in this town that I cannot abide, it is Major Josef Van Buren.''

''We'll be on passage to Moreton Bay,'' Murdo reminded him. ''The Governor, too,'' he added, his normal cheerfulness restored. ''Mrs. Van Buren will have to make do with Colonel Erskine and Archdeacon Scott and perhaps some of the clan Macarthur for her scalps.''

''So she will,'' Justin agreed mildly. ''Come on—we're late, and Jessica will have dinner waiting.''

Jessica met them at the door of the cottage on the waterfront, with Red and his younger brother, John Lachlan, crowding excitedly behind her.

''You have just missed two very welcome callers,'' Jessica said. ''Rick Tempest and dear little Katie. They have come from Pengallon for Katie's confinement and are staying with the Dawsons. Rick was very anxious to see you, Justin dear, but he said he would come back later on.''

It was almost a year since he had seen his partner, Justin realized. Pengallon, the grant they shared, was on the Macquarie River, a dozen miles from Bathurst across rugged country, and settlers in the area did not often undertake the long journey to Sydney over the treacherous mountain road. But Katie Tempest's last pregnancy had almost cost her life and, he knew, had ended in stillbirth, so clearly this time they had decided to take no chances.

He bent to kiss his wife's smooth cheek, conscious, as always, of the fresh, warm scent of her and the softness of her skin under his lips.

''It will be good to see Rick. And—you said they had

come down for Katie's confinement. Are they expecting to stay long?''

"The baby's not due for three or four weeks," Jessica said. "But Rick told me he will be going back in a day or so. He's taking Dickon with him . . . poor Rick! He would dearly love a son, and Dickon is the apple of his eye, in spite of his handicap. And the boy worships him. Did you know—" Jessica's face clouded over. "Justin, did you know that they lost their little girl?"

"No," Justin answered, shocked. "I didn't. How did it happen?"

"The poor little soul was afflicted with a virulent fever, from which they believed her to have recovered. But—" There was a catch in Jessica's voice, and her eyes were moist as she looked up at her husband. "Oh, Justin, Katie found her dead in her cot one morning. About three months ago, I think."

Justin's gaze went, involuntarily, to his two sturdy young sons, and he sighed. "I'm truly sorry. It's tragic for them. We're very fortunate, my love, thanks be to God!"

"We have been," Jessica agreed, and then added, a trifle tartly, "up till now. But when you take Red to sea with you . . . oh, dear goodness! He met the Van Burens' boy, Claus, this morning, when I delivered that package you left with me, and heard all about the wreck of the *Flinders* from him. And he's talked of nothing else, Justin."

"Of the wreck, do you mean?"

She shook her head. "No, of going to sea."

Justin met Murdo's gaze and put a finger to his lips. Over their meal, he thought—then he would tell her of the Governor's invitation, choosing a moment when, it was to be hoped, she would be relaxed and less likely to reproach him.

"Is dinner ready?" he asked, attempting to change the subject.

"It has been spoiling this hour past." Jessica had noted the movement of his finger, and she saw her brother's answering nod. Her cry came from the heart. "Oh, Justin, no! Not yet—he's still only a little boy. And there's his schooling. Mr. Cape says he is making such good progress.''

The boys were both out of earshot, but Red, as if some instinct had warned him, came warily back to where his parents were standing.

''Dad,'' he began uncertainly. ''Please, Dad, I—''

Murdo grabbed him by the collar and spun him round. ''Inside with you, you scamp,'' he commanded, with mock severity. ''Some things are not for your ears, understand? In any event, you'll get to know what concerns you soon enough.''

''It will only be a short voyage, Jessie my love,'' Justin said defensively, when the boy had preceded them into the house. ''Three weeks, probably. I'm to take the Governor to Moreton Bay. And it was his suggestion. He—we— thought it would give young Red a taste of the sea. He can go back to school when we return, and—''

''You know he will not,'' Jessica flung at him bitterly. ''He's your son. Once he's had a taste of the sea, there'll be no getting him back to school.''

She evaded the arm he sought to put round her, led the way into their living room, and gestured to him to seat himself at the head of the table. Murdo and the two boys, already seated, maintained a tactful silence.

Jessica served their meal and, having done so, left them to eat it, her very back a reproach as she closed the door behind her. Justin stared after her guiltily, reminded of his own mother's reaction when, twenty years before, he, too, had sought her consent to his going to sea with his father, under poor, dead Matt Flinders's command.

He closed his eyes, his laden plate untouched, as the memories came flooding back. He had gone on board the *Investigator* when she had put in to Port Jackson to refit and provision, after Flinders had surveyed the southern coast in the wake of the two French ships under Captain Baudin's command. And Flinders had told him of the loss of his sailing master, John Thistle, caught in a tide rip and drowned, with six seamen, when their boat had foundered in Spencer Gulf. He himself, not Flinders, had been responsible for his father's volunteering to take Thistle's place, well knowing that, as the sailing master's son, he would be accepted as a member of the *Investigator*'s crew. . . . Justin felt the muscles of his throat tighten.

He could see his mother now, her arms white from the flour with which she had been baking and her eyes filled with tears, as he had talked excitedly with his father about the forthcoming voyage. The *Investigator* was being provisioned for twelve months, her destination the Great Barrier Reef, Endeavour Strait, and the Gulf of Carpentaria, and none of them could be certain that they and their small, ill-found King's ship would ever return.

He had said, bubbling over with eagerness, Justin recalled, "It's a chance that may never come again, Mam!"

"For you, Justin?" his mother had questioned. "Or for you and your father?"

"Matt Flinders needs a master, Jenny," his father had said. "And he's my friend. But you are my wife. . . . I'll only go with your consent, and the boy, too."

His mother had given her consent, biting back the tears. "Off you go, then," she had bidden them. "I'll not stand in your way."

The scene was as vivid in his mind as if it had been enacted yesterday, not twenty years ago—yet he had scarcely thought of it in those intervening years. He looked across the table at his elder son, but the boy, subdued, did not meet his gaze. Abruptly, Justin rose from the table, pushing his plate away. He found Jessica in the small, dark kitchen and, startled by the coincidence, saw that she, too, was baking, and, as his mother's had been, her arms were powdered with flour.

He said, the words wrung from him, "I'll only take Red with your consent, Jessie. I haven't told him anything about it."

Jessica faced him, dry-eyed, her heartbreak in her eyes yet bravely controlled. "You can tell him," she answered. "If it's what you both want, I'll not stand in your way."

Justin reached for her thin little hands and drew her to
him. This time she did not try to evade his embrace, but as
he kissed her, he could taste the salty bitterness of her
tears on his lips.

Salt as the sea, he thought ruefully, and held her close,
his cheek on hers.

"I'll take good care of the lad—I promise you, Jessie.
And he *will* go back to school!"

But *he* had not gone back, Justin remembered. The
year-long, nightmare voyage under Matthew Flinders, during which they had circumnavigated Australia, weathering
cyclones and losing almost half their number to scurvy and
Java fever and native attack, had been his initiation to life
at sea. Perversely, perhaps, he had wanted no other life,
for all its perils and uncertainties, its hardships and its tests
of his manhood. And Jessica . . . He looked down into her
tear-wet face and summoned a smile.

"You tell him, my love," he begged her. "It will come
best from you."

Jessica did not answer him, but she mopped at her
brimming eyes with a corner of her apron and then went,
her head held high, to obey him.

CHAPTER VI

Abigail Dawson's heightened color was evidence of her ruffled feelings as she descended the stairs and paused in the shadowed hallway to regain her composure.

It was always the same these days, and her stepdaughter Julia was invariably the cause of her ruffled feelings, Abigail thought wearily . . . although the good Lord knew to what lengths she had gone in the hope of bringing harmony to their relationship.

Julia had never been easy to handle. During her childhood, she had bitterly resented her father's decision to remarry, and Abigail, despite all her efforts, had failed to win the girl's affection or her trust, gaining, at best, her sullen obedience . . . and only that, because Timothy had insisted on it.

Now, at twenty-four and still unmarried, Julia had become a disruptive influence in what was otherwise a happy and united family. Her younger sister, pretty, gentle little Dorothea, was on the best of terms with everyone, courteous and helpful and a delightful companion, much sought after by Sydney's most eligible beaux. True, Julia attempted to dominate her, but . . . Abigail managed a smile. Little Dodie had a will of her own, and her elder sister's power over her had long since begun to wane. The more so, of course, now that Dodie had ardent suitors for her hand, while Julia's romances, for all they had been numerous, had not culminated in proposals of marriage.

For this, however, Abigail reflected severely, Julia could

blame no one but herself. She set her sights too high. Not for her the hardworking young farmers and pastoralists who were their neighbors in the Hawkesbury Valley or friends of her brother, Alexander, at Portland Place.

"They smell of tainted wool and the dung heap," Julia was wont to assert scornfully. "And most of them are native-born. I'd sooner remain a spinster than be wife to one of their kind."

Even Colonel Erskine's officers failed, for the most part, to meet with her approval. They were too liberal, they mixed too freely with the emancipists—albeit at their colonel's behest—and, unlike the officers of the 46th, who had been their predecessors, few of them had, according to Julia, the attributes of gentlemen.

There had been George De Lancey, of course. Abigail repeated her sigh and moved toward the rear door into the garden, thinking to take a breath of air before joining Rick and Katie and her husband, Tim, for the ritual of afternoon tea in the withdrawing room.

Julia had set her cap at George De Lancey when he had first arrived in the colony . . . understandably, perhaps, since he possessed all the attributes she valued. He was handsome, a barrister-at-law, and he had served with distinction as a cavalry officer in the Peninsular campaign and at Waterloo. The fact that he was American by birth had been outweighed, in Julia's eyes, by his aristocratic connections and his Huguenot ancestry.

"The De Lanceys were Loyalists," she had informed all who had cared to listen. "They did not betray their allegiance to the King when the American colonists rebelled. And Mr. De Lancey's brother was knighted for his services."

She no longer spoke of him thus. Poor girl, Julia had suffered deep humiliation when George, seemingly indifferent to her beauty and her partisanship alike, had married Rachel Broome, whose parents had been emancipists and who had neither dowry nor position to bring to their union. And before that—Abigail caught her breath, conscious of an illogical feeling of pity for her stepdaughter. Before that, there had been the scandal linking him with Katie Tempest, which, she was aware, had cut Julia to the heart. George and Katie had been betrothed once, before George had left America; chance had reunited them in Australia, and it was whispered that they had resumed their friendship, and had even had an affair. . . . Abigail shook her head sadly. It had been just talk, after all, and no one who cared about the two had given it any credence, though admittedly it had strained the marriage of Rick and Katie. And its effect on Julia had been little short of catastrophic. . . . Small wonder, then, that the girl was so difficult and unresponsive. Abigail chided herself; she must not allow her own feelings to be ruffled, but rather must try to make allowances for her stepdaughter and gain her trust, at least—even if she could not hope to win her affection.

From the house a gong boomed, and Abigail started to retrace her steps in response to it.

In the spacious, elegantly furnished withdrawing room she found Tim waiting for her, with Rick and Katie. Since their arrival that morning and a short call on the Broomes, Katie had kept to her bedroom, sleeping off the effects of the long, exhausting journey from Bathurst by ox-drawn wagon. She still looked wan and tired, Abigail noticed with concern, all the bright color gone from her cheeks, and her eyes sunken and lackluster. But she summoned a smile when Abigail poured tea for her and asked after her health, assuring her sister-in-law that she was quite well and would be even better after a good night's sleep.

"I can still feel the jolting of the wagon," Katie admitted ruefully. "Mr. Cox's road is not improved, I'm afraid, although some of the steeper sections have been leveled off somewhat. But it's wonderful to be here, Abigail—truly wonderful to see you all again. And an immense relief to know that dear Kate Lamerton will be with me when my time comes. God grant," she added gravely, "that this may be third time lucky!"

"Please God it may," Abigail echoed. Pouring tea for

her husband and brother, she chided herself for having allowed Julia to upset her. Julia's problems, her complaints and her accusations, faded into insignificance when set against Katie's need and her evident unhappiness. Because of her stiff New England pride, Katie would not complain; she would hide her hurt, would refuse to speak of it, and yet, Abigail sensed, it was there, simmering beneath the surface.

Did it stem from her marriage, she wondered; had Rick's love for his wife—or hers for him—in some way failed to compensate for the harsh, pioneering life they led, its loneliness and isolation? She looked searchingly at Rick, but he was deep in conversation with Tim, their subject the absorbing one of wool trading. By contrast with Katie, Rick looked tanned and fit, but there was an unaccustomed tenseness about him, a wariness, as if—despite the enthusiasm with which he was talking to Tim—he were keeping a guard on his tongue.

"I'm taking a leaf from Macarthur's book," Abigail heard him say. "Aiming for a comparatively small but purebred flock. Unlike him, I'm going in for more beef cattle, though, because the land is more suited to cattle than sheep, and they're less work. When they're ready for slaughter, they can be driven down from Bathurst on the hoof, with little or no loss of condition, and the same drovers can bring back store cattle, for fattening, to replace them. Sheep don't travel well over that road, but wool's no problem—and those merino rams I bought from Macarthur, for all they were damned costly, have certainly improved my yield."

Tim smiled. "They were costly all right, Rick. But didn't you say you were going in for horse breeding now? Or did I imagine it?"

"You didn't imagine it—I am." Rick sounded complacent. "I've got the paddocks and the buildings—we've expanded quite a lot since you last came our way. And Macarthur sold me an Arab stallion, which is a gem. Also costly, of course—John Macarthur never lowers his prices—but that animal has got me some beautiful foals. Given another year or so, Berber will have repaid his cost three times over, believe me. . . ."

He talked on, with Tim displaying a keen interest, and Abigail left them to their own devices and again turned her attention to Katie.

"Are you still finding it lonely at Pengallon?" she asked, replenishing her sister-in-law's cup. "And do try some of this cake. It's freshly made, from a recipe of my mother's."

Katie accepted a thin slice of cake and munched it appreciatively. "It's delicious, Abigail—and a long time since I've tasted anything so—so feminine. My household is all male, and the meals tend to be satisfying and stodgy. That's why I miss my poor little Annabel so much . . . I'd been looking forward to bringing up a daughter and sharing a few refinements with her, when she was old enough to enjoy them." She set down her plate, her expression momentarily darkening. "But . . . Pengallon is not as lonely as it used to be, not as isolated, because more grants have been taken up in the area. Governor Macquarie, as one of his last acts, chose ten young—I think you call them currency lads; anyway they're all Australian-born and all men in their early twenties. He chose them very carefully and gave them land on the Bathurst Plains—much less than ours, only fifty acres each. But they've done wonders with their grants, and one of them, Will Lee, has started breeding red shorthorn cattle with great success. It was he who gave Rick the idea of cutting down on sheep and running cattle instead. And now, of course, it's horses. But that—" Katie glanced across at her husband and shrugged. "That was Mr. Macarthur's idea. Rick met him in Parramatta when he went to select the merino rams. I sometimes think—" She broke off, flushing.

"What do you sometimes think, Katie?" Abigail persisted.

"Oh, nothing, really. I—it's just that Rick had no experience of farming before he left the navy, and of course I had none, either.''

"You have Jethro Crowan," Abigail reminded her. Tim, she remembered, had insisted that Jethro, the shepherd who had come out with Lucy and herself, should go to Rick, as manager and adviser, to compensate for his initial lack of experience.

"Yes," Katie agreed flatly. "We have Jethro, and it was very good of Tim to let us have him. But Rick won't listen to him, I'm afraid. He says all Jethro cares about are sheep. They fell out when Rick decided to cut down on the number of sheep we run. I think Jethro would like to return to you at Upwey. In fact, he as good as told me so.''

"Well, Tim would take him back, I'm quite sure," Abigail answered. "And so would I." She owed old Jethro Crowan a great deal, she reminded herself, and smiled as Katie eyed her in surprise.

"It was Jethro who brought Dickon into the world," she said softly. "I fancy I would have died if it hadn't been for Jethro. Indeed, I—" She was interrupted by Julia, who burst unheralded into the room, brandishing a letter.

"This has just come, addressed to you, Aunt Abigail," she announced, without apology. "It was delivered by that Javanese butler of Aunt Lucy's. And there's one for Katie, too. It's an invitation to the reception she's giving, I'm sure it is, and—"

"What reception?" Abigail asked icily. "I've heard nothing about a reception, Julia."

"But *I* have," Julia asserted pertly. "When I was at the Bowmans' they received an invitation, delivered in the same manner by the Javanese. Aunt Lucy is to give an evening party—a musical evening, it's to be, Mary Bowman said. I don't know how she heard, but she told me that Aunt Lucy has invited Lady Brisbane's sister, Miss Mackdougall, to play the harp."

"Oh!" A trifle nonplussed, Abigail exchanged a glance with her husband. Tim Dawson laughed.

"Miss Mackdougall is even more retiring than the Governor's lady," he said deprecatingly. "And I very much doubt whether she can be prevailed upon to exchange the comforts of Parramatta for the discomforts of Sydney's Government House, which is falling to pieces before our eyes! Besides, Lady Brisbane has only recently presented His Excellency with a son, has she not? She will be in no state to travel, either. Lucy has timed her party-giving somewhat injudiciously, I fear."

"But it's not to be until the sixth of May, Papa," Julia protested. "And it will be elegant and lovely—Aunt Lucy always plans her entertaining so lavishly, just as she used to when she was living in Batavia. You will accept, won't you? I wouldn't miss it for anything, truly I wouldn't."

Her enthusiasm found no echoes from her family.

Abigail sighed. "We shall have to accept, of course—Lucy will expect it of us, since we are her closest relatives. But . . ."

Again she glanced at her husband, who returned bluntly, "Devil take it, I suppose we shall have to! Though, speaking for myself, I must confess that a little of *Mijnheer* Van Buren goes a long way. He has a genius for rubbing people up the wrong way, whether intentionally or not. At the last dinner party he attended, he contrived to insult his hostess and at least half the male guests—including Major Goulburn. And James Erskine was incensed when he remained seated when the loyal toast was drunk at a mess dinner. I think he would have taken him to task for it, except that the Forty-sixth are leaving soon and he decided it was not worth putting himself out for."

Julia, looking offended, left the room as abruptly as she had entered it, and Rick said, "My acquaintance with Van Buren is slight, but from what you say of him, it seems something of a pity that Justin Broome went to his rescue."

"He told you about that, did he?" Tim took pipe and tobacco pouch from his pocket and rose, but Abigail signed to him to sit down again.

"Smoke if you wish," she bade him. "But let us hear about the rescue. There are all kinds of rumors concerning it, but I haven't heard the full story as yet. Did Justin tell you about it, Rick?"

Rick nodded. "Yes, this afternoon, when I went to call on him. He had been at the Governor's council meeting all the forenoon, so I missed him when we first called. Justin didn't say much—he never does—but I understand that Van Buren ran the *Flinders* onto the rocks at Cape Hawke." He repeated the brief account Justin had given him and shrugged. "Justin loved that little sloop, you know, and he was heartbroken at her loss. He wasn't too enamored with Van Buren's behavior either, I gathered, though he didn't say why. Something to do with one of the sloop's crew, who was injured, I think. He said the man is in the hospital and Van Buren has just washed his hands of him, although the poor devil's a Malay whom he signed on in Batavia." He added, his gaze going to Katie's face with odd intensity, "George De Lancey was with him on board the *Elizabeth*."

Katie said nothing, but she swiftly lowered her gaze, and Rick went on evenly, "They had been off to inspect the old penal settlement on Norfolk Island, with James Meehan. It appears that the Colonial Office wants it reopened and that there's also a possibility of a new settlement at Moreton Bay, for capital respites and incorrigibles and their like. Justin said that the Governor wishes to inspect the Moreton Bay site for himself, and the *Elizabeth* is under orders to take him there in a week or so. He told me that—" Katie scrambled awkwardly to her feet, and Rick broke off. "Katie, are you all right?"

Katie inclined her bright head, but every vestige of color had drained from her cheeks, and she was grasping the edge of the table for support, her slight body distorted by the swelling curves of her pregnancy. The coming child was not due for another four or five weeks, yet . . . Abigail moved toward her, but Katie gestured to her to resume her seat.

"I'm all right," she asserted. "Just very tired. If you will have the goodness to excuse me, Abby, I think I will go and lie down for a while."

Rick's hesitation was momentary. Then, concerned, he went to offer her his arm and, with a murmured apology, led her to the door. It closed behind them, and when their footsteps had receded, Abigail glanced across at her husband in mute and anxious question.

Tim, puffing at his pipe, answered her unspoken thoughts. "No, my dear, all is *not* well with those two, I'm afraid," he said regretfully. "Though God only knows why—I'd always supposed they were ideally suited to each other. Katie's a city girl, of course. Maybe she's not cut out for the hardships of a settler's life."

"She has plenty of courage," Abigail defended. "But I think she's probably lonely, Tim. She dreaded Pengallon's isolation before she and Rick were married, and apart from her convict maid, she seldom sees another woman from one month to the next. It's not only that, though—she admitted to me just now that she is worried that Rick was falling too much under the influence of Mr. Macarthur."

"He would not be alone. A great many of the new settlers *are* influenced by John Macarthur, and invariably to Macarthur's profit, if not always to their own. Rick told me he'd purchased an Arab stallion from him, in addition to the merino rams. And that *will* have cost him a pretty penny!"

Abigail nodded, frowning. "Yes, I heard him telling you that, and I wondered how he could possibly afford it. Unless . . ." She lowered her head, as if not wanting to complete the thought. "I can understand why Katie is worried."

Tim tapped out his pipe. He rose and started to pace the room, his heavy brows knit in a frown. "John Macarthur's an extraordinary fellow," he observed. "In a way, I suppose, he offers a challenge or, at any rate, an example. He's the richest man and the largest landowner in the whole of New South Wales; even the Reverend Samuel Marsden cannot

hold a candle to him—though, with God's help, he tries!
But men like Rick tend to forget how long Macarthur's
been at it. Even when they kept him in London, he never
lost sight of his objective or permitted his wife to forget
it.''

"Elizabeth Macarthur is a wonderful woman, Tim,"
Abigail insisted, with genuine admiration.

"So she is," Tim conceded readily. "But Macarthur is
the moving spirit, the planner . . . the schemer, if you
like. He gets what he wants, however long it takes him.
To cite just one example—he finally persuaded Lord Bathurst to grant him the five thousand acres in the Cow
Pastures that both Bligh and Macquarie refused to let him
have. Because they wanted to retain it as government
land—quite rightly, in my view. But Macarthur would not
give it up or accept other land in lieu. He had a battle royal
with Secretary Goulburn and John Oxley over it; he fell
out with the judges, Barron Field in particular . . . and
they blocked his appointment to the magistracy. He quarreled with Macquarie, and he waited—God in heaven,
Abby!—he waited over twenty years, and he never let up,
never gave the Colonial Office any peace. He found a way
to enlist Commissioner Bigge in his cause, and he did the
same with the present Governor. Lord Camden originally
granted him ten thousand acres in Bligh's time, but Bligh
only permitted him to take half. Well, now he owns the lot
. . . ten thousand acres of the finest grazing land in the
whole colony, in addition to his farms at Parramatta and
Belmont!''

Warming to his theme, Tim halted his restless pacing
and went on forcefully, "Abby, John Macarthur may have
been deprived of the magisterial appointment he wanted,
but what is that to him? He owns over eight thousand
sheep, about a thousand head of cattle, and probably a
hundred horses, including the Arabs—and he has a virtual
monopoly in merino rams. He sold the land he bought
from Foveaux at Toongabbie at a vast profit, and he's said
to be after land in Rick's area on the Bathurst Plains.

Leaving aside his political activities and the fact that he should have been hanged for treason, can you wonder that Rick listens to him and tries to emulate him? They all do, all the new monied settlers the home government is sending out here.''

"But Rick isn't a new settler," Abigail objected. "He had no love for John Macarthur when he was serving in the navy at the time of the rebel administration, had he?"

"Times change, my dear," Tim answered with a shrug. "I hold no brief for John Macarthur and I never have—the man's an opportunist and a rogue. But even I have to admire his achievements. Apart from everything else, he has done more to build up our wool trade than any man living, and we all profit from that. Indeed, I'd go as far as to say that, a hundred years from now, Australia's prosperity may well be attributed to his efforts." He smiled without amusement. "By then, of course, his part in ruining three governors and deposing a fourth will conveniently have been forgotten."

"I expect you are right," Abigail said. "All the same, Tim, I am worried about Rick. You don't suppose, do you, that he—" She broke off, still reluctant to broach the subject.

"Suppose what, Abby?" Tim urged.

She hesitated, unwilling to suggest, even to Tim, that her brother might be capable of deceit. But Tim would never betray a confidence, least of all hers, she knew, and she said uneasily, "Well, do you recall those gold nuggets Rick found in the river, when he and Justin first went to Pengallon?"

"Certainly I do." Once again, Tim read and answered her unspoken thoughts. He shook his head emphatically. "He would be breaking the terms of his leasehold, Abby. Governor Macquarie specifically had mineral rights excluded from it for twenty years, and—Rick isn't a fool. He knows that he could forfeit the grant and be liable to criminal proceedings if he broke those terms."

"That's true, Tim, but . . . oh, dear, I think you should ask him, I—"

"He wouldn't admit it, even if he is secretly obtaining gold. And besides," Tim added unanswerably, "how could he dispose of it, supposing he is? Who could he trust to buy it from him?"

"No one in the colony," Abigail conceded. "Even the worst felon would be too much afraid of the consequences to buy it from him, I imagine. But even so, I—oh, Tim, Rick is my brother, and I care for him very deeply. I don't want to see him in trouble—any sort of trouble. If it isn't the gold, if he's running himself into debt in order to buy stock from Mr. Macarthur, then I . . ."

Tim put an arm round her and smiled. "Abby my dear, if Rick is in debt to Macarthur, it will be with Macarthur's full connivance, don't worry. He'll have covered himself; he always does. But I would be most reluctant to question your brother on the subject, if you'll forgive me. I should only insult him and forfeit his trust. As matters stand, we are on excellent terms with him, are we not? If he has got himself into debt, I feel sure he will ask us for our help, since he knows very well that we should give it gladly."

He was right, Abigail thought. As always, Tim was right . . . Rick *would* resent being questioned; but if he were in serious financial trouble, he would know, without being told, that he could depend on Tim and her for help. Tim was a rich man; not as yet in the same class as John Macarthur, but one of the colony's major landowners all the same. He had worked hard for what he had; even his inheritance from Jasper Spence had been well earned, and he had a reputation for honesty and fair dealing that few could match. She turned to kiss his cheek, and Tim said, his smile widening, "Is this a moment when I might ask a favor of you, Abby?"

"Oh, Tim, you don't have to ask," she began. "You—" The door opened and cut her short, and she turned, startled, to see Rick standing in the aperture. He looked pale and distraught, and Abigail wondered for a moment whether he could have overheard her conversation with Tim.

But his first words banished all such thoughts from her head. "It's Katie," he told them. "She has gone into labor, I'm afraid."

"Already?" Abigail was on her feet in an instant, shocked and apprehensive. "But surely it is too early, Rick?"

"A month too early," her brother answered bitterly. "But it's worse than that, Abby. I called Kate Lamerton to attend to her, and she says it is a breech presentation and the birth may be difficult. Mrs. Lamberton wants a doctor to examine her. I'm going to the hospital now, but I thought I'd better tell you first."

"We can send a servant," Tim offered. "No need for you to go, Rick."

"There's nothing else I can do to help, is there?" Rick countered, an abrasive edge to his voice. "The last time Katie was brought to bed, only the convict girl Mary and I were there to do what we could. And it wasn't enough—the poor infant was stillborn, and Katie nearly died. *This* time I'm taking no chances . . . she shall have a doctor, and I intend to see that he's on hand before the birth. I only wish that Dr. Redfern hadn't retired; but I suppose Bowman is competent?"

"He's said to be," Abigail assured him. She glanced uncertainly at her husband, and Tim nodded in assent.

"I'll go with you, Rick. And, Abby—"

"I shall go and see Katie at once," Abigail promised. She left them and hurried upstairs to the room Katie had occupied since her arrival. The curtains were drawn, and the room was in semidarkness. Kate Lamerton met her at the door, a finger to her lips.

"The poor lass has dropped off," the stout midwife whispered. She let the door close softly behind her. " 'Tis best she should sleep, Miss Abigail, for she's as weak as a kitten. She'll need all the rest she can get before the doctor comes."

"Is it a breech presentation, Kate?" Abigail asked anxiously. "Are you sure?"

"Aye, it is." Kate, her round, honest face reflecting the regret she felt at having to impart such news, went into details. " 'Twill be a difficult birth—she's that small, you see, an' with her only a few weeks from term, well . . ." She spread her hands in a gesture of resignation. "Dr. Redfern might have been able to save her babe, but with anyone else, I don't know what chance there'll be."

"*You'll* be with her, Kate," Abigail managed huskily. "And Dr. Bowman should not be long. My husband and Mr. Tempest have gone to the hospital to call him."

But, to her dismay, it was not Dr. Bowman with whom, an hour later, the two men returned. The doctor was out of town; in his place came a young assistant surgeon who, full of confidence, introduced himself as Hamish Macnab and admitted to having arrived in the colony only a few weeks before.

Abigail took him to Katie's room and left him with an openly mistrustful Kate Lamerton; after that, there was nothing to do save wait and, in Abigail's case, silently pray that all might go well, however slim the chance. The time dragged by on leaden feet; dinner was served, but Rick made barely a pretense of eating, while emptying a decanter of Cape brandy. He was restless and ill at ease and, as the night wore on, became increasingly morose, and Abigail, seeking vainly to cheer him, was thankful that Julia had elected to spend the evening with friends. Dorothea and Dickon, her own deaf and dumb son, were subdued and of little help when it came to dispelling Rick's gloom. Both took their leave as soon as the meal was over, Dickon—a slim, handsome eighteen-year-old, with the trusting mentality of a child of half that age—manfully hiding his hurt when his adored uncle failed to acknowledge his presence or to reply to his halting attempts to communicate.

It was to Abigail's intense relief that Dr. Bowman made his appearance just before midnight. He looked worried when she told him how long Katie's labor had lasted, but his words were reassuring and noncommittal as he followed her upstairs.

"Be so good as to wait here, Mrs. Dawson," he requested. "I will examine the patient and then give you my opinion as to her condition."

Abigail obeyed, her heart sinking when, through the open door, she heard Katie's weak, agonized cries. Dr. Bowman's examination occupied a scant fifteen minutes. Abigail waited, her lips moving in disjointed prayer, and he was beside her before she was conscious of his return.

He said gravely, "Mrs. Dawson, there is no fetal heartbeat. I am exceedingly sorry to have to tell you that the child is dead. To save the mother I must use forceps to make the delivery without delay. But continue to wait here, if you please. It will not take very long."

"Very well, Doctor," Abigail managed in a choked, unhappy voice. "But should not her husband be told? He is here and—"

Dr. Bowman shook his head, his thin, angular face betraying a cold anger that, at first, Abigail found hard to comprehend. Then he said flatly, "It is on her husband's account that Mrs. Tempest prevailed on my young colleague to delay beyond the point when it was safe to do so. She would not permit him to make a forceps delivery because she feared injury to the child. She told Dr. Macnab that her husband held her to blame for her previous stillbirth and for the death of their elder child. No doubt she was delirious when she made this claim, but . . . she seems convinced of it. And she has been asking for you, Mrs. Dawson. I will call you when it is over."

Poor little Katie, Abigail thought as she settled down once more to wait, trying vainly to shut her ears to the cries that reached her from the room beyond, rising shrilly above the low, muted voices of the two doctors and Kate Lamerton's husky burr. Could Rick really have blamed her for her failure to give him a living child, or had she, perhaps, imagined it, against all reason? She had been

prepared to risk her own life, that was evident from what
Dr. Bowman had said, but . . . Abigail caught her breath
on a sob. Surely that was proof enough of her love for her
husband, not the reverse? Surely—

"Miss Abigail, dear . . ." Kate Lamerton was coming
out onto the landing, tears mingled with the streams of
perspiration coursing down her plump red cheeks. " 'Tis
over now, and the poor young soul is out of pain. The
babe was a boy, Miss Abigail, an' she's near beside
herself with grief, goin' on an' on 'bout what Mr. Rick's
goin' to say 'cause she couldn't born him. These past
hours I was beggin' her and the young doctor, too—let
him do what he must, Miss Katie, I said. But she wouldn't
have it. No, she said, no—not whilst there's a chance my
babe will live."

"It's not your fault, Kate dear," Abigail asserted. "I'm
sure you did all you possibly could."

Kate mopped her eyes with a corner of her stained white
apron and smothered a sigh. "She's wantin' to see you,
Miss Abigail. The doctor says 'tis all right, but will you
stay just for a few minutes, if you please?"

"Very well," Abigail agreed. The two doctors passed
her, bowing politely as they moved toward the head of the
stairs.

"I will break the sad news to Mr. Tempest," Dr.
Bowman volunteered kindly. "I am truly sorry that it must
be bad news. Good night, Mrs. Dawson."

Numbly, Abigail thanked him and followed Kate into
the sickroom. In the big, four-poster bed, Katie lay hunched
up, her small, pinched face as white as the pillows on
which her head rested. Kate Lamerton had set the bed to
rights; there were clean sheets and a fresh coverlet, and
Katie herself was wearing a pretty lace-trimmed nightgown,
her hair neatly braided and brushed to golden smoothness.

At the sight of Abigail, she attempted to sit up, and,
dry-eyed, her soft young mouth bravely compressed, she
whispered, "You know? They told you?"

"Yes," Abigail confirmed. "And I am most truly sorry,

dearest Katie. But try not to grieve—please, please, do not blame yourself. You—"

Katie cut her short. She said, quite calmly and quietly, "Abigail, I cannot go back to Pengallon. May I stay here with you until—that is until I can find suitable lodgings?"

A dozen questions sprang to Abigail's mind; she wanted desperately to urge the girl to wait before coming to a decision, to plead with her to see and talk to Rick, to let time heal her grief, but the look in Katie's blue eyes restrained her, and she answered gently, "Of course you may stay, for as long as you wish, Katie."

"Thank you," Katie acknowledged. The stark pain in her eyes did not diminish, but for all that, she seemed relieved and let herself fall tiredly back onto her pillows. "Will you tell Rick, please, that I am staying?"

"If you want me to," Abigail agreed reluctantly. "But won't you—Katie, dear, won't you see him? I'm sure he will be anxious to see you, even if it's only for a moment."

The refusal she had half expected did not come. Katie's eyes closed. "If he wants to see me, then of course, let him come up. But I am very weary, I—let him come at once, if you please."

Abigail hesitated and then, pityingly, bent to kiss her, shocked by the ice-cold cheek as her lips brushed it, meeting no response.

Downstairs, the withdrawing room held only Tim and Rick; the doctors, clearly, had decided not to linger. Rick, looking strained and uneasy, went to pay his visit to his wife, but he was gone for only a few minutes. When he returned, he announced baldly, "I gather, from Katie, that she would like to stay on here for a while and that you're willing to have her, Abby. Well, I've no objection, naturally—indeed, I'm very grateful. I'll leave for Pengallon in the morning, with young Dickon. I've some business to conclude in Parramatta, but it won't take long. I—thanks for all you've done, both of you. Good night."

He strode out, walking quite steadily, and Tim observed dryly, "Your brother can hold his liquor better than any man I know, Abby my dear. And maybe it's helped him to get over his disappointment, which is understandably keen. But . . . I'm afraid what I said earlier about their marriage is only too true, alas. All is not well between them, is it?''

Abigail shook her head, feeling suddenly unbearably weary and despondent. "No," she confirmed. "It is not. Perhaps if that poor babe had lived they might have been able to reconcile their differences.'' She let a sigh escape her. "But, Tim, Katie must love him—I don't know whether Dr. Bowman told you, but it seems she was willing to risk her life to save that child, because Rick wanted it so much.''

"He mentioned it, but I'm not sure whether Rick took it in." Tim stifled a yawn and put his arm about her shoulders. "Let's get some sleep, Abby my love. I'm tired, and you must be worn out. We've done all we can tonight, and maybe we shall be able to put a fresh slant on things in the morning.''

"Yes, all right," Abigail agreed. On their way upstairs, she remembered that her husband had been about to ask a favor of her when Rick had interrupted them. Pressed to reveal what it was, Tim gave her a rueful smile. "It's of no account, Abby.''

"Tell me, all the same," she insisted.

He shrugged. "Very well—but truly, it *is* of no account. I was going to ask you to intercede with your sister Lucy, that's all. To try to persuade her to accept the deeds for the house and farm at Portland Place, in settlement of her claim on Yarramundie. I'm anxious to make a settlement, and the vineyard and wine vats might appeal sufficiently to Van Buren to make him swallow his pride and permit Lucy to hold the lease. But—'' Tim yawned again, unable this time to stifle it. "That infernal reception will afford me an opportunity to raise the subject with Van Buren myself . . . and you could probably talk to Lucy then, too. Normally, as you well know, my dear, I avoid such damned functions like the plague, but on this occasion it may prove useful.''

"I hope it will, Tim," Abigail answered, her words lacking conviction. But Lucy's claim in respect of the property they had jointly inherited had worried her even more than it had worried Tim, and she added, as they went into their bedroom together, "Dear Tim—it's good of you to offer to give up Portland Place. How I wish, though, that it might have gone to Rick and Katie instead. My heart bleeds for both of them, but especially for Katie."

As had been her habit since childhood, she knelt down at the bedside to pray as soon as she had disrobed. There was solace in prayer, and Abigail felt at peace when, ten minutes later, she slipped into bed and into Tim's sleepy but welcoming arms.

"Dear Tim," she murmured softly. "Dear Tim—I do love you."

But he was already asleep, and she could not be sure if he had heard her.

CHAPTER VII

George De Lancey consulted his watch and set off at a brisk pace down King Street. The court sitting had gone on longer than he had anticipated, and he would, he realized, be late for the Van Burens' reception by the time he had changed. This knowledge worried him very little personally, but Rachel was looking forward to the occasion, and he did not want to disappoint her, since these days party-giving seemed to be in abeyance in Sydney.

Government House receptions and dinners were, in any event, few and far between, and with Sir Thomas Brisbane on passage to Moreton Bay on board the *Elizabeth* and Lady Brisbane in Parramatta, none was in prospect. The garrison regiment was in the process of leaving for India, and its replacement, the 40th Regiment of His Majesty's Foot, having only just arrived in the colony, was not yet ready to assume its social responsibilities. For the rest . . . George sighed, wishing that his position as one of the two high court judges did not place him so inescapably in the elitist camp, with the obligation to entertain and be entertained by people with whom he had little in common.

Rachel enjoyed parties, of course, and that was understandable. His wife was only twenty-one; she had lived most of her short life in the isolation of her mother's or her stepfather's farms, and to her, dining out was still something of a novelty. A chance to play the lady and to dress in keeping with her new role . . . but, he thought indulgently, the novelty would wear off. Like her mother, by all accounts, and certainly like her brother William, she was more happily at home amid a rural community and in the surroundings she knew and loved.

An expert horsewoman, Rachel had, for all her youth, a profound knowledge of husbandry in all its forms and an eye for stock that even her brother William respected. There were times when, wearying of the clacking tongues and the absurd pretensions of Sydney's self-styled respectable inhabitants, she urged him to resign his legal appointment and apply for a land grant; and indeed, George reflected, there were times when he was tempted to do so. Or—he swung into Macquarie Street, tapping the dust from his boots with his cane—or at least do so in part. The Governor had offered him two thousand acres of prime farming land in the Hunter Valley, together with the post of judge of the Court of Requests—a new post, to be set up in Newcastle when the Hunter Valley area was opened for general settlement. Meanwhile he would be required to act as circuit judge and preside over courts in Liverpool and Windsor, alternating with a newly arrived barrister named Douglass, a pleasant fellow, well versed in civil law, with whom, he knew, it would be pleasant to work.

Such was the shortage of men qualified in the legal profession that, were he to ask for it, a similar opening would be found for him, the Governor had hinted, virtually anywhere else in the colony that he might choose.

George quickened his pace, glancing about him at the lengthening shadows. The street was crowded, with most of the passersby on foot and the occasional curricle or carriage compelled to proceed at a snail's pace by the press of people.

Apart from soldiers in the King's scarlet and a few ship's officers in uniform, the folk abroad at this time of the evening presented a drab appearance. Most of the chain gangs and other convict working parties had been herded into the Hyde Park barracks for the night, so that those who remained were, for the most part, either the poorer settlers, ticket-of-leave convicts employed as clerks or household servants on errands for their masters, or farmers seeking brief distraction after attending market. It was difficult, if not impossible, to distinguish one from another, for virtually all were clad in garments made from locally produced woolen cloth, spun and woven at the women's factory at Parramatta, where some six hundred female convicts were employed to toil at the looms, or at the Botany Bay mill, owned by the enterprising Simeon Lord.

George thrust his way through the crowd, coming to a halt outside the door of his chambers. Since his marriage, he had built on a pleasant, two-story dwelling house at the rear of the rooms he had rented on first arriving in the colony. The front door and main reception rooms were in Hunter Street, but access could be obtained through his clerk's office, and since this saved time and a considerable walk, he used it when coming from the court. He inserted his key, fumbling to unlock the heavy wooden door, only to find, to his surprise, that it swung open at his touch.

It was long past the time when his clerk normally left, and he paused in the entrance lobby, listening intently. A faint tapping sound reached his ears, coming, as nearly as he could judge, from a cupboard halfway up the stairs, used for the storage of brooms and cleaning materials. Puzzled and suspicious, George grasped his cane in both hands and, as silently as he could, started to ascend the narrow wooden staircase . . . but before he could reach the cupboard, a dark-clad form hurled itself down from the landing above. The intruder, employing fists and booted feet, knocked him off-balance and sent him staggering back to the lobby, winded and unable to cry out.

When he picked himself up, the man had vanished, the door slammed shut behind his disappearing back. George, breathless and shaken, had a confused recollection of a thin, pale, but not ill-favored face and a pair of steely gray eyes that, for a moment, had bored into his. For the rest, however, he was utterly at a loss and doubted whether, should they meet again, he would be able with any degree of certainty to recognize his assailant. He dabbed at his bruised and bleeding mouth and then, pulling himself together, mounted the stairs to the cupboard, from which the tapping was now both louder and more urgent.

As he had half expected, it was his clerk, young Rodney Akeroyd, whom he found, bound and with a roughly fashioned gag in his mouth, incarcerated there. Freed of his bonds and given a few mouthfuls of brandy from George's flask, the young emancipist gave a graphic account of his misadventures.

"I was just getting ready to go home, seeing Your Honor had told me I should not stay late," he explained. "In fact, sir, I was at the door when two men accosted me. One was a big fellow—very powerfully built, sir, with red hair, close-cropped, obviously a convict, though he wasn't wearing convict garb. I spotted the mark of irons on his wrists. He grabbed ahold of me before I'd any idea of what they wanted and dragged me back into the lobby. The man with him was—" He hesitated.

Goerge prompted, "Go on, lad. Was he thin—thin-faced, I mean, with gray eyes?"

"Aye, that's right, sir. Well dressed, too, and well spoken, and he—well, this may sound farfetched, but I took him for a gentleman. That is, sir, until he kneed me in the groin, the way no gentleman would think of doing." Akeroyd's tone was indignant, and George, for all the discomfort the gray-eyed man had caused him, could not suppress a smile at his young clerk's criteria for what constituted gentle breeding.

"They asked for Justice Forbes, sir," Akeroyd went on. "I told 'em these weren't his chambers, but they didn't believe me. 'Twas after that they tied me up and pushed me into the cupboard. I heard 'em going upstairs to your room, and then I heard you come in, sir, so I started banging on the floor as loud as I could, in the hope that Your Honor would hear me."

"The men did not say what they wanted?" George questioned.

Rodney Akeroyd shook his head. "No, sir, they didn't.
'Cept the smaller one. He said something about court
papers and a transcript of his trial—his trial in England, I
took him to mean. The big fellow, he must have left first,
just before Your Honor came in. They'd been in your
room for quite a while . . . half an hour at least, as near as
I could judge, sir."

"Then we had better go and see what damage they've
done, if you're feeling up to it," George decided.

"I'm fine, sir," Akeroyd assured him. "Just a mite
stiff, that's all."

The upstairs room, which he used as an office, showed
no sign that a search had been made of it, to George's
surprised relief. Indeed, he thought, looking about him,
nothing appeared out of place. The papers on his desk still
lay in the neat piles in which he had left them, and the
contents of drawers and filing cabinets were in their usual
order. Whoever had searched the room had done so
skillfully, as if seeking to hide the fact that a search had
been conducted. He did notice that his legal books had
been examined, several of them replaced in shelves in
which he did not normally keep them, and one—a treatise
on appeal court findings—was missing. So, too, was a small
sum in cash, taken from the pocket of his working jacket,
which hung on a hook behind the door of the closet.

The most serious loss, discovered belatedly by Akeroyd,
was of the heavy cavalry pistol he had acquired during his
army service, which, like the jacket, had hung out of sight
in a closet where deed boxes were stored. The search, he
realized, had indeed been thorough, for the closet door,
which was flush with the wall and concealed by a curtain,
would not be noticed by the general run of his callers.
George gave vent to a muffled oath.

"I'd be obliged if you would inform the police of the
break-in, Rodney, on your way home," he said. "I'm due
at a reception—indeed, I'm late for it already—but the
theft of my pistol must be reported as soon as possible. If
you're correct in thinking that the intruders were convicts,

it could be a serious matter, I'm afraid. But—'' He frowned. ''There's damned little to go on, is there? A couple of vague descriptions, which could fit half a hundred of Sydney's inhabitants. I suppose you didn't chance to hear them addressing each other by name, did you?''

The young clerk considered the question. Finally he said uncertainly, ''I fancy I heard the name Nick, sir, but I can't say which of the two it belonged to. I was shut up in the cupboard when I heard it, and their voices were muffled, you understand. It might help the constables to trace them, I suppose—Nick will be short for Nicholas, and Nicholas isn't a very common name, is it, sir?''

It was hardly uncommon, George reflected, but clearly it was the best he and young Akeroyd could do. He consulted his watch and started to move toward the passageway that connected his chambers with his private dwelling, pleased now that he had taken the precaution of having a stout lock fitted to the access door.

He found Rachel, dressed and prettily coiffured for the Van Burens' reception, in the nursery, bidding good night to their little daughter, Magdalen. The child, auburn-haired like her mother and of the same happy nature, was the apple of his eye, and late though he was, George could not resist picking her up in his arms and hugging her. Magdalen responded joyfully, her small arms clasping him about the neck and her eager cries of ''Dada!'' touching him to the heart.

''It's long past her bedtime,'' Rachel reproved him gently. ''And you haven't changed yet.''

George reluctantly laid his daughter back in her cot— willing himself to ignore her wails of disappointment—and Rachel, leaving the child in the care of her convict nursemaid, followed him to their bedroom. His evening clothes were laid out ready for him on the bed, shaving water and his razor on the washstand.

''I'll not be long, dearest,'' he promised, divesting himself of his coat and stock and starting to lather his face.

"What made you so late?" Rachel asked. "Did the court sit late?"

George nodded. "That—and a burglary in my chambers." He gave her a brief account of the break-in, omitting to mention the attack on himself.

"Sydney's getting worse," Rachel observed. "The Governor is right, George, I'm sure he is. With such a high proportion of ne'er-do-wells permitted, for one reason or another, to roam the streets at night, no one is safe. Newly arrived convicts *should* be assigned to work on farms outside the town until they've proved themselves capable of leading honest lives. Or, if they are needed to stay here to work, they should *all* be locked up in the Hyde Park barracks overnight. I've heard that those with money are able to bribe the jailers to let them out."

George had also heard this rumor, but he merely grunted and set to work with his razor. In all probability, if Rodney Akeroyd's guess was correct, the men who had robbed him of his pistol were new arrivals in the colony, and the gray-eyed fellow Akeroyd had initially taken for a gentleman had been possessed of enough money to buy his freedom from restriction. Or perhaps he was one of the educated class of felons who, because their skills were always needed, were able to assume ticket-of-leave status virtually as soon as they landed from the transports bringing them out to New South Wales. Almost all the government offices were staffed by such men; they were employed as clerks, storekeepers, teachers, even in some cases as court officials and constables. Few betrayed the trust their education had won for them, but . . . there were always exceptions.

Michael Robinson, who had enjoyed the privileged position of clerk to Governor Macquarie's secretary, John Campbell, and who had been the colony's poet laureate in Macquarie's day, had only recently been brought before the court, charged and found guilty of forgery. The same crime, George reflected wryly, for which the Oxford University fellow had originally been deported. . . . He cupped his hands and splashed water on his face, washing the soap from his freshly shaven cheeks.

Rachel said, holding his starched evening shirt for him, "William is here, George—in Sydney, I mean. He brought a flock of culls down from Ulva to market."

"You invited him to stay here, I hope?" George responded. He liked Rachel's second brother as much as he liked the elder, Justin Broome. William managed the farm his mother had owned on the Nepean River, and had done so since his boyhood, his schooling—like that of Justin's firstborn—a constant bone of contention between them.

Rachel shook her head. "He's staying at Justin's. Jessica is on her own and welcomed him warmly. But he is staying only for a couple of days, and—" She hesitated, eyeing him doubtfully as he tied his cravat, and then went on, "George dear, he wants me to go back with him for a short visit. He says my stepfather is far from well and wants to see me."

"Then of course you must go," George asserted. Andrew Hawley, a retired royal marine captain with a distinguished war record, was another man for whom he had conceived a strong liking. A valuable man, his wife's stepfather, who had come out initially as one of Admiral Bligh's aides and had contributed much to the colony's well-being. He was in his middle sixties now and in failing health, and Rachel was devoted to him. "Of course you must go," he repeated. The cravat tied to his satisfaction, he let Rachel help him into his green velvet tailcoat.

"What about little Magdalen?"

"My love—" George was startled. "You weren't thinking of taking her with you, surely?"

"Well, yes, I was," Rachel admitted. "Only that would mean taking the curricle, and you have to go to Windsor next week."

"Magdalen can stay here. The girl—Dorcas—is quite competent to look after her, is she not? And if you're not going to be away for very long . . . it would be a trying journey for a little girl, Rachel, in this weather. I can postpone my visit to Windsor or ask Douglass to go in my place. Magdalen will be quite all right with me." He was almost pleading, George realized, so reluctant was he to be parted from his adored little daughter. To his relief, Rachel gave her agreement without protest, and he took her into his arms, kissing her tenderly.

"The drought is very bad, William told me," she added when he released her. "And if it's just the two of us, we can ride over in half the time it would take in the curricle, of course. And I'm worried about Andrew, you see—really worried, George. It seems he's losing weight and is barely able to walk. I think perhaps he needs me more than you and Magdalen do . . . and Dorcas is very good with her, as you say."

"Yes, I know she is." George buttoned his coat and turned, smiling, to offer her his arm. "Needless to say, I shall miss you, my love. Well . . ." His smile widened. "I'm ready at last, and you are looking quite lovely—too lovely to waste your charms on the Van Burens and their infernal reception. But I suppose there's no help for it—we must put in an appearance. Will your brother be there, do you imagine?"

"William?" Rachel's tone was restrained, but George sensed her resentment. "Lucy Van Buren would not invite William. We were at school together, and I used to stay at the Spences' with Abigail and Lucy, but *I'm* only invited because I'm your wife. In any case"—her resentment faded and she echoed his smile—"I have reason to believe that William is courting."

"Is he, by Jove!" George was delighted. "Has he told you whom he's courting?"

"Oh, no. He's very secretive about it. But I have my suspicions."

"Which are?"

Rachel's blue eyes were suddenly bright with pleased anticipation. "George, I think it's Dodie Dawson. But

don't breathe a word, will you, dearest? Because it would
set Julia against them, if she found out, and Julia is—''

"I know what Julia is," George returned with unconcealed bitterness. "And you may rest assured that I shall
keep a still tongue in my head where that young woman is
concerned. But I think it would please Abigail—and
Timothy, also."

"Yes, I'm sure it would." Rachel's fingers tightened
about his arm. "Shall we just peep into the nursery, before
we go? We're so late already that two minutes won't make
much difference."

They tiptoed together into the darkened room where
little Magdalen slept and, for considerably longer than
Rachel's specified two minutes, stood looking down at the
child's small, peacefully sleeping face. . . .

"*Not* that way, Saleh—serve the ladies and gentlemen
with *Mijnheer* Macarthur's party first!"

Lucy Van Buren's voice was lowered, but it was harsh
with exasperation. The reception, she thought bitterly, was
close to becoming a social disaster, instead of the brilliant
gathering of Sydney's elite that she had planned with such
care and forethought.

The Governor was away, on some voyage of inspection;
his wife and her sister, Miss Mackdougall, had refused the
invitation, giving no reason, and Colonel and Mrs. Erskine
were on their way to India, taking their officers with them.
The new Lieutenant Governor and the officers and ladies
of the relieving regiment had not yet returned any calls,
and so—Lucy sighed. Etiquette precluded their being invited.
There had been a number of other refusals, politely couched
and offering plausible excuses, but . . . Looking about her
at the guests moving among the elaborately set-out buffet
tables, Lucy was compelled to admit that—with a few
notable exceptions, such as the Macarthurs, Justice Forbes,
and Archdeacon Scott—the cream of the colony's society
was conspicuous by its absence. Of course, her sister and
the Dawson family were there in force; she had known that

she could count on Abigail's loyalty and support. . . . Still, she had made preparation for over a hundred guests, and the hired marquee was barely half full.

Biting her lower lip to still its angry trembling, she watched Saleh going obediently with his tray of champagne glasses to the group that surrounded John and Elizabeth Macarthur. Their sons were with them, tall, well-favored young men, who did their parents credit; Hannibal, John Macarthur's nephew and himself a wealthy landowner, was there with his pretty wife and his elder daughter; and Dr. and Mrs. Bowman were standing nearby and seemingly enjoying themselves, judging by the laughter a chance remark had provoked. But then, to her dismay, Lucy saw and understood the reason for it. Her husband, Jos, immaculately dressed and adhering to his promise to permit no drop of liquor to pass his lips, had, in spite of this, managed to draw attention to himself by falling full-length over one of the guy ropes by which the marquee was secured.

He was up at once, but, his dignity ruffled and his face like thunder, he turned on Dr. Bowman in angry protest. The doctor's laughter ceased abruptly, and he appeared about to reply in kind, but Elizabeth Macarthur stepped swiftly between them. Lucy was not near enough to hear what she said, but clearly it was placatory and well-chosen, for Jos was smiling and kissing her hand, and Saleh was at his elbow with a brimming glass, ignoring her signal. Jos took it and raised it in a toast to the man whose laughter, a few moments before, had so annoyed him, and Lucy, relieved, felt the tension drain out of her.

Pausing to greet the late arrival of George De Lancey and his wife, she moved among the guests, slowly but purposefully making her way toward the bandstand, where the small orchestra she had engaged for the evening was setting up its instruments.

"Play," she bade them impatiently. "Waste no more time—do what I am paying you for!"

Their leader looked hurt, for he had not finished tuning

his battered violin, but he bowed politely, and a few
minutes later strings combined with woodwind and piano
to produce a succession of the gay, light airs for which she
had asked.

Lucy moved on. The De Lanceys, she saw, had joined
Abigail and her party; her servants, well trained and aware
of her presence, plied them with champagne and offered
trays of Dutch sweetmeats and savory concoctions that her
excellent cook had prepared with such care for the occasion.
Claus, clad in the same white jacket and tight-fitting white
trousers as the other male servants, was assiduous in his
attention to Judge De Lancey, Lucy noticed with some
surprise, and the judge, even more to her surprise, was
chatting to him as if to an equal. De Lancey had, of
course, been aboard the *Elizabeth* when Justin Broome had
gone to Jos's rescue, she recalled, so that perhaps . . . She
came abruptly to a standstill.

A girl's voice, high-pitched and, she could only suppose,
intentionally loud, reached her above the melodious strum-
ming of the orchestra.

"You see that boy—the half-caste they call Claus? George
De Lancey is talking to him over by the bandstand . . .
yes, that's the one. Aunt Lucy pretends he's a servant, but
he's not, you know."

A softer voice answered her, expressing doubts, and
then the first, which Lucy had no difficulty in recognizing
as that of her niece, Julia Dawson, went on derisively,
"Dear Aunt Lucy's handsome husband had a native wife
before he married her. . . . Claus is his son. Truly, Dodie,
you've got to believe me. You—"

"You are making it up," her sister Dorothea accused.
"Just out of—out of spite, Julia!"

White with indignation, Lucy started toward them, conscious that heads were turning and that, without a doubt, a
number of people besides Dorothea had heard Julia's malicious claim. And they would probably believe it, she
thought wretchedly as the girl continued, still in the same
shrilly raised voice, "I'm *not* making it up! Dickon is

friendly with Claus; they play together sometimes in our garden. And I *heard* him telling Dickon who his father was, so there! I—''

Abigail reached her before Lucy could do so. She said, with icy authority, ''You will fetch your cloaks, both of you—I'm sorry, Dodie, but you will have to go as well. Your father will take you home, and I shall make your adieus to Aunt Lucy. No, not another word—'' as Julia attempted to argue. ''You have said more than enough, Julia. You have a wicked and deceitful tongue and should be ashamed of yourself. Go—at once, do you hear? I declare I am mortified by your behavior.''

Dorothea, pink with embarrassment, grasped her elder sister's arm and almost dragged her away. Lucy made no attempt to detain her. The harm, she thought bitterly, was done, but only those in her immediate vicinity had overheard the wretched girl's spiteful words. Jos, thank heaven, was deep in conversation with Archdeacon Scott and William Balcombe, the colonial treasurer, and was blissfully unaware of the slur cast upon his reputation. It would only set more tongues wagging if she were to demand an apology in the presence of her guests . . . better by far to put a brave face on it and act as if nothing untoward had happened, Lucy told herself.

Nevertheless, she was angry, and she vented her anger on Abigail. Drawing her sister aside, she said in a harsh whisper, ''That girl is insolent and vindictive, Abby—you really should try to control her.''

''I do try,'' Abigail assured her. ''But she isn't a child, you know—she is twenty-four years old.''

''And unmarried.''

''Yes, alas. And I *am* sorry for what she said, Lucy, believe me. I shall see that she writes you a letter of apology. It was—oh, dear, it was a most outrageous suggestion to make, and I cannot imagine why she saw fit to make it.''

''Except,'' Lucy retorted disparagingly, ''that it happens to be true, more's the pity. My handsome husband doesn't only drink to excess, he sees no harm in bedding native women—in or out of wedlock. All the same, Abby, I do not want *that* fact made public here. It is necessary to keep up appearances, as you well know, so I'll thank you to respect my confidence. And, if you please, make sure that Julia keeps a guard on her tongue.''

Abigail looked shocked at this admission, her blue eyes widening in disbelief, but she recovered herself quickly and gave Lucy the assurance she wanted. Anxious to change the subject and in the hope of turning away her sister's wrath, she ventured, "Tim has been talking to your husband, Lucy . . . about making over poor Jasper Spence's old property at Portland Place to you. It has a delightful farmhouse, as you know, and Tim has done well with his vines there. He—''

"And what was my husband's reaction?" Lucy put in.

"He accepted," Abigail answered. She smiled thinly. "After some argument about putting the leasehold in your joint names. To which Tim agreed, provided official sanction can be obtained. He's promised to see Mr. Oxley about it as soon as possible. He—that is, we both want to settle the question of your compensation for Yarramundie, once and for all, Lucy.''

"I *am* entitled to compensation," Lucy pointed out, still with a hint of aggression in her voice. But her anger was subsiding; Portland Place was a fine property, and the house, as Abigail had reminded her, was indeed delightful. It was close to Sydney on the turnpike road, and Tim had worked extremely hard to bring the vineyard into successful production, even employing a German expert to set up wine vats and cellars on the property. In addition, there were at least eight hundred acres of grazing land and arable, from Jasper Spence's original grant. Of course, it would have been the vineyard that appealed to Jos. . . . She laid a hand on Abigail's silk-clad arm. "Thank you, Abby. It's a generous settlement, and *I'll* accept, even if the powers that be still refuse to relent in Jos's case. He is a Dutchman, after all, is he not? And,'' she added maliciously, lowering her voice to a faint whisper, "most of his countrymen in the Dutch spice islands breed with the native women, you know. There are virtually no white women for them to marry, and the Dutch Company *encourages* the *lip-laps*. It's their idea of colonizing."

Abigail was silent, reddening a little, and Lucy gave her sister's arm a pat and moved away, searching for Claus. The miserable little *lip-lap* should be punished for his indiscretion, she decided—Saleh should be ordered to flog him in the morning. She beckoned for the older servant and was about to give him the order when, to her dismay, she heard Jos's voice raised in drunken fury. He had been talking with Mr. Balcombe and the archdeacon the last time she had caught sight of him, but now, she saw, he was with a group that included Major Goulburn, the colony's secretary, and George De Lancey. It was against De Lancey that he was engaged in an angry tirade, in which only the words "damn the *Flinders*" could be heard, rising above the music and chatter.

Before she could reach him, however, Mrs. Macarthur intercepted her, with extended hand, her husband and his nephew close at her heels. Charming, as always, Elizabeth Macarthur offered her thanks for the hospitality, which, she insisted, they had greatly enjoyed. John Macarthur bowed, a trifle distantly, Lucy thought, and did not echo his wife's thanks. He took her arm, his limp very apparent and his face pale, and murmured that his gout was playing him up—a seemingly truthful excuse for his party's early departure. Hannibal was no more forthcoming, although his wife, like Elizabeth, spoke graciously, and the three Macarthur sons contented themselves with courteous bows.

Saleh, again summoned by Lucy, escorted them to their carriages, but they had scarcely departed when a general exodus began, headed by the De Lanceys and swiftly followed by Justice Forbes and the Balcombes. Even Timothy Dawson, returning from the supervision of his daughters' premature departure, announced that he had an early start in prospect next morning and took Abigail away.

Within the next half hour the marquee emptied and Lucy found herself alone, apart from the servants, with her husband. Jos was slumped in a chair, snoring loudly, the contents of a spilled glass of brandy staining his once immaculate shirtfront. The sight of him thus repulsed her, and she was hard put to it to hide her disgust. Somehow she contrived to do so, and with what dignity she could muster, she bade Saleh assist him to his room. The orchestra, engaged to play until midnight, struck up a lively gavotte, and Lucy turned on them in cold fury.

"That is enough—go, for heaven's sake go!"

The gavotte petered out, and the leader, eyeing her apprehensively, ventured, greatly daring, to request his payment.

"Call tomorrow morning," she ordered, controlling the impulse to strike him. "My steward will pay you. Take your instruments and go."

They obeyed her without argument, chastened and overawed, for they were emancipated felons, aware of the danger of incurring an adverse report. The servants slipped out after them, leaving the disordered tables and the un-eaten delicacies as mute reminders of what, Lucy thought wretchedly, had been one of the unhappiest evenings of her life.

She stood there in the flickering light of the whale-oil lamps and the spluttering candles and found herself, once again, racking her brains for a means of bringing her marriage to an end. The boy Claus chose that moment to accost her.

"My father wishes to speak with you, *mevrouw*," he began. "He says—" He got no further. Lucy struck out at him with a beringed hand and then, seizing him by the shoulders, shook him savagely.

"He is not your father, *lip-lap*!" she shrieked. "And tomorrow I shall have you beaten to teach you that he is not! Never, as long as you live, are you to dare to make such a claim again!''

Claus fled from her in terror. Very slowly, Lucy followed him from the marquee, and gaining her bedroom, flung herself down on the bed in a paroxysm of weeping.

CHAPTER VIII

Ulva, Rachel realized as she and William came in sight of the homestead, was suffering very severely from the prevailing drought. Indeed, she thought uneasily, in all the years that she had lived there, she could not remember so many dried-up creeks, or so many acres of sun-scorched brown earth, where before there had been water and lush grass in plenty for the stock they carried.

William, on his own admission, had sold more stock than he had intended or wanted, in order to save the exorbitant cost of taking feed and water out to the far paddocks.

"Even so, I've had to buy feed," he had told her glumly. "And take on two extra men, just to keep the breeding ewes alive. Labor costs money these days, and it's damnably hard to come by as well. Andrew didn't want me to sell any of Mam's horses, but I had to let a couple of them go—they were eating their heads off, and we didn't need them for work. Oxen are better, and they drink less."

He had told her little more than that, Rachel reflected, studying him as he rode beside her, taking in his broad-shouldered, muscular frame and his healthily tanned face. It was not like William to be secretive. She had tried to question him tactfully about where he had gone and whom he had seen in Sydney, but he had evaded her questions, changing the subject whenever she had dropped hints concerning Dodie Dawson or, come to that, any other young, marriageable girls of their acquaintance. Yet, for all his evasiveness, she had sensed that her brother was laboring under some sort of shadow . . . and that, too, was unlike the normally contented, easygoing William.

As children, with only a year between them, they had been brought up together and had quarreled frequently; William, as a boy, had been jealous of their elder brother, Justin, resenting his achievements and the successful career he had made as a sea officer, yet . . . Rachel smiled to herself, remembering. William had never wanted to emulate his brother, never wanted any life but the one he led, on the land, and as he grew up, the jealousy had been forgotten, the childish quarrels had become a thing of the past. He was deeply attached to Justin—they both were— but, oddly, it was Andrew, the stepfather he had once so bitterly opposed, to whom he now gave his devotion and loyalty. And it was evident that he was worried about Andrew, although, being William, he had shied away from putting his anxiety into words.

"He's not well, Shelley," was all he had said, using her childhood nickname with affection. "And he needs you. I think, if your husband can spare you, that you ought to stay with me awhile at Ulva."

She, too, was devoted to Andrew, of course. Her memories of her own father were dim; all she could recall were his very blue eyes and his ready laughter and the fact that he was tall. Andrew, big, stalwart, gentle giant that he was, Andrew had been the father she knew and loved and, yes . . . regarded with pride. He . . . William turned suddenly in his saddle and said, lowering his voice, although there was no one to hear him, "You'll see a great difference in Andrew, Shelley. But try not to let him think you've noticed any change. He tries to hide it, even from me."

Rachel nodded. "Yes, of course. But what sort of change, Will? It's . . . oh, goodness, it's almost a year since I saw him, you know. He didn't come to Magdalen's christening, as I'd hoped he would."

"He wasn't well enough," William defended. His tanned, angular face was gravely set. "I don't know for sure, since I'm no physician, but I fancy it's his heart. Or maybe he's had what they call a stroke. He has lost the full use of his right hand, and at times, when he's tired, his speech is slurred and he finds it difficult to remember things. But that doesn't stop him working—damn it, *I* can't stop him working! That's why I wanted you to come back with me. If you're in the house, perhaps he'll stay there, so as to be with you, and give himself a rest."

"I'll do all I can to persuade him," Rachel promised.

"And try to make him eat."

Rachel was shocked. "Doesn't he eat?"

William shook his head. "Not enough. Since you went off and married Judge De Lancey, we've had to make do with Nelly's cooking. You remember Nelly Finch, don't you—the convict girl Aaron Finch married?"

"Yes, I remember her," Rachel confirmed. Poor Nelly had been deported as a child of ten, for stealing potatoes from a London street hawker's barrow. She had been a heavy-featured, unlovely child, and Mrs. Macquarie had taken pity on her and removed her from the Female Factory and its inevitable corruption, and when the Macquaries had left Sydney, Jessica Broome had employed her for a while. Aaron Finch, one of the men who had worked for years at Ulva, had astonished them all, she recalled, by wedding the girl, despite the fact that she was half his age. Rachel glanced inquiringly at her brother.

William shrugged. "The marriage has worked out well. Old Aaron is as happy as a king. They live in the cottage Mam built for Tom and Nancy Jardine—Tom has his own farm now, as you know. But I'm afraid Nelly's cooking is not up to Nancy's standard and never will be, though she's pleasant and willing enough. It will be a pleasure to sample yours again."

Rachel laughed. "I'll do my best for you, Will. But I'm a little out of practice. George has to entertain a good deal, so we employ a staff, including a very good cook, which enables me to play the hostess without a hair out of place.''

"Do you like your new life?'' William asked curiously.

"I enjoy the novelty,'' Rachel admitted. "But I fear it is starting to pall . . . on both of us, really.'' She told him of the Van Burens' reception, making a bitter little comedy of it, and at the mention of Julia Dawson's unseemly revelation, William reined in his horse with a smothered exclamation.

"Do you suppose it's true? Julia is—oh, the devil take her! She's a spiteful, jealous bitch; there's no other word for her! But surely even she would not dare to lie about a—a matter of that kind. The Dutch colonials *do* marry native women, or so I've heard.''

"Yes, I believe they do. I have to confess that I find Major Van Buren a most repulsive person, and George cannot abide him. If that poor little boy Claus *is* his son, they certainly don't treat him as such. All the same,'' Rachel qualified, "Julia had no right to say what she did in public and while she was the Van Burens' guest.''

"Julia enjoys making trouble,'' Will asserted. He reddened and kneed his horse on, avoiding Rachel's gaze. "I suppose you guessed that I was on my way to see Dodie, when I called on you the other evening?''

It was as near as he had come to confiding in her, and Rachel answered warily, "Well, yes, it did occur to me, Will. You're fond of Dodie, aren't you?''

William's color deepened and spread. "I've always been fond of her, since we were children. But I . . . keep it to yourself, Shelley, please. We've been meeting whenever I come to Sydney, which isn't often, as you well know. I love her and I want to wed her, and she . . . well, I believe she feels the same way about me. Or she did, until Julia started making trouble. Dodie's influenced by her, you know, and Julia is very much the exclusionist.''

"Yes, I know.'' Pityingly, Rachel studied her brother's red, shamed face. "What happened the other evening? Did you not see Dodie, then, after all?''

"Oh, I saw her . . . but Julia was there, too. And she stayed, putting in snide comments, reminding Dodie of my family background, comparing it with theirs. She called me a common sheepherder, whose parents came out here in chains. 'Our father employs convicts to do the work William Broome does,' she kept saying. 'Look at his hands, smell his clothes—he stinks of the dung heap, Dodie!' and Dodie *listened* to her."

"It's very hard *not* to listen to Julia," Rachel offered, trying to make a jest of it. "When she's in full cry."

The jest fell flat. William said miserably, "But Dodie's supposed to care for me, and she just let her go on and on. I left in the end, when Julia started comparing me— unfavorably, of course—with some newly arrived lieutenant of the Fortieth Regiment who is to be one of Governor Brisbane's aides. I don't know his name, but it seems he's been calling on the Dawsons and had invited Dodie to go to some darned boat picnic with him."

It could be worse, Rachel thought; clearly, the Governor's new aide had not yet progressed to serious courtship, and Dodie Dawson, although admittedly under her elder sister's influence, had a mind of her own. Besides, there was Abigail to be taken into account—Abigail was no exclusionist, and she would permit Julia only to go so far.

She tried to tell William this, but he was unreceptive and glum, perhaps regretting his decision to confide in her and anxious to change the subject. They reached the farmhouse, and he dismounted to open the gate, putting out a hand to take her horse's rein.

"I'll take care of the animals, Shelley—you go to Andrew. He'll be eager to see you, of course. But don't forget—he *has* changed. Try not to let him realize that you see any change."

"I'll be careful," Rachel promised. Yet, despite William's warning and her own resolve, she was hard put to it not to betray her concern when Andrew rose from his chair at the sound of her voice and came limping to meet her. The change in him was alarming. He had always been a big

man, broad-shouldered and robust, but now he seemed
strangely to have shrunk, and his clothes hung on him,
looking as if they had been made for someone else. The
military bearing was there; he still walked stiffly erect,
with his head held high, but his ruddy cheeks had lost their
healthy color, and his hair was white.

"Rachel, my dearest child!" He was flatteringly pleased
to see her, and his embrace was warm. "Will said he
would try to persuade you to come back to us for a little
while, but I feared that he would not succeed. Needless to
tell you, I'm overjoyed that he did. And you're looking
radiant! Marriage and motherhood evidently agree with
you."

"Oh, yes, indeed they do," Rachel managed, kissing
his lined cheek and clinging to him as she had been wont
to do as a child. He asked for George and for little
Magdalen, his brow furrowed when he tried to explain his
absence from her christening.

"We missed you, Andrew dear. But we understood."

"I'm not the man I was," Andrew said ruefully. He
released her, smiling. "You'll wish to wash away the
stains of travel, I don't doubt. It's infernally dusty on the
road with this drought, which, alas, shows no sign of
breaking. Off you go—your old room is ready for you,
and Nelly Finch will have tea waiting, when you've done.
Have you a valise? You'll want to change, perhaps."

"William will bring it, when he's stabled the horses."
Rachel, feeling her throat tight, planted a parting kiss on
his cheek and slipped away, thankful that she had managed
to maintain her composure. Her old, familiar bedroom was
cool and welcoming, and Nelly Finch had thoughtfully laid
out a change of clothing for her, with a ewer of warm
water, soap, and towel ready to hand. The dress was one
she had long since discarded, but it still fitted her, and she
donned it, realizing as she did so that the room had been
kept just as she had left it, two years before, the closet
containing half a dozen childish garments she had supposed that Andrew would have given away. The fact that

he had preserved them moved her deeply, and she felt tears stinging her eyes.

Back with him, in the living room, with its threadbare carpet and worn, makeshift furniture, it was as if she had never been away. Nelly brought tea in the huge brown china pot that, Rachel remembered, her mother had always used, and, beaming with goodwill, offered bread and a cake of her own baking, both heavy as lead but touchingly decorated with sprigs of wattle, with which she had lined the serving platters.

Andrew declined to eat but sipped his tea thirstily; William came in with her valise and left them alone together, on the plea of work to be done, after gulping his tea and reluctantly accepting a slice of the doughy bread. Rachel leaned back in her chair, feeling almost as if time had stood still and she had never left Ulva, the contrast between her new life and the old oddly poignant and even painful.

Andrew eyed her thoughtfully. "You are happy, are you not, child? And that husband of yours is good to you?"

"Oh, yes," she assured him. "I'm very happy. And I love George very much. He is more than good to me. And we have our daughter, Magdalen—we both adore her."

Andrew's expression relaxed. He let her talk on about Magdalen and then began gently to question her about the state of affairs in Sydney under Governor Brisbane, and George's work, displaying a shrewd interest in both, his mind as alert and perceptive as ever.

Rachel talked freely and realized that she had revealed more than she had intended when, still smiling, Andrew asked whether she would not prefer to live again on the land.

"I suppose I would, really," she admitted. "And we have thought about it. George does not care greatly for Sydney society, though I know he admires and supports the Governor. He does find some of the viceregal staff— well, if not openly disloyal, more concerned, perhaps, with their own advancement. Particularly Major Goulburn."

"Governor Macquarie was not enamored of Frederick Goulburn," Andrew volunteered. "It's he who, by all accounts, is the strongest advocate for the wealthy settler policy, I'm told. And he's hand in glove with John Macarthur . . . or so Will Redfern informed me. He called here a week or so ago, just on a friendly visit. But he's glad to be out of what he's pleased to call the rat race, and he's doing extremely well with his cattle at Airds. I think he has forgotten his bitterness at the way the home government treated him—at all events, he never mentioned it, apart from observing that Commissioner Bigge's influence still prevails."

Why, Rachel wondered uneasily, had Dr. Redfern called on him? Had it been, as Andrew claimed, purely a friendly visit, or . . . She searched her stepfather's gaunt face, but it betrayed nothing of his feelings and seemingly no anxiety.

"George has been offered a judicial post in the Hunter Valley," she said. "And a land grant, when the area is opened for free settlement. The Governor intends to close Newcastle as a penal settlement—the convicts are to be sent to Norfolk Island and some new prison, which is to be established at Moreton Bay." She supplied such details as she could and saw that Andrew was again looking thoughtful.

"Does your husband seriously think of quitting Sydney?" he asked.

"I believe so. He's never said anything definite, but we have discussed the proposal more than once."

Andrew was silent, filling his pipe. When it was alight and drawing, he appeared to come to a decision, for he put out a hand to reach for hers and held it tightly.

"One of the reasons I wanted to see you, Rachel child," he said, "was to tell you that I—well, I haven't much longer. Dr. Redfern says I have a failing heart. No—" as Rachel started to speak. "Hear me out, lass. I know you're sorry, but I'm not. I'm tired, and I don't greatly like being a deadweight here. And I miss your mother. As each day passes, I miss her more . . . she was the moving spirit of this place, just as she used to be at Long Wrekin. I want to go to her, wherever she is now, Rachel. And as you know, lass, I'm a God-fearing man, and I believe in an afterlife, the way the Scriptures tell it. I'm sure my Jenny is waiting for me somewhere.''

He saw the swift tears in Rachel's eyes and grinned at her with his old good humor.

"Spare no tears for me, lass. I'm not a mite afraid. Lord, I faced death often enough when I was fighting the French, and God preserved me. He let me find your mother again and wed her and live with her and her children for more than my fair share of happy years. I've no regrets.''

Rachel lifted his big, work-scarred hand to her lips. Unable to stem her tears, she hid them behind his hand. "Does—does Will know?'' she asked.

"He guesses,'' Andrew answered. "Dr. Redfern came when he was in Sydney Town, so he doesn't know for certain. I'll tell him, when he comes in, but it will be no surprise to him. He does the work of two men on this land, and he's seen me failing. He—'' Andrew paused, drawing on his pipe, the smoke rising in a thin blue spiral above his head. "Will's restless, Rachel. This drought is ruining all his plans—we're losing valuable stock every day, and we don't have any capital behind us. Will's only staying here for my sake.''

Rachel lifted her tear-wet face to his, startled.

"You don't mean that Will wants to quit Ulva, do you? He never said anything of that to me.''

"He wouldn't,'' Andrew rejoined. "But there's talk of vast acres of good land to be had for the asking—or even without it—in Van Diemen's Land. And the climate is good there, the best there is for sheep rearing, with no fear of drought. If it weren't for me, I fancy Will would pull up stakes and start anew in the Launceston area.'' He shook his head. "Something's unsettled your brother, Rachel—a woman, maybe. He keeps his own counsel on that score, but I know him too well to be mistaken. And this is a small property; Will can't expand—even without this infernal drought, he could not.''

Rachel impulsively knelt beside her stepfather's chair. Sensing his need for reassurance, she asked, ''What can I do, Andrew? Is there anything that we—George and I—could do?''

Andrew stroked the bright head resting against his knee. ''Not till I'm gone, dear lass,'' he told her quietly. ''But then—Ulva is willed to you and William; that was your mam's wish. Let the lad sell up, if he has it in mind, or ask your husband to buy out his share. He could put a manager in to run it. The stock is Will's, but you could come to some arrangement with him over that.''

It would go against the grain to sell this house, Rachel thought, but . . . perhaps George might buy it. She looked up, forcing a smile. ''You may rely on us, Andrew dearest. But you've not gone yet, and—'' She broke off, for Andrew seemed not to have heard her. His eyes were closed, she saw, and he had laid his pipe down.

In an oddly emotional voice, he said, ''Think of the flocks and herds this land will sustain, the crops it will grow . . . look at it, children, for it is your future spread out down there. . . .''

There was a brief silence; then he roused himself, reached for his pipe again, and said, in his normal deep, faintly accented voice, ''Nay, lass, this won't do! I told Aaron Finch to kill a young hog ready for your coming, and I'd planned that we should feast on it tonight. But if it's left to Nelly to cook, it's liable to be uneatable.''

Rachel jumped up, wiping her tears away with the back of her hand.

''I'll go and help her, Andrew,'' she promised. ''And it shall be a feast!''

She left him smoking contentedly and made for the cookhouse, suddenly glad of the mundane task she had set herself.

*   *   *

All Sydney turned out to witness the arrival of His Majesty's ship *Tamar*, of twenty-six guns, and she made a brave sight as she sailed down the harbor, her signal gun firing the customary salute and her seamen lining her spotless upper deck as she brought-to at the entrance to the cove.

In common with everyone else, George De Lancey went to seek a vantage point on the lawns of the Government Domain in order to watch her come in. It was Sunday, and having attended divine service in the church of Saint Philip, he was at a loose end. His little daughter, Magdalen, was having her afternoon nap, and Rachel, his wife, had been gone for almost two weeks; so, having no particular reason to return home, he lingered in the pleasant sunshine, enjoying the fresh southerly breeze, exchanging a word now and then with passersby who were known to him, and relishing the peace of his surroundings.

It was with a shock of surprise that he saw Katie Tempest in the distance, his surprise engendered by the fact that, for a moment, he did not recognize her. She was still as beautiful as he remembered her, but painfully thin, her shoulders drooping and her gait a trifle unsteady. As he approached her, he was struck by the deathly pallor of her small, piquant face, half hidden beneath an elaborate flowered bonnet, which became her so ill that George wondered whether it had been borrowed . . . from Julia Dawson, perhaps. Julia, he recalled wryly, had a fancy for such unbecoming hats.

"Mrs. Tempest . . . Katie—" The sound of his voice clearly startled her, for she turned with an exclamation, looking up at him in confusion.

"Oh—oh, it's you! I hadn't expected—that is, I did not imagine you would have time to spend on—on sight-seeing."

"It is Sunday," George reminded her.

'Is it? I—I'd forgotten; but of course it is. How stupid you must think me."

"I shall never think you stupid, Katie. Unhappy, perhaps, but not stupid."

Waves of embarrassed color flooded her pale cheeks, and George remembered belatedly what Rachel had told him—that Katie had lost the child she had been expecting. He had not taken in the details, had not wanted to, for no reason that he could have explained to his wife, but . . . He looked down at the girl he had once loved so deeply, and could have bitten his tongue out for the thoughtlessness of his remark.

"The arrival of one of His Majesty's ships is always an occasion in Sydney," he suggested, trying to cover up his error. Damn it to hell, of course the poor girl was unhappy, and with reason, he reproached himself, and . . . she was alone. Tempest was not with her, and he could see no sign of Abigail or her husband or even of the two Dawson girls. "I understand she's the frigate *Tamar*, under the command of Captain Bremner, who is charged with the task of establishing a new settlement on the northern coast."

"Yes, I believe so," Katie answered. She recovered herself, the hectic color fading from her cheeks, and again George was conscious of how ill she looked. He offered her his arm, motioning to a rustic bench a few yards from them.

"Shall we sit down? It's a long time since I've seen you, Katie."

"Over two years." She took his arm and permitted him to lead her to the bench, seating herself with what was unmistakably a sigh of weary relief. "I've been living in the wilds. But you . . . you're a high court judge now, are you not?"

"Yes," he confirmed, unable to follow this as a conversational lead.

Katie, however, seized on the topic. "Did you ever imagine, in the old days in Boston, that you would become a judge in New South Wales?"

George shook his head. "Not in my wildest dreams, Katie! The most I hoped for in those days was to set up as an attorney in what I regarded as the land of my birth.

We've both come a long way from that dear land, have we not?''

"Yes, we have.'' Katie's tone was wistful. He saw her lower lip tremble, but she went on, quite composedly, "I want to go back, George. I don't think I shall ever feel at home here. But you do, do you not?''

Did he, he asked himself, and knew, without a shadow of a doubt, that he did feel at home, as Katie had put it, and had no desire to go back. The war had contributed to his feelings, of course; the war, with its culmination at Waterloo and his brother's tragic death, had left him with a longing to put down roots, to find peace and a worth-while purpose in life. And these he had found; he had a wife and child, professional satisfaction in the work he did, a stake in the future . . . what more could any man want?

He answered Katie's question honestly. "Yes, Katie, I do. But you . . . I'm sorry you want to go back, sorrier than I can tell you. Perhaps it was living in the wilds— we're not all of us cut out for that sort of life, you know.''

"No," she conceded flatly. "But if anything, I prefer Pengallon to Sydney. At least it has no clacking tongues, no cruel gossips, no . . . no bitter social rivalries or elitist factions. One is so conscious of the barriers here, which preclude friendship between the free and wealthy and the poor onetime felons. That even extends to the second generation—the native-born Australians, the ones Julia Dawson calls currency brats.''

"Julia is an extreme example," George protested.

"Yes, I know.'' Katie stifled a sigh. "I'm living in her shadow at present, so perhaps I'm prejudiced.''

"There are other places less isolated than Pengallon, Katie. Would not your''—he hesitated before pronouncing the word—"your husband consider making an exchange? The Hunter Valley is soon to be opened for settlement, with grants of a thousand acres available—more in some cases, I believe. Or there's—''

Katie cut him short, her headshake emphatic. "Rick

would not hear of leaving Pengallon. I've tried to persuade him and failed dismally. I . . . oh, George, it's truly not that I have failed to—to adapt to conditions there. I can ride very well now. I can herd cattle and sheep, wash fleeces, and cook, and I can grow vegetables. When I'm busy, it is not unbearable, but Rick doesn't like me to do what he calls men's work. I'm supposed to be confined to the kitchen—and the nursery. Only—'' Her teeth closed fiercely about her lower lip. ''Only the nursery is empty now, you see. My darling little girl, my Annabel, died three months ago, and I—I lost the baby I was carrying. I came here for the birth, but it didn't help. Rick wanted a son so much, and so did I, but he . . . the poor little soul was stillborn.''

George was moved by her confession. Sick with pity and at a loss for words to express it, he took one of her small, cold hands in his and bore it gently to his lips. To his dismay, he became acutely conscious of a longing he had believed long since dead, and he released Katie's hand as if it had stung him, ashamed of the strength of his own emotions.

She said, avoiding his gaze, ''I don't know why I'm telling you all this. I—I've no right to, no right at all. Forgive me, George, I—''

''You have every right, Katie!'' George interrupted explosively. ''For God's sake, haven't we known each other almost from childhood? Were we not raised in the same country, the same city? If you cannot talk to me, to whom can you talk?'' He almost added, ''And I love you,'' but contrived somehow to hold back the all too revealing words. Instead he said lamely, ''Surely I'm your oldest friend?''

''Oh, yes,'' she agreed, sounding relieved. ''Dear George, of course you are! And it has helped me to talk to you. I—I seem to have had to bottle up my feelings for such a very long time. Even with Abigail, who is one of the kindest women in the whole wide world.''

''Then talk away, Katie my dear,'' George invited,

controlling his voice with some difficulty. "If it is of the smallest help to you. But I hope very much that you will *not* leave Australia."

Katie looked up at him then. "I know I can't, George. I only said I *wanted* to go back to Boston, and that's the truth—I'd give anything to go back. But I shall stay here for a few weeks, and then—then I shall go to Pengallon. I promised Rick, and I know my duty."

She spoke quietly but with conviction, and George had again to swallow the words he longed to say and the questions he wanted desperately to ask. It was evident that Katie had no inkling of the feelings she had aroused in him and would be appalled if she had . . . but it was also evident that her marriage to Rick Tempest was in a precarious state. As it had been before, he recalled with a pang, when she had come to him and requested that he arrange her passage back to America. Then he had taken her into his arms and promised to go with her, because the cruel gossip that had linked their names together had been, even for him, too much to endure.

But everything had changed now. He was married to Rachel, and the gossip had died a long time ago, together with the dreams he had once had of Katie and the life they might have shared. Besides, there was Magdalen. . . .

As if to echo his thoughts, Katie asked, with a swift change of tone, "You have a child, have you not, you and Rachel? Abigail told me you had."

"Yes, indeed we have. A delightful little daughter who is named Magdalen, after my brother's widow. She is just starting to talk, and she's into every sort of mischief you can imagine."

As he spoke, George had a vision of his small daughter standing up in her cot, her chubby arms extended to welcome him and an impish smile playing about her lips as she called out, "Dada! Dada!" He adored the child, he reflected—no, more than that, he was besotted by her, and . . . "Poor Katie," he said awkwardly. "I can understand how you must feel. I don't know what I would do if I lost Magdalen. You must have been heartbroken.''

"Yes," Katie admitted. "I was, and the loneliness was more than I could take. When Annabel was there, I could chatter to her, you see, and . . ." She broke off, flushing again. "One is so helpless when one is dealing with a sick child; I . . . But enough of my troubles. I will not impose on you anymore. And the King's ship, the *Tamar*, is at the anchorage now, so there's not much more to see, is there? Except—is that not Justin Broome's ship, lying off the government wharf?''

"Yes, that is the *Elizabeth*," George confirmed. "She returned from Moreton Bay yesterday, with the Governor on board. I believe she is to accompany the *Tamar* to Raffles Bay, but probably not with Justin in command. Rumor has it that he's to be given the *Mermaid*, to enable him to remain on this station.''

"That will be a relief to Jessica," Katie said. She rose, to stand facing him, swaying a little and grasping the back of the seat for support. Instinctively, George put out a hand to take her arm, but she backed away, shaking her head.

"I'm quite all right. It's only a little dizziness, and Dr. Bowman says I shall get over it. I'll walk slowly back to the gate—don't worry, the fresh air and exercise are what I need. I've been playing the invalid for too long.''

"At least permit me to escort you," George urged, concerned for her obvious frailty, but again she shook her head.

"Abigail is to pick me up in her carriage at five, and we are to go for a drive and then listen to the band concert.'' Katie smiled faintly. "All Sydney society will be there, no doubt, so perhaps, even now, it might be as well if we're not seen together, George . . . dear friend though you are. But thank you for allowing me to pour out my sorrows to you. And . . . au revoir.'' She gave him her hand, but so briefly that it barely touched his, and George let her go with an odd mixture of regret and relief.

He followed her at a discreet distance to the gates of the

Domain and saw her climb into a waiting carriage, in which three ladies were already seated—Abigail, he presumed, and her two stepdaughters. Waiting until the carriage had drawn away, he was strolling at a leisurely pace toward Macquarie Place when he heard a voice, calling him urgently by name.

"Mr. De Lancey—Your Honor! Please wait, sir, I've been seeking you everywhere." Rodney Akeroyd, his clerk, came to a breathless halt beside him. He was in his shirtsleeves and perspiring freely, and George eyed him with unconcealed surprise.

"Well," he prompted, "you've found me. What is it?"

"I've come from the Rocks, sir," Akeroyd told him. "I thought I recognized one of the men that broke into the chambers—the big fellow, with red hair. I followed him into a tavern, and I was wondering whether to tax him with it when a drover came in, sir, from Emu Ford. And what he said put everything else out of my mind, save finding you. There's a bad bushfire on the east side of the Nepean River, the drover claimed, south of the Government Farm, where he'd come from. And that's where Mrs. De Lancey went, was it not, sir?"

It was, George thought, his heart sinking . . . dear God, indeed it was! And with the long drought of the past few months, the bush would be tinder dry, needing only a spark to turn it into a raging inferno. He thanked young Akeroyd, holding himself under iron control.

"I'll ride out there at once," he added. "And perhaps you'd be good enough to deliver a message to Justice Forbes. Tell him what's happened and say that I will be back as soon as I can."

He broke into a run, suddenly filled with a sense of terrible foreboding.

CHAPTER IX

It was William, who had gone out at dawn, from whom Rachel learned of the fire. He came into her bedroom, his face blackened by smoke and his shirt sodden with sweat, to blurt out the details of the outbreak in a few terse words.

"The wind's southeasterly, and as long as it stays that way there's little danger to the house and buildings. But if it changes, I'm going to have to drive the stock to the river and maybe across it, and that'll take Aaron and me and the two men all our time. Will you ride out to the Government Farm, Shelley, and ask for help? We'll need to clear firebreaks, to stop it spreading . . . and it's in their interests, as well as ours, because the fire's heading their way."

Rachel sat up, startled, rubbing the sleep from her eyes. She did not need to be told of the danger; past experience of the awful havoc such fires created was clear in her mind, and she was out of bed and starting to dress before her brother had finished speaking.

"I've left Minstrel saddled for you," William ended.

"What of Andrew?" Rachel asked. "Have you told him?"

"No." William's headshake was firm. "He's still asleep. I've warned Nelly Finch, though, and I'm leaving two of the workhorses and a wagon, in case the fires reach here. I'll see they're hitched up before I go." He smiled thinly. "Ride as fast as you know how, Shelley—and warn the

Dicksons as you pass their place, if you can. Rafe will want to move his stock, too. 'Bye—and God keep you!''

He was gone. Rachel hurriedly donned the rest of her clothes and, pausing only to make sure that Nelly Finch knew what to do, ran to the stables. William had been as good as his word; the gray gelding known as Minstrel was saddled, ready for her, and an open wagon stood ready also, the two workhorses tethered beside it and eating, contentedly enough, from nosebags.

As yet none of the animals showed signs of alarm, but as she led Minstrel out into the fold yard, the pungent smell of smoke assailed her nostrils, and in the distance she could make out an ominous black cloud, hanging low over the waving tops of the gum trees that bordered the river. The river was low, she knew; in places only the merest trickle of water flowed over its dried-up bed. Fortunately, close to the Ulva property frontage and some hundred and fifty yards from the buildings, there was a creek that had never dried up, as far as she could recall, even in the most prolonged drought.

If worse came to worst, sanctuary could be found there, at least for Andrew and the men's wives and children, she told herself . . . and the wide expanse of the riverbed should act as a natural firebreak, if the wind did not change. But William would have his work cut out if he had to drive the livestock across, for the far bank was steep rock, overhung by trees, on which even the most agile sheep would have difficulty in finding foothold.

Rachel dug her heels into Minstrel's sides, and the big horse broke into a long, loping gallop, head down and needing no further urging. It was a scant five miles to Emu Ford and the Government Farm, but a creek at the edge of the neighboring property necessitated a detour of almost a mile. Even if she made a further detour to the Dicksons' farmhouse, Rachel decided, she ought to reach the ford in less than an hour . . . and in all probability, Rafe Dickson would have seen the smoke clouds and require no warning.

The Ulva land had long been cleared of brush and

timber, save near the river's edge, and the first part of her journey over pasture and cultivated land was swiftly accomplished, with Minstrel keeping up a steady pace and scarcely breaking sweat. Reaching the boundary of the Ulva grant, she opened the paddock gate and slowed down for long enough to liberate two brood mares with their foals, and they cantered slowly behind her through a tree-grown section of the Dickson land. Still neither they nor Minstrel appeared nervous, and glancing back over her shoulder as she drew clear of the timber, she saw that although the smoke clouds were now tinged with red, they had come no nearer. But some of the wildlife was alarmed; ahead of her, a screeching flock of parakeets took wing, and she glimpsed upward of a dozen kangaroos bounding through the trees and making at speed for the river.

At the Dicksons', she was disconcerted to find no one about and was compelled to waste ten precious minutes while Rafe and his wife roused themselves from what had evidently been very sound sleep.

"Bushfire, you say, Miss Rachel? Oh, Gawd, and with the whole countryside as dry as a bone!" Rafe swore loudly and then apologized. "You're on your way to the Government Farm for help, are you? Well, there's a convict working party not half a mile from here, along the cart track—leastways there was yesterday. Might save you time if you can find 'em."

He gave her vague directions, and Rachel thanked him, wishing that he had offered to send one of his sons with her to aid in locating the working party. The Dicksons had four strapping sons, and their farm was small, their stock consisting mainly of hogs and goats, with a flock of about sixty or seventy Bengal sheep, bred for meat rather than wool. Rafe and his sons would have ample time to round them up and, if need be, drive them to safety . . . even if, like their parents, the boys were sleeping off what, she suspected, had been a night of heavy drinking.

She shook her head to his offer of refreshment and rode on, skirting the creek and finding herself once more on uncleared land amid eucalyptus and stringy bark trees. But she had somehow missed the cart track Rafe Dickson had mentioned, she realized, and in her effort to find it had lost sight of the river. Anxious to make up for lost time, she urged Minstrel on, bending low in the saddle to avoid the thickly growing tree branches that constantly threatened to impede her. From somewhere not far away she heard the thud of hooves; a horse neighed, and Minstrel whickered in answer. Rachel turned, supposing the brood mares to be following her still. Her attention was distracted for only an instant, but in that instant Minstrel stumbled over an exposed tree root and fell to his knees, while she was hurled over his head, to land heavily on the hard ground.

Instinctively she attempted to retain her hold of his rein, but he scrambled up, jerking it from her grasp, one iron-shod forefoot catching her a glancing blow on the chest as he made off into the trees, snorting his alarm. Rachel lay where she had fallen, the breath knocked out of her and dark mists closing about her and robbing her of her senses.

She came to, with no idea of how long she had been unconscious, to find a man bending over her and three others standing by, one of whom held Minstrel, whose gray sides were lathered and coated with dust. A fourth, a few yards away, held the party's horses, from which they had evidently dismounted in order to come to her aid.

Rachel looked from one to the other of them uncertainly, taking in their unkempt appearance and ragged clothing, her first thought that they must be the convict work party for whom she had been searching. But they were unfettered and were not wearing the distinctive prison garb all the convicts at the Government Farm were compelled to wear, and . . . two of them were armed, with muskets slung from their shoulders. She tried to sit up, suddenly afraid as the realization sank in that they were in all probability convicts on the run.

Then the man who was kneeling beside her said gently, "I do not think you are too badly hurt, young lady. Let me help you to your feet, so that we can make sure that there are no bones broken.''

His voice was educated, the unmistakable voice of a gentleman, and as he assisted her to rise, Rachel saw that he was tall and respectably dressed, with a thin, high-boned face and a pair of strikingly alert gray eyes, which were studying her intently.

"I—I'm all right," she managed shakily. "I—thank you for your help and . . . for catching my horse. I was in some haste, you see, and—"

"And your animal fell and threw you?" He smiled, a hand tentatively on her arm to steady her. "Well, he's all right, too—which is just as well, for that fire is coming nearer and destroying everything in its path. It will not be wise to linger here much longer. Permit me to put you back in the saddle, and we will be on our way. You are making for Emu Ford, I take it?"

"For the Government Farm, in search of help." Rachel explained her mission and saw her rescuer frown when she indicated from where she had come. But he said nothing until she was once more astride Minstrel, and then he directed her to look behind her.

"I fear your farm will have been overwhelmed and help will come too late. Look—the fire is everywhere."

Stunned, Rachel turned and saw, with a sinking heart, that he had spoken no more than the truth. The wind must have changed while she had lain unconscious, for now it was driving the flames in the direction of Ulva, and . . . she could not hold back a cry of dismay. Had Andrew seen the danger and left, with Nelly and the laborers' wives, in the wagon William had prepared for them? She had no means of knowing, and could only guess for how long she had been lying helpless; judging by the position of the sun, it must have been for at least two hours.

"We will escort you to the ford," the gray-eyed man volunteered. He gestured to one of the men, a dark, bearded giant in stained moleskins. "My horse, Giff, if you please."

The man seemed disposed to argue. He led the horse

over but engaged in a low-voiced altercation, of which Rachel caught only a few words. They sufficed, however, to convince her that her first impression had been right. Despite the gentlemanly accent and the well-tailored clothes of the man to whom she had been talking, these were convicts on the run, escapers and probably bushrangers into the bargain, whose reluctance to go anywhere near the Government Farm was understandable.

She said, catching her breath, "Don't concern yourself with me, I beg you. I am going back to the farm, to Uiva, not to the ford. I *must* go back!"

Her rescuer attempted to stop her, but anticipating his attempt, Rachel was too quick for him. She kicked Minstrel into motion, and his grasping hand missed her rein by inches.

"You're going to your death, child!" he shouted angrily. "Come back—in God's name, come back!"

He was on his own horse and starting after her, but as she turned her head to look back in panic, she saw that the black-bearded giant had halted his rush, jerking his mount back onto its haunches with savage strength.

Rachel dug her heels into Minstrel's sides, intent on putting as much distance as she could between herself and any pursuit. But there was no pursuit, only a voice borne faintly to her ears, which she could not be sure she had heard correctly. It sounded like a promise to deliver her message to the Government Farm . . . and might have been precisely the reverse.

In any event, she thought numbly, even were help to be sent by the farm superintendent, it would probably be too late, as the gray-eyed escaper had warned. She could only pray that Andrew had evacuated the farmhouse before the fire reached it, and . . . She felt her throat ache. And that William and the men he had taken with him had succeeded, against the odds, in saving the stock.

She rode on, having to urge Minstrel now with voice and hands, for he was frightened, starting at shadows and nervously reluctant to increase his speed. He was tiring, too, stumbling with increasing frequency, his ears laid back, as if to shut out the crackling roar of blazing brush and timber. Reaching the creek, she saw that the Dicksons' buildings were untouched, and then, having made the necessary detour, realized with a shock that she was now behind the fire and following in its wake.

Flames glowed redly below the rising smoke, and all about her was a scene of terrible desolation, blackened timber and great gums reduced to ashes and, here and there, the shapeless corpses of animals—wild and domestic— that had failed to escape the relentless onslaught of the fire.

She turned toward the river, her nerves strung almost to breaking point when she heard the blood-chilling, half-human cries of a terrified kangaroo that had been cut off by the flames. Close on a score of others went leaping and bounding over the ash-strewn ground in a frantic bid for safety. Their concerted onrush and the strange sobbing sounds they emitted added to Minstrel's unwillingness to go on, and expert horsewoman though she was, Rachel knew that her strength was ebbing, and with it her ability to compel her mount's obedience.

A sow, with a litter of piglets—escaped from the Dicksons' land—proved the last straw. The creatures emerged from the smoke almost at Minstrel's feet, squealing and grunting, and he reared in alarm and then came to an obstinate halt, his whole body quivering as the piglets scampered wildly after their mother from the underbrush.

Rachel slipped from the saddle, choking and gasping from the smoke. Holding the big gray steady with difficulty, she managed to rip off her skirt and use a strip torn from it as a blindfold. A second strip, wrapped round her nose and mouth, kept out some of the smoke, and she plodded on, on foot, leading Minstrel by the bridle. He submitted for perhaps a hundred yards and then jerked his head free, to vanish at a headlong gallop in the direction from which they had come. Rafe Dickson would take care of him,

Rachel thought wearily, and probably the brood mares as well, so long as the fire did not again change course.

She stumbled on, half blinded and near to exhaustion in the airless, smoke-filled heat, and at last came in sight of Ulva . . . or what was left of it. The buildings had gone, the stables, the granary with its precious store of corn. The fold yard and the paddock fences were blackened skeletons, shapeless and as unrecognizable as the corpses of the animals had been. But to her stunned astonishment, she saw that the house still stood, its stone foundations virtually untouched and its shingle roof scarred but still in place. In front if it yawned a shallow pit—a firebreak, which had miraculously held the flames at bay, and as she staggered wearily toward the house that had been her home, she glimpsed a slumped figure, half lying, half sitting on the veranda steps.

It could only be Andrew, Rachel knew, and despite her weariness she gathered up the folds of her trailing petticoat and ran to where he lay, a silent, inarticulate prayer on her lips. He was alive but barely conscious, his breathing uneven and labored, his face and his whole body bathed in sweat. With an anguished cry, Rachel dropped to her knees beside him and clasped him in her arms.

"Andrew—oh, dearest Andrew! Why did you stay? The wagon was there—William had left it ready and the horses hitched to it. Why didn't you go?"

To her surprise, it was Nelly Finch who answered her. The girl came stumping from the interior of the house, an earthenware beaker in her hand, her plain, square face red from her exertions and her clothing as smoke-grimed and filthy as Rachel's own.

"The master wouldn't hear o' going, Miss Rachel," she said. "He were set on saving the house, you see. He packed the women an' their kids off in the wagon, soon as he seen the fire was coming this way. 'If I can clear the trees an' brush from the front,' he says, 'then maybe the house'll be safe.' An' that's what he done, Miss Rachel—

working like a madman, he was, and wouldn't stop, even to draw breath.''

"And you stayed to help him, Nelly," Rachel managed in a shaken voice. "You didn't go with the others."

Nelly went to kneel on Andrew's other side, holding the beaker to his lips with red and blistered hands. "Course I stayed, Miss Rachel," she returned laconically. "Bin good to me, has Cap'n Hawley, so I weren't about to leave him." Her voice softened, took on a pleading note. "Won't you drink this, master? 'Tis a drop o' your best brandy, and 'twill do you good, sir, truly it will."

Andrew sipped obediently. After a while his eyes opened, and seeing Rachel, his gaunt face lit with a smile. "Thanks be to God, you're safe, child! And your mother's house is still here. Have you any news of Will?"

Rachel was compelled to shake her head. "No, not yet, Andrew."

"He had time to get the cattle clear. But I fear the sheep may be another matter. Did you get through to Emu Ford?"

"I was able to send a message. I—"

"You should have stayed there," Andrew chided her. "Dearest child, you shouldn't have come back."

Nelly rose to her feet. She wiped the perspiration from her face with a corner of her dress and suggested practically that, now there were two of them, they should move Andrew into the house.

"I couldn't manage him on me own," she confided, lowering her voice to a hoarse whisper. "He wilted quite sudden-like, you see. One minute he was wielding his ax, and the next . . ." She sighed, deftly slipping her hand under Andrew's limp knees and bracing his head against her ample bosom. "Like so, Miss Rachel. I seen him have these turns afore, but he's mostly all right if he rests for a while."

But this time, Rachel's instincts warned, Andrew would need more than rest. He could not walk, could barely move hand or foot, and he lapsed into unconsciousness when, with great effort, she and Nelly managed to carry him into the house and lay him gently on his bed. There was a single bucket left of the water Nelly had stored in the kitchen; with this, they sought to cool and refresh his fever-hot body and burning face so that, as the girl put it, he could rest in comfort. But the air, both inside and outside the house, was still heavy with smoke and ash, the buildings continuing to smolder, and Andrew's breathing became more labored, the pulse at his wrist fainter and harder to find.

Rachel sat with him, clasping one of his hands in hers. Nelly brought her a beaker of tea, and she drank it gratefully, refusing any other offer of refreshment.

"He's going, ain't he, Miss Rachel?" the girl said sadly, pausing by the end of the bed to look anxiously at Andrew's still face. "And there's nowt more as we can do, I'm fearing. He spent himself, clearing that firebreak. But 'tis God's will, I reckon."

Or Andrew's, Rachel thought, recalling the way in which he had spoken of his future to her on the night of her arrival . . . his uncertain future, measured, perhaps, in months or even weeks by Dr. Redfern. His words came back to her, as if he were speaking them now.

I don't greatly like being a deadweight here. And I miss your mother. As each day passes, I miss her more. I want to go to her, wherever she is now. Rachel's fingers tightened about his big, motionless hand—blistered, as poor Nelly's were, from their brave toil with spade and ax. *I'm a God-fearing man,* he had said, *and I believe in an afterlife, the way the Scriptures tell it. I'm sure my Jenny is waiting for me somewhere. . . .*

He moved suddenly, opening his eyes and looking straight at her. Rachel tensed as his hand gripped hers.

"Why, Jenny," he said, quite clearly and distinctly. "It's so good to see you again, my dear love. It's been a long time, but . . . now you're here, praise be to God."

In the dim half-light he had mistaken her for her mother, Rachel told herself, for there had always been a strong resemblance between them, and she had her mother's auburn hair. But . . . Andrew was looking beyond her, and he was smiling, she realized, the gaunt, haggard countenance oddly smoothed into youthful lines.

Then he was still; his hand relaxed its grip on hers, and his eyes lost their light but remained fixed, yet sightless, on some point above her head. Gently she leaned forward and closed them, herself dry-eyed, aware that she could not grieve for his passing, since he had gone without regret and in the firm belief that the woman he had loved had come to meet him.

When William came in, a little while later, Rachel was still sitting by the bedside. Her brother took in the situation at a glance and came to stand behind her, his hands resting on her shoulders.

"Nelly told me what he did, God rest his soul. He looks—Shelley, Andrew looks twenty years younger. And *happy*."

"Yes," she agreed. "Happy and at peace, Will. He knew it was coming; Dr. Redfern had told him, and he told me that he wasn't afraid. He believed that Mam was waiting for him."

"Maybe she was," William said quietly. He raised her to her feet, and they went out together. "The men from the Government Farm are here, but there's not a lot they can do now. They're bedding down here overnight, and the overseer's promised that they'll put up some pens and help me get the sheep into them at first light."

"You managed to save them, then?"

William shrugged. "The cattle mostly saved themselves— all we had to do was knock down the fences and let them out. We saved about half the breeding ewes and two of the rams. The rest—" He sighed. "The rest are ashes, like the buildings, alas. There were too many of them, and they were too scattered, Shelley, and crazy with fear. We lost two dogs, trying to round them up."

"I'm terribly sorry, Will. Does it mean—"

"That I'm ruined?" He repeated his shrug. "I suppose

it does. Oh, the land will recover; the fire will burn itself out and the drought will break, eventually. But it will take a man with capital behind him to put this place back into production, restock it and clear up the mess. One of the wealthy adventurers Andrew was always so dead against, perhaps—one of Commissioner Bigge's prize settlers. I shall quit, Shelley. If Andrew had lived, I'd have stayed, for his sake, because this place—and this house—meant so much to him. But now that he's gone there's no reason to stay.''

Rachel recalled what Andrew had told her, and she asked doubtfully, ''Will you go to Van Diemen's Land, to Launceston?''

William stared at her and then gave vent to a mirthless laugh. ''So Andrew *did* guess—I didn't fool him! Though, damme, I tried hard enough.''

''*Is* that where you want to go?'' Rachel pursued.

''I've thought about it,'' her brother admitted. ''But again, it's a question of money. I did sell my culls quite profitably, and I could take the breeding ewes with me . . . and the land's free, I believe. Acres of it.''

Let the lad sell up, if he's a mind to, Andrew had said. *Or ask your husband to buy out his share.* She could do that, Rachel thought—indeed, she would do so, if William really did want to leave Ulva. She started to say as much, but William stopped her.

''You've not seen the damage the fire's done yet, Shelley,'' he warned. ''And I've not toted up the losses. They'll be heavy, and the crops are all burned out. There's not much left, except this house, thanks to Andrew and brave Nelly Finch. But if anyone has Ulva, I confess I'd like it to be you.''

Rachel left it at that. Nelly had somehow fixed up a meal for them, and they ate it, with Aaron and the two weary convict laborers, all of them subdued and stunned by Andrew's death.

* * *

George came riding in, on a lame and lathered horse, the following morning. His frantic anxiety for her moved Rachel deeply, the fact that he had ridden throughout the night a measure of his loving concern, and she clung to him, her tears released at last as she told him of Andrew's death.

He stood staunchly at her side when the laborers' wives returned, unscathed but with a terrible tale to tell of the fire's ravages throughout the whole area. Only Rafe Dickson's place and the Government Farm at Emu Ford had escaped, thanks to the change in the wind's direction, which, Rachel realized, must have taken place while she lay unconscious, three miles from her destination.

"Four o' the convicts ran," one of the women, Dorcas Cain, went on. She shuddered. "Dangerous fellas, the superintendent told us, all of 'em highway robbers not long out from England. It seems they was in a work party near the Dicksons', and an armed man—well dressed and well spoken—held up the overseers and stole their muskets an' their horses. We was scared we might run into 'em, being women on our own, but we never seen hide nor hair o' them, thanks be to God."

But *she* had encountered them, Rachel thought guiltily, and wondered why she had kept silent, even when she had talked to William of her failure to reach Emu Ford. They had done her no harm; rather they had helped her, caught Minstrel for her, and—at heaven knew what risk—the gray-eyed man with the voice of a gentleman had somehow delivered her request for aid to the Government Farm superintendent.

She glanced uncertainly at her husband, but George, misunderstanding the mute question in her eyes, offered gently, "Your brother wants Andrew Hawley buried here, my dearest. He says that's what he would have wanted, and I'm inclined to agree, if you are. This was his land, and we've found a place by the creek that the fire did not reach. It is green and peaceful, and we can have a headstone put up later on."

Rachel's hesitation was brief. "Yes," she said. "I believe it's what Andrew would have wanted. But Will wants to leave here, to sell the property—his share of it, that is. The other share is mine."

George put his arm about her waist, drawing her to him. "We'll buy his share, my love—I told him that. Aaron Finch can manage it until I leave the bench. That's what *you* want, is it not?"

She looked up at him gratefully. "Yes, it is. I . . . thank you, George."

The simple funeral service was held that evening, after William returned from rounding up his scattered stock. Rachel watched through tear-dimmed eyes as the rough-hewn coffin was lowered into the ground, and William took a spade with which to cover it over, first with soil and then with turf.

It was, she again told herself, what Andrew would have wanted. Bathurst, where her mother lay at rest, was too far away, but surely that no longer mattered, since Andrew himself had been so certain that his spirit had gone to wherever his Jenny was waiting.

Nelly Finch, sobbing loudly, her angular face red and swollen with grief, put a sprig of wattle into her hand. It was scorched and wilting, but its yellow blooms smelled sweet, and Rachel took it and laid it on the squares of turf covering the grave. They would unite, she told herself, and God willing, when the rain came to replenish the parched land, the wattle would bloom again in all its golden glory, and this would be a fitting place for the fine, brave man who had been Andrew Hawley to sleep his last, long sleep.

She turned, and George was waiting to give her his arm and take her back to the house.

CHAPTER X

In the small, carefully tended garden of Justin Broome's cottage on the waterfront, Murdo Maclaine stood with his sister, Jessica, watching as the convict transport *Mary Anne* was warped from where she had lain at anchor overnight to tie up to the public wharf, prior to unloading.

Beyond her at the anchorage, and dwarfed by her bulk, lay the brig *Amity* and the *Mermaid* cutter, Justin's new command, with lighters alongside and men busy on their upper decks.

They were preparing to sail for the new prison settlement at Moreton Bay, Murdo was glumly aware, for he was under orders to accompany them, and he said irritably, "Damme, Jessie, I did not ask to go! I wanted to join Hume and Hovell on their expedition to Spencer Gulf, but—supposedly because I went there with the Governor—Henry Miller has picked me as his second-in-command. And Captain Bishop backed him up, plague take him! I'm beginning to regret having transferred to the Fortieth. The new Lieutenant Governor is much less sympathetic to our exploratory expeditions than Colonel Erskine was."

"It will not be forever, Murdo," Jessica offered consolingly. "And Justin is going also."

"He will not have to stay, once the *Mermaid* has delivered our men and the stores," Murdo countered, refusing to be consoled. "But I'll be there for at least a couple of months, acting as an infernal building supervisor, while

Henry plays the commandant and Oxley demands the impossible.''

"Perhaps you will be founding a city," Jessica suggested, gently teasing. "And it will be called after you!"

"On the strength of a prison, a guardhouse, and a few huts?" Murdo retorted scornfully. "In any case, it has already been named Edenglassie, the Lord only knows why—some eccentricity on Oxley's part, no doubt." He hesitated and then asked warily, "Are you permitting young Red to sail with us? The lad shaped uncommon well on our last voyage, for all he's so young. He impressed the Governor with his aptitude for navigation by the stars."

"How can I stop him, after that?" Jessica answered resignedly. "Justin says that His Excellency promised him volunteer status and a midshipman's berth when he's twelve. To be honest, I almost wish that Red hadn't impressed him, but . . . it is his choice, is it not?"

"Aye," Murdo agreed. His gaze returned to the convict transport, now nearly alongside the wharf, and to the military guard formed up there to await the disembarkation of the convicts. "I'll have to go, Jessie—I'm in command of the guard." He smiled without amusement. "The *Mary Anne* is carrying a hundred and thirty female convicts— there will be an unholy rush of officers and so-called gentlemen to inspect them. And my lads will be all eyes too, if I'm not there to keep them in hand."

He dropped a light kiss on his sister's cheek. "I'll see you before we sail. And don't worry too much about Red. The boy's as bright as a button, and the only schooling he needs now is what he'll learn at sea. Justin's very conscious of his responsibilities, believe me."

"I do," Jessica admitted. "I do believe you, Murdo. But all the same . . ." She shook her head resignedly. "Deal kindly with those poor women on the *Mary Anne*, won't you?"

She was giving him a tall order, Murdo thought wryly as he set off for the wharf. Officially the assignment of convict labor—whether male or female—was strictly con-

trolled, but a certain latitude was invariably shown where
the female convicts were concerned. There was no government work for them, save in the Female Factory at
Parramatta, which was overcrowded, and the unwritten
policy was to permit those who were offered employment
as domestic servants to accept it. An official blind eye was
turned as the civilian administrators and the officers of the
garrison took their pick, even when the women went to
bachelor establishments and despite the fact that concubi-
nage was frowned upon by the authorities and vehemently
condemned by the Reverend Samuel Marsden and Archdeacon
Scott. Emancipists and ticket-of-leave convicts were
encouraged to choose wives from among the new arrivals,
and the rank and file of the garrison regiment were
accorded the same privilege . . . although marriage was
not always the outcome.

Murdo sighed. He himself had been guilty of that omission more than once during the limited time he had spent
in the Sydney garrison, but the women he had taken
briefly had been of easy virtue, and he had suffered no
qualms of conscience on their account.

Reaching the wharf, he returned his sergeant's salute
and then stiffened, recognizing the well-known figure of
the Dutchman, Major Jos Van Buren, among the small
crowd waiting to board the transport. Van Buren was not
alone; he had his Javanese houseman with him, in the
starched white coat and crested headband he affected, and,
Murdo saw, the Javanese carried a length of chain, to
which wrist fetters were attached. Clearly the major had
come with the intention not only of choosing one of the
Mary Anne's female convicts, but also of taking the woman
of his choice back with him—a practice the authorites
expressly forbade.

Murdo was about to intervene and to remind the Dutchman that the necessary paperwork had to be completed
first, when he saw Major Goulburn, the colony's secretary,
step up to the gangway and wave Van Buren to precede
him. It was the normal practice for either the secretary or

the Governor himself to board each newly arrived transport and make a brief address to the convicts, following which the prisoners' documentation was formally handed over by the ship's master, whose responsibility for them then ceased.

Murdo marched his men aboard, ready to relieve the transport's guard, and stood them at ease. The women were lined up on deck, looking woebegone and apprehensive in the somber dark clothing that was the regulation issue, waiting patiently for someone to tell them where to go. As always, the long voyage and the cramped conditions in which they had made it had drained the spirit from them; they stood with downcast eyes, seemingly resigned to whatever fate might be in store for them. One or two of the bolder spirits leered at the soldiers, but for the most part the women were docile and silent, and no dissenting voices were raised when Secretary Goulburn began his address.

It was the usual harangue, delivered rapidly, with heavy emphasis on the consequences to be expected should the new arrivals misbehave and a passing assurance that exemplary conduct would reap its due reward—a promise that evidently failed to carry conviction, judging by the sullenness in which it was received.

Murdo, conscious of the imminence of his departure from Sydney, studied the faces before him with indifference, aware that no women were to be included in the Moreton Bay work party. But suddenly, almost against his will, he found his gaze lighting on a girl standing a little distance from the rest, whose small, comely face seemed to him to express such misery that his heart went out to her in pity.

She was not weeping; her melancholy was given no release in tears, and there was defiant pride in the way she held her head high and stood erect. By contrast with her immediate neighbors, she was young—sixteen, at most, Murdo decided—a slim child, with a mass of chestnut-brown hair curling tightly about her head. Her clothing, though the same as all the others', yet looked clean and wholesome, the pinafore she wore spotlessly white and carefully pressed.

Behind him he heard a man's voice say disparagingly, "That is the girl I mentioned to you, Major Van Buren— the one standing by herself at the larboard rail. Her name is Fairweather, Alice Fairweather. She's young and a mite rebellious, I concede, but if your lady wife is in need of a personal maid, she could do worse. Alice is a trained seamstress and a milliner, or so she claims. I had her caring for my laundry on the passage out, and certainly she performed her task to my satisfaction and, indeed, with no little skill."

Murdo did not hear Van Buren's low-voiced question, but he was able to guess its purport by the answer it elicited.

"Why, as to that, sir, you need anticipate no reluctance. I experienced none, though I confess that her lack of sophistication tended to pall, and I looked elsewhere for my distraction."

For no reason that he could have explained, Murdo turned angrily on Jos Van Buren's companion. To his surprise, however, he found himself facing a pleasant-looking, dark-haired man of about his own age, slim and tanned and, from his appearance, a gentleman. The stranger bowed and introduced himself.

"Robert Willoughby, late of His Majesty's Navy and a prospective settler in this colony. And—" He indicated a man of somewhat similar appearance, who was standing at his elbow. "My friend Henry Daniels, also a new settler. You, sir, I take it, are an officer of the garrison regiment?"

"Michael Dean, sir, serving with His Majesty's Fortieth Regiment," Murdo responded stiffly. But his anger subsided; the girl was nothing to him, her distress not of his making, and if Van Buren wanted her, then there was very little he could do to prevent him from taking her.

"A pleasure to meet you, Mr. Dean." Willoughby was smiling, his manner disarmingly open and friendly. "Major Van Buren will be well known to you, of course." Van

Buren nodded curtly but did not speak, and Willoughby went on, "The major is seeking a suitable young woman to serve his wife, and since I have spent the past one hundred and twenty-two days on board this ship, I can at least claim a nodding acquaintance with the female felons we have brought out here. So I am acting as adviser . . . no official objections to that, are there?"

Before Murdo could reply, Van Buren said aggressively, "I have the Colonial Secretary's authority to select whom I wish. Lieutenant Dean can scarcely overrule that, Mr. Willoughby."

Murdo kept his temper. Major Goulburn, he saw, was on the point of concluding his inspection of the women, and his clerks were collecting their papers, preparing to depart. Murdo said quietly, "And the woman you have selected, Major—am I to take it that, on Mr. Willoughby's advice, you have made your choice?"

Willoughby answered for him. "The young woman's name is Alice Fairweather. She's standing over there—" He pointed, and the girl, seeing his gesture, attempted to engage his attention. He ignored her, and his friend Henry Daniels broke into a loud guffaw of laughter, murmuring something Murdo did not hear. The girl looked stricken, the color draining from her small, thin face, and Murdo was again conscious of a feeling of intense pity, coupled with admiration for her courage, for though distressed, she continued to hold her head high, refusing to have recourse to tears.

Clearly there had been something between her and Willoughby during the *Mary Anne*'s passage—something more, at all events, than merely providing him with clean linen—and perhaps the girl had been expecting him to claim her. But that, it seemed, he had no intention of doing. . . . Murdo drew himself up.

He said formally, "I will have a word with the girl. It is customary to ascertain the women convicts' willingness to accept domestic employment when it is offered." That was not strictly true, but Murdo experienced no twinges of conscience as he strode across to where the girl was standing and came to a halt in front of her with exaggerated military precision.

"Alice Fairweather?"

She gazed at him in wide-eyed alarm and answered nervously, "Yes, sir, that is my name."

"I am Lieutenant Dean. Don't be afraid, Alice; you have done nothing wrong." Seen thus, at close quarters, she was beautiful, and again Murdo found himself instinctively drawn to her. But the devil take it, he thought bitterly, his infernal posting to Moreton Bay could not have come at a worse time! He would have to let her go to the Van Burens. . . . "You are to be offered domestic employment, here in Sydney," he told her reluctantly. "And I have to ask if you are willing to take it."

"Yes, sir." Her eyes were downcast, her voice low and devoid of expression, but he sensed her fear. "Is the offer from Mr. Roberts, sir?"

Puzzled, Murdo stared at her. "Roberts? I don't know any Mr. Roberts."

Alice Fairweather raised her eyes to his. "That is the name Mr. Willoughby has been going by, during the voyage. But I fancy his real name is Willoughby, sir."

"Well, the offer is not from him. It is from Major Van Buren—the tall gentleman with Mr. Willoughby. His wife requires a lady's maid. Major Van Buren is Dutch, but his wife is English, and they are well-to-do. They—"

She cut him short, leaving him no chance to enlarge on what her employment in the Van Burens' household would entail. "I will accept most gladly, sir. So long as the offer does not come from Mr. Rob—that is, from Mr. Willoughby, I . . . thank you, sir, I am beholden to you. It is a fine opportunity."

"There might well be other opportunities," Murdo began, but she shook her head.

"Domestic service is to be preferred to work in the Female Factory, sir. We heard on the prison deck what *that* is like." The girl shivered, but, Murdo saw, her fear had vanished and, for the first time, she was smiling, the smile lighting her whole face to radiance. He felt his pulses quicken in response to it and, for a moment, was filled with so strong a desire to touch her that he almost yielded to it, forgetful of his duty and the role he was playing.

Major Goulburn's voice restored him to sanity.

"Damme, Dean, is the matter of a servant for Van Buren resolved?" He sounded irritable and gestured impatiently to the two clerks at his heels, both of them laden with the convict manifests they had collected. "I have work to do—my damned office is piled high with infernal papers. The confounded fellow will give me no peace until he gets what he wants, and these women should be taken off the ship. Which one does the Dutchman want?"

Murdo stiffened. Wordlessly, he indicated Alice Fairweather, and Goulburn said, in a more placatory tone, "Then let him have her." He studied the girl for a long moment, grunted, and laughed shortly. "Tell him he'll not need fetters for this poor child. All right, Dean—carry on, will you, please? And . . ." He hesitated, as if belatedly remembering. "Perhaps you'll be so good as to direct Mr. Willoughby and his friend to Parramatta and tell them where they can hire horses. Willoughby has an introduction to Mr. Macarthur."

"Very good, sir," Murdo acknowledged woodenly. He called out an order to his sergeant, and as the women were being ushered into single file, preparatory to disembarking, he handed Alice Fairweather over to her new master. His last sight of her was on the crowded wharf; she was walking demurely beside the Javanese houseman, who had discarded the chain fetters and was, instead, carrying the small bundle of her possessions and talking to her volubly.

Perhaps his misgivings were unjustified, he thought; perhaps she would be happy in the Van Burens' household, and . . . He suppressed an oath. Perhaps his posting to Moreton Bay had saved him from making a damned fool of himself over a convict wench of whom he knew nothing.

He turned to find Robert Willoughby at his side and, as he had been bidden, supplied him with directions to the Parramatta turnpike and indicated the location of a livery stable from which he could hire horses or a curricle and pair.

Willoughby thanked him courteously.

"Of your kindness, Mr. Dean, oblige me and Mr. Daniels with some more information."

"Certainly, Mr. Willoughby," Murdo returned with equal courtesy, and found himself wondering why, for no logical reason that he could conceive of, he suddenly mistrusted the new settler's overly effusive manner. "I have these women to disembark, but that will not take long. My sergeant can march them to the hospital, and I will be at your service as soon as they are on their way."

But the two young men did not wait. By the time Murdo had dealt with the convict women and their escort, Willoughby and Daniels had left the wharf—having, Murdo could only presume, obtained the information they wanted elsewhere. Instead, Justin came ashore, with young Red proudly commanding his gig.

"We're ready to sail," Justin announced. "And Henry Miller assures me he can have his soldiers and the thirty convicts on board the *Amity* by noon. We are to have the pleasure of Mr. Oxley's company, as well as yours. Is your kit ready? I'm sending a party to pick up Oxley's from the survey office now, in the hope that he'll bestir himself."

"I left mine at your cottage with Jessie," Murdo told him. "But why the haste? I understood you didn't intend to sail until tomorrow morning."

"I want to get under way while this wind holds—it's liable to drop before evening. So if you are free, we had better go and make our farewells now." Justin turned to his son. "Off with you, Red, and tell your mama we're coming." The boy sped away, and Justin lowered his voice. "Murdo, I've just heard that the Governor is to be replaced—Captain Piper told me. It seems the *Mary Anne* brought out a copy of the London *Times*, in which it was announced. Her master showed it to him when he went out to her at the Heads yesterday, with the pilot. Piper says he does not think that the Colonial Office has yet informed His Excellency officially—or if they have, the Governor hasn't mentioned it.''

Murdo pursed his lips in a silent whistle of astonishment. "Why should he be replaced, Justin? For what *reason*, for heaven's sake?"

"For the same reason that Governor Macquarie was replaced, my dear fellow." Justin's tone was cynical. "Because private letters are sent to Lord Bathurst and complaints are made behind his back to the Colonial Office and members of the home government. Sir Thomas told me himself that Major Goulburn has been intriguing against him—and you don't have to look far for the others. Every damned official who's not given preferment blames the Governor, and virtually every landowner and every merchant has some complaint he wants to air. And there's Macarthur, of course. According to John Piper, he's accused the Governor of overspending and wasting the colony's resources!''

"But why the devil does Lord Bathurst heed such complaints?" Murdo questioned.

"Because they are many, and the Governor is alone . . . and because overspending is the ultimate crime in Bathurst's eyes. Mind you—" Justin's tone changed, and he laid a hand on Murdo's arm. "Keep this to yourself, Murdo, but I don't fancy that Sir Thomas will be either greatly surprised or greatly put out when he receives his recall through official channels. He may even have offered his resignation.''

"You really think so?"

Justin nodded. "From what he said to me, when I took him to Moreton Bay and we studied the stars together during the night watches, I believe he'll be glad enough to go. He's prepared a paper to read to the Royal Astronomical Society in London, and he told me he plans to set up an observatory at his Scottish residence near Kelso when he goes home. By my reckoning, Murdo, Sir Thomas Brisbane is a master of nautical astronomy. He didn't only teach Red—he taught me a great deal, you know.'' He smiled. ''If he had not gone into the army, if he'd chosen the navy instead, I truly believe he would have rivaled Cook and Bligh as a navigator! And lesser men would not have been able to make him haul down his flag. Strange, is it not, how things work out?''

''Yes,'' Murdo agreed. ''It's passing strange.'' He and Justin started to walk toward the end of the wharf as a convict chain gang was marched onto it, no doubt to start unloading the *Mary Anne*'s cargo, their overseer bawling to them to pick their feet up or taste his lash. What, he wondered, was the convict girl doing now in the Van Burens' opulent residence? Alice Fairweather . . . he savored the name, seeing in memory her small, sweet face and the shapely head she had held so high, not bowed in defeat, as those of the chain gang were. As Justin had said, it was strange how things worked out. Had he not been ordered to the infernal new settlement at Moreton Bay, he might have been able to prevent the unpleasant Dutchman from taking her, might have taken her for himself, and . . . oh, the devil!

He thrust the thought of what might have been from his mind and asked, more to distract his thoughts than from genuine interest, ''Who is to be the next Governor, Justin, do you know?''

''The *Times* stated that it's to be a very distinguished general by the name of Darling,'' Justin answered, ''and that he will arrive next year. According to John Piper, he's said to be something of a martinet. He served under Sir John Moore at Corunna and was recently Governor of Mauritius . . . where,'' he added dryly, ''Piper says he made himself extremely unpopular.''

Murdo shrugged. Almost against his will, his thoughts returned to the convict girl, and he asked, without much hope, ''Are there no women to be permitted in the new prison settlement—no wives?''

Justin shook his head. "Most definitely not. Moreton Bay is to be a segregated prison for the worst offenders—escapers, bushrangers, and capital respites, all male. There is to be a chaplain, I believe, and a surgeon. Maybe the officers will be permitted to take their wives with them—I don't know. Why do you ask?" He eyed his young brother-in-law with amusement. "Were you thinking of getting married?"

"Good God, no!" Murdo denied hotly. "And I'm not thinking of staying in plaguey Edenglassie for longer than I can help, either!"

Justin grinned at him. "Perhaps, like the Governor, you chose the wrong profession, old man. If you were an officer in the King's Navy, now—"

Murdo aimed a playful punch at his head.

"I did not choose my profession," he retorted. "It was chosen for me."

He had a sudden vision of Nick Vincent, who had rescued him from the prison van, and of the two recruiting sergeants to whom Nick had introduced him in the inn at Buck's Oak. It was a vision dredged up from the past and one he had hoped to forget. He shivered involuntarily and then forced a smile, as they entered the garden of the Broomes' cottage and Jessica came to meet them.

CHAPTER XI

Alice Fairweather had been a member of the Van Burens' household for almost three weeks, but, she realized miserably, she was no nearer feeling at home there than she had been when the Javanese majordomo, Saleh, had brought her from the convict transport.

The language difference was a barrier between her and the other servants, though Saleh, it was true, understood more English than he was willing to admit, and the boy Claus—whose status still puzzled her—spoke it well but with a strong accent.

With the exception of these two, the servants had not received her kindly. Alice, plying her needle diligently, paused a moment to inspect her work. In part, she supposed, their coldness was due to jealousy. The others were Malay or Javanese, who worshiped heathen gods and resented her white skin and her ignorance of their language and customs; and the woman whom their mistress addressed as Leah had double cause for resentment, since she had previously acted as lady's maid but was now relegated to the kitchen. Leah was spiteful, Alice had learned to her cost, and not above acting in a manner calculated to bring down her mistress's wrath on her supplanter's head.

Mrs. Van Buren was, as the young officer had told her on the day of her arrival in the colony, an English lady, but she had apparently lived for several years in the Dutch Indies, and in addition to speaking both Dutch and the native patois with ease and fluency, she had seemingly

become imbued with many of the qualities that characterized her husband's race.

Neither rose early, and both indulged themselves in rich
foods, which had to be impeccably served, often late at
night. Worst of all, Mrs. Van Buren's temper was as
unpredictable as his, and if either was displeased, the
whole household trembled. When Major Van Buren drank
to excess, as he often did, even Saleh went in terror of
him, aware that he might be abused and sometimes brutally beaten.

All the servants were severely punished if they offended
in any way. Saleh was ordered to beat them, and he did
so, watched coldly by their mistress to ensure that he did
not let them off lightly. . . . Alice turned the garment she
was hemming and expelled her breath wearily.

She herself had twice earned a beating for quite trivial
offenses, but the one who was most frequently in trouble
was poor Claus. The boy—he was scarcely more than a
child, Alice reflected pityingly—was consistently ill-treated,
for all he worked so hard and willingly and did all he
could to merit approval. Mrs. Van Buren seldom addressed him by name; she called him the *lip-lap*, which,
Saleh told her, was the contemptuous Dutch term for those
of mixed race, with both white and native blood in their
veins.

"And this he has," Saleh had concluded, an odd gleam
lighting his dark eyes. "For which *Mevrouw* Van Buren
will never forgive him, as long as he shall live."

He had said no more, leaving Alice to arrive at whatever
conclusions she chose, but it was evident that his sympathies
—insofar as he dared to display them—were with Claus.

The light was fading now, but Alice stitched resolutely
on. Mrs. Van Buren had insisted that this dress must be
finished by the evening, since she was dining with her
sister and wished to wear it then, and there was still much
to be done to it . . . over a score of tiny pearl buttons to
sew at the neck and on the bodice, and tucks to be taken in
at the waist. It would consume all her time to complete the

work; her mistress would change at seven thirty, she had said, and . . . In her haste, Alice let the needle slip and ran its tip into her finger. The sharp point drew blood, and before she could prevent it, two red spots appeared on the flimsy white material of the frilled collar, and she cried her dismay aloud. It would be impossible to wash the stains off, she knew, without leaving visible traces of her clumsiness, but . . . perhaps the frill could be made to hide them. She bent anxiously to the task, brows knit in a frown of concentration.

The long voyage out here had taken its toll of her skill as a seamstress. Such sewing as she had done in the cramped prison quarters of the *Mary Anne* had been restricted to mending and patching for Mr. Roberts—no, his name was not Roberts, it was Willoughby—and for his friend Mr. Daniels, and occasionally for one of the ship's officers. Alice felt her cheeks burn as she remembered the voyage and the pain and humiliation she had endured, all of it caused by Robert Willoughby.

She had been innocent and naive when she had boarded the *Mary Anne,* she thought bitterly; strictly brought up by hardworking, God-fearing parents who had asked no more of her than that she follow in their footsteps and earn a living, until some decent young man of their own class should take her to wife. They had apprenticed her to the village dressmaker and milliner when she reached her twelfth birthday, and she had served her time with that good woman, winning her praise and her parents' affectionate approval.

But then . . . Alice felt tears come to ache, unshed, in her throat. She had met the young man—Tom Digby, the son of a farmer, big and gentle and with prospects that, she had known, set him above her, since her father was only a laborer who had no land of his own and who had worked all his life for Tom's uncle.

Fool that she had been, she had sought to better herself, so that she could meet him on equal terms—or almost equal terms—and he need not be ashamed to court her.

The milliner in Honiton had advertised for an assistant; she had applied for and been given the post, and although she had not liked her new employer, the shop in Honiton had offered the step up that she had wanted, and the promise of instruction in lace making had been tempting.

One of the tiny pearl buttons fell to the floor, and Alice laid the dress down and dropped to her knees to search for it, reliving the nightmare that had led to her arrest and sentence. She had borrowed a card of lace—only borrowed; she had never intended to steal it—with which to deck a bonnet to wear when Tom took her to the harvest festival supper at their church. But she had foolishly omitted to tell her employer what she had done, and the woman had been angry and had given her in charge for theft. . . .

The button found, Alice returned to her chair, first moving it closer to the window so as to have the benefit of what daylight still remained. She had a candle, but candles were strictly rationed by Saleh, and the one she had was almost burned out.

Tom, she recalled with a pang, had done all in his power to help her. He had borne witness, before judge and jury at the assize court in Exeter, that she was of previous good character and that it was his intention to wed her, if the court would relent and clear her of the charge. But the court had not relented; her employer's word had carried more weight than Tom's, and after an unhappy stay in jail, she had been sent on board the *Mary Anne* at Plymouth with a hundred and twenty-nine other female convicts, many of them prostitutes or hardened criminals.

She had not seen her parents again; they, poor souls, had been too shamed to attempt to see her after the court hearing, and Tom . . . Alice caught her breath, remembering, her needle still. Tom had been on Guy's Wharf to wave her farewell, but she had not seen him again after that. And after what Robert Willoughby had done to her, she would willingly have died, rather than see Tom again. . . . The tears came then, threatening to overwhelm

her, but she brushed them away, and picking up another
button, stitched it swiftly into place.

Robert Willoughby had used her cruelly and heartlessly,
but she would not weep on his account. Twice more, after
that first terrible experience at his hands, he had had her
sent to his cabin and taken his will of her, but then she had
plucked up the courage to appeal to the captain, and the
summons had not been repeated. She had done his laundry,
but that was all; the other women had laughed at her,
telling her she was a fool to abandon voluntarily the
chance to exchange the prison deck for a wealthy passenger's
snug cabin, and two or three of them had accepted the
mate's escort to the 'tween decks in her place. But at the
Cape, the captain had fallen ill, and while he was confined
to his bunk, with the ship's surgeon in constant attendance,
the mate had told her that her presence was again required,
and . . . it had all started anew.

"You'll live to regret it if you refuse," the mate had
threatened. "Because I'll see to it that you're put on half
rations and kept chained up in the brig, if you do. In any
case, girl, 'twill be the best course you can take—that
young gennelman has a right strong fancy for you. When
we make port in Sydney Town, he'll likely take you with
him an' look after you. He's got money, he has, an' you'll
live like a queen."

Willoughby, Alice recalled, had made her a similar
promise—but he had not kept it. Instead, he had given her,
like a discarded toy, to the Van Burens, and she, in her
foolishness, had seized the chance to escape from him and
been glad of it. Only . . . her lips twisted into a bitter
smile. Her escape had been, as the old proverb put it, out
of the frying pan, into the fire, for surely not all the female
convicts who took domestic employment in the colony
were treated as the servants in this household were.

There was Mrs. Van Buren's sister, for example—Mrs.
Dawson, who had been to the house a few days ago and
had talked to her kindly, even troubling to compliment her

on one of the dresses she had made. But . . . there was a soft knock on the door, and it opened to admit Claus.

The boy had a livid bruise on his cheek that had not been there earlier, but he shook his head to Alice's concerned inquiry and said, in his quaintly accented English, "*Mevrouw*—I am meaning Mrs. Van Buren—has sent me to ask you if her gown is yet finished?" He regarded Alice's handiwork with a critical eye and, pointing to the row of buttons, offered gravely, "They must take much time. Would you wish that I help you to sew them on?"

She hesitated, not wanting to hurt his feelings by rejecting his offer, and he said, with an eager smile, "But I can! My mother has teached me. Give me one of your needles and I show."

Still uncertain whether or not to believe his claim, Alice did as he asked, and he swiftly made light of her doubts, stitching with a speed and skill she could only just match.

"Your mother taught you well, Claus," she told him.

"My mother fine woman," Claus asserted proudly. "But she dead. You do skirt now—I do buttons, then we finish soon, not? *Mevrouw* be much pleased, maybe."

"All right, then—thank you," Alice agreed. They worked in companionable silence, and then, prompted by curiosity concerning him, she asked, when the last button was in place, "Did your mother die in Batavia before you came here?"

"In Coupang," the boy answered, with seeming indifference. "A long time ago, when I still a child. My father order her to be made dead when she try to attack *mevrouw*, see? That was—" He frowned, searching for the right word. "That was foolish; but she was not wicked woman, only much afraid."

Alice eyed him in bewilderment, but before she could ask him to explain this extraordinary statement, Claus added anxiously, "I must not say he is my father. He beat me if he know. You—please, Alice, you don't tell him, promise me!"

He could only mean Major Van Buren, Alice thought,

shocked as she attempted to piece together the odd-sounding story. And if he did, then . . . She reached out a hand to him, seeking to assuage his fears. "Of course I won't tell him, Claus."

"You promise?" His thin brown fingers twined about hers, the dark eyes pleading.

"I promise," she said solemnly, and was rewarded and happily surprised when Claus flung his arms round her neck and hugged her.

"We be friends—we help each other," he offered enthusiastically. "You, me, and Abdul."

"Yes, gladly—but who is Abdul?"

"Abdul Wetar. He is very good seaman, but he was hurt when the *Flinders* went onto rocks. His leg broke, but now he much better. Good English doctors at hospital make him well. He is now to work for Mr. Lord, not go back to Batavia." Claus was beaming; evidently, Alice decided, the good seamen Abdul, who was now to work for Mr. Lord, was a particular friend of his. She smiled back at the boy and, rising, started to shake out the folds of her mistress's dress, pleased by the final appearance of it.

"It is ready," she said. "Would you tell Mrs. Van Buren, please, Claus? Say that I—" She was interrupted by a loud, imperious summons from Mrs. Van Buren herself, and they looked at each other, startled, their fragile moment of happiness abruptly shattered.

"Better I go," Claus whispered. "You take her pretty dress, Alice. She be very much pleased."

But Mrs. Van Buren, to Alice's dismay, was not pleased. She inspected the dress, quick to find fault with it, but was somewhat mollified when, assisted nervously to don it, she found that it fitted her perfectly and that, when the folds and frills were shaken out, the garment was undeniably becoming.

"Yes . . ." With critical eyes she studied her image in the full-length mirror in her bedroom. "Yes, it will do. All those buttons on the bodice are tiresome—be sure you are up when I return from my sister's, because I shall need you to undo them for me. And those shoes are the wrong color—fetch me my black pumps from the closet; I think they will be better."

Alice knelt at her feet, buckling and unbuckling the various shoes her mistress tried on, careful to betray no sign of impatience or resentment. Then there was her hair to be dressed—a protective cape first thrown over the frilled collar of the new gown—with gentle, prolonged brushing to precede the braiding of her dark locks, and the ribbon that must be tied, with infinite care, at the nape of her neck.

"You do my hair better than Leah," Mrs. Van Buren conceded thoughtfully, when at last she was satisfied. "And you have, I hope, more common sense than she possesses and, perhaps, stricter morals. But tell me—has Major Van Buren made any advances to you since he brought you here?"

Alice was taken aback by the unexpected question and reddened furiously. "No, ma'am, never."

And it was true, she reflected: Major Van Buren had so far confined his attentions to the disgraced Leah, with whom, it was common knowledge, he slept . . . when not too far gone in his cups.

"He will," the major's wife said, making no attempt to disguise her scorn. "And if you wish to continue as my personal maid, take care that you do not accede to his demands."

"Yes, ma'am," Alice acknowledged dutifully, keeping a tight rein on her emotions but reminded, nonetheless, of Robert Willoughby, to whose demands she had been compelled to accede. Greatly daring, she ventured to ask, "But how, ma'am? As his assigned servant I—"

"You are assigned to *me*," Lucy Van Buren reminded her, with heavy emphasis. "All you need do is to inform me, should any demands be made on you. You are not a whore, are you? It was not for prostitution that you were deported?"

"No, ma'am, certainly not!" Bitter indignation played momentary havoc with Alice's control. "I was strictly brought up, in a God-fearing family. I . . ." Her indignation faded. That, she remembered, had been the defense she had first used against Robert Willoughby, and he had brushed it aside, as of no account. And . . . had he not made her a whore, for all her pleas and her strict Christian upbringing? Was she any less a whore than the women with whom she had shared the *Mary Anne*'s deck throughout the long, endless months of the passage to New South Wales? No decent man would want to wed her now, after what Robert Willoughby had made of her; not even her loyal, devoted Tom. . . .

"Then . . ." Lucy Van Buren rose, and their eyes met in the reflected glow of the candle-lit mirror. "I need not concern myself on your account. You know what you must do."

"Yes, ma'am," Alice responded with humility. She handed her mistress cloak and gloves, as she had been trained to do, and then hastened ahead of her, so as to warn Saleh to summon the carriage.

The vehicle had scarcely drawn away from the front of the house when she saw Leah come from the kitchen and make her way on swiftly running feet to Major Van Buren's room. The woman gave her a faintly malicious smile as she passed, and then the door closed behind her slim, dark-robed figure. Alice heard Saleh release what could only be a sigh of relief.

"Come," he invited, in unexpectedly good English. "Is there not a saying in your country as to what mice may do, when the cats are away? Tonight we shall feast ourselves, Alice Fairweather, and he who is called the little *lip-lap* shall join with us also, without fear of punishment."

It was with a lifting of her flagging spirits that Alice followed him, to find the scrubbed wooden table at which the Van Burens' servants normally ate their frugal meals set with what truly was a feast. Saleh piled a plate high with rice and spiced fish and meat and placed it in front of her, laughing at her astonishment. Then his expression changed.

"Not all of us are bad people like those we serve," he told her gravely. "We do what we must and try to avoid trouble." He gestured to a small, brown-skinned man seated with Claus at the end of the table. "That man is Abdul Wetar, who is our friend and the friend also of Claus, to whom he owes his life. We drink a toast to him now, for pleasure that he is well again."

The small stranger jumped to his feet, holding his glass aloft. He said something in his own tongue, which Alice did not understand, and then he turned, the glass raised in Claus's direction.

"Abdul wishes that the toast be drunk to Claus," Saleh explained. "Rise and we will do as he desires."

There were tears in the boy's expressive dark eyes as the toast was drunk, but they vanished when his plate was put before him and he attacked it with hungry relish.

"He has been without food for two days," Saleh whispered. "As punishment ordered by *Mijnheer* Van Buren because he was insolent." He shrugged his slim, white-clad shoulders. "But we take care of our own. You are one of us now, Alice Fairweather, although you are white— and we will take care of you, since Claus asks that we do."

For the first time since her arrest in an England that was now half the world away, Alice was conscious of the dawning of hope. Perhaps, after all, she thought, she could make a new life, here in this strange land and with these alien people. She had come here as a convict, and when her time expired, she would be free; but they . . . they were slaves, Mrs. Van Buren had once told her, for whom there would be no freedom. They . . .

Claus looked up from his plate, spooned the last morsels of rice into his mouth, and beamed at her happily.

"I am telling them that you are good woman like my mother, Alice—and that when I am old enough, I will wed you. So now we are all friends, not?"

He was twelve years old, Alice thought with a pang, but she smiled back at him warmly, conscious of the compliment he had paid her.

"Yes, Claus," she answered gratefully. "Now we are all friends."

There were two unexpected guests at the Dawsons' for dinner, and when she had first been introduced to them, Lucy Van Buren had been annoyed, for she had looked forward to a confidential talk with her sister, Abigail, when the meal was over. As the evening progressed, however, her attitude underwent a change. The two young gentlemen were personable and clearly well off, and the older of the two, Robert Willoughby, was, she decided, attractive and worth cultivating, with a hint of recklessness about him that she found intriguing.

He and Henry Daniels had arrived recently in the *Mary Anne* transport; they had brought stock with them from the Cape and, Lucy gathered in the course of conversation, were now in the process of claiming grants of a thousand acres each in the Macquarie River area.

"That was Mr. Macarthur's advice," Robert Willoughby explained. "I had an introduction to him and also, of course, to the Governor, thanks to my father. As a retired rear admiral, it's amazing how many influential people he knows."

Also in the course of conversation, he let it be known that he was the eldest son of the distinguished admiral and heir to his baronetcy and that he himself had served in the Royal Navy at the battle of Algiers. He passed on all this information in a casual manner, making light of his achievements and glossing over his impeccable credentials, but Lucy was impressed, and even Timothy—who had made Willoughby's acquaintance in the 40th's mess and issued the dinner invitation—appeared to be much taken with the new arrivals.

Henry Daniels was also well connected. The son of a wealthy London merchant, he, too, had apparently held a commission—in a cavalry regiment that, he admitted regretfully, had had the misfortune to be stationed first in India and then in Ireland, so that he had been unable to take part in the Peninsular campaign and had, as he disappointedly expressed it, "missed Waterloo."

Julia Dawson was bubbling over with excitement as the two young men talked of their experiences and enlarged on the latest news from England, with emphasis on the London scene and political gossip, subjects on which Henry Daniels appeared exceptionally well informed. But the girl played her cards too openly, Lucy observed scornfully, earning Abigail's unspoken but obvious disapproval and a rebuke from her father for a clumsy interruption. Daniels ignored her overtures, directing his studied witticisms at Katie Tempest, who pointedly failed to respond to them and appeared, to Lucy's critical eyes, so preoccupied with her own thoughts that she was unaware of his attempts to ensnare her.

Rick's wife was looking more beautiful than ever, despite her pallor and a noticeable loss of weight, but she maintained her aloof and oddly brooding silence until Robert Willoughby announced that he intended to take the first opportunity to inspect the area in which his claim was situated.

"We'll ride up to—what's the name of the place? Bathurst, is it not?—next week, probably, when we've engaged some convict labor. We both have stock eating their heads off here, at vast expense, so the sooner we can drive them up to the Macquarie Plains, the better I'll be pleased."

"You will need to be patient, Mr. Willoughby," Katie told him, a distinct edge to her voice, "as I must. There have been extensive bushfires south of Emu Ford, and the country is devastated. It will be a while before you can drive stock through it."

Willoughby's face fell. "Mr. Macarthur mentioned the fires," he admitted. "But since they did not touch his land, I had supposed—oh, a plague on it! We shall have to find somewhere to accommodate our stock, Henry, and go up there without them.''

Daniels nodded, without much interest, and turned once more to Katie. ''Are you also waiting, Mrs. Tempest? Do you perhaps live in the devastated area?''

''No,'' Katie answered, her tone flat and faintly repressive, as if regretting her outburst. ''My husband has a land grant on the Macquarie, and I am anxious to return there as soon as I can. But he, too, has stock to drive up, and I am compelled to wait until the road is once more passable.''

''You could come with us,'' Daniels suggested persuasively. ''Could she not, Robert? That is, of course, if you can make the journey on horseback. I'm ignorant of conditions in this country, but I've been told that the road over the mountains is somewhat hazardous.''

Katie's refusal of his offer was polite but firm, and Timothy broke an awkward silence by asking what stock the two new settlers had purchased at the Cape and the prices they had paid.

''Hundreds of sheep were lost in the drought,'' he told them, ''before the fires ever started. Many of the smaller landowners are facing ruin, and a very old and dear friend of ours lost his life in an attempt to save his buildings— Andrew Hawley, late of His Majesty's Royal Marines.'' He sighed, his face clouding over, and then, conscious of his obligations as host, he changed the subject. To Lucy's surprise, however, Robert Willoughby returned to it.

''If settlers in the Emu Ford area have lost stock,'' he said thoughtfully, ''presumably they will want to replace their losses, will they not?''

''When the rain comes to restore their grazing, yes, they will,'' Timothy agreed.

''Then we should stand to make a profit if we sold our Cape flock, sir?'' Willoughby suggested.

''A considerable profit, I imagine.'' Timothy's tone was dry. ''But I had understood that you were desirous of settling on land of your own.''

Robert Willoughby laughed. ''That was my initial

intention, sir. But if I can make more money and lead a less strenuous life by trading, then I'd as soon become a trader—even a seagoing trader, seeing that I've been at sea since my eleventh birthday.''

Lucy's interest quickened. Apart from being handsome and well-bred, Robert Willoughby had other qualities, she realized—qualities that might be turned to good account, if he could be dissuaded from isolating himself on a land grant at the back of beyond. Jos wanted land but was proscribed from owning any by the Governor's prejudice against a onetime French ally. . . . Her gaze lingered on Willoughby. Rumor had it that this Governor was leaving, and his successor might be less prejudiced, but—even if he were not, a partnership of the kind her brother, Rick, had entered into with Justin Broome might be a possibility. Jos, if *he* were the one to be isolated at the back of beyond, would leave her free of the hated matrimonial ties she now so deeply regretted. She would be spared his arrogance and his drinking, his supposedly secret infidelities and unpleasant company, and if he were removed from the Sydney social scene, she might herself reenter it and resume the friendships his uncouth behavior had cost her.

Ignoring the general conversation, she studied Robert Willoughby, becoming increasingly aware of his masculine attraction and the recklessness she had earlier sensed in him. Not entirely to her surprise, he returned her scrutiny without making any effort to hide the fact from her, and for the rest of the meal he turned his back on Dorothea, beside whom he was seated, and talked across the table to her in amusing and uninhibited fashion.

When Abigail rose, to signify that the gentlemen should be left to their port and cigars, Lucy followed her from the room reluctantly.

''Those are two charming young gentlemen,'' she observed. ''They will be a great asset to the colony, don't you think, Abigail?''

Her sister, pouring coffee, murmured abstractedly, and Julia declared, in gushing tones, that she found both guests delightful. "Who knows," she added eagerly, "perhaps coming out here to settle may become fashionable, and we shall see more gentlemen of their caliber arriving in Sydney, instead of fly-by-night army officers and dreary little clerks and parsons sent by the Colonial Office."

But there were two dissenting voices: Dorothea, predictably, announced that she thought Mr. Willoughby's manners left something to be desired, and Katie, with what for her was unusual vehemence, said that she liked neither of them.

"Mr. Daniels is boastful, and Mr. Willoughby has, I feel sure, something to hide. I would trust neither of them, for I believe they are adventurers who have come out here purely in the hope of making money." She set down her coffee cup untasted, and before Lucy could take her to task for her condemnation of the two new arrivals, she pleaded a headache and asked Abigail to excuse her. Dorothea planted a swift kiss on her stepmother's cheek and followed Katie from the room.

"Dodie is becoming most boring," Julia said in a voice loud enough to carry, even before her sister had closed the door. "She and Katie hardly opened their mouths during dinner—they made no effort to join in the conversation, so what could they expect? I really do think that you should talk to Dodie, Abigail, and try to make her more aware of her social obligations."

"You, at least, seem to be very much aware of yours," Abigail returned, eyeing the girl with pity. "If you were less free with your opinions, you would make a better impression, Julia, believe me."

Julia was instantly offended. "You always take her part," she accused.

"Only when I believe her to be in the right," Abigail countered.

"And do you believe she's right to let William Broome court her? Because that's what she's doing, Abigail! And if she runs off with him, don't say I didn't warn you."

Abigail looked startled, and Lucy was about to intervene

when the door from the dining room opened and Timothy ushered her guests in, with an oddly tense expression on his face. He offered no explanation, however, only exchanged a silent glance with his wife, which Abigail evidently understood, for her tone was cool as she invited their guests to be seated. Both young men looked round the room; Henry Daniels's face fell when he realized that Katie was no longer there, but Robert Willoughby crossed with slow deliberation to Lucy's side, courteously asking her permission before joining her on the sofa.

Julia, at Abigail's behest, went sullenly to the piano, but she brightened perceptibly when Henry Daniels followed her, with an offer to turn the pages of her music. She accepted, and soon they were singing in tuneful unison, Daniels in a very pleasant baritone, which blended well with Julia's small but well-trained voice.

"Henry's no mean performer, Mrs. Van Buren," Robert Willoughby volunteered. "Many's the evening that he kept us entertained during the voyage—he and a most talented young scapegrace named Turner, who left Plymouth with us in the *Mary Anne* but was, unhappily, compelled to leave us at the Cape."

"For what reason, Mr. Willoughby?" Lucy asked curiously.

He shrugged. "He was involved in a duel, poor Tony, and the Cape authorities put him in arrest. Had it not been for that, there would have been three of us in partnership here, instead of just Henry and me." He turned to her thoughtfully. "I don't know what view you may hold, ma'am—you've been out here much longer than I—but I fancy that two or three men in equal partnership, each contributing a thousand acres and livestock, would stand a better chance of commercial success than one man on his own. Resources would be pooled, the labor to which each partner was entitled would work for all, and an experienced manager could be put in charge of the combined venture."

"It is an ingenious idea," Lucy agreed. He was playing
into her hands, she thought, and smiled at him warmly.

Robert Willoughby echoed her smile. "I can claim only
partial credit for it," he admitted. "It came to me when I
visited Mr. Macarthur's estate at Camden. He now possesses ten thousand acres of grazing land in what I believe
is called the Cow Pastures, and alongside his grant are
those owned by his friend and longtime associate, Mr.
Davidson, and his nephew, Hannibal Macarthur. They
jointly employ more labor than anyone else in the colony
and, in consequence of their association, are far and away
the wealthiest settlers in the country. And Mr. John
Macarthur, I'm led to understand, has interests in a number of trading vessels, plying from here to the Pacific
islands, as well as to England and the Cape."

"Mr. Macarthur is a very shrewd businessman," Lucy
assured him. "But at the root of his prosperity lies the
sheep-breeding policy he adopted very soon after he came
out here." She enlarged on this, conscious of Tim's eyes
fixed on her, as if seeking to convey a warning, but she
ignored his frowning gaze and concentrated on the man at
her side, stimulated by his unconcealed interest, which, it
became evident, was more in herself than in the subject of
her discourse.

"You are most knowledgeable, Mrs. Van Buren," he
said, with flattering humility. "Tell me—" He leaned
closer. "Your name is Dutch, is it not? May I presume to
ask whether your husband is Dutch?"

Lucy inclined her head. "You must meet him, Mr.
Willoughby."

"Actually, we've met informally, but I'd appreciate a
proper introduction," Robert Willoughby replied. "Provided—" His voice sank to a whisper. "Provided meeting
him affords me the opportunity to renew my acquaintance
with you."

"You could take dinner with us. Or luncheon, if you
prefer it."

"I should be overjoyed to do either. I'm at a very loose

end at the moment. Neither Henry nor I can do anything until the government surveyor returns from Moreton Bay. He's helping to build some new prison there, I understand—infernal fellow! He should be attending to his duties here, not gallivanting off building stockades for—what are they called? Bushrangers and capital respites? They should be hanged and have done with 'em, in my view!''

Abigail had gone to the piano, to join in the singing of a song that was a favorite of hers, and, Lucy saw with relief, Timothy's gaze had followed her. Freed of his scrutiny, she laid a slim, white hand on Robert Willoughby's and bestowed on him the full warmth of her smile.

"Then make it luncheon tomorrow—anyone will direct you to our residence," she told him. "You mentioned the stock you have brought with you—is it accommodated in the government pound?''

He nodded ruefully. "Indeed yes—at exorbitant cost.''

"It is possible that we may be able to offer you temporary accommodation at a property we own near Parramatta, at a quarter the cost. You must speak to my husband about it. And—'' Lucy's eyes were very bright as they looked into his. "Major Van Buren has trading interests in the Dutch islands, Mr. Willoughby. He has two vessels under charter, which he is always saying are poorly commanded. I feel sure that, with mutual goodwill and a little ingenuity, some sort of arrangement could be devised that would be satisfactory to all of us. My husband is no seaman, so that . . .'' She left the sentence unfinished, the promise it held out implied, and Robert Willoughby's fingers tightened about hers.

"I shall be looking forward to luncheon tomorrow, dear lady,'' he assure her, and raised her hand to his lips.

Lucy made her good-byes then; there was, she decided, nothing more to be gained by prolonging her stay, and she would have to be up much earlier than her usual hour to ensure that Jos was properly briefed concerning their luncheon guest and that he did not start drinking when he broke his fast—a habit he had fallen into of late.

The carriage took her the short distance to her own house, and Saleh and the convict maid, Alice Fairweather, were in the hall, waiting to attend her. The girl's cheeks were flushed, and as she hurried forward to help relieve Lucy of her cloak, she was smiling, even willing and helpful, where before she had been sullen and resentful.

Suspiciously, Lucy subjected her to a searching scrutiny, at a loss to understand what had wrought the change, and then, catching a whiff of her breath, she exclaimed indignantly, "Alice, you have been drinking!" The girl hung her head, making no attempt to deny the accusation, but Saleh stepped forward. He said smoothly, in his own tongue, "The young woman fainted, *mevrouw*. I gave her a little *arrack* to revive her. But she is quite sober and able to wait on your ladyship." He hesitated, his dark eyes oddly challenging, and then added quietly, "If *mevrouw* wishes, I can send for Leah in her place."

Lucy stifled an angry retort, guessing, from his manner, whence Leah would have to be summoned.

"No," she returned curtly. "That will not be necessary, Saleh. But remember, convicts are not permitted alcohol in this colony. Alice must be given water, should she faint again."

She swept past him toward the door of her own room, and at a nod from Saleh, Alice followed her, the ghost of a smile still playing about her lips.

CHAPTER XII

John Oxley, the government surveyor, returned from Moreton Bay ten days after the Dawsons' dinner party, and at Major Van Buren's suggestion, Robert Willoughby agreed that they should wait on him together, in the hope of speeding up matters pertaining to Willoughby's land grant and that of his friend Daniels.

"I truly believe that the beautiful Mrs. Van Buren was right," Robert said thoughtfully as he and Daniels set off on foot for the survey office. "I confess I do not greatly fancy the major, but . . . we can derive mutual benefit from an association with him, I am confident. He has money and trading interests—all he lacks is land."

Henry Daniels laughed derisively. "Oh, come now, Rob!" he exclaimed. "Do you think I am blind, for the Lord's sake? It is the major's wife you fancy, and you need not waste your breath to deny it."

"Then I shall not deny it," Robert retorted, unabashed. "She is a woman I most sincerely admire—not only is she beautiful, she's also very shrewd, with a sound grasp of conditions here and the wit and wisdom to exploit her knowledge. Van Buren is a drunken, ill-mannered oaf who does not deserve such a jewel of a wife."

"He could be dangerous if you arouse his jealousy," Rob," Daniels warned. "I'd think twice before I'd cross him."

"I do not intend to," Robert assured him. "Give me credit for some subtlety, old man. The lady, I deduce, is ripe fruit for the picking, but I shall bide my time. You could assist me in my endeavors, though, if you've a mind to.''

"I have nothing else to do. The lady *I* could fancy is seemingly devoted to her husband and is, I'm led to understand, setting off in a day or so to rejoin him.'' Daniels sounded disconsolate. "Under escort by the military, I was told. The subaltern's command at Bathurst is to be relieved, and Mrs. Tempest will travel with the relief party.''

"It need not be very long before we follow her, Henry,'' Robert pointed out. "Now that this elusive fellow Oxley is back from Moreton Bay, we should be able to obtain the required authority for our land grants without further delay.''

"I fear you are being unduly optimistic,'' Daniels countered glumly. "Nothing in this benighted place is done without delay. But''—he eyed his companion a trifle warily—"you invited my assistance, did you not? In what way can I assist you?''

Robert smiled at him. Daniels, he told himself, was not blessed with a great deal of intelligence, but he was proving to be a loyal and useful friend. "It is very simple, Henry my dear fellow. Van Buren has agreed to accommodate our livestock on the property at Parramatta, as you know, until we can transfer ourselves to Bathurst. Suggest, when we meet him, that you and he go there when the stock is moved . . . make any excuse you can devise. Say that you are interested in the vineyard at Portland Place and the wine making. Or tell him you want to buy a horse from him—anything you like.''

"That does not sound as if it would be beyond my capabilities, certainly,'' Daniels conceded. "I take it that what you want is for me to keep the fellow at Parramatta for as long as I can, so as to leave you a clear field to ingratiate yourself with his wife?''

Robert's smile widened. "You have it in a nutshell, Henry. Time is what I want—enough time to lay siege to her . . . although, as I indicated, I don't anticipate too much resistance.''

"Suppose the Dutchman is awkward and does not wish to leave Sydney Town?" Daniels said doubtfully. "If I had a wife like Lucy Van Buren, I would not leave her unguarded, least of all with a rogue of your caliber in the offing!''

Robert sighed. He explained patiently, "Henry, you'll have no trouble with Van Buren, I promise you. He needs us, and he needs me, in particular. He seeks the promise of a partnership in my Macquarie River grant, and I've hinted that I'm prepared to consider giving him one. He would also jump at the chance to put me in command of one of his chartered trading vessels, because, as he has told me frequently, the masters he has are incompetent and untrustworthy. As I mentioned just now, we have common interests, but I don't intend to let him suspect that one of these is his lady wife.''

"Just so long as you don't, Rob—''

"Set your mind at rest, my dear Henry. I'll tread carefully.'' And he would, Robert thought, although it was becoming increasingly difficult. Lucy Van Buren stirred his blood as few women ever had, and her response to the tentative advances he had made—of necessity restrained, in her husband's presence—had threatened, at times, to tempt him to throw caution to the wind. Since the initial meeting at the Dawsons', he and Henry had been frequent visitors to the Van Burens' Bridge Street house, invited to luncheon and dinner and lavishly entertained, sometimes on their own and sometimes with other guests, whose acquaintance, Lucy Van Buren had insisted charmingly, would be useful to them in the future.

The only fly in the ointment was Alice Fairweather. . . . Robert's fists clenched and unclenched nervously. He had recommended her to Van Buren, as maid to his wife, purely on impulse, in order to avoid having to carry out the promise he had made her, in a weak moment, before the *Mary Anne* reached Port Jackson. The impulse was one he now deeply regretted; if the miserable girl talked, she could do irreparable harm to his courtship of her mistress, and he had no means of knowing whether or not she would talk.

Certainly, as yet, she had not, judging by Lucy's attitude toward him, but it might be prudent to ensure her silence. He could say that she was dishonest—after all, she had been sentenced for theft—and attempt to persuade Lucy to cancel her assignment, and . . . yes, of course! There was a woman's factory, at or near Parramatta, to which recalcitrant female convicts were sent—if Lucy had the girl sent there, it would not matter if she talked her head off, for no one would pay her any heed.

Robert brightened and heard Henry Daniels say, "Look, there's Major Van Buren, punctual to the minute. I'll do my best to talk him into taking me with him to Portland Place, Rob. But I can't guarantee how long I'll be able to keep him there." He added, with feeling, "You would have been wiser to stick to that little convict lass from the *Mary Anne*, truly you would. Damme, you're asking for trouble, Rob—and Van Buren's the type to give you trouble, make no mistake on that score!"

"He won't," Robert asserted defiantly. But, for all that, he experienced some misgivings as he studied the man who came smiling to meet them. Josef Van Buren cut a gross figure, despite his height; his face was red and fleshy, and he moved ponderously, but he was as powerful as an ox, and his dark eyes held an oddly malicious gleam, which the smile did not dispel. He would, as Henry had said, make a dangerous enemy. . . . Bracing himself, Robert went to meet him, his hand outheld.

"I give you good day, sir. And I trust—"

Van Buren brushed the greeting aside. He said forcefully, "I demanded a sight of the survey maps of the Macquarie River area, Willoughby—Meehan showed them to me, before his superior came in. The whole area has been surveyed, the grants already made noted and numbered—Mr. Wentworth's, Captain Cox's, Mr. Broome's, and Mr.

Tempest's are the largest. But even the fifty acres given to the emancipists are shown on the maps. Willoughby, you should tax Surveyor Oxley with this—he is being dilatory, even deliberately obstructive! There is no reason for delay.''

Robert hid his surprise. "All right," he said. "I'll tell him so. Are you coming with us?''

Van Buren hesitated and then shook his head. "No, it may be best if you tackle him alone. I fear I may lose my temper. But come to my house when you have completed your business and tell me what has happened.''

He strode off, shoulders hunched, and Robert exchanged a quizzical glance with Daniels before leading the way into the surveyor general's office. To his surprise, John Oxley proved friendly and very cooperative. He looked pale and ill, but whatever pain he was enduring did not impair his efficiency, and he dealt briskly with Robert's questions and requests.

There were grants of up to twenty-five hundred acres available, he explained, and he indicated their widespread location on his map. New settlers were required to supply proof of the capital sum each had to invest, a cargo manifest detailing the livestock purchased on passage, and authority from the Colonial Office.

"You and Mr. Daniels have lodged the necessary documents with my deputy, so all that remains is for you to select, from the available uncultivated land, which it is your wish to occupy. Under new regulations imposed by the Colonial Secretary, Lord Bathurst, you will be required to maintain one convict laborer for each hundred acres of your grant and to agree to spend on development of the land one quarter of its value. After seven years a quitrent of five percent will have to be paid yearly, and the grant may be canceled, should you fail, after seven years, to bring it into satisfactory production. . . .'' He talked on, going into painstaking detail and offering maps for perusal, illustrated by his own descriptions of the type of country and the possibilities for development in each area.

"If you intend to grow wheat, land in the vicinity of

Frederick's Valley is fertile and well watered—Mr. William Wentworth owns a large property in that locality and at Summerhill Creek, much of it leased to smallholders. But if, as I suppose, you aim to become graziers, since you have brought sheep and cattle with you, then—'' His slim forefinger jabbed at the map in front of him. "The Bathurst and O'Connell plains are already fairly heavily settled, mainly by the emancipist farmers whom the late Governor established there on small, fifty-acre grants. Mr. Tempest farms two thousand acres on the Macquarie River, in partnership with Mr. Justin Broome. He calls the property Pengallon, and most of it is pastoral land. And Captain Cox's original holding was—''

Daniels, losing patience, interrupted him. "Mr. Oxley, is there land available in the vicinity of Mr. Tempest's?''

"Yes," the surveyor general admitted. "Not in the immediate vicinity, but—'' He consulted his map, doing a rapid calculation. "Twelve miles north of his boundary."

"On the Macquarie River?" Robert put in.

"That is so, yes. The land there is valued at five shillings an acre—it is virgin land, uncleared, but it provides good grazing. It has been offered for sale, according to the latest Colonial Office instruction, at a quitrent of one and a half percent, but—''

"But there were no takers?" Robert suggested shrewdly.

"A gentleman named Van Buren expressed some interest," Oxley answered. "His Excellency, however, was unwilling to authorize the purchase." He shrugged. "I have had my troubles with Van Buren. But if you two gentlemen are considering land in the Macquarie River area, I fancy it can be arranged for you to claim your grants there as soon as the necessary paperwork can be completed. Mr. Tempest is, I presume, known to you—a friend, perhaps? Like you and me, he served in the Royal Navy before settling here.''

Robert tensed. Oxley, he had ascertained, had retired from the Royal Navy in 1809 and would therefore have no knowledge of his court-martial and dismissal from the service, but Tempest was much younger and might well know of the ignominious end to his naval career. . . . The devil take Henry Daniels for his insistence that they take land near—what did Tempest call his property? Pengallon. He glared at his friend, warning him to remain silent, and said offhandedly, "I've never met Tempest. He wasn't in the fleet action off Algiers under Lord Exmouth, was he? That was my last experience of active service—I was a supernumerary lieutenant in the *Queen Charlotte,* which bore His Lordship's flag."

His adroit change of subject succeeded. A gleam lit Oxley's dark eyes. "And mine was under the gallant Duncan at Camperdown. I mind well the speech that the admiral made to us before the battle. 'The duty I am charged with,' he told us, 'is to keep the Texel closed, and I intend to do that—with ships or without them.' It was just after the Nore mutiny, you may recall, and his command consisted then of only the *Venerable* and the frigate *Adamant.* 'This ship shall fight till she sinks,' he said to us on board *Venerable,* and he meant it, too! I was a mid at the time, and I'd just joined the ship. . . ." He launched into a vivid description of the battle, and Robert listened, his patience wearing thin.

When Oxley came at last to the end of his recital, Henry Daniels said testily, "About our land grants, Mr. Oxley—I take it we are at liberty to inspect the area before we commit ourselves?"

"Certainly, if you wish." Oxley eyed him with disfavor. "But a buyer for this particular grant might well come forward while you are making up your mind. And in view of Major Van Buren's interest, I fancy the land is good— perhaps even undervalued. Besides, there's the question of your stock and, of course, the convicts to be assigned to you. You will want to move your stock as soon as possible, will you not?"

Robert nodded emphatically. "Yes, that's so, sir. We'll take the grant. Perhaps you would be so good as to have—

er—the necessary paperwork completed expeditiously. We've been held up long enough.''

"The deeds will be ready for your signatures in—" Oxley frowned. "Damme, I'm short of staff, you know. But let us say within a week. Will that suit you, gentlemen?''

It would take more than a week to arrange to move the stock, Robert thought, and at least that long to obtain horses and an ox wagon for the journey to Bathurst . . . and there was Lucy Van Buren to be considered. Henry Daniels could go to Portland Place, with some of the convicts—he would have a valid excuse for doing so now, and even a plausible reason for inviting Van Buren to accompany him.

He rose, bestowing on the surveyor general his most disarming smile. "Indeed, Mr. Oxley, I thank you. But do not overwork your clerks. Within the next two or three weeks will suit us admirably. When I used the word 'expeditiously' I had not taken into consideration the time it will take to put all our arrangements in hand, of course. And I—'' He intercepted an alarmed glance from Daniels and laid a precautionary hand on his friend's arm, continuing to smile. "I thank you again, sir, for your cooperation, which we greatly appreciate. It is on the advice of Mr. John Macarthur that we decided to take our grants in the Macquarie River area, and I feel sure that his is very sound advice.''

"I don't doubt that, Mr. Willoughby,'' Oxley answered, with unexpected sourness. "Mr. Macarthur and his family now own over twenty thousand acres of prime land in this colony. Lord Bathurst has just authorized a further grant to him of ten thousand seven hundred acres at Cawdor, at an annual quitrent of only one hundred and forty-two pounds!'' He grunted his disgust. "For myself, Mr. Willoughby, I have found it necessary to drop the gentleman's acquaintance, but you, of course, are free to seek advice and friendship wherever you find it most expedient. I give you good day, gentlemen.''

Outside the survey office, Henry Daniels laughed with

more than a hint of malice. "For once, Rob, you carried your boasting a mite too far! Were you not aware that Oxley fell out with John Macarthur and that they hate each other's guts?"

"No," Robert admitted sullenly. "I was not, plague take them! For what reason did they fall out?"

"Over some merino sheep, I believe. Oxley sold crossbreds as pure merinos to a new settler, and Macarthur took him to task for it. They haven't spoken to each other since, I was told. Apart from that—" Daniels shrugged. "Oxley and his assistants from the survey office have been responsible for discovering and exploring most of the new lands beyond Bathurst and for opening them up for settlement. His salary is fifteen shillings a day, he doesn't take bribes, and he owns less than a tenth of the acreage granted to Macarthur! You may imagine how it riles him when Macarthur invokes his interest in high places and, without stirring a foot, persuades Lord Bathurst to go over the Governor's and the surveyors' heads and grant him another ten thousand acres of the best grazing land in the whole colony."

He could imagine Oxley's wrath, Robert thought, and the man's bitter sense of injustice.

"You are well informed, Henry," he conceded less grudgingly. "I was not aware of all that."

"I keep my ear to the ground, Rob," Daniels said. "It pays in this place, where everyone seems to be feuding with everyone else. I confess it will be a pleasant change to live in isolation by the Macquarie River—I'm even looking forward to it!"

"Then let us bestir ourselves," Robert suggested. He lengthened his stride. "We must report our successful dealings to Major Van Buren."

Henry Daniels hurried to keep pace with him.

"You're not still expecting me to go to Parramatta with him, are you?" he asked apprehensively. "For God's sake, Rob—there's not time! And if we are to take him into partnership, it would be the height of folly to involve yourself with his wife. I tell you, Van Buren is a dangerous fellow, and—''

Robert rounded on him irritably. "Of course I am expecting you to go with him to Parramatta—and to keep him there until we're ready to start for Bathurst in about three weeks' time. There will be plenty for you both to do. Let Van Buren supply horses and stores and the wagon— that will keep him occupied. I'll deal with the paperwork here and select the convicts we'll take with us. We shall need a good overseer, too—but you can leave that to me."

"Well, if you insist," Daniels said weakly. "But I wish you'd leave Van Buren's wife alone. For the Lord's sweet sake, Rob, there are plenty of women here for you to amuse yourself with! Sydney Town may be lacking in many things, but it has no lack of women."

"I am not merely seeking amusement," Robert assured him loftily. "And I swear, Henry, that there is only one woman in this town—damme, in this whole colony—to whom I am drawn! And she draws me irresistibly."

His own ardor surprised him a little, but what he said was, he recognized, no more than the truth, and as they strode briskly down Bridge Street together, he felt his pulse quicken at the prospect of seeing and talking to Lucy Van Buren again. Even with her arrogant oaf of a husband present, the prospect was still one that excited him, for all the risks it might entail.

He had known many women in his life, Robert reflected, but they had almost all been of the same type. From his early days in the navy there had been the seaport whores, who came on board when fighting ships were provisioning or refitting and shore leave for their companies was seldom if ever granted. Brief stays in port had permitted only brief interludes with women whose names he seldom troubled to ask and whose faces he swiftly forgot.

Ashore it had been much the same; the only women of his own class whom he had met had been the wives or daughters of brother officers, and as such they were forbidden to him, with very few exceptions. One exception had

been Leonard Neville's beautiful, promiscuous wife. . . .
Robert could still feel the anger rise within him as he
recalled the disastrous consequences of that unhappy affair.

Leonard Neville had been his captain, a dull, humorless,
middle-aged man of little talent, who owed his rank to an
uncle on the Board of Admiralty and who, when he
learned of his wife's infidelity, had been willing to perjure
himself in order to exact revenge. And he had done so. . . .
Robert's face fairly burned, remembering. Neville had
brought him before a court-martial on what, as he had told
his father, were trumped-up charges. The court had believed them and sentenced him to be dismissed from the
service . . . and Dora Neville had gone back to her husband without uttering a word of sympathy or apology to
the lover whose career—no, plague take it, whose life—
she had ruined.

And then there had been Becky—Becky and her infernal
rogue of a father, who between them had completed his
ruin. If he were prudent, he would regard the consequences of both unfortunate involvements as a warning
and steer clear of Lucy Van Buren, as Henry Daniels had
advised, but . . . oh, the devil! He had never been a
prudent man, and this was a new country, a new life,
perhaps even a test of his manhood. He turned to flash a
challenging smile at his companion, deriding his caution.
Poor old Henry's only crime was the fact that he had been
compelled to flee from his creditors, but out here he would
be tolerably well off, since his father had promised him a
regular remittance of generous proportions so long as he
remained in the colony.

Unlike the damned Lord High Admiral, his own father,
Robert thought resentfully, who had cut him off with a
miserable two thousand pounds, and who intended to leave
his very considerable fortune to the little milksop Jamie.
Jamie, who had not the guts to say boo to a goose, damn
his eyes, would not know how to make the most of his
inheritance. Their sister Emily, for all she was a female,
would have put it to better use than Jamie. Indeed, she

. . . They reached the front door of the Van Burens' imposing residence, and Daniels stepped forward to beat a hesitant tattoo on the highly polished brass knocker.

It was answered promptly by the dark-skinned Javanese manservant, Saleh, who ushered them into the withdrawing room, where Van Buren, a half-empty glass in his hand, rose ponderously to greet them.

"Well," he demanded, motioning Saleh to serve them, "did you succeed in making Oxley bestir himself?"

"That we did," Robert asserted. "We've taken the grant on that land on the Macquarie River that you were interested in purchasing at one time, but—"

"But which the Governor refused to allow me to purchase," the Dutchman put in, with asperity. He spread his plump, freckled hands. "However, as no doubt you will have heard, *this* Governor—the almighty Sir Thomas Brisbane—is to be recalled. Perhaps his successor will harbor fewer prejudices against those of my nationality."

Robert shrugged indifferently. He had not yet met Sir Thomas Brisbane in person, although both he and Henry Daniels had signed the Government House visitors' book and left the obligatory cards. The Brisbanes, it seemed, spent more time in Parramatta than they did in Sydney and were not renowned for their hospitality.

"The new Governor is also a major general, sir," Daniels supplied. "He served under Sir John Moore on the retreat to Corunna, and they say he's something of a martinet. I take leave to doubt whether you are likely to find him more—ah—more amenable than the present Governor."

Josef Van Buren stared morosely into the liquor in his glass. "Then a partnership with you would seem to be the best course I can follow—if you are willing?" He looked up to meet Robert's gaze, and once again his dark, narrowed eyes held an oddly malicious gleam. "*Are* you?"

"Yes," Robert assented. "Provided the terms are acceptable, sir."

"We will work out suitable terms after luncheon," the

Dutchman promised. "In the meantime, my young friends—fill your glasses, and we will drink to our future association. And you can tell me precisely what terms *you* were able to negotiate with Mr. Oxley."

During the next hour, to Robert's ill-concealed annoyance, he kept them talking, demanding to know the smallest detail of their interview with the surveyor general. All the while he drank steadily, and his questions became more searching. Of his wife there was neither sign nor mention, but Henry Daniels did, at least, contrive to extract from him the promise that they would go to Portland Place the following day in order to arrange for transport and the moving of the stock.

"We will ride up to Bathurst with half a dozen of your assigned convicts," Van Buren told them decisively, "as soon as the necessary deeds are signed and sealed. I shall be adding to the stock, of course, and I have a reliable man at Portland Place who can act as overseer and take charge of the drovers. The country around Emu Ford is still in a state of devastation after the recent fires, and the road over the mountains is difficult . . . and plagued by the infernal rogues they call bushrangers. We shall be armed, of course, and on horseback, but it will take three or four weeks to drive the sheep as far as Bathurst, if they are to arrive in good condition . . . and they will require an armed escort."

Once more he went into meticulous detail, and Robert's impatience grew. Van Buren, it was evident, intended to make himself the senior partner in their joint enterprise, but Robert stifled the impulse to raise objections, buoyed up by the thought that by next day the Dutchman would be fifteen miles away on the Portland Place farm. And woe betide Henry Daniels if he failed to keep the fellow there until the time came to start for Bathurst and the Macquarie River!

"Convict labor is a mixed blessing," Van Buren declared. "It is free, admittedly—the men get their keep but no wages. Some work well, and some are idle layabouts. You will need to choose your men carefully, Willoughby, for the responsibility will be yours, if Daniels and I are at Portland Place. I shall undertake the horse buying and—"

Reminded suddenly of Alice Fairweather, Robert cut him short. "Major Van Buren," he exclaimed, with exaggerated contrition, "I have a most abject apology to offer you! The girl I recommended to you as lady's maid to your wife—Fairweather is her name, if I remember aright."

Van Buren eyed him from beneath scowling brows. "What of her? My wife is satisfied with her, as far as I know. She works well and is an expert seamstress."

"She is also, I regret to have to tell you, a persistent thief and a female of loose moral character," Robert insisted. "These facts have only come to my notice recently—the mate of the *Mary Anne* warned me that I had made a grave mistake in advising you to employ her." He saw Daniels looking at him in openmouthed astonishment, and warned him, with a gesture, to hold his tongue. But Van Buren, too, seemed surprised, and he added hastily, "Of course, if the girl is giving Mrs. Van Buren satisfaction, I'll say no more. But I felt I should pass on the mate's revelations, since it was I who—in good faith, I assure you, sir—gave her a recommendation. Indeed, I—"

At that moment, Lucy Van Buren entered the room. She looked so beautiful, in a shimmering jade-green taffeta gown, her dark hair piled high about her head and a warm smile on her lips, that momentarily she took Robert's breath away. Her smile was directed at him; she held out her hand to him in welcome, and the mere touch of her fingers on his palm seemed to burn through him, setting his blood on fire.

Sweet God in heaven, he thought, no woman that he had ever known could hold a candle to this lovely, seductive creature, with her pale, soft skin and shining, deep-set dark eyes! Desire for her throbbed with every pulse of his blood, blinding him to caution, and he was hard put to it not to betray himself as he read the message in her eyes.

She was not indifferent to him, he sensed; the desire was there, as strong and compelling as his own. . . .

But when she freed her hand from his clasp, her smile faded and she spoke with unruffled calm.

"Were you talking of my maid, Mr. Willoughby? What did the mate of the *Mary Anne* reveal concerning the girl?"

Robert recovered his composure. He repeated the accusations he had made earlier, and this time Henry Daniels supported them, adding, with a malicious grin in Robert's direction, his belief that Alice Fairweather had been a favorite of the ship's master.

Lucy Van Buren merely shrugged. "Most of the females they send out here are of easy virtue—one endeavors, whenever possible, to reform them. But if Fairweather is a thief, that is another matter. She will have to be sent to the Female Factory, I suppose. Will you see to it, Jos?"

"I leave for Portland Place in the morning," her husband objected, "with Henry Daniels. We have great plans—a partnership in prospect, when he and Willoughby take up their land grants on the Macquarie River, my dear. We are planning—"

Lucy Van Buren put in coolly, "Luncheon is ready—we can talk of the matter as we eat, can we not? Needless to tell you, though, I am delighted." She laid a small, beautifully manicured hand on Robert's arm, and again, as he looked down at her, he read the message in her eyes.

"Is it necessary for you also to go to Portland Place, Mr. Willoughby?" she asked as they walked together to the dining room.

Robert shook his head, aware that his whole body was tense, and his heart thudded as he heard her add, in a soft whisper, "Then I hope that you will dine here tomorrow evening. I don't like to eat alone."

"It will be my pleasure, Mrs. Van Buren," he managed hoarsely. "My—my very great pleasure."

"And mine, Mr. Willoughby." She took her place at

the long, elegantly furnished table and waved him to a seat at her side.

Van Buren shambled in after them, his brandy glass still in his hand. His voice more than a little slurred, he extolled the merits of a horse he had for sale, as Henry Daniels listened resignedly. Catching Robert's eye, Daniels jingled the coins in his pocket in warning.

"It is an Arab, you know, Daniels—a stallion—one of those the Governor imported," Van Buren persisted. "Worth its weight in gold here and better by far than any of Mr. Macarthur's, I can promise you."

Before Daniels could voice the expected refusal, Robert said recklessly, "We'll buy the animal, sir—subject to Henry's inspection and approval, of course."

"But of course." The Dutchman beamed at him and settled back in his chair as his Javanese manservant hastened, unbidden, to refill his glass.

CHAPTER XIII

Lucy Van Buren lay in her ornate four-poster bed and looked down indulgently at the sleeping face of her new lover. Robert Willoughby lay with his dark head resting on her breast, his thick hair ruffled and one muscular brown arm clasping her to him, as if he feared that she might escape him while he slept.

But there was no fear of that, Lucy thought. His love-making had been the reverse of gentle, it was true, but she had gloried in his passionate hunger for her and in the pulsating thrill of their coupling and its climax. His body was lean and hard, in sharp contrast to her husband's corpulent, flaccid frame, and the demands he had made were so different from Jos's drunken fumbling. She had responded to even the most outrageous of those demands, giving herself to him with almost wanton abandon, her mind and body aflame until, exhausted and satiated, they had both lain still and slept.

She had wakened first, while he still stretched in drowsy oblivion at her side, his lips parted in a lingering smile, and Lucy knew that she would not have the heart to rouse him and send him away from her bed, although caution required that he must be gone before the servants wakened and went about their duties. Saleh was always the first, but he was discreet; a small bribe would ensure his silence, she was confident. But the convict girl, Alice Fairweather, was an unknown quantity . . . and she was due to bring tea to the bedroom at eight o'clock.

Glancing at the shuttered window, Lucy realized that the sun had not yet risen and let herself relax. The girl was to be sent to the Female Factory, she remembered—Robert had warned Jos, in no uncertain terms, that she was dishonest and not to be trusted. It was a pity, for she was an excellent needlewoman, punctilious in the performance of her duties, and on good terms with the Javanese servants, now that she had settled down. Saleh had made no complaint against her, and as to her morals . . . Lucy's lips tightened. Leah's were infinitely more reprehensible, and . . . Her slight movement wakened Robert; he stirred sleepily and then opened his eyes.

"My love, you are here! I had feared that I might waken and find that last night was a dream. Oh, Lucy, you are so beautiful, I—I can find no words to tell you how happy you have made me!"

He turned over onto his back and reached for her, his slim fingers toying with her breasts as he drew her down beside him. She made to kiss him gently, teasingly; but instantly his mouth found hers, and his arms imprisoned her, his tongue forcing her lips apart.

"I wanted you, you know," he whispered, lifting his head to look down at her, "from the first moment I set eyes on you at that dinner party at the Dawsons'. It's a wonder I did not betray myself to you then."

"You did," Lucy told him, laughing. "Dear Rob, I knew . . . and I wanted you, too."

His deep-throated laughter echoed hers and then abruptly faded. "But you were married to the unspeakable Dutchman! Why, in God's name, did you wed him, sweet? He is uncouth—a gross, unpleasant fellow, unworthy to enjoy your loveliness. Why did you tie yourself to him?"

"It is a long story, Rob," Lucy evaded. "And he was not always uncouth."

"But he is old," Robert protested. "And you are young. Was it his money that made you choose him?"

"No," she denied. "I was friendless and alone. I was the only survivor of a shipwreck. They took me to Coupang, on the Dutch island of Timor. . . ." She told him the story of the *Kelso*'s last, ill-fated voyage, a sob in her voice, and Robert took her into his arms. He kissed her again, with swiftly mounting passion, his hands continuing to caress her, moving from breasts to thighs and setting her whole body throbbing with desire.

"Do I please you?" he demanded roughly. "More than that old man ever did? Do I, Lucy?"

"God in heaven, of course you do! How can you ask such a question, when you know the answer? Take me, Rob—I belong to you!" She clung to him, unable to curb the longing he roused in her, but he held her off, a hand beneath her chin, his eyes boring into hers.

"For how long will you belong to me? Lucy, my love, this cannot end after a few stolen hours," he warned her gravely. "I'll not give you back to the Dutchman!"

"He never touches me now, Rob—I swear he does not. It has been a long time—" Lucy looked up at him with swimming eyes, suddenly afraid that she might lose him. "A long time since any man touched me. I need you, Rob—dear God, I need you!"

He yielded to her then, unable to control his own desire, and she cried out in mingled pain and ecstasy, shaken to the depths of her being by the emotion his lovemaking had aroused in her. Even in the first blissful months of their marriage, Jos had never stirred her so, and as for Luke Cahill . . . Lucy shivered, hiding her burning face against Robert's naked shoulder as the tears came and she found herself powerless to stop them.

Robert, too, was shaken. "I fear," he confessed, as she lay limply in his arms, "Lucy my dearest love, I fear that I'll never be able to let you go. Whatever the consequences, whatever your husband does should he find out."

"He will not find out," Lucy whispered. She mopped at her brimming eyes. "It has long been his wish to own land, to farm, Rob, and the Governor's ban has made him the more determined. He could be induced to stay on the

Macquarie River grant—you will have to see to it that he does.''

Robert's eyes were narrowed and pensive as they met her gaze. "It's certainly not *my* intention to stay there, Lucy—particularly if he elects to do so. I shall come back to Sydney at the first possible moment . . . to Sydney and to you, my love!''

"It will not be easy for us even then," Lucy pointed out uneasily. "Sydney is full of clacking tongues—there are few liaisons here that remain secret for long, you know. It is a veritable hotbed of gossip.''

"And there are your servants," Robert reminded her. "There is that girl—the convict girl whom I mistakenly recommended to you.''

"My servants will not talk—they speak little English. And I shall send the girl to Parramatta, to the Female Factory," Lucy assured him.

"Soon," he urged. "Devil take it, Lucy, she will know that I stayed here with you tonight! And she's not to be trusted.''

His urgency puzzled her a little, but she inclined her head in acquiescence. "As soon as it can be arranged, Rob dear." Lucy glanced again at the window; time was passing all too swiftly, but there were no sounds of movement from below, and as yet no shafts of sunlight had come to penetrate the slats of the window shutters. They would have a little longer. . . . She leaned back against him, lifting her lips to his, and he kissed her with unexpected tenderness.

"I've fallen in love with you," he told her softly. "I'd give my soul to wed you, if only you were free! You are the only woman in the world I've ever wanted to wed, Lucy—and that's the truth; I give you my word.''

She smiled up at him. "Tell me about yourself, Rob," she invited, suddenly curious. "I know so little about you, save that you served in the Royal Navy and that your father is an admiral.''

Robert shrugged. "There's not much to tell you, sweet.

My father is Admiral Sir Francis Willoughby, who was honored with a baronetcy when he retired.''

"A baronetcy—which you will inherit?"

"In the fullness of time, yes. I'm the eldest son."

Lucy's interest was kindled. "Did your father serve under Admiral Nelson? Mine was with him at Copenhagen and was badly wounded in the battle. So badly that he was invalided, and . . . he died on the voyage out here."

Robert's mouth tightened. "Papa went to the West Indies with Hood, and he stayed there, amassing vast sums in prize money. I was with him for over three years as a volunteer, when he commanded the old *Monarch* in the Mediterranean—officially designated a captain's servant, which in my case was literally true. My share of the squadron's prizes amounted to exactly six guineas!"

"But you are the eldest son . . . you are his heir, are you not? Won't it all come to you?"

"Well, I . . ." Robert's hesitation was lengthy and a trifle puzzling, and Lucy was about to repeat her question when he answered it in a voice that was fraught with bitterness. "Yes, I'm the eldest son, and I'm heir to his title. But I incurred his displeasure—he did not want me to quit the service. He cut me off with a pittance and made my young brother his heir. Jamie is still in the navy—he was a cadet at the Naval College when I left England, and I presume he's now at sea as midshipman. He's a nice enough lad, but—" He swore under his breath and then apologized. "That was the reason why I came out here, Lucy. I—damn it, I could hardly stay in England in those circumstances, could I?"

"No, I suppose not." Sensing that he had not told her the whole story, Lucy was about to beg him to tell her more, but once again he forestalled her question.

"My father took me to sea with him when I was eleven years old—he never asked me what I wanted to do, and he took me to spite my poor mother. She, God rest her sweet soul, fell gravely ill while we were with Nelson's squadron on the wild-goose chase to the Caribbean after Villeneuve.

The old *Monarch* was barely seaworthy, so she was left behind when Nelson went back to England and finally caught up with Villeneuve at Trafalgar. I did not see my mother again until three years later, although my father received dozens of letters from her, pleading with him to send me back. She was virtually an invalid then, and she died in childbirth eight years ago, believing I'd deserted her.''

"Were you unhappy in the navy?" Lucy asked.

"Oh, no, not all the time. It was not so bad when I was commissioned and appointed to a ship my father didn't command. But he used his influence and saw to it that I never spent more than a few weeks at a time in England. I was four years on the East Indies station, when my mother needed me most . . . and that was *his* doing. I hated my father, Lucy." Robert expelled his breath in a deep, angry sigh. "And he always hated me."

"Because of your mother, Rob?"

"Perhaps. I never came up to his standards, though. But I was in the fleet action at Algiers, under Lord Exmouth, as fifth of the *Queen Charlotte*, and was commended—that was the only time he ever praised me. The only time I ever did what he expected of me, damn his eyes! But then he had me sent to the *Columbia* frigate, commanded by a swine named Neville, who was one of his protégés. Neville hated my guts, and . . ." Robert broke off, two spots of angry color burning in his cheeks.

Lucy took one of his hands, caressing it gently and holding it against her lips. "Poor Rob," she said, with genuine pity. He lapsed into a moody silence, and she asked, hoping to distract him, "Have you others in your family, apart from—what did you call your brother? Jamie?"

"James Saumarez Willoughby," Robert told her derisively. "After Admiral Sir James Saumarez. I, unhappily, was christened Robert Horatio after the incomparable Lord Nelson, under whom my father served in the *Agamemnon* in 'ninety-four." He repeated his sigh. "I have a sister named Emily, who is ten years younger than I and who keeps house for my father. Emily—Emmy—has brought up our two younger sisters, who are children of eight and nine—Charlotte and Biddy. Emmy's a sweet girl, very pretty. She could have married half a dozen times, but my father made sure that she did not. He's retired and a widower, so she is indispensable to him. When I left home, she was attempting to carry on a clandestine courtship with a local physician. Needless to tell you, my father forbade him the house, but I think they were meeting in secret.''

He raised himself on one elbow and eyed her quizzically. "An odd family, mine, is it not? I doubt you can match it."

She could, Lucy thought wryly. Her own father had come close to ruining her life. He had gambled away their home and every penny he possessed and had shot himself on the passage to Sydney, leaving Abigail and her as wards of the unscrupulous Caleb Boskenna. But she smiled and shook her head. Few people in Sydney now remembered her unhappy story, and for years she had schooled herself not to talk of it—and Abigail, happy and serene in her marriage to Timothy Dawson, had probably long since erased the memory of those early days from her mind.

"Your brother, Rick Tempest," Robert began, "was he not—" Lucy waved him to silence, her quick ears catching the sound of footsteps on the landing outside. They were light, pattering footsteps, and she guessed that Claus had come in from the servants' quarters to perform his early morning chores. He would collect glasses and dishes from the night before and take them to the kitchen to wash, a task that would not take him long. But it was time for Rob to go, for the whole household would shortly be astir; and there was the convict girl, Alice Fairweather, who must be sent to the Female Factory lest she talk out of turn.

The pattering footsteps faded, and Lucy reached for her robe. "Rob my dear," she warned him regretfully, "the time has come, alas . . . but I shall be waiting for you this evening.''

Robert did not argue. He dressed quickly and, following her directions, left the house through a side door leading into the garden.

Saleh watched from behind the concealing slats of the kitchen shutters and waited until his mistress's visitor was out of sight before drawing them back to admit the pale early morning sunlight. His dark face was inscrutable, and he said nothing when Alice—whose sleeping quarters were in the attic—came down to make preparations for the ritual service of tea. But then Claus joined them, with his tray of used cups and glasses and, ignoring Saleh's warning headshake, announced innocently that a hat and cloak had been left on the hall stand.

"They belong to the gentleman who came last night for dinner with *mevrouw*," he said in Dutch, addressing Saleh. "*Mijnheer* Willoughby. He has forgotten them." Alice's head turned toward him, startled by the name, and Claus translated his announcement into English. "The one who is known to you from the ship."

Robert Willoughby, Alice thought. Her hand shook a little as she poured boiling water from the great iron kettle onto the tea leaves in Mrs. Van Buren's delicate china teapot. Since being assigned to the Van Buren household, she had feared that he might make a belated claim on her, and she had kept out of sight, anxious to avoid him, whenever he and Henry Daniels had called at the house. Her duties did not include waiting at table, and the previous evening, after she had assisted Mrs. Van Buren to dress for dinner, she had been dismissed with instructions to work at her sewing. At the time, she had thought nothing of it, but . . . She caught her breath, as understanding dawned.

Robert Willoughby had come alone; Major Van Buren had left earlier for the property at Portland Place with Henry Daniels, and they had taken Leah with them. . . .

She looked up to meet Saleh's dark, sardonic gaze, momentarily forgetful of her task.

"What—" she began, and then had to stifle a cry of pain as water from the heavy kettle spilled over onto her hand.

"You are clumsy this morning, Alice," Saleh reproved her. But he smiled, robbing his words of any harshness, and took the kettle from her. "I will take *Mevrouw* Van Buren's tea to her, since you have scalded your hand, and Claus will fetch the cook's salve for you." He added softly, as the boy ran to do his bidding, "You need no longer fear that *Mijnheer* Willoughby will make a claim on you, little one. That has been your fear, has it not, since he has been coming so frequently to this house?"

"Yes. Yes, it has," Alice admitted. "But I don't know how you guessed."

"A good servant," Saleh told her gravely, "sees all and says little—that is a lesson you must learn. It is, perhaps, easier for me, since those I serve do not know that I speak your English language." His expression relaxed, and he lowered his voice. "I have just seen *Mijnheer* Willoughby make his departure through the garden—that is why his hat and cloak were forgotten. But if my lady should ask me, I shall tell her that I saw nothing, and you also, if you are wise, will keep a still tongue in your head regarding *mijnheer*. Whatever he may have been to you on your voyage here, you understand?"

Shamed color flooded Alice's cheeks. "Yes," she assured him humbly. "I understand, Saleh. I—I am grateful for your advice."

He laid a comforting brown hand on her arm. "I, too, understand, little one. They plucked you from your home and put you on board the ship in chains, did they not? The manner in which your countrymen treat the women they send out here as felons is no secret. It is worse, I believe, than the manner in which our Dutch masters treat my people . . . and the poor *lip-laps* they father. They—" He broke off as Claus returned with the salve. Deftly setting his mistress's tea tray, he picked it up, adding a plate piled high with the sugary cakes she fancied. An oddly enigmatic smile played about his lips. "Take care of your future bride, little *lip-lap*," he advised the boy teasingly. "That is a nasty scald she has."

Left alone, Claus did as he had been bidden, applying the salve with a liberal hand. "Saleh is making fun," he complained. "But I am most serious. If no man has made you offer of marriage before I am sixteen, I will wed you. I make solemn promise to you, Alice."

Alice looked down at his bent head, feeling tears come to her eyes. "We have a few years to go until you are sixteen, Claus," she responded, with the gravity he clearly expected. "But I shall never forget the honor you have done me."

He beamed back at her, carefully replacing the lid on the jar of salve. "Does your hand feel better now? Does it make you less hurt?"

"Yes," she assured him. "It is much better, thank you. Indeed, it scarcely hurts at all."

"But you will have trouble when you do your sewing. If that is so, tell me please, and I help you. I am good at sewing, you know."

"Yes, I know you are. But perhaps Mrs. Van Buren will not be pleased if you help me. We must be careful."

"Of her?" Claus challenged scornfully. "I not respect *Mevrouw* Van Buren longer. She bad woman, not like you and my mother."

Startled, Alice stared at him. Saleh had supposed that Claus had not understood the significance of Robert Willoughby's abandoned hat and cloak, but—the boy's dark eyes held the same scorn as his voice, and he gave vent to a word in his own tongue that, although she did not understand its exact meaning, was by implication clear enough.

"You must not speak so, Claus," she reproached him, and added, recalling Saleh's sage advice, "It is best to keep a still tongue in your head."

"Oh, yes, I keep my tongue still, save when I forget. But I hear voices which come from *mevrouw*'s sleeping chamber—her voice and *Mijnheer* Willoughby's. And my father is not here. Alice, I—" The arrival of the Javanese cook and his sleepy-eyed scullion interrupted him, and Claus shrugged his thin shoulders and said no more as the cook started to make preparations for breakfast. As on every other morning since she had come to this house, Alice reflected, the routine was the same.

Mrs. Van Buren's breakfast would be taken up to her, in bed; Leah would come into the kitchen and wait, in silence, for the heavy meal their master took on waking; when that was served, she herself would carry a brass can of hot water to her mistress's room and aid her to dress and do her hair. But Major Van Buren was not here this morning, and neither was Leah, so that . . . Saleh came back, slamming the door of the kitchen behind him, and they all turned, in swift alarm, sensing trouble, for Saleh usually moved like a shadow, making no sound.

He spoke in his own tongue at first, spitting out the words in cold fury, and the eyes of all of them were suddenly turned on her. To her bewilderment, Alice read pity in them, and when Saleh came to put his arm about her shoulders, she knew that whatever tidings he had brought concerned her and were likely to be bad.

"What is it, Saleh?" she managed. "Have I—have I done wrong?"

"I do not know," Saleh answered. "It must be that you have. *Mevrouw* has ordered that I lock you in your room, and you are not to be permitted to leave it."

Alice was numb with dismay. Unable to think of any reason for her mistress's order, she could only stare at him, bereft of words, and Saleh went on flatly, "The carriage is ordered for midday. *Mevrouw* will go to see *Mijnheer* Goulburn. But first I am to deliver a note to him, which she will write when she rises." Claus started to protest, but Saleh shook a disapproving head at him, and the boy lapsed into stunned silence.

"You will go with the carriage," the Javanese instructed him. "And keep your ears open, to find out what you can. I think it is on Alice's account that *mevrouw* will call on the Major Goulburn, but I am not sure." He translated what he had said in response to the cook's urgent request and, amid a chorus of indignant voices, led Alice to the door. "I must do as she commands me," he told them apologetically. To Alice, he said with great gentleness, "Do not fear, little one. We will let no harm come to you—and I shall see to it that you do not starve."

Despite his assurances, Alice was gravely frightened. Food was brought to her, once by the cook and once by Claus, but neither was able to enlighten her as to the reason why she should be confined in the hot, airless attic for hour after hour without a word of explanation.

Mrs. Van Buren's call on Major Goulburn had been postponed until the afternoon, Claus told her, apparently at the major's request. Her note to him—which Saleh and one of the English grooms had managed to decipher—had been merely a request to see him on what she had described as "a matter of some urgency."

"I shall do as Saleh said and keep my ears open," the boy promised. "And I shall at once tell you what I find out."

But he returned having found out nothing, and once again Alice was left alone, her fears growing with each hour that passed, as she sought vainly to find a plausible reason for the treatment she was enduring. That it must have something to do with Robert Willoughby she did not doubt, yet even so she could think of no justification—unless, of course, he was anxious lest she speak of her previous relationship with him to her mistress. But merely to have her locked in her room would not ensure her silence, and in any event, it was Mrs. Van Buren who had ordered the seemingly pointless incarceration, not he.

Darkness fell, and Alice was nearing the limit of her endurance when the key grated in the lock of her door and Claus entered on tiptoe, a finger to his lips.

"He is here—*Mijnheer* Willoughby," he whispered. "And Saleh heard them talk of you, when he was serving them. Alice, *Mevrouw* Van Buren has arranged that you will be sent to the Female Factory at Parramatta. In the morning, a constable will come to take you there, and . . . it is a most terrible place!"

The boy was close to tears, his small face puckered in distress, his voice choked. "The women in the factory, they are all wicked and wanton—you cannot go there! I will not let them send you to such a place!"

Alice was numb with shock, scarcely able to take in what he was telling her. She had heard of the dreaded Female Factory—the women on board the *Mary Anne* had hinted of its horrors, their information gleaned from the seamen—but surely she had done nothing for which she deserved to be sent there?

Surely . . . She turned pleading eyes on Claus, her own voice as choked as his had been. "But why, Claus? *Why* am I to be sent to the factory? What have I done? I have been happy here, and—and I have worked hard to please Mrs. Van Buren."

"Saleh says that—oh, Alice, I know well it is not true! He says that *Mijnheer* Willoughby claims you are a thief. And also—" Claus hung his head, unable to meet her gaze. "That you are a loose woman and were beaten many times on the ship for bad behavior. *Mevrouw* Van Buren, she has told this to *Mijnheer* Goulburn of the government."

"It is not true, Claus," Alice defended bitterly. She drew a deep, shuddering breath, fighting to control her fear and disillusionment. That Robert Willoughby should make such accusations was monstrously unjust, since it had been he who had robbed her of her virgin innocence and sought to corrupt her, for no better reason than his own warped amusement. She remembered her first encounter with him, when the *Mary Anne*'s bullying, rapacious mate had brought her to his cabin, and shuddered again, recalling how both men had lied to her and how the promises they had made had been broken.

"Is it—Claus, is it tomorrow that I am to be sent away?" she asked wretchedly. "Tomorrow morning?"

Claus inclined his head. "So *mevrouw* has told *Mijnheer* Willoughby, in Saleh's hearing. But I will not let you go, Alice—I will not permit them to take you away."

"How can you prevent them?" Alice asked. "I am a convict—I have to go wherever they choose to send me. Convicts who try to escape are severely punished, Claus."

"Saleh is saying that *mevrouw*'s sister is a kind and good lady . . . Missus Dawson is her name, and she is living quite nearby." The little boy brightened. "Alice, I will go to Missus Dawson. I will ask her help. There is a boy there who cannot speak—Dickon, he is called, and we are friends. He will help me." He was suddenly excited, eager to depart on his mission, and Alice did not try to dissuade him; but when he left her, turning the key once more in the door of her temporary prison, she sank down onto her bed and let the despairing tears flow unchecked.

Mrs. Dawson was Mrs. Van Buren's sister—she would not go against her sister or take the word of a little half-caste boy, however fervent Claus's pleas on her behalf might be. It was useless to hope—as useless as it would be if she were to attempt to run away. Convicts did escape, it was true, but they were men, and even men were apprehended, sooner or later, to be given heavy sentences or banished to some distant penal settlement whence few ever returned. For a woman alone, escape was fraught with danger, and for one who, like herself, had only recently arrived in the colony, it would be virtually impossible. Since being brought here from the *Mary Anne*, she had never set foot outside the Van Burens' house, and she would have difficulty even in finding her way to Mrs. Dawson's, for all that Claus had said it was nearby.

Despite these despairing thoughts, the sound of the key turning in the lock, two hours later, set her heart beating faster. Claus came softly in, and her hopes rose when she glimpsed his smiling face.

"Oh, Claus—did you see Mrs. Dawson? Will she—"

He shook his head. "She is not there, alas. She is gone with *Mijnheer* Dawson to their farm on the Hawkesbury River—it is called Upwey."

Alice's heart plummeted. "Then it's no use hoping. It is—"

"There is hope," Claus told her, and his smile, as much as the confident tone of his voice, carried conviction. "Dickon was not there also—he is gone to the Macquarie River with his uncle. First I saw the lady who is called Miss Julia, and she told me to go away, but there is another lady, Dickon's sister, Miss Dorothea. She was most kind, and she let me speak of you. Alice, she say that for sure Mrs. Dawson will help you."

"But if she isn't here, Claus, how can she help me?"

Claus's smile widened. "I take you to her," he stated simply. "Now, when it is dark and no one see us. *Mevrouw* dines with *Mijnheer* Willoughby; she will pay no heed. We take one horse from the stable and we ride, you and me together. The cook will give us food; Saleh has told him. We go first to Parramatta, Miss Dorothea say, by turnpike road, then to Windsor. See—" He fumbled in his pockets and brought to light some loose coins and a slip of paper. "Money for toll, and letter of authority."

"Letter of authority?" Alice questioned. "What is that, Claus?"

"Miss Dorothea write it," Claus explained. "To show constables, if we stopped on road. It tells that we go to Upwey Farm, to *Mijnheer* Dawson."

He had thought of everything, Alice realized, and in wordless gratitude she hugged him. Claus clung to her for a moment and then warned her that they must hurry. "You take belongings, Alice. All that belong you."

Her possessions were few enough. With the boy's help, they were bundled up, and together the two of them crept downstairs, Claus carrying the small bundle and leading the way on tiptoe. Saleh was standing at the foot of the stairs, a tray of glasses and used plates balanced on the flat of one hand. He gestured with the other to the closed door of the dining room and then waved them past him in wary silence.

"Come!" Claus urged, and they were running through the side door and into the kitchen garden. In the stables at the rear of the house, the old cook was waiting, and by the light of a single lantern, Alice saw that one of the carriage horses had been saddled, ready for her escape. She eyed it nervously, but . . . Claus cupped his hands, motioning for her to step up. She did so, and with surprising strength he boosted her onto the animal's broad back. Her bundle of clothing was laid across the animal's withers, and a moment later the boy was in the saddle in front of her, warning her, in a sibilant whisper, to hold on to him.

"Round my waist . . . so! Do not fear, I shall go slowly. You will be quite safe."

Releasing his hold on the reins, the cook raised a thin brown hand in farewell, extinguished the lantern, and hastened with it back to his kitchen.

Claus dug his heels into their mount's sides and clicked his tongue, and the big animal moved forward obediently into the unlit street at the back of the house. As they emerged into George Street, which was illuminated by oil lamps for part of its length, Alice's heart was in her mouth, but the few passersby they encountered paid them no heed, and after a while her panic subsided and her heart ceased its wild beating.

Claus exclaimed jubilantly, "Soon you will be free! And the moon will light us on our way when we reach the turnpike. We have nothing to fear, sweet Alice!"

"We have stolen a horse, Claus," Alice reminded him soberly. "That is—must be a crime."

But Claus was not to be deterred. Turning, with a flash of white teeth, to grin at her impishly, he amended, "We only borrow the horse—I shall take it back. *Mevrouw* will no doubt be angry, and she will tell Saleh that he must beat me. But she is often angry, and I am often beaten . . . I do not worry, so you must not. We make a great adventure, you and me. That is better than the factory, is it not? It is

just a pity that I am not older, for then we could—what is
the word in English? Elope, I think.''

He kicked the horse into a canter, laughing aloud, and
as the lamp-lit turnpike gates came into sight, Alice found
herself infected by his reckless optimism. Both hands clasped
tightly about his waist, she threw back her head and joined
in his laughter.

CHAPTER XIV

The Reverend Nathan Cox climbed, with some reluctance, into his hired curricle outside the Woolpack Hotel, Parramatta, and prepared to continue his journey. His destination—the township of Windsor, on the Hawkesbury River—was twenty miles distant, and the day was already promising to become unpleasantly hot. But there was, he knew, no help for it, since the colony's principal chaplain, the Reverend Samuel Marsden, had failed to offer him the hospitality he had expected at the rectory, on the grounds that Mrs. Marsden was unwell.

Nathan picked up the reins, nodding to the Woolpack's ostler to release his horse's head. He had arrived in the colony only two weeks ago, in the transport *Minerva*, which had brought out a hundred and seventy male convicts, along with sad tidings of the death, in July, of a former Governor, General Lachlan Macquarie. The esteem in which the general had been held had both surprised and impressed him; he had seen people weeping in the streets when they heard the news—ordinary folk, emancipated felons, poor clerks and minor officials, farmers and smallholders and their women, even some of the children.

Arrangements were being put in hand for a memorial service, to be held in Sydney, at the church of Saint Philip, and he had wished that he might have stayed, in order to attend the service, but his meager funds precluded such an indulgence. His appointment—the first he had ever had, since taking Holy Orders—was as a chaplain in

the colony's prison service. As yet, however, he had not
been told officially to which penal settlement he was to be
sent, and to his intense chagrin, no one appeared to be in
any hurry to make use of his services.

"You could call on Mr. Marsden, at the rectory of Saint
John's in Parramatta," one of Archdeacon Scott's parish
clerks had advised, when he had confided his anxiety to
find gainful employment. "He is the principal chaplain.
No doubt he will know of a temporary vacancy you might
fill, while you are waiting. There are changes being made
at present—penal settlements are being closed down at
Newcastle and Port Macquarie and reestablished at Moreton
Bay and Norfolk Island. It seems probable that you will be
appointed to one or the other, Mr. Cox, when the convicts
are moved to their final destinations."

The clerk had given no details, to Nathan's disappointment, beyond telling him that prison buildings were in the
process of construction in both localities, but he had said a
great deal about the Reverend Samuel Marsden. The principal chaplain was, it seemed, one of the richest and most
successful sheep breeders in New South Wales, the owner
of pedigreed Spanish rams presented to him by the King
himself some fifteen years before, and the holder of over
three thousand acres of prime agricultural and grazing
land. Recently he had been granted more land in the
Bathurst area, the clerk had told him, and—apparently
unaware of Nathan's shocked astonishment at these revelations concerning a man of the cloth—had gone on to
relate, with gusto, that the Reverend Samuel Marsden
owned a trading schooner, which plied profitably between
Sydney and New Zealand and other islands in the South
Seas.

"It is a pity, young sir," the kindly old gentleman had
ended, with genuine regret, "that you have not come out
here under the auspices of the Church Missionary Society.
Had this been the case, you would, I feel sure, have been
on your way to New Zealand or Otaheite already, with Mr.
Marsden's blessings heaped upon your head! The mission

he founded in Whangaroa Bay for the Maori people is very close to his heart . . . closer, even, than his work here, I'm inclined to think.''

Nathan whipped the jaded horse he had hired into a shambling trot and pulled the brim of his hat down, in the hope of shading his eyes from the sun's fierce glare. His brief sojourn with the principal chaplain was not one he remembered with pleasure. True, the aging, obese Marsden lived as befitted one of the colony's richest landowners; his rectory was large and pleasantly situated, furnished with excellent taste and staffed by well-trained convict servants. Nathan had liked Marsden's elder daughter, Anne, and his son Charles; he had admired the healthy-looking sheep he had been permitted to glimpse in the breeding pens and, when pressed, had agreed that the well-stocked library at the back of the house was appropriately chosen to suit the needs of a convict population.

But he had not much cared for Mr. Marsden himself. For one thing, the principal chaplain was clearly of a very Low Church persuasion; and for another, when acquainted with the news of the late Governor's demise and the proposal to hold a day of mourning throughout the colony, he had displayed, on his round, red face, an expression that belied his protestations of regret. In the light of the public reaction in Sydney, Marsden's lack of grief had seemed extremely odd, if not callous.

Perhaps there was a reason for it; perhaps Governor and chaplain had not seen eye to eye during the years they had served in the colony together. Even so, Nathan—brought up in the belief that one spoke no ill of the dead—had been taken aback when his host had gone on to declare sourly that it was blasphemous to speak too highly of any man, as, it seemed, the people the Governor had once ruled were now intent on doing.

''In the twelve long years that he was Governor here, General Macquarie behaved as if he were a king. He affected to be God-fearing—but men in power often like religion only so long as it accords with their political measures and tends to support their dignity and consequence. Well, now he has been called to the bar of divine justice, before the King of Kings, and he must answer for all he did and all that he left undone.'' And Marsden had added sanctimoniously, ''I thank God that I am not in his shoes!''

To Nathan's bewilderment, he had then abruptly dropped the subject of the late Governor and had questioned him about himself and his own circumstances.

''So you are an only son,'' he had summed up, with a scorn he had not attempted to hide. ''Educated expensively, and a Cambridge graduate to boot! Consecrated a priest of the Church of England and accepted for a chaplaincy in the penal service . . . and, since your father's death, the sole supporter of your widowed mother. Why, Mr. Cox, did you not remain in England and support the poor soul by taking a curacy?''

Nathan sighed in exasperation. He had tried to explain that a curate's stipend, in an English parish, would not have come near to keeping his mother in the state to which, all her life, she had been accustomed. The two hundred and fifty pounds a year he had been offered, if he joined the colony's prison service, had been his answer to the problem—and one that his mother, who had never yearned for his company, had approved. Besides, he had come out to New South Wales with a sense of mission, eager to do all in his power, by spiritual means, to aid in the reformation of those unfortunates whom the law had condemned to transportation. His Bible classes and the sermons he had preached on board the *Minerva* had inspired him with the hope that he had something to give to the colony's felons, but when he had started to say so, the Reverend Samuel Marsden had cut him short.

''You'll not find much response from the capital respites and the bushrangers you'll be ministering to on Norfolk Island or at Moreton Bay,'' the harsh Yorkshire voice had informed him, with derision. ''For that's where you'll be posted, I don't doubt—and Norfolk Island's my guess, in maybe six or eight weeks' time. You're not married, are you?''

He had admitted he wasn't, Nathan recalled, and Marsden had wagged a reproving finger at him. ''My advice to you is that you take advantage of the time you have left here to find yourself a respectable lass and wed her. Norfolk Island's a lonely place, and Moreton Bay is even lonelier . . . you'd find a wife a great solace. But be careful as to the kind of lass you choose, boy. No convict woman would be suitable—most of them are whores, or even if they were virgins when they left England, they will have been corrupted on the passage out. But you'll find a number of decent, well-brought-up young women in the families of our clergy. In fact—'' The principal chaplain's red, bulbous nose had suddenly twitched, as if on the scent of game, and he had brought one large, heavy hand down on Nathan's shoulder. ''I'll have you appointed temporarily as curate to Mr. Robert Cartwright, who is the incumbent at Windsor. He has a large family and several marriageable daughters. He'll not be able to afford a stipend, but your salary will be paid by the government, and the Cartwrights will accommodate you, so you will live free. I'll give you a letter to him, and you can go to Windsor at once.''

The note was in the breast pocket of his sober black jacket, Nathan reflected resignedly; and in obedience to the Reverend Samuel Marsden's instructions, he was now on his way to the township of Windsor, with an estimated six to eight weeks in which to find himself a wife! The prospect alarmed him. When he had boarded the *Minerva*, he had supposed he would not be likely to marry for at least the next four or five years; and in England he had had very little to do with the opposite sex—his mother had seen to that. Even at Cambridge, as a student of divinity, he had been expected to behave with circumspection, and the *Minerva*, with her cargo of male felons, had offered no temptation to him to become corrupted or to corrupt others. Such female passengers as there had been on board the

transport were either married or too young for matrimony. . . . Nathan took out his kerchief to wipe his moist
and heavily perspiring brow.

The jaded hireling he was driving took advantage of his
momentary lapse of concentration to slow to a walking
pace, and he sighed again, lacking the energy to compel
the animal to move faster. Twenty miles, he thought, and
an almost completely deserted road, with the sun now
blazing down on him from a cloudless blue sky, and
insects—hordes of them—launching savage attacks on his
person from a clump of trees on his right. He would have
been wiser to wait, as the hotel keeper at Parramatta had
suggested, until the heat of the day had passed. Still, the
kindly fellow had supplied him with a meal of sorts,
wrapped up in a clean white napkin, and a flagon of ale
with which to slake his thirst on the journey. The trees, for
all the horde of flies they had let loose on him, offered
shade . . . and he was as hot and weary as his horse.

"Whoa!" he bade the flagging animal, and started to
pull off the road, to be startled, a moment later, by the
realization that he was not alone in his choice of a stopping
place. Beyond him, half hidden by the screen of trees, a
handsome bay horse was tethered, its riders—there were
two of them, Nathan saw—seated cross-legged on the
ground a few feet away. They were an oddly ill-matched
pair . . . a young girl of perhaps sixteen or seventeen, as
pretty as a picture with her tightly curling chestnut-colored
hair and small, pale face, and a dark-skinned boy, who
appeared to be a few years younger. Both were neatly
dressed, the girl in starched gingham covered by a white
pinafore, and the boy in white duck trousers and a checkered shirt, the sleeves of which were rolled up to give his
arms full play.

Below them a small, almost dry stream trickled past,
and his horse, resisting Nathan's efforts to restrain it,
made for the water, causing the boy and girl to jump to
their feet to avoid being struck by the near wheel of the
curricle. The boy, unbidden, made a quick grab for the

horse's head and brought it to a standstill, but not, however, Nathan saw to his dismay, before the wheel of the curricle had gone over and crushed the food that the pair had been eating and which they had spread out on the grass between them.

He apologized confusedly and leaped from the driving seat, dropping to his knees in an attempt to salvage what he could from the wreckage of their picnic. It was a vain attempt; all that he could save were a half-eaten apple and a mud-spattered crust of bread, but the boy smiled at him quite cheerfully and assured him that they had finished eating.

"Your horse needs to drink," he said, in a sibilant, strongly accented voice. "I will unhitch him and take him to the water, *mijnheer*."

He did so, handling the awkward animal with obvious skill, and Nathan, finding the girl eyeing him with apprehension, sought to put her mind at ease by introducing himself. She took in his clerical garb and nodded, her apprehension fading.

"You are a man of God?" she suggested shyly.

While he would normally have hesitated to describe himself thus, Nathan inclined his head. "I am a chaplain," he explained. "Recently arrived in the colony by the transport *Minerva*. And you?"

"I am Alice Fairweather," the girl responded. "And my companion"—she gestured to the boy, standing ankle-deep in the stream while Nathan's horse drank thirstily from it—"my companion is called Claus." She gave him no surname and went on quickly, "We are on our way to the Hawkesbury—to Windsor, and thence to the farm of Mr. Timothy Dawson. Upwey, it is called."

The name Dawson meant nothing to Nathan, but struck by the coincidence in their destination, he smiled.

"I, too, am going to Windsor, Miss Fairweather. Perhaps we could complete our journey together. Of course—" Belatedly he recalled his own untouched provisions. "Of course not before you have lunched with me. See—" He took the napkin-wrapped bundle from the curricle and spread it out on the ground at her feet. "I have ample for all three of us, and perhaps it will make up for my clumsiness in spoiling yours."

It was Claus who answered him, his dark eyes bright as he glimpsed the appetizing array. "I will tether your horse, sir, and then we shall be much pleased to take luncheon with you." He grinned, pointing to three apple cores lying in the mud. "Our provisions were finished before you came here. We have been on the road all night, you see."

Nathan puzzled over his statement but did not question it. The cook at the Woolpack had more than earned the small tip he had been offered—there was bread, a hunk of mutton ham already sliced, a chicken leg of ample proportions, two hard-boiled eggs, cheese, and some fresh peaches, probably picked from the tree that morning, their skins golden. He fetched the ale, and they sat down together on the sun-warmed grass, Claus rewarding his generosity with another happy grin.

As they ate, they talked of the homes they had left, and Nathan learned, without surprise, that Claus hailed from one of the Dutch islands, and Alice from Devon. "We are almost neighbors," he told her delightedly, when she mentioned Honiton. "My home was in Taunton. I spent my boyhood there. My father was a doctor, with a large rural practice. Unhappily, though, he liked to play cards, and when he died, he left my poor mother with very little, save a heavily mortgaged house and a great many unpaid bills." He shrugged, biting hungrily into one of the peaches and feeling, for the first time since his arrival in the colony, happy and completely at his ease.

The boy Claus was endearingly friendly, and Alice Fairweather, although a trifle reticent concerning her own immediate past, was easy to talk to and only too eager to share his nostalgia for the places they had both known and loved.

And besides . . . He studied her covertly as he demolished the peach. She was enchantingly pretty; slim and

graceful as the young deer he had once hunted with bow
and arrows—a boy, pretending to be a red Indian—among
the wooded slopes of the Quantocks. Her people had been
farmers, she told him—poor but honest folk, he surmised,
listening as she spoke of them with affection and pride—
but she herself had been apprenticed to a milliner and
seamstress, in the village near her home.

What, he found himself wondering, had brought her to
New South Wales, seemingly alone, since she had made
no mention of her family having accompanied her? Without any conscious desire to pry, but merely to assuage his
curiosity, he asked the question casually and was startled
when he saw her cheeks flood with color and tears come
welling into her blue, intelligent eyes.

Claus came fiercely to her defense. He said, before she
could speak, "Alice is a good woman, Mr. Cox. A good
woman, like my mother! But bad people in England, they
make false accusation against her and send her here. And
then—then they make her assigned to *Mevrouw* Van Buren
as a servant, like me. And she happy with us, with Saleh,
with Arifin, with Tjoe and Abdul . . . we love her! She
work most hard, all day long sewing dresses for *mevrouw*.
But that not enough—*Mevrouw* Van Buren is cruel. She
send Alice to Female Factory in Parramatta for no
reason. . . ." His English became almost unintelligible,
and Nathan could only stare at him in openmouthed astonishment as the truth slowly sank in.

This gentle, lovely young girl was a *convict,* one of the
corrupt breed against whom Samuel Marsden had warned
him! Shamefaced, he looked at her, deeply regretting the
thoughtless question that had provoked the little boy's
outburst and wishing, with all his heart, that he had not
indulged his idle curiosity, since by so doing he had
obviously caused her pain and humiliation—quite apart
from what it had done to her young companion.

He said, a catch in his voice, "I did not know—I—
forgive me, Miss Fairweather. It never occurred to me that

". . . I mean—" He was floundering helplessly, his cheeks as red as hers.

"It never occurred to you that I was a convict, Mr. Cox?" she finished for him, with quiet dignity.

Nathan shook his head. "No, I—it was the last thing I expected."

"I am not only a convict," she went on, still very quietly. "I am what they call here an escaper, and Claus is helping me to escape."

The whole story came out then, and Nathan listened in disbelief as the girl and boy, between them, revealed what had led to their presence on the road to Windsor. He did not doubt the truth of what they told him; his disbelief was rather directed against a system that could place a girl like Alice Fairweather—a good girl, as Claus repeatedly reminded him—in such a situation, leaving her vulnerable and defenseless, at the mercy of the cruel woman to whose service she had been assigned. It smacked of slavery. Mrs. Van Buren, it seemed, could have her flogged, could condemn her to the Female Factory without even telling her why . . . simply on a whim or, perhaps, for some still less worthy reason.

It was the first he had heard of the Female Factory; Samuel Marsden had not mentioned it, and although he had passed its forbidding walls only the previous day, he had had no inkling of the horrors hidden behind them, or of the sort of women who were more usually sent there.

"So you stole a horse from Mrs. Van Buren's stable?" he suggested. "Was that not taking a terrible risk?"

"The horse," Claus retorted crisply, "is only *borrowed*. I take it back, after I take Alice to Mrs. Dawson."

"Mrs. Dawson is at Upwey, a farm near Windsor?" Nathan pursued. "But will Alice be safe there? Cannot Mrs. Van Buren demand her return, or—or have her arrested?"

"We have letter for Mrs. Dawson, sir," the boy said. Patiently, he supplied details. "She Mrs. Van Buren's sister, but she very good woman. I show letter of authority to constables in Parramatta, and they say 'All right, go on.' "

"But you will get into trouble when you return the horse, will you not?"

"Oh, yes." Claus's tone was indifferent. "We all be in trouble—Saleh, too. But if Alice is with Mrs. Dawson, that not matter, Mr. Cox. She will have assignment changed; Alice work for her then." He added, with conscious pride, "Alice must serve sentence, seven years before she free. But she free before that, if she marry. And *I* will be old enough to marry her in four years, see?"

"You!" Nathan exclaimed, unable to hide his incredulity. "*You* would marry her, Claus? But—" He intercepted a warning glance from Alice Fairweather and sought vainly for words that would temper the hurt he knew his skepticism must have inflicted on the boy. Claus was a brave boy, heaven knew, selfless in his devotion, and he had taken a dangerous risk in aiding the girl's escape. "You would be gaining a beautiful wife," he managed at last. "But four years is a long time to wait, is it not?"

"Long time, yes," Claus conceded. "Maybe we find good man before that who want to wed her."

Nathan lapsed into pensive silence, suddenly uncomfortably aware that it lay within his power to offer a solution. Yet the notion was crazed, he told himself; he did not know the girl, and she was a convict . . . but he did not know the Reverend Robert Cartwright's marriageable daughters, either. They might well be anathema to him— bluestockings, who would put him to shame; buck-toothed or otherwise unattractive; perhaps even empty heads or overly genteel young ladies, with whom he would have little or nothing in common, particularly in the lonely isolation of a penal settlement like Norfolk Island. And that was, in all probability, where he would be sent, six or eight weeks from now—with or without the wife he had been so strongly advised to acquire.

He looked again at the girl beside him. Chance had thrown them together—pure, blind chance, or . . . His

theological training caused him to dismiss the supposition
that it had been by chance. Rather it was God's will, he
thought, the choice made for him by divine providence, in
recognition of his need. And . . . he would have time to
become properly acquainted with this girl before he need
commit himself—time enough, surely, in six weeks. She
smiled, sensing his eyes on her, and the smile was so
warm and lacking in coquetry that Nathan's last lingering
doubts were dispelled. His God had chosen well.

He said decisively, "I will drive you to Windsor, Miss
Fairweather, and to Mrs. Dawson's farm. Claus can go
back to Sydney with the horse, and perhaps if he returns
quickly, Mrs. Van Buren will find it in her heart to forgive
him." He added, as Claus started to speak, "Do not
worry, Claus—Alice will be safe with me. I will deliver
her to her destination, I give you my word, if that is where
she wishes to go."

Claus hesitated, looking from the girl's face to his and
then back, once again, to the girl's. He did not speak, but
she answered his unvoiced question by putting her arms
about him and hugging him tightly, and her voice shook a
little as she said, "It will be best if I go with the reverend
gentleman. And perhaps, as he says, if you return quickly
with the horse, Mrs. Van Buren will not punish you. I . . .
oh, Claus, I shall miss you so! But as long as I live I shall
not forget what you have done for me. And Saleh, too; and
the others. Tell them I thank them and—and that I shall
pray for them all."

The boy's reply was inaudible, and Nathan guessed that
he was fighting to restrain his grief at a parting he had not
supposed would come so soon. But clearly he saw the
practical need for it, and, his small, dark face devoid of
expression, he crossed to where the borrowed carriage
horse was tethered, freed the rein, and scrambled onto the
animal's back.

"I beg you to take good care of Alice, sir," he said, his
young voice clipped. Then he dug his heels into the big
bay's sides and was off at a brisk canter along the dusty

road. Alice watched him until he was hidden by the dust
his horse's pounding hooves had raised. She hesitated for a
moment, her back turned to Nathan; then, to his surprise,
she bobbed him a curtsy and asked, in a quiet, controlled
voice, "Is it your pleasure that we continue on our way,
sir?"

"It—why, yes. Yes, of course," he agreed.

"Then if you will hitch up the horse, I will pack up the
remains of our meal and put my belongings into your
equipage," she offered, then added apologetically, "Although I was brought up on a farm, sir, I never had to do
with horses. I am a little afraid of them."

His own experience of the equine breed was also limited,
Nathan thought—his father had employed a groom—but
he managed the task of returning the animal to its place
between the shafts tolerably well, and a few minutes later
they were seated side by side on the curricle's box, talking
away as if they had known each other all their lives.

Nathan was enchanted; in Alice's company, the loneliness he had felt so keenly since his arrival in New South
Wales no longer plagued him, and if homesickness affected them both as they spoke of the England they had
left behind them, it was shared, and the pain of it lessened
on that account.

His God, the young clergyman thought again, had chosen well, and he would be lacking in faith were he to
question the workings of divine providence on his behalf.
They were nearing the small township of Windsor, its
church spire already plainly to be seen, when he made his
proposal of marriage with due humility.

"You will be free, as my wife," he added, when Alice
was silent, her gaze averted and the color suddenly draining from her cheeks. "And I—oh, Alice, you will make
me very happy if you will consent to share my life. I am to
be appointed to one of the new penal settlements as chaplain,
I believe. Perhaps that is not the life you would have
chosen, but if we are together, it would be bearable. And
together we could work to improve the lot of those poor

unfortunates who are condemned to penal servitude—
together we could try to do God's work among them,
could we not? I . . ." She continued to hesitate, and
Nathan put out his hand to take hers. "I will love you,"
he promised gravely, "and be true to you all my days. I
. . . oh, Alice, I feel sure that young Claus would approve,
if we could ask him."

His last words, it seemed, decided her. She looked up at
him, her eyes brimming with tears, and answered softly,
"If you truly want me, knowing what I am, then I will be
proud and happy to become your wife, Mr. Cox."

"Nathan," he amended. "My name is Nathan. And I
know what you are. You—Alice, you are a gift from
God!" He carried the hand he held to his lips and then,
galvanized into action, released it and raised the carriage
whip, startling the half-slumbering horse into a reluctant
trot.

"We will ask the Reverend Cartwright to call our banns
and wed us as soon as it is possible," he told her exultantly.
"You have made me the happiest, most fortunate man in
this whole colony, dearest Alice!"

Alice stanched her tears with the corner of her pinafore,
and she was smiling as they drove into Windsor's main
street. Among the town's pretty, white-painted wooden
houses, they found that of the rector beside the churchyard.

Proudly, Nathan helped her to alight from the curricle
and offered her his arm.

"I expect there will be certain formalities," he warned.
"But we will deal with them. And—" He gestured to the
little church. "That is where, God willing, we shall be
wed, my dearest love." He halted and, a hand beneath her
chin, tilted her face to his, to kiss her gently. "Are you as
happy as I am, sweet?"

"If it were not that I am anxious for Claus," Alice
confessed, "I should tell you that this is the happiest day I
have known since coming here."

"We will pray together for Claus," Nathan offered,
"before making ourselves known to Mr. Cartwright."

Arm in arm, they entered the small, stone-built church and, in its cool dimness, knelt side by side in silent prayer.

There, in his soiled working clothes, after a difficult calving in his cow barn, the Reverend Robert Cartwright found them and, warmly welcoming, led them to his rectory to be introduced to his numerous family.

The formalities, he assured the anxious Nathan, would take a little time, and Alice would be required to appear before the magistrates' bench next day. She would almost certainly be released on his recognizance, and provided that her former mistress brought no charges of a criminal nature against her, permission to marry would be granted and the banns could be called.

The good rector's bevy of marriageable daughters proved to be as friendly and well-disposed as he, and all of them were pretty; but looking at the radiant face of the bride he had chosen, the Reverend Nathan Cox experienced no regrets.

Claus had ridden fast, and a little after sundown he led his weary horse into the stables at the rear of the Van Buren's house. One of the convict grooms, Amos Bryant, took his mount from him and told him, grinning, that he was in luck.

"Madam never spotted as the 'oss was missin'—didn't want the carriage all day, for a wonder. An' what the eye don't see, the heart don't grieve about, eh? You cut along, young Claus, an' leave 'im to me. I'll rub 'im down an' feed 'im, an' she won't never know 'e's bin away. Did you deliver the little lass safe an' sound?"

Claus nodded, too spent to do more than mumble his thanks. In the kitchen, all the indoor servants crowded round him, asking the same question, and again he answered it with a wordless inclination of his small dark head.

Arifin, the old cook, set a steaming plate of savory rice before him; Tjoe, the scullion, brought him water; and Saleh said, regarding him with unfeigned approval, "You have done well, little *lip-lap*, exceedingly well. To have returned so soon has removed all danger of discovery, I think. I have told *mevrouw* that the constable came for Alice in the early hours, before she had risen, and she did not doubt my word—neither did she ask for you. She has other things on her mind, and all day she has been out with *Mijnheer* Willoughby, going in a sailboat across the harbor.''

He paused, patting Claus gently on the head. ''Only the constable had doubts, but to him I said that we had ourselves taken Alice to Parramatta and did not need his help. He grumbled a little, but I gave him a glass of *mijnheer*'s best brandy, and he departed in happy humor, Allah be praised!''

Claus ate hungrily, enjoying the general interest and approval, but he would, he knew, have to tell them that his swift return was the result of the encounter with the young English man of God, when he and Alice had been only some five or six miles beyond Parramatta. He waited, crouched over the table, cramming rice into his mouth with his fingers.

Then Saleh asked, ''How did *Mevrouw* Dawson receive the little one?'' and there was no way that he could avoid admitting the truth.

''I did not take her to *Mevrouw* Dawson's, Saleh,'' he blurted out.

''You did not take her to Upwey Farm?''

Claus hung his head. ''No, I . . .'' He gulped. ''We met a young gentleman on the road, driving in a small carriage. He was a man of God, what the English call a chaplain—a good man, I am sure. He was on his way to Windsor, as were we also, and he offered to take Alice there in his carriage, to enable me to return here quickly with *mevrouw*'s horse. She was willing—Saleh, Alice said she would go with him. So I did not protest.''

There was silence. Saleh stood frowning down at him.

''The gentleman, the man of God—he was young, you say?''

"Yes, and newly arrived here, he told us. In the ship that lies still at the anchorage—the *Minerva*."

Saleh's frown lifted. Smiling, he put his arm about Claus's thin shoulders. "I think perhaps you will lose your bride, little *lip-lap*," he said, with gentle mockery. "For the sake of our poor Alice, I must hope that you may. You—" A bell rang an impatient summons, and he got to his feet, suppressing a sigh. "*Mevrouw* returns . . . I must go to her. Take your rest, boy, and have no fear. Our lady has eyes only for *Mijnheer* Willoughby."

CHAPTER XV

Rick Tempest was in a cheerful mood as he rode back from the river, intending to take luncheon with his wife and spend the rest of the afternoon at home in her company, as proof of his pleasure at her return.

His pleasure and, he knew only too well, his relief, for the terms on which they had parted, following her confinement at his sister Abigail's house, had been such as to cause him to fear that she might elect to stay in Sydney and not come back to him at all. True, Pengallon was isolated, and their neighbors were few and far between, but Katie's reluctance to live with him here was not, he knew, solely on that account. It stemmed from a much deeper cause, which had its roots in the loss of their little daughter, followed—so tragically soon—by that of their stillborn son.

Katie blamed herself for both losses, he knew, and nothing he could do or say would convince her that, in his eyes, she was completely blameless. He had tried, heaven knew; she listened, smiled a sad little smile, and gave his words and his pleas no credence. Since her return, however, she had seemed happier. The stay in Sydney and the influence of his sister Abigail had clearly done her good; she talked to him more and appeared glad to have resumed their normal life together, and she no longer wept when the name of their little dead daughter was mentioned.

There was hope, Rick thought, for they loved each other and . . . He smiled to himself. George De Lancey, whom he had once feared as a rival for Katie's affections, was himself happily married to Rachel Broome and the father of a child whom he adored, so there was nothing to fear from that quarter.

Lips pursed, he started to whistle a gay little tune, expressive of his present mood of optimism. He enjoyed the life he led, up here in the new lands beyond the Blue Mountain barrier. By any standards, he was well on the way to being a successful farmer, despite his initial lack of experience. He had three hundred head of beef cattle—half of them bred from William Lee's shorthorn bulls—which were thriving mightily on the lush hill pastures of his own grant. On the land he shared with Justin, there were close on to twice that number of merino and half-merino sheep, which, under Jethro Crowan's skilled care, were now producing high-quality wool and remaining healthy, while those of some of his neighbors went down with foot rot or liver fluke. And there were the horses he was breeding from John Macarthur's Arab stallion. . . .

Best of all, though . . . Rick felt in the pocket of his coarse homespun jacket, fingering the two sizable gold nuggets he had that morning retrieved from the bed of the river. Of necessity, he had to keep his gold finds secret— even from Katie—under the terms Governor Macquarie had imposed on his lease. For that reason, the sieves and pans he used to obtain the gold had to be carefully hidden, and his search conducted at infrequent intervals, when he was certain that he was safe from discovery. By trial and error he had devised and learned to use the primitive tools his search required, but often he drew a blank, when hours of work yielded only aching muscles and a pile of worthless pebbles.

Initially, too, he had been faced with the problem of how to dispose of the gold, for he dared not offer it for sale openly to anyone in the colony. An emancipist named Hensall, who was employed by the mint as an assayer and coiner, had purchased the first nuggets, and had even set himself up in business as a jeweler on the profits. But—

although purporting to believe that Rick had acquired the nuggets outside the colony—the man had been too curious, had asked too many questions, and deciding that he was not to be trusted, Rick had never attempted to sell to him again. For a while it had been necessary to hoard the gold—and that had gone very much against the grain, when he needed money for expansion. But then . . . Again Rick smiled to himself.

His difficulties had been largely overcome by the return to Sydney of old Silas Crabbe, the onetime sailing master of H.M.S. *Kangaroo,* now a civilian and in command of a trading brig of which he was part owner. Silas was a good friend and the soul of discretion, and furthermore, his trading voyages took him to India and China, as well as to the Dutch East Indies, where the gold found a ready market and no questions as to its origin were asked.

Thanks to the deal they had struck, he had accumulated as much money as he needed to build up his stock, Rick reflected with satisfaction . . . the money to purchase merino rams and Arab horses from the Macarthurs and fine red shorthorn cattle from the enterprising Lee. Katie, he knew, worried about what she saw as his profligate spending, but most people believed his claim that he was spending only his naval prize money, and he was at pains to conceal the fact that he had financed Silas Crabbe's trading and was reaping a handsome profit from that also. Indeed, he . . .

A horseman came cantering toward him, and Rick recognized Dickon, his sister Abigail's son, and raised a hand in greeting. Dickon, too, had been a willing, if unwitting, partner in his dealings with Silas Crabbe. The boy was deaf and dumb, but aside from that, he was intelligent and completely trustworthy, and when Silas's ship came into port and it was difficult to get away himself, he had sent Dickon to Sydney with the gold, concealing it carefully, so that if the boy were ever questioned, he could with truth plead ignorance of what he carried. Not that he had ever suspected anything. Dickon was eighteen, tall and well grown for his age, but possessed of an innocence that was at once childlike and endearing. He was on intimate terms with the aborigines in the area and, in particular, with Justin's protégé, Winyara, and, Rick thought, as he watched the lad's approach, it was probably on Dickon's account that the blacks never raided his stock or fired his crops as, not infrequently, they raided his neighbors' when game was scarce.

Dickon, for all his handicap, seemed able to communicate with the black people and they with him; he hunted and fished with them and was more at ease in their company than he was in that of the white farm workers—with the sole exception of Jethro, to whom he was devoted. Jethro probably stayed on at Pengallon because of Dickon, Rick suspected, and Jethro was worth his weight in gold as a sheep breeder—although they had almost fallen out when, against Jethro's advice, he had sought to reduce the size of his flock in favor of more cattle.

He reined in as Dickon came abreast of him; the boy looked concerned, his tanned face twisted into the odd grimace he always resorted to when attempting to impart some item of information he considered urgent.

"Well, what is it, lad?" Rick prompted.

Dickon let the rein fall on his horse's neck, in order to leave both hands free. He talked with his hands, displaying extraordinary eloquence when he did so, and Rick watched him, interpreting each expressive movement aloud and mouthing the words, so that Dickon could read his lips and confirm or amend his interpretation.

"Three men were coming—mounted men?"

A vigorous nod and more hand movements, describing a small face, and Rick guessed, "Three mounted men with an aborigine boy? No . . . not a blackfellow, but a boy, right? And one of the men is heavyweight—a big man, who is smoking a pipe? Not a pipe, a cigar? And—hey, Dickon, what do you mean? He is angry? Why should he be angry?"

Dickon shrugged, clearly unable to supply the answer to

the last question. His hands moved across his own thin, muscular belly, forming a semicircle above it, and then, with fingers spread out, to his chin, as if he were stroking an invisible beard, and Rick grinned at him. A gross fellow with a beard, smoking a cigar . . . "Major Van Buren?" he suggested. "And the boy is your young friend Claus, eh?"

Another affirmative nod. But, for all Dickon's expressive gestures, the identity of Van Buren's two companions remained a mystery. Rick motioned his nephew to pick up his reins.

"We'd better go and find out what they want, I suppose. Are they in the house? Has Katie offered them refreshment?"

Dickon nodded, still looking worried, and Rick clapped his heels into his horse's sides.

Katie met them outside the door of the log-built farmhouse, and leaving Dickon to deal with their horses, Rick hurried to join her.

"Dickon found you, thank goodness!" She glanced back at the house apprehensively and, in a lowered voice, said, "Rick, I don't know what it's all about, but Major Van Buren called here nearly an hour ago, with two new settlers who—"

"New settlers? Here? Have they been granted land up here, Katie?" Rick asked, frowning.

"Yes," Katie said. "I think so. I met them at Abigail's when they first arrived. Robert Willoughby and Henry Daniels. Mr. Willoughby used to be in the Royal Navy, and Mr. Daniels was—"

Rick smothered an exclamation. "Willoughby's the son of Admiral Sir Francis Willoughby, I'm almost sure. Sir Francis was port admiral at Plymouth when I—"

Katie interrupted him. "Never mind about his father— Rick, they've quarreled, he and Major Van Buren. I don't know why, except that it has something to do with Mrs. Van Buren—with Lucy."

"The obvious, I imagine," Rick said cynically. "Lucy may be my sister, but that doesn't mean that I hold any brief for her or for the infernal Dutchman she married. But why have they come here, for the Lord's sake? Am I supposed to try to patch up the quarrel?''

Katie shook her head unhappily. ''It has gone too far for that. They—they intend to fight a duel.''

''*Here?* Plague on them, why here?''

''Major Van Buren requires a second. He wants *you* to act for him.''

''The devil he does!'' Rick was angry.

''That was all they told me,'' Katie said. ''And I had to put them in different rooms to wait for you. Oh, Rick, dueling is illegal, is it not? Can you stop them?''

''I'll have a damned good try,'' Rick promised, and stalked off toward the door.

His efforts were, however, abortive. He talked first to Jos Van Buren, who met him with an adamant refusal, insisting that his honor had been impugned. The boy Claus, Rick gathered from his brother-in-law's furious outburst, had inadvertently revealed the fact that Robert Willoughby had spent several nights in the Bridge Street house during Van Buren's absence. The Dutchman, Rick gathered, had been at Portland Place with Daniels, where they had been making preparations to move stock up to Bathurst.

''And he admitted the truth!'' Van Buren asserted, white with anger. ''This rogue Willoughby, whom I trusted— with whom, devil take him, it was my intention to enter into partnership! He boasted of having made love to my wife—boasted of it, and made accusations against me which do not bear repeating! God's blood, we journeyed up here for over a week in close company, in comradeship, and Willoughby said nothing. We were as brothers, I tell you—there was trust between us. I had even offered him command of one of my ships . . . but then, from the boy, this stupid, innocent boy, I learned what had occurred in my absence, and I could have killed him! Damn his soul, I *will* kill him—but it must be in honorable fight. We must face each other with pistols, adhering strictly to the rules that govern such matters. For that, I require you to act as my second and witness, Rick. That is why I am here.''

Rick's gaze went to the boy Claus, who was crouching in abject terror in a corner of the small, dark room, the tears running down his ashen cheeks.

"Off you go, lad," he suggested pityingly. "Go find Dickon. He's in the stables, I think, and he'll look after you. Go on—no need for you to stay."

Van Buren raised no objection. Indeed, as he continued his tirade, he seemed scarcely to notice the little boy's departure. It was useless to attempt to argue with him; with difficulty, Rick contrived to excuse himself and go in search of Willoughby and his companion. He found them in his bedroom, where both, it appeared, had made themselves at home, with Robert Willoughby stretched, fully dressed, on the neatly made double bed, and Daniels, a trifle less at his ease, seated on the room's only chair.

They had the grace to rise when he entered, and Willoughby made the introductions, his manner elaborately casual. "I apologize, sir, for this intrusion," he said smoothly. "And for involving you in what amounts to a purely personal quarrel. But Major Van Buren insists that our—er—our differences can only be settled in time-honored fashion, with pistols. Daniels here is willing to act as my second, and I hope, since you are related to him by—er—by marriage, that you will be willing to perform a like office for Van Buren. I take it you've talked to him?''

"Yes," Rick agreed, with distaste. "I have listened to the accusations he has made regarding your relations with his wife.''

"Who is your sister, I believe?" Willoughby put in, smiling. The smile was insolent, the implications deliberately offensive, and Rick's hackles rose. Be damned to them, he thought—let them settle the affair in any way they wished! He was, in any case, powerless to stop them; the duel would take place, whether he seconded Lucy's husband or not. All he could do was to ensure that, as Van Buren had said, they adhered strictly to the rules that governed such matters. There would be no surgeon present, of course, but . . . He gave Robert Willoughby an icy smile and said flatly, "That is so. I will second Major Van Buren, and since no good purpose can be served by delay, perhaps Mr. Daniels would adjourn with me now so that we can agree on terms and conditions."

Daniels bowed. "By all means, Mr. Tempest."

But once he was alone with Rick, pacing the yard outside, his confidence evaporated. "I wouldn't have let it come to a duel if there had been any way to prevent it," he admitted anxiously. "But they would have shot it out in the bush with no damned rules at all, if I hadn't intervened. A duel is at least an honorable way of settling things, between gentlemen—only it *is* against the law here, is it not, as it is in England?"

Rick shrugged. "Between officers holding the King's commission it is a court-martial offense here, as elsewhere—if the fact that a duel took place becomes known to the authorities."

"We are all civilians, sir," Daniels pointed out, sounding relieved. "And up here, in the—in the wilds, surely the authorities aren't likely to find out, are they?"

"No . . . unless one of the duelists is killed or dies of his wounds. And the nearest surgeon is at Bathurst, at the army hospital." Rick hesitated, eyeing the younger man searchingly. "Will they be satisfied if they draw blood, do you suppose, or will they try to kill each other?"

Daniels shivered. "Rob would be satisfied, I'm pretty sure. But I'm not so sure about the Dutchman, Tempest. He went berserk when he—that is to say when he found out that Rob had been playing around with his wife. If only that idiot boy had kept his mouth shut! Not that he meant any harm—in truth, I don't think he realized what he was saying or the significance of it, anyway. And Rob could have denied it, but he did not, he . . . Devil take it, Tempest, he gloated in quite insufferable fashion! I think he wanted to bring matters to a head."

"He has certainly succeeded," Rick retorted. "Well, I

suppose we can reduce the charges when we load the pistols. I take it you have pistols and that they are the weapons to be used?''

Daniels nodded, becoming businesslike. "Yes, I have them here—Rob's and mine. They are new; we purchased them in Sydney from the same gunsmith, and Van Buren's agreed to use them. He's not carrying a pistol, only a hunting rifle. Please examine both weapons and satisfy yourself that they are virtually identical.''

Rick did as he was asked and expressed himself satisfied; the conditions for the duel were agreed without argument, and Daniels accepted his suggestion as to a suitable site—a clearing a mile or so from the homestead and screened from it by a belt of eucalyptus trees.

"What about your laborers?" Daniels inquired, with a return of his earlier apprehension. "We want no witnesses.''

"Do not concern yourself with them," Rick reassured him. "We are dipping sheep, and my men are fully occupied." He shrugged. "Well, let us be about it, shall we? The sooner this is over, the better I shall be pleased, I don't mind telling you.''

"I, too," Henry Daniels admitted. "I had hoped to make a start settling my new land grant, but I fear this has changed things very radically. I mean—there will be no partnership now between us and Van Buren, will there?''

"That seems unlikely," Rick returned. He added formally, "Be so good as to acquaint your principal with the terms we have agreed upon, Mr. Daniels. I will lead the way with my principal in—shall we say ten minutes?''

Van Buren was somewhat less agitated when he followed Rick to the stables to collect their horses; he passed Willoughby and Daniels, already mounted, without word or glance, but Rick sensed his fury and saw the evidence of it in the big man's heightened coloring and in the trembling of his hands as he picked up his reins.

"You would be as well to calm yourself, Josef," Rick advised. "We've a way to go—use it, if you can.''

"I have fought duels before," Van Buren flung at him sourly. "I am a good shot."

And so, probably, was Robert Willoughby, Rick thought; certainly he was a cool customer, and if his friend Daniels was to be believed, he had provoked Van Buren into a fight, though to what end—unless he hoped to kill his opponent—was anybody's guess.

They reached the place he had chosen and dismounted, tying their horses to a nearby tree. A flock of parakeets rose in a multicolored cloud, screeching shrilly at the intrusion as they circled overhead and then made off, their noisy flight disturbing a bunch of wallabies that had been dozing in the bush fifty yards away, lulled by the hot sunshine. Then all was quiet, and Rick joined Henry Daniels, to go through the formal ritual of pacing out the distance by which the duelists were to be separated and loading, priming, and inspecting their pistols.

Rick found himself thinking of his sister Lucy and wondering what her feelings were for the man she had apparently taken as her lover. Robert Willoughby was personable enough, and compared with the red-visaged, overweight Dutchman she had married, he cut a much more attractive figure. All the same, there was something about him that—although Rick was unable to define the reason for it—aroused a feeling of acute mistrust. Willoughby seemed very sure of himself, almost arrogantly so, and in comparison with Van Buren, he displayed an almost icy calm.

When called upon to do so by Daniels, both men came to stand back to back, each taking his loaded pistol in his right hand. Van Buren's hand was trembling visibly, and beads of perspiration had gathered on his brow, but he grunted his assent when asked if he was ready.

Daniels stood back. "I shall call out the paces," he announced. "At the count of ten, when twenty paces separate you, you will halt, gentlemen, turn to face each other, and fire. Is that understood? Very well—Mr. Tempest will give you the word to start walking."

Feeling his mouth suddenly dry, Rick braced himself and gave the word, hearing, as if it were coming from a long way away, Daniels's voice, monotonously counting. "Eight . . . nine . . . ten! Turn and fire!"

Van Buren's pistol spoke first. He had turned, with remarkable speed for one of his build, and fired as he turned, not waiting to steady himself. His shot went low and wide, the ball burying itself in the sandy ground a few yards to the rear of its intended target.

Willoughby, Rick saw, was smiling, his eyes bright with the assurance of victory as he faced his helpless opponent. Taking his time, as if he were merely at practice, he took careful aim, and Van Buren's guttural cry of pain echoed the exploding shot. The big man slumped heavily to the ground, clutching his chest, his empty pistol falling from his grasp to lie unheeded at his feet.

With one accord, Rick and Daniels ran to him and, together, turned him onto his back. His white shirt was stained with blood, and at first Rick sought for the wound in his heart, fearing that Willoughby's deliberate aim must have killed him. But Daniels said breathlessly, "It's his arm—look, he must have held it in front of him! Praise be to heaven, it's only a flesh wound after all!"

He was right, Rick realized as he rolled up Van Buren's shirtsleeve, using it temporarily to stanch the bleeding. Robert Willoughby had aimed for the heart, no doubt of that, but Van Buren's wound was in the fleshy part of his left arm—painful enough, but unlikely to prove fatal. Rick expelled his breath in relief.

"We'll bandage the arm," he said, "and get him back to the house, if you'll lend me a hand."

Van Buren was conscious, swearing and furiously angry. He submitted to having his arm bandaged and then scrambled to his feet unaided. Ignoring Willoughby, who stood silently by, he stumbled unsteadily over to where his horse was tethered and managed to drag himself onto its back, shaking off Daniels's hand when the younger man attempted to help him.

Rick mounted his own horse and rode after the wounded man, leaving the other two to their own devices. "Josef, you must come back to my house," he urged, "to let us clean and dress your arm properly."

Van Buren turned an inflamed and resentful gaze on him. "Is the ball still in my arm?" he demanded.

"Yes, I'm pretty sure it is. But—"

"Then I need a surgeon. I shall ride to Bathurst. The boy—Claus can go with me."

Rick tried to dissuade him, advising rest and promising his own escort to the army hospital when the heat of the day was over, but the Dutchman brushed both offers aside ungraciously. When they reached the homestead, he consented to have his bandage renewed, and Katie, very white of face but determined, led him into her kitchen and, with Rick's help, washed the wound, dressed it carefully, and fashioned a sling to hold the arm immobile. It was, Rick confirmed, only a flesh wound, but the ball, as he had feared, was still there. His brother-in-law accepted Katie's ministrations with a bad grace, swearing at the slight pain she occasioned him and quaffing two large beakers of brandy with neither thanks nor acknowledgment. Finally he lurched to his feet and stumped outside, shouting for Claus and demanding his horse.

Rick brought him his horse, but the boy did not respond to the Dutchman's raucous summons, and he said wrathfully, "The cowardly little rogue is doubtless in hiding. Send him after me when you find him." He scrambled awkwardly into the saddle, emitting an agonized groan as the pommel caught his injured arm and he slumped against the horse's neck for a moment, cursing freely in his own language.

Rick was about to repeat his invitation to him to stay, at least until it was cooler, but Robert Willoughby, who was standing by the stable trough, watering his horse, turned disdainfully to look at him.

"Devil take it—he's making much of it, isn't he, Henry? And I only winged him, for the Lord's sake!"

Daniels reddened in embarrassment and did not reply, but Van Buren straightened himself in the saddle and made to ride his tormentor down. Willoughby stepped swiftly aside and, a hand on the big Dutchman's bridle, turned the oncoming horse in the opposite direction and, releasing it, gave the animal a resounding slap on its hindquarters. It bounded forward, almost unseating its rider, and Van Buren, controlling it with difficulty, turned furiously to curse him.

"This is not the end, you blasted rogue! You've not seen the last of me, God's blood you have not! I'll make you rue the day, if it is the last thing I do!"

Then he was gone at a thunderous gallop, leaving a thick cloud of dust in his wake.

Willoughby pursed his lips in a silent whistle and made an elaborate pantomime of mopping his brow.

"You didn't have to do that to him," Henry Daniels exclaimed reproachfully. "It was adding insult to injury, Rob—you know it was. You've made a damned dangerous enemy, and it's all your own doing. I want no more part in your affairs, devil take you!"

Robert Willoughby was unrepentant. "Don't be an idiot, Henry," he retorted sharply. "Van Buren's not dangerous—he's a drunken oaf. Our fight was honorable, and I bested him. Just wait till the gossips of Sydney Town get wind of *that*—the fellow won't be able to hold his head up." He turned to Rick and said, with unrestrained politeness, "May I avail myself again of your hospitality, Tempest? I'm covered with dust and as dry as a bone, so perhaps you would be so kind as to give me a drink and water to wash myself. I—"

Rick, at the end of his patience, cut him short.

"You have abused my hospitality, Willoughby, quite apart from the trouble you have caused Major Van Buren's wife, who is my sister. I'll thank you to take yourself off now—at once. And unless you want to fight a duel with me, you'll keep your mouth shut about what happened here today. It will not redound to your credit, I assure you."

Willoughby looked offended, but he controlled himself and bowed stiffly. "You are right, of course, and I'm sorry—I was carried away. I—as to your sister, sir, I beg you to believe that my feelings for her are sincere. I intend her no harm; indeed, I would do anything in my power to protect her from the unpleasant fellow to whom she is married. You will concede, surely, that the marriage is an unfortunate one?"

Rick's hands bunched into fists at his sides. He disliked the man his sister had married, he was forced to concede, but she had married him, and that, of necessity, had to be the end of it. He said coldly, "Unless you prefer to repair with me to the clearing we have just left, Willoughby, you will get on your horse and rid me of your presence forthwith. You have, I trust, somewhere to go?"

Daniels answered him, in subdued tones, "Yes, sir, we have. Our tents are pitched on my new land grant, where our convict laborers are commencing work on buildings for our stock. We'll leave at once, Mr. Tempest. And— may I offer you my personal apologies?" He offered his hand diffidently, and after a momentary hesitation, Rick accepted it. Daniels, he thought, was not a bad fellow, but like Lucy's choice of a husband, Henry Daniels's choice of a friend was undoubtedly unfortunate. Daniels bowed. "Come on, Rob," he pleaded. "We have outstayed our welcome."

Willoughby spread his hands in a gesture of resignation and, putting a foot in the stirrup, swung himself onto his horse's back.

"I give you good day, sir," he said stiffly to Rick, and not waiting for Daniels to mount, he cantered off onto the dusty track. Daniels suppressed a sigh, bowed again, and, climbing lightly onto his own horse, gathered up his reins and went after his friend.

Rick watched them go, his frown not disappearing, and then returned to the house. Over lunch, he replied as evasively as he could to Katie's worried questions, anxious to spare her the sordid details of Lucy's affair. But it was evident from her distress that she had guessed the reason for the duel and had worked out most of the details for herself.

"I've always detested Major Van Buren, Rick," she confessed. "And after his behavior here today, I pray I may never have to set eyes on him again. But I cannot say I fancy Mr. Robert Willoughby very much, either. There's something about him that—oh, I don't know. Something that doesn't ring true, I think."

"I share your sentiments completely, my dearest Katie," Rick assured her. "My sister Lucy has displayed a deplorable lack of taste, I'm afraid." He sighed. "Have you seen the two boys—Dickon and young Claus?" Katie shook her head. "Well, if you do, send Claus to Bathurst, will you—Van Buren wants him."

"Must we?" Katie objected. "The poor child is terrified of Major Van Buren."

Rick relented. "Well, I suppose we could keep him overnight. Van Buren's probably halfway to the township by now, so the boy won't be of any assistance to him. Poor little devil, he doesn't have much of a life, although there's a rumor that he's Van Buren's son."

"Do you think it's true?"

"The Lord knows—I suppose it could be. The Dutch officials intermarry with their Javanese subjects, I believe. But Lucy's never admitted it, of course."

"Lucy is a strange person," Katie mused. "So different from you and Abigail."

"She always was," Rick said. "And I don't think her sojourn in the Dutch East Indies did her much good." To avoid further discussion of what had become a painful subject, he excused himself and rode out to the river, expecting to find Dickon and Claus fishing there. But there was no sign of either, and the native boy, Winyara, whom he encountered in his search, shook his head emphatically when asked if he had seen them.

"No—but men come," he volunteered, holding up one hand, the fingers separated, to indicate that there had been five of them. "Bad men, runaways. Make camp alonga there—" The hand pointed to a distant clump of trees. "By billabong. They have fire-sticks. Shoot kangaroo."

Escapers, Rick thought with annoyance. As if he had not had enough for one day, devil take it! And armed escapers were dangerous men, bushrangers, liable to raid and steal stock and crops whenever an opportunity to do so presented itself. He had better get back to the farmstead, which, with Jethro and the shepherds busy with their dipping of shorn ewes two miles away, would be virtually unguarded. He thanked Winyara and set off for home at a brisk canter.

It wanted about an hour to sunset when he pulled up in the fold yard of the farm, tethered his horse to the rail, and hurried toward the house, to find that, once again, Katie was at the door waiting for him . . . and this time she was in tears. Alarmed, he ran to her and took her in his arms.

"For God's sake, Katie, what's wrong? You've had no unwelcome callers, have you? Nothing's happened to Dickon, has it—or Claus?"

"No, not that. But . . ." Katie lifted her tear-wet face to his, making a brave effort to control herself. "Harry—" She gestured to one of the stockmen, a gray-haired ticket-of-leave convict named Bowyer, who was standing, hat in hand, in the doorway behind her. "Oh, Rick, Harry found two bodies—naked bodies—in the gully the aborigines call Waratah. They had been shot, and . . ." She broke off, trembling. "You'd better let Harry tell you."

Harry Bowyer gave his account with hoarse brevity. "I was rounding up some strays, Mr. Tempest. They ran into t'gully, see, and I follered 'em down through the trees. They was just lying there, naked as the day they was born—two of 'em. I didn't stay long, just long enough to make sure they was dead. And they was, both of 'em—shot an' dead as doornails."

Rick stared at him in shocked dismay. He did not have to ask who the men were. Katie's face told him what she feared, and he found himself sharing her fears. Waratah

Gully was about three miles away, on the route that Willoughby and Daniels would have followed when returning to their campsite.

"You say they were naked, Harry?" he asked thickly. "What about their horses?"

The stockman shrugged in a gesture of ignorance. "There was hoof marks in the mud, but no sign o' any horses, Mr. Tempest. An' no muskets nor pistols, neither."

The escapers, Rick thought bitterly, of whose presence Winyara had warned him. Escapers always wanted weapons and horses, and against five such desperate men, Robert Willoughby and his friend Daniels would have stood no chance—particularly if the villains had sprung an ambush from the thickly wooded slopes of the gully. He glanced skyward, realizing that the light was fading.

"Go and fetch a couple of lanterns, Harry," he said. "And your horse. We'll have to ride out and bring the bodies in." His arms tightened about Katie's slim waist, and he added gently, "Katie my love, go inside and lock the door. Jethro and the shepherds will be back very soon, but until they are, don't open the door to anyone, understand? I'll send the women to join you."

She was still trembling, but she nodded, prepared to obey him. "Rick, do you think—who could have done this—this terrible thing?"

"There are some absconders in the neighborhood, sweet— Winyara told me. But they'll be miles away by this time; I'm sure they won't come here." Rick frowned, recalling his nephew's absence. "Has Dickon come back? Or the boy, what's his name—Claus?"

"No, they haven't. They—"

"We'll look for them," Rick promised. He bent to kiss her, and his heart quickened its beat as Katie clung to him, her lips soft and yielding under his. "Remember, my dearest—keep the door locked. I'll be as quick as I can."

Harry Bowyer came back, leading both their horses, the lanterns suspended from his saddlebow and a musket slung across his shoulder.

"Jethro's on his way, sir," he offered, to Rick's intense relief. "And looks like Mr. Dickon an' the other youngster's with 'im."

Rick called out this welcome news to Katie and swung himself into his saddle.

The light was all but gone when they reached the gully, but even before Bowyer had contrived to light one of the lanterns, Rick had seen enough to confirm his worst fears.

Willoughby and Daniels lay where they had fallen, beside the small, sluggishly flowing stream. A single shot in the back of the head had seemingly killed Daniels outright, but Willoughby had been shot twice. The second shot—apparently fired at close range—had been to the heart, and he had died in a pool of his own blood.

Holding the lantern in a shaking hand, Bowyer said, sickened, "The blasted rogues! Never gave these poor devils a chance, did they? May they rot in hell, the bloody swine!"

Rick got to his feet, choking back the bile that rose in his throat. "We'll have the soldiers after them. I'll ride to Bathurst at first light, Harry, and report this to the commandant." He would call at the hospital also, he thought—to inquire for Josef Van Buren and inform him of what had happened. Because he would have to be told and, alas, the boy Claus, his son, restored to him. "Lend me a hand, will you?"

"Right, sir," Bowyer said, recovering himself. Together they lifted the two limp bodies onto their horses, then made their way slowly back to Pengallon.

Claus had gone, Katie said apologetically, after Rick had rejoined her in the lamp-lit living room and confirmed the bleak news of the two deaths.

"He insisted, poor little fellow, although Dickon and I did all we could to persuade him to wait until daylight. He kept saying that Major Van Buren would be angry with him if he stayed, and he seemed so frightened that I had not the heart to detain him. But it has upset Dickon,

Rick—I think he's very fond of Claus. At all events, he refused to eat, and he's gone to bed."

"Where I'm going as soon as I've eaten," Rick said wearily. "It has been a hell of a day, Katie my love—and I shall have to be up at the crack of dawn in the morning. The sooner I report what has happened to the commandant, the sooner the troops can make a search for those murdering rogues of escapers. If need be, I'll accompany them or use my men to aid the search. Those swine have got to be brought to justice."

Katie set a plate of steaming food in front of him, and he fell upon it hungrily.

"I suppose . . ." She hesitated, her expression troubled. "Rick, are you sure that it was the escapers who killed those two poor young men?"

"Who else could it have been, dearest?" Rick countered. "Who else would have stolen their clothes and their horses?"

Katie lapsed into a thoughtful silence. Finally, becoming aware of it, Rick pushed his empty plate away and reached for her hand.

"What's on your mind, Katie?" he asked. "Because something is troubling you, is it not?"

"Yes," she admitted reluctantly. "But it's probably foolishness. I'm sure you are right, Rick, and the bushrangers, the escapers, stole the horses and the clothing. But did they need to kill those two young men, just to steal from them? They could have held them up—you said there were five of them, did you not? Would they add murder to their other crimes?"

"Desperate men do desperate things," Rick reminded her. He stifled a yawn. "Lord, I'm all in! Let's go to bed, shall we?"

Later, as Katie lay in his arms, loving and responsive—as she had not been, Rick reflected, for longer than he cared to remember—she again expressed her doubts.

A trifle impatiently, he lifted his head from her breast. "Then who?" he challenged. "Who except the absconders could have set an ambush and killed them?"

''Major Van Buren,'' Katie whispered tensely. ''He had a rifle, and—oh, Rick, there was murder in his heart when he left here! He wanted Mr. Willoughby dead—and he would be capable of murder.''

''Van Buren went to Bathurst with a pistol ball in his arm,'' Rick said dismissively. ''Waratah Gully's in the opposite direction. Besides, he had lost a good deal of blood, and he could hardly sit his horse. He might have wanted Willoughby dead, but I swear he was in no state to kill him. Anyway''—he let his head fall, drawing her to him—''I will call on him at the hospital tomorrow, if it will set your mind at rest. Katie, I love you! I need you, Katie my dearest . . . don't hold yourself aloof from me any longer, I beg you. We could have other children, you know, if we want them badly enough.''

Katie tensed only momentarily, and then her arms went round his neck, and his lips found hers. . . .

Next day, in Bathurst, Rick delivered the two bodies and made his report to the garrison commander. That task completed and his offer of help in the search accepted, he went to the hospital. His visit was brief.

Major Van Buren was there, and the army surgeon confirmed that he had been admitted the previous evening in a state of near unconsciousness, having been found on the road and brought in by a settler.

''I removed a pistol ball from his left upper arm, Mr. Tempest, and it should heal quite satisfactorily in time. At present, however, he's running a fever, and the only visitor he has expressed a desire to see is a Javanese boy, who is with him now. Perhaps you would care to leave a message, and I will see that it is delivered to him.''

Rick hesitated and then shook his head. ''It will keep, sir, thank you. At the moment, I have more pressing business to attend to. I'm joining one of your patrols to hunt for a gang of murdering bushrangers, who killed and robbed two new settlers on my property.''

''Then I wish you luck, sir,'' the surgeon offered warmly.

"There's a perfect plague of their kind in this area now. They must be stamped out, by heaven they must! I trust you will catch up with the scum before they do any more harm."

Forty-eight hours later, after an exhausting chase, the escapers were apprehended, and Rick was able to identify the horses and the clothing stolen from the murdered men. The five prisoners were brought into Bathurst and heavily ironed, and despite their frantic denials and their reiterated claims that they had come across the two bodies when both victims were already dead, all five were to be charged with robbery and murder and sent to Sydney to await trial.

Their leader, a well-dressed man with the manners of a gentleman, gave his name as Nicholas Vincent and the crime for which he had been deported as highway robbery.

His lingering doubts dispelled by this revelation, Rick returned to Pengallon and to Katie.

"The absconders are guilty, my love," he told her. "You need not worry anymore about Josef Van Buren, I promise you."

CHAPTER XVI

"A safe voyage, Mrs. Cox!"

"Farewell, dear Alice—we shall hope to see you both again before too long!"

"Let us hope that you will not be kept at Norfolk Island for more than a year. We shall miss you sorely!"

Seated once again in Nathan's hired curricle, Alice smiled shyly in response to the chorus of good wishes from the family and servants of the Reverend Robert Cartwright, who had gathered outside the rectory at Windsor to make their good-byes. On the third finger of her left hand, the wedding ring Nathan had placed there ten days ago gleamed in the early morning sunlight. It was not gold, but brass, and had been fashioned by one of Mr. Cartwright's convict parishioners; yet looking down at it now, Alice's heart swelled with happiness and pride, for the ring was a symbol and the most precious of her few possessions.

She remembered the small, stone-built church and simple ceremony that had changed her status from that of female felon to respected wife, and given her freedom within the colony and the right to hold her head up high in any company. With a sudden misting of the eyes, she recalled the vows Nathan had made and that she had echoed so eagerly, hearing in memory Mr. Cartwright's voice as he had joined their hands together and declared them man and wife.

"Alice Mary, wilt thou have this man to thy wedded husband?" the old rector had asked. "Wilt thou obey him and serve him, love, honor, and keep him in sickness and in health and, forsaking all other, keep thee only unto him, as long as ye both shall live?''

Forsaking all other, Alice thought, and while still smiling at the Reverend Robert Cartwright's wife and daughters, she could not suppress a shiver of apprehension, which was mingled with fear and guilt. She had not told Nathan of Robert Willoughby; half a hundred times, while they had waited for the formalities to be completed and their banns to be read, it had been on the tip of her tongue to tell him. Yet . . . her teeth closed over her lower lip, as she felt it trembling and knew that her smile had faded. She had lacked the courage to tell him, and then, when the shocking news of Robert's death—Robert's *murder*—had reached Windsor, she had decided finally to keep silent.

It had been a cowardly decision, she knew, but she had assuaged the pangs of conscience by telling herself that to reveal how Robert had used her on the voyage out from England would hurt Nathan and rob him of the joy their marriage had brought him. Nathan was so gentle and diffident a lover; there had been no woman in his life before, and he had harbored no suspicions concerning her, so that it had not been difficult to deceive him. And . . . Alice turned in her seat to look at him, standing there, engaged in a last earnest conversation with the good Mr. Cartwright, his grave young face upturned to that of the man who had been his friend and mentor during their brief stay in the Windsor rectory.

Little Claus had wanted to find a good man to wed her, she recalled, her smile returning, and . . . bless his heart, aided by chance he had done so, for Nathan was truly good. He might lack the years that had given Mr. Cartwright his aura of saintliness, but the two men were cast in the same mold. Both were strong in their faith, both were generous, self-sacrificing, and kindly, and both practiced Christianity as, she felt sure, the Lord Jesus Christ had shown, by His blessed example, that it should be practiced. It made no difference to either if those who needed their help or their counsel were convict or free, and, Alice reflected, she had been at the Windsor rectory long enough to see the love the Reverend Cartwright's flock felt for their pastor and the respect in which he was held. Nathan could have had no better teacher, and indeed he—

"Alice, my child—" Mrs. Cartwright was beside the curricle, offering up a small parcel in her big, work-roughened hands. She was a plain woman, forthright in her opinions and inclined, at times, to tartness, but she was as hardworking and practical as her husband, and Alice had conceived a strong affection for her.

"This is a shawl I thought would come in useful, when you are on passage to Norfolk Island. It's not new, but it is made from Shetland wool and will protect you in the strongest wind. No, take it, please—" she insisted as Alice hesitated, unwilling to deprive her of what had evidently been a treasured possession. "Mr. Cartwright and I will be taking no sea voyage until his retirement— and that is likely to be some time off, unless the government relents and grants him a pension. Unlike some others I could name, my dear husband has not made his fortune here." She lifted her face for Alice's farewell kiss, her expression faintly forbidding, as it always was when she spoke of her husband's humble circumstances. But it relaxed as she added, "God keep you, child, and may He give you the strength and courage you will need!"

Alice clung to her for a moment, attempting to voice her thanks, but the old rector's wife brushed her expressions of gratitude aside, reddening in embarrassment.

"I did nothing . . . and it was a pleasure to have your company and Nathan's. I am only glad that I was able to help you to gain your freedom."

Yet she had done so much, Alice recalled. It had been Mrs. Cartwright who had made the long, hot journey to Sydney, in order to talk to Mrs. Van Buren and ensure that her erstwhile employer brought no charges against her for absconding. She had reported that Major Van Buren had returned from Bathurst, with his injured arm in a sling

and the boy Claus with him, and had spoken, with out-
raged pity, of the murder of Robert Willoughby and his
friend by a band of escapers.

"Poor Mrs. Van Buren seemed dazed by the tragedy,"
she had exclaimed, in innocent bewilderment. "She could
talk of nothing else and appeared scarcely to remember
your name, Alice. Of course, her husband had intended to
go into partnership with those two unfortunate young men,
and they were friends—it must have come as a double
blow to both of them. But at least the evil murderers were
apprehended and are to be brought to trial. One, Mrs. Van
Buren told me, was a notorious highwayman, who had
escaped within a few days of being landed from the transport that brought him here."

She had talked to Claus, too, Alice thought gratefully,
but the boy—although he had apparently been overjoyed to
learn of her forthcoming marriage to Nathan—had rejected
Mrs. Cartwright's well-meant overtures, and that good
woman, hurt and puzzled by his attitude, had described
him as "a secretive little fellow, who does not take to
strangers." Well, perhaps he was, but if that were so, it
was the life poor Claus was forced to lead in the Van
Buren household that had made him wary of strangers and
inclined to keep his own counsel, lest a word spoken out
of turn land him in trouble.

Since the arrival of Nathan's orders, instructing him to
embark in the government cutter *Mermaid* for passage to
Norfolk Island, Alice had known that they would be returning to Sydney Town—perhaps for several days, before the
Mermaid was ready to sail. She had made up her mind that
somehow, even at the risk of incurring Mrs. Van Buren's
wrath, she would try to see Claus, and Saleh, too, if it
were possible. With that end in view, she had sent a note
by the mail carrier, and . . . Nathan climbed onto the box
beside her and reached for the reins.

"We must be on our way, my dearest, if we are to reach
Sydney Town before nightfall," he said reluctantly. He
raised his carriage whip in salute, as the chorus of fare-

wells broke out afresh and the youngest of the rector's daughters, greatly daring, blew him a kiss from behind the cover of her hand.

"They are a truly delightful family," Nathan said, with sincerity. "I cannot remember ever being treated with so much kindness. Yet they are in a perilous financial state, thanks to the Colonial Office, which has failed to keep a promise made five years ago to increase the poor rector's stipend. With so many mouths to feed, he cannot afford to buy a horse to take him on his parish rounds and must, in consequence, make them on foot. But Mr. Marsden—who is one of the wealthiest landowners in the colony—has had *his* annual emolument increased by a hundred pounds!"

"I did not know," Alice confessed. "Although Mrs. Cartwright has hinted as much to me. She said just now that her husband could not think of retirement unless the government relents and grants him a pension. Do you think they will relent?"

Nathan sighed. "I do not know, my love. But I felt ashamed when the poor old gentleman told me how much he earned and I realized that I—a newcomer—shall be paid the same amount for doing duty in a penal establishment."

He whipped their horses into a brisk trot and lapsed into silence. Alice puzzled over his last statement, wondering at the injustice of it. The Cartwrights, she knew, had been in the colony for over seven years, but . . . perhaps the prison service was more exacting than the work of an ordinary parish and chaplains were reluctant to undertake the task. Certainly they had to endure isolation—the new convict settlements were being set up in places that were remote from civilization, to render escape impossible and punishment more severe, and like the officials and the wardens, the chaplains would be required to share that exile. She had heard Mr. Cartwright talking of "capital respites" and knew, from what he had told her, that these were men who had been sentenced to death and then reprieved, being given, instead of the death penalty, a life sentence, against which there was no appeal. Norfolk Island had been reopened to accommodate such men, and it was not intended—according to Mr. Cartwright—that any of them should be permitted to return to New South Wales.

Alice shivered, and—uncannily, as if she had spoken her thoughts aloud—Nathan said bleakly, "His Excellency the Governor has decreed that Norfolk Island is to be a place where punishment short of death is to be inflicted on all who are sent there. I pray to God, my little love, that you will find the strength to face life there."

Of the two of them, Alice reflected grimly, she was probably the more likely to find that strength. She had been a convict and he had not; she had been brought out in chains and had been beaten, humiliated, and . . . and corrupted and robbed of her innocence by Robert Willoughby. But he was dead and could never betray that secret, and she would be wise if she were to put the fear of betrayal from her mind and remember only that she was Nathan's wife, the wife of—what had Claus called him? A man of God. Summoning a smile, she put out her hand to touch his and said consolingly, "We shall be together, Nathan dear. However bad Norfolk Island proves to be, we shall have each other."

"Yes," he agreed. "Thanks be to God, we shall have each other."

They halted in Parramatta for luncheon at the Woolpack Hotel—an extravagance, Alice knew, but one her bridegroom insisted on—and, rested and replete, completed the last fifteen miles over the well-surfaced turnpike road at a good pace, reaching Sydney Town just before sunset. Nathan booked them a room for the night in the small hotel in George Street where he had previously lodged, and from its window the next day they were able to see the ships that were to convey them, along with a hundred convicts, to Norfolk Island.

The *Mermaid* lay in the outer anchorage, a graceful vessel, her gilded figurehead gleaming brightly in the sunshine and men busy on her decks. Alice could clearly make out the hulk *Phoenix*, where the capital respites had been imprisoned; a procession of boats plied between her and the colonial brig *Brutus* with their melancholy cargoes of heavily fettered convicts. There were some women and children, Alice saw, being taken out to the *Mermaid*—the wives and families of the condemned men, she could only suppose, who had agreed voluntarily to accompany them into exile.

After breaking their fast, they walked the short distance to dockside, where Nathan learned that they would be expected to be on board the *Mermaid* by noon, which left her very little time in which to seek out Claus and Saleh, in order to make her farewells. She was fearful of going openly to the Van Burens' house, lest, even now, Lucy Van Buren might decide to make some claim on her, but to her relief, Claus made his appearance, running joyfully into her arms as she hesitated uncertainly on the quay.

"I have watched each day for your coming," the boy told her as she hugged him. "They said that the man of God Mr. Nathan Cox would sail to the Norfolk Island, and I was sure that you would be with him. He is now your husband, is he not?"

"Yes," Alice confirmed. "He is my husband, Claus."

"And you are happy with him? He is good man, always kind to you?"

"Oh, yes! He is always kind, and I am happy. Did Saleh not receive my letter, to tell you this?"

"There was a letter," Claus agreed. "But—" He shrugged. "None of us could read it; not even Amos, though he is English and he tried."

Alice was instantly contrite. "Oh, Claus, I'm sorry—I should have realized."

"It is no matter," Claus assured her. "Saleh was listening to what was said when he was waiting at the table, and when Missus Dawson and the Miss Dorothea dined, they spoke of your marriage. And . . ." He hung his head. "I do not like to tell you this, dear Alice, but *Mevrouw* Van Buren was saying that you would go to the Norfolk Island

and it was the right place for you. She is a most unkind
lady . . . more unkind than before, since she was hearing
of the death of *Mijnheer* Willoughby, and—'' The boy
broke off, his dark cheeks suddenly drained of color. ''I
must not speak of that matter, even to you. My fath—I
mean *Mijnheer* Van Buren, he say he wring my neck like a
chicken's if I speak of it.''

Alice did not press him. Had there been more time, she
might have done so, but Nathan was waving to her from
the far side of the quay, and a boat from the *Mermaid*, she
saw, was approaching the steps. Their baggage—most of it
Nathan's—had been brought from the lodging house in a
barrow and was waiting to be loaded. . . . She would have
to go.

Claus saw the wave, and his eyes filled with tears.
''You must go now to the ship, Alice?'' he whispered.

''Yes, I must. I'm sorry, Claus. I had hoped that we
might have had a few days here and that I might have seen
Saleh and the others to thank them and say farewell. Will
you do that for me?''

Claus blinked back his tears, nodding vigorously.

''I wish so much that I might come with you,'' he said.

''I wish it also,'' Alice admitted huskily. ''Oh, dearest
Claus, how I wish it!''

''You have the man of God, your husband,'' Claus
reminded her. ''I would come, were you alone, Alice. But
Mijnheer Van Buren—he was wounded, shot in the arm
when he and *Mijnheer* Willoughby were fighting with
pistols, in what is called a duel. He is my father, I must
care for him. I am *door de plicht gebonden*—in duty
bound, I think you say in English.''

''Yes, that is what we say.'' Alice bent to plant a kiss
on his dark head, her throat tight. ''God bless you, Claus—
God bless you and keep you always.''

''You write to me,'' the boy urged. ''I learn to read
English—it not take too long. And to write also.'' He
flashed her a smile. ''Already I learn drawing from Dickon.
I draw you picture, until I learn proper to write, see? And

maybe I pay you visit at the Norfolk Island, like before, when *Mijnheer* Van Buren go to there in ship.'' He was cheerful again, his eyes bright with anticipation, and when Nathan came to join them, Claus was his usual polite and smiling self, offering his hand with adult dignity.

Nathan wrung it warmly. Then, his farewell said, he took Alice's arm and they made their way to the waiting boat.

The *Mermaid*'s commander was on the cutter's deck to greet them, a tall, handsome officer with the bluest eyes Alice had ever seen.

''The Reverend Nathan and Mrs. Cox, I believe? I am Lieutenant Justin Broome, Royal Navy—welcome aboard! We are giving passage to fifty male convicts, six wives, and six children, in addition to yourselves, and the *Brutus* is carrying a like number. Granted fair winds, we should make the island in eight or nine days, and we shall do our best to make you comfortable during the passage.'' He nodded to a small, red-headed boy standing alertly at his elbow. ''My son, Murdoch Broome, who is known as Red— he will show you to your quarters, and I shall look forward to making your acquaintance in a more leisurely fashion over dinner.''

Nathan thanked him, and as he and Alice followed the captain's young son to the after hatchway, a small figure could just be seen, waving to them vigorously from the quayside.

Alice waved back, conscious of a lump in her throat, and young Red said curiously, ''That's Claus Karimon, is it not, ma'am? Do you know him well?''

''Yes,'' Alice confirmed. ''Very well.''

''He is a good fellow,'' Red told her, with conviction. ''Mind the hatch coaming, ma'am. Your cabin's on the larb'd side, Mr. Cox, sir, just for'ard of where you're standing.''

It was very different, Alice thought, from the manner in which she had been received on board the *Mary Anne* transport, almost a year ago, and the light, airy cabin into which the captain's son had ushered them was in striking contrast to the overcrowded orlop deck to which they had taken her in chains.

Sensing her husband's eyes on her questioningly, she gave him a swift, happy smile and went into his waiting arms. "I love you, Nathan," she whispered.

"And I adore you," Nathan answered, holding her to him, his voice oddly shaken. "And I thank God for you!"

"His Honor Justice De Lancey, Your Excellency," the manservant announced. He bowed and stood aside to permit George De Lancey to precede him.

The new Governor, Lieutenant General Ralph Darling, was seated at his desk, but he rose, his hand cordially held out, and said crisply, "Ah, Mr. De Lancey—I'm delighted to make your acquaintance, sir. Be seated, I pray you. I understand you wish to see me in connection with a criminal trial you have recently conducted."

George took the chair the Governor had indicated. Darling, he thought, had the look of the martinet he was reputed to be. His bearing was stiffly military, his uniform impeccable, and his gaze searching, the shrewd blue eyes seeking to penetrate the thin veneer of social courtesy the brief exchange had generated. A man, clearly, who would appreciate plain speaking—even one who would demand it, viewing any attempt to dissemble with annoyance. And an efficient man, judging by the precise order of the papers on his desk, from among which—without waiting for George to detail the reason for his visit—he picked out the bulky file containing the transcript of the trial in question.

"You are referring to the trial of an absconder by the name of Nicholas Vincent, I take it?"

"Yes, Your Excellency," George confirmed, "I am." He waited for the Governor to glance carefully through the transcript, saying nothing until the papers were replaced neatly in their folder and Darling's cold blue gaze returned to his face. Then he added quietly, "I have come to request Your Excellency to remit the death sentence imposed on Vincent and his companions.''

General Darling was taken visibly aback, his thick brows lifting in astonishment. ''But you yourself imposed the sentence, did you not? You tried the case, and the men were found guilty of murder and robbery, damme! They had absconded from the Government Farm at Emu Ford—Vincent organized their escape, having himself absconded from the jail here.''

''He was granted ticket-of-leave, sir. As an educated man, he was made clerk to Captain Piper, the port naval officer, and—''

''He left his employment,'' the Governor interrupted sharply. ''And took to the bush, carrying arms. He and the men he helped to escape from Emu Ford became what I believe you call bushrangers—footpads and robbers. I understand that when apprehended, such criminals are usually hanged—is that not so, Mr. De Lancey?''

''Yes, sir, it is,'' George conceded. ''But those who commit no violence are often respited. The death sentence has to be imposed by law, but it is within the Governor's province to remit the sentence, if there are any extenuating circumstances. Capital respites, sir, are sentenced instead to life imprisonment at the new penal colony at Moreton Bay or to the reopened prison on Norfolk Island.''

The Governor's face darkened. ''Devil take it, De Lancey—these men committed murder! They shot and killed two new settlers—two ex-King's officers—and robbed them of their weapons, their horses, and even of their clothing! Did not another ex-naval officer—what is his name? Tempest, is it not?—did not Mr. Tempest state in evidence that he found the bodies of those two unfortunate gentlemen naked?''

''Yes, sir, he did. But Nicholas Vincent and the four men with him swore on oath that they found Mr. Willoughby and Mr. Daniels already dead. Vincent admitted taking their weapons and clothes and also their horses.

But—'' George shrugged. "He insisted that neither he nor the men with him murdered them.''

"And you believed him?'' Darling snapped.

"Yes, sir. I was convinced that he was speaking the truth.''

"The officers who sat with you on the bench did not agree. They brought in verdicts of guilty against all six men.'' The Governor was scowling.

George inclined his head. His jury had been composed of officers of the newly arrived 57th Regiment, sitting for the first time in judgment, and one of them—Captain Patrick Logan, a hard-eyed, bewhiskered Peninsular veteran—had swayed the others, scornfully dismissing their doubts. Logan was to be Captain Bishop's successor as commandant of the Moreton Bay penal settlement, he recalled, and was only waiting for a ship to take him there. . . . "The evidence was not conclusive, sir,'' he asserted. "And there was the time factor.''

"What time factor?'' Darling demanded.

"You will find it in Mr. Tempest's evidence, sir. If I may—'' George reached for the file and, riffling through it swiftly, laid the requisite sheets out on the desk. "Mr. Tempest states that he and an aborigine he employs placed Vincent and his fellows some five miles from where the bodies were found at the time when, all are agreed, the murder was committed. Here, sir.'' He indicated the appropriate lines of neat script on the transcript.

The Governor read the page and thrust it from him. "What does this prove, Mr. De Lancey? The rogues were mounted, surely?''

"Not all of them; and it would have taken them over an hour, in that country, to reach the scene of the shooting, sir,'' George argued. "And their horses were spent, they said.'' He hesitated and then added emphatically, "And there was a duel, sir. That must place a new complexion on the matter.''

"Yes, that infernal duel!'' Darling exclaimed wrathfully. He passed a hand through his thinning hair. "I should take action on that, I suppose, although it's probably wiser to turn a blind eye to it, since two of the protagonists are dead, poor devils." His eyes narrowed. "For heaven's sake, De Lancey, you're not suggesting that the Dutchman—Van Buren—lay in ambush and shot the two poor fellows, are you?"

"Sir, I consider that there is room for doubt," George returned flatly. "Josef Van Buren is an odd fellow, with a violent temper. And he had no reason to like young Willoughby. They were opponents in the duel, and he considered his honor impugned. Besides that, sir, Van Buren's loyalty is . . . well, in some doubt." Briefly, he described the Dutchman's visit to Norfolk Island and his rendezvous with the French frigate and saw the Governor's brows rise once again in astonishment.

"But the man was wounded—he had a pistol ball in his arm, did he not?"

"Yes, that is so, sir," George conceded. "But he was able to sit a horse—he was able to ride over twelve miles to Bathurst. The time factor applies also to Van Buren, sir."

"Damme, I suppose it does! But you've no proof, have you?"

"No, sir, none."

"Well, then?"

"The proof that Vincent and his fellow absconders committed the murder is, in my view, also lacking . . . and I do not believe that they are violent men. Following their escape from Emu Ford, sir, they were of service to my wife, when a bushfire was raging." Choosing his words carefully, George repeated the story Rachel had told him. "They risked recapture in order to return to the Government Farm and summon help, sir. And far from harming my wife, they caught her horse and assisted her to remount and ride to safety." He did not deem it wise to add that Vincent and one of his friends had also, in all likelihood, been the ones responsible for the earlier break-in at his own chambers on Macquarie Street—Vincent's possession of the stolen pistol had all but confirmed this, and, George now realized, they must have been after some of the very records now on the table before him. All the same . . .

"So you believe that Nicholas Vincent is what the gutter press is pleased to call 'a gentleman of the road,' do you?" Darling suggested cynically. "He was transported for highway robbery, was he not?"

"I understand he was, sir. But he was never charged with any form of violence. I've looked up his record. It was because of that, sir, that he wasn't hanged in England. His sentence was commuted."

"And you think I should commute the sentence you've just imposed on him, do you?"

George drew himself up, meeting General Darling's searching gaze squarely. "That is the reason for my calling on your, sir, to appeal on Vincent's behalf for clemency."

"It's somewhat unusual for the judge who tried him to make such an appeal—even in New South Wales, is it not?" Darling suggested.

"Yes, sir, I confess it is. But as a judge, I am anxious not to be party to what I sincerely believe would be a miscarriage of justice in this case."

"I see. Well—" The Governor continued to subject him to a pensive scrutiny, but finally his expression relaxed into a wintry smile, and George felt the tension drain out of him. His appeal was, he was only too well aware, unusual, but he had been obliged to make it. The evidence had not been convincing; proof *had* been lacking, and Van Buren's behavior in court had aroused his suspicions and led to his dismay at the verdict the six 57th officers had brought in—and this despite his summing up, which had urged acquittal of all five convicts on the capital charge. They were guilty on the lesser charges, of course, and to a man had not attempted to refute them, so even if the Governor were to exercise his prerogative and remit the death sentence, they would still have to serve an almost equally heavy sentence.

"Men sent to Moreton Bay go there for life, I believe," Darling said. "And there is no possibility of escape."

"No, sir, none," George assured him.

"Then I will not confirm these death sentences, Mr. De Lancey, in view of what you have told me. Indeed, I am grateful that you have brought the—ah—the matter to my attention, because—" The smile faded, and General Darling's expression again hardened. "An eye must be kept on Josef Van Buren, and, damme, there must be no more duels! My instructions from Lord Bathurst are to ensure that good order and discipline shall prevail throughout this colony, and I intend to carry out those instructions to the letter. I've not been here long, as you're aware, but already I am finding that certain administrative departments are in a state of chaos. The surveyor's office is understaffed, the port authority can produce no accounts for the past two years, and—yes, devil take him, convicts like this man Vincent are put into positions of trust, which they abuse!"

He talked on, a distinct edge to his voice, and George listened politely but with a certain foreboding. The new Governor, it was clear, intended to initiate a substantial reorganization of the colony's civil service, and—whether or not his efforts met with success—inevitably he would make himself unpopular. But it would be of little use to attempt to warn him. He had been for a number of years at the Horse Guards, as a senior staff officer and then as deputy adjutant general, George knew, and evidently had a staff officer's mentality. But . . .

General Darling changed the subject. "You were a cavalry officer, Major Ovens told me—you served in the Peninsular campaign and at Waterloo, I believe?"

"Yes, sir," George acknowledged. "I started my military career as an ensign in the Fifty-second and ended it with the Scots Greys at Waterloo."

"Sir William De Lancey was your brother, was he not?"

"Yes, he was, sir."

"His death was a sad loss," the general said with obvious sincerity. "I commanded the Fifty-first on Sir John Moore's retreat to Corunna, and I met your brother when I first went to the Horse Guards. He was a fine officer, with exceptional organizing ability. I recall that the Duke sent for him before Waterloo, to act as his chief of staff in place of that infernal idiot Hudson Lowe, did he not?"

"Yes, sir, he did," George confirmed. "My poor brother had just celebrated his nuptials when the summons arrived. Indeed, sir, he—" But Governor Darling was not listening.

"I wrote to him, you know," Darling said with undisguised bitterness. "I wrote personally to the Peer, begging him to give me a command in Belgium, but I received no reply until after Waterloo had been fought. And then, damme, De Lancey, he reprimanded me! Staff officers, he told me, were seldom suitable material for the command of fighting divisions, and he considered me no exception to that rule. I was deeply mortified, as you may well imagine. However, there have been compensations—staff officers are, it would seem, suitable material for appointment to governorships. I was Governor of Mauritius before I came out here, you know."

"Yes, sir, so I believe. You—" But once again General Darling abruptly changed the subject.

"Sir William De Lancey was American by birth, wasn't he?" he asked. "Which means that you—"

"I'm American by birth, sir," George answered, without hesitation. "Our family was of Huguenot descent, and we were what are now called American Loyalists."

"I see." The cold blue eyes held an unvoiced suspicion, but George made no response to it.

There was a knock on the door, and Major John Ovens came briskly into the room. He had remained as secretary to the Governor after Sir Thomas Brisbane's departure, and with the departure of Major Goulburn following swiftly thereafter, rumor had it that he was angling for promotion to the influential post of secretary for the colony.

"Sir," he reminded the Governor, "You have an appointment with Mr. William Wentworth and Dr. Waddell. Shall I bring them in now?"

Darling nodded, though with a forbidding scowl. "Infernal fellows—they intended to start a newspaper, I believe, and—" A loud thud, coming from the anteroom next door, caused him to break off. "Damme, what's that? See what's going on, will you, Judge?"

George was already on his way to the anteroom. Major Ovens, he saw, had collapsed, and lay, his florid face denuded of color, on the floor, with Wentworth and Waddell bending over him.

"I fear he has suffered a stroke," the young barrister Wentworth exclaimed. His raised voice brought aides and servants running, the Governor with them. They lifted the unconscious man onto a daybed, but their combined efforts did not succeed in rousing him, and, moments later, his fitful breathing abruptly ceased.

George, feeling for a pulse or a heartbeat, could find neither; his gaze met Wentworth's in mute dismay, and Waddell said, in a low, shaken voice, "I greatly fear, Your Excellency, that the poor gentleman is dead."

"God rest his gallant soul," the Governor responded. He was visibly upset, shaking his head in disbelief. "He— good God, he wasn't forty! My predecessor said of him that no public officer rendered him better service or the colony more benefit. To be struck down so suddenly, in the prime of his life is—oh, quite appalling! Although I had only known him for so short a time, I—I feel as if I have lost my right hand."

He left the room, his scarlet-clad shoulders hunched, and William Wentworth observed, more to himself than to those standing in a silent group around him, "My father warned poor Major Ovens years ago that his heart was weak. Yet he went exploring with Currie and Oxley and wore himself out in the administrative work of government, poor fellow. But I think he had a premonition that his life was soon to end—only a few weeks ago he asked me to draw up his will for him.'' Wentworth smiled wryly. "In it, he made the request that he might be interred beside the grave of his friend the late Ellis Bent. Odd, is it not, that they should have become friends? John Ovens was Governor Macquarie's man throughout his term of office, and Bent and his brother did all in their power to ruin the poor old Governor . . . and yet, in death, that's whom he chooses to lie beside! I find it more than passing strange, I must confess.''

No one answered him, but later, when Major Ovens's body had been removed and they were leaving Government House, George fell into step beside William Wentworth. They had encountered each other several times in court, but until now their relationship had remained on a purely professional basis. Now, however, intrigued by the young barrister's recent remarks, George decided to rectify his earlier omission and seek Wentworth's acquaintance.

Dr. D'Arcy Wentworth's son had, he knew, been born on Norfolk Island, where his father had been serving as a surgeon. His mother had been a convict girl there, who later had married the good doctor. The elder Wentworth, now retired, had become the colony's principal surgeon and Sydney's chief magistrate, having won the respect and trust of the whole community and the warm friendship of successive Governors. His elder son had been granted a commission in the army, and William Charles, after taking part in the first crossing of the Blue Mountains, had been sent to England to complete his education and read for the English bar . . . leaving a minor scandal in his wake, in the form of a scurrilous poem, issued anonymously, intended to defend the late Governor Macquarie against the calumny of his enemies.

Now about thirty, William was said to have outgrown his youthful aggressiveness, although those who knew him well claimed that he had merely learned to control it. He was a curiously awkward man, always untidily dressed, with a cast in one eye and an unruly thatch of auburn hair, but he had a fine brain and an intellectual stature few in the colony could match, and since his return, he and his fellow barrister Waddell had built up a lucrative legal practice. Considering the grants of land he already possessed, he must, George thought, be a comparatively wealthy man—though from his appearance and the shabby clothes he habitually wore, no one would have guessed it.

They talked amicably enough as they walked toward Macquarie Street in the warm sunshine, Wentworth grinning derisively as he admitted that the poem he had entered for the chancellor's medal at Cambridge had failed to win the coveted prize.

"I titled it 'Australasia,' and it was a decided improvement on the 'pipe' I composed about the late unlamented Colonel Molle, Judge," he said. "But it was merely an also-ran, as the racing fraternity term it. However, sir, I did succeed in getting published two volumes on the subject of our settlements here before I left London, and my work was well received by the reading public. Indeed, it ran into a third edition and has given me incentive for my next venture."

"And what is that?" George questioned, his curiosity further aroused.

William Wentworth's grin widened into a puckish smile. "My friend Robert Waddell and I intend to set up a newspaper—he has previous experience; he was for a time editor of the *Statesman*, and we have brought the necessary plant and machinery with us."

George studied his face in pensive surprise, and the younger man went on, "There's a need for it here, sir. It will be a crusading newspaper, and we have decided to call it the *Australian*. In its pages we shall campaign vigorously for liberal principles—for the introduction of trial by jury, freedom of the press, elected representation on the Governor's council, for instance. But above all we shall support the late and, by me, greatly lamented Governor Macquarie's policies in relation to the emancipists. Governor Brisbane did not uphold them, and I fear that this new holder of the office will be unequivocally on the side of the 'pure merinos.' "

"What makes you think so?" George countered, frowning. "He did not give me that impression, although I understand that he intends to reorganize the various government administrative departments. And *that's* not too soon, Wentworth."

"No, Judge, it's not," Wentworth conceded. "But within twenty-four hours of his arrival here, General Darling told Vance Donaldson—Captain Donaldson, of the Fifty-seventh, who is newly appointed commandant of Norfolk Island—he told him, sir, that emancipists should be treated 'as a lower class of persons, who must never be permitted to aspire to either social recognition or political power.' Those were his exact words, I'm told. Damme, sir, even Colonel Molle never went so far!"

This still further contradicted his own impression of the new Governor, George reflected, but he challenged mildly, "May we anticipate another pipe before long, then?"

William Wentworth shook his head vehemently.

"No, Judge—I'm forging a better weapon to fight for the causes I believe in," he asserted with conviction. "As I told you, sir, the columns of the *Australian* will fight all my battles on behalf of the underprivileged in the future. It will fight them fairly, I give you my word, but with heart and spirit and without fear of intimidation, whosoever may attempt to silence its voice!" His expression relaxed and became again oddly boyish. "Truly better than a mischievous pipe, would you not agree, Your Honor?"

"I will reserve judgment, Mr. Wentworth," George responded, echoing the younger man's smile. "But I shall deem it an honor if you and Dr. Waddell will dine with my wife and me in the near future."

"We shall be more than pleased to do so, Judge," Wentworth assured him.

They parted company at the door of George's chambers, a strange, unspoken truce between them, which, on reflection, George decided might well be put to the test before long, for William Wentworth was very evidently in earnest.

To Rachel he said, when he joined her two hours later for luncheon, "I think, my love, that I shall accept the appointment to the Hunter Valley judiciary, if it is again offered to me—or even a circuit commission. I've had enough of Sydney, and we could take land in the Hunter Valley very soon—the convicts are leaving. Unless, of course, you have your heart set on returning to Ulva."

"No." Rachel shook her head. "Ulva will do well enough with Aaron and Nelly Finch in charge—we still cannot run much stock there. I should like to break new ground, George, and if you want to leave Sydney, I shall leave with you very gladly." She added, a trifle wistfully, "Once Will goes, Ulva will not be a place I hanker after." Then, glimpsing the expression on his face, she came to put her hand in his. "Why do you want to quit Sydney, George dear?"

Was it an instinctive reaction to his interview with the new Governor and his subsequent talk with the younger Wentworth, George asked himself, or was he reluctant to engage in battle on one side or the other? Sydney society was too sharply divided; he was weary of the quarreling between elitist and emancipist, of the constant rivalries, the jealousies and the wagging tongues. He had felt a bond of loyalty to Sir Thomas Brisbane because they had served together, but General Darling was a stranger—and Wentworth and his proposed crusade would only inflame the present situation. Besides, Rachel was pregnant with their second child.

He touched her swelling stomach with gentle fingers. "I hanker for peace and quiet, my love," he told her. "For you and our children. And I want finally to turn my sword into a plowshare."

Rachel lifted her face to his. "So be it," she answered softly.

Part Two

THE MILLS OF GOD

CHAPTER XVII

The funeral service was over, and the last of the considerable crowd of mourners had left the house, with expressions of sympathy and regret mingled with well-intentioned advice as to the future, to which Emily Willoughby had listened with downcast eyes and a swiftly growing resolve.

Her father was dead. After a lengthy illness, Rear Admiral Sir Francis Willoughby had died in his sleep, and the Royal Navy, according to custom, had taken charge of all the funeral arrangements, with naval pallbearers, his flag draped over his coffin, and volleys of musketry fired over his grave.

Emily, worn out by the strain of nursing him, had walked dazedly behind the hearse, her two little sisters holding anxiously to her hands, and her brother Jamie—a tall, slim stranger in his white-patched midshipman's uniform, grown out of all recognition—walking a few paces in front of her.

It had been touch and go whether Jamie would be given leave to attend the funeral. He had been appointed to His Majesty's frigate *Success,* commanded by Captain James Stirling, which was due to sail from Portsmouth to Sydney, Australia, on the twenty-fifth of January. Fortunately, the *Success* had been ordered to put into Plymouth on her way, and the captain had given Jamie permission to rejoin her there. Emily suppressed a weary sigh and glanced uncertainly at her younger brother. Since being graduated in the top ten cadets from the Royal Naval College, Jamie had spent a year at sea, and this was the first time she had seen him, apart from his brief graduation leave, for over a year.

They had yet had no time to talk, with the bustle of the funeral and the constant coming and going of callers at the house, and now, as they awaited the arrival of their father's lawyer for the reading of the will, Jamie was oddly silent and withdrawn. In the old days, he had always confided in her and sought her counsel, but now, seemingly overwhelmed by the new responsibilities that would face him as their father's heir, he appeared anything but eager to resume their childhood intimacy.

Emily braced herself for a rebuff and picked up the teapot that had stood untouched for the past ten minutes on the tray that the butler, Hawkins, had set for them.

"Would you like some tea, Jamie?" she asked diffidently.

Jamie inclined his dark head in assent but did not break his silence until he had drunk his tea thirstily and passed his cup to be refilled. Then he burst out, with unexpected vehemence, "I hated him, Emmy, you know! It's a—a dreadful admission to make, when Papa is barely cold in his grave. But I can't pretend to grief I don't feel, especially to you."

"I should keep your voice down, though," Emily cautioned. "We don't want the servants to hear . . . or Charlotte and Biddy."

Her brother reddened. "All right, I will. But I want *you* to understand, Emmy. I respected him, I even admired him until that awful day when he summoned us all to his study—you and Rob and me. That was what made me hate him—the way he treated poor Rob. Cutting him off as he did, forcing him to go out to Australia . . . and giving me Rob's inheritance. I never wanted it—I don't want it now."

"If it is willed to you," Emily pointed out, "you will have to take it, Jamie."

"I know I shall. But—" Jamie's dark eyes were suddenly bright. "I will make sure that the lawyers make adequate provision for you and the two little girls. And whatever's left—the residue, I think they call it—I shall hand over to Rob when we reach Sydney. In a way, it is a stroke of luck that Papa died when he did, because it means that I can take the money out to him.''

"Did you always mean Rob to have it?" Emily asked.

He nodded. "Oh, yes, of course I did. He's the elder son. But it would have taken a good deal longer if the *Success* had sailed before Papa died. When I volunteered to join her, it was in the hope that I might be able to see Rob, perhaps quit the navy and join up with him, if he wanted me to. I'll be doubly welcome if, when I see him again, I'm in a position to give him back his inheritance, will I not?"

"I imagine you will, Jamie dear," Emily agreed. The faint dryness of her tone passed unnoticed. Jamie, with a return of his old affectionate attitude to her, put out both hands to grasp hers. "Dearest Emmy, you *do* understand, don't you? Whatever Papa wanted, whatever he accused Rob of doing—I could not take what is rightfully his, could I? Now he will inherit the baronetcy and the money, and perhaps, God willing, he'll come home. And this house will be waiting for him."

"He may be happily settled in Australia and not wish to leave," Emily argued.

"He wasn't keen to go."

"No. But that was because Papa insisted that he should. By this time he may have a farm and sheep and cattle. In his last letter, he told me he had applied for a land grant in what he called the 'new lands' beyond the Blue Mountains."

"Was that the only letter you received?" Jamie asked. "Apart from the one from the Cape?"

"Yes," Emily admitted. "He sent it in the care of Mr. Yates—Dr. Simon Yates, old Dr. Vine's assistant. I . . ." She broke off, with heightening color. She had not told Jamie her news and had hesitated to do so, for he had seemingly held himself aloof from her, offering and inviting no confidences. But it was momentous news, and she said eagerly, "Jamie, I . . . when we knew that poor Papa

had not very much longer to live, Simon asked me to—to
wed him. He has been accepted by the Missionary Society
and is to be stationed in New Zealand after a probationary
period in New South Wales.''

Jamie let out a joyous exclamation. ''Oh, Emmy, that's
wonderful! You accepted his proposal, I hope?''

Recalling Simon's proposal of marriage, only a few
days ago, Emily's color deepened and spread.

''I love you!'' he had said. ''And I cannot bear the thought
of leaving you behind. Come with me, my dearest little
love, as soon as you are free. I know your father did not
approve of me, did not think me worthy of you . . . and I
am not. But there's no one else, is there, Emmy? For
you—as there can never be for me, darling, as long as I
live!''

She had been so pleased that he had at last found the
courage to ask her to become his wife, and pleased also
because it would mean for her, as well as for Jamie, a
reunion with Robert . . . the whole family together again,
for Simon had insisted that they must bring her two little
sisters with them.

''I accepted,'' she said. ''Oh, yes, of course I accepted
his proposal. I never dared to tell Papa, Jamie, but Simon
Yates and I . . . we have been in love with each other ever
since he came to Murton. And when we go, he wants us to
take Charlotte and Biddy with us. He's promised to be a
father to them.''

''Emmy, I'm so very happy for you!'' Jamie drew her
to him, kissing her warmly on the cheek. ''It will be a
wonderful family reunion, on the other side of the world!
All of us together, even the little ones. Do you know when
you're sailing?''

Emily shook her head. ''We could not arrange anything
while Papa needed me. But the Missionary Society will
pay Simon's passage and mine, I think, and—''

''I will pay Charlotte's and Biddy's,'' Jamie offered.
''It should not take too long for the lawyers to settle
Papa's estate. But even if I have to leave before it is

settled, I can surely make provision for you and the girls."
He glanced about him at the shadowed room. "What of
this house, Emmy? Ought we to sell it?"

"I suppose we should," Emily agreed.

"Rob might want it, if he comes home."

"We don't know whether or not he will come home."

"No." Jamie frowned. "We could ask the lawyers' advice.
But there does not seem very much point in keeping this
vast place, does there, if it is to be unoccupied? Except for
the servants—Hawkins in particular. He's been with Papa
for over twenty years. Unless we—" His expression relaxed.
"Why not bring him with you, Emmy, if he wants to
come? And the girls' nursemaid. You will need servants
when you reach Australia."

"Missionaries do not usually employ servants, Jamie,"
Emily reminded him gently. "But if they do want to
come—Hawkins and Bella, at least—I think we should
offer to pay their passage. Or perhaps, if they prefer to
stay, you could arrange for pensions for them."

"I'll talk to Papa's lawyer about it," Jamie promised.
He glanced at the clock on the mantel. "I wonder how
much longer he'll be?"

As if in answer to his question, old Hawkins knocked on
the door to announce the lawyer's arrival.

"Mr. Augustus Peake, sir," he said. "I've shown the
gentleman into the library. I took the liberty of serving him
with a glass of sherry."

Jamie rose, glancing across at her questioningly, but
Emily shook her head. "You see him, Jamie. It's you he's
concerned with, not me. I will go and read the girls a
bedtime story while you're talking to Mr. Peake."

A year or so earlier, Jamie would have begged her to
accompany him, but his time at sea had given him self-
confidence; he nodded his agreement and followed Hawkins to the library. Emily went upstairs, to find her small
sisters being prepared for bed by their nursemaid, Bella,
a buxom country girl to whom they were both much attached.

"They'm right sorely tired, the pair o' them, Miss

Emily,'' Bella said. '' 'Twas a long enough day for them, an' with all the 'sitement, why I do reckon they'll fall fast asleep afore you've finished their story.''

Her forecast proved accurate. Emily had scarcely read two pages from the book of fairy tales she had given Charlotte for Christmas when the two small, dark heads started to droop, and by the end of the page both little girls were sleeping soundly.

Their father, she knew, had indulged them far more than he had ever indulged his elder children, but despite this, they had not gone in awe of him, and his passing had left them comparatively unaffected, for all the elaborate pomp and ceremony of his funeral. Each night, under her tutelage, they had prayed earnestly that "Dear Papa might be made well again," but their visits to his sickroom had been made reluctantly and at times even under coercion.

She tucked them in and, dropping a light kiss on each small, flushed cheek, went downstairs and back to the morning room to wait for Jamie.

It was another half hour before he emerged from the library and she heard heavy footsteps crossing the flagged hall as Hawkins escorted Mr. Augustus Peake to the door. Jamie came into the morning room, his young face almost drained of color, to slump down onto the sofa at her side, as if, Emily thought apprehensively, whatever their father's solicitor had told him had come as a profound shock.

Wisely, she did not press him for an explanation but instead ordered a glass of the cider he was usually partial to and sat in silence while he drank it. Finally her brother set down his empty glass with a far from steady hand and regarded her uncertainly.

"Emmy, I don't know how to tell you this," he began, the stammer that affected him when he was nervous or upset making itself apparent. "B-but I—"

"Just tell me simply," Emily begged. "And try not to distress yourself, Jamie dear. Whatever it is, I won't be shocked, I promise you."

But, for all her bravely expressed confidence, Jamie's next words succeeded in shocking her.

"There's almost nothing for me to inherit," he said. "Papa was living on his capital, his prize money, Mr. Peake said—and spending it without regard for the future. He had a naval pension, of course, but that ceases with his death. And there's this house and the furniture, the carriage and his horses—they will all have to be sold if the girls' fare to Australia is to be paid, and Hawkins's and Bella's. Or pensions provided for them and the other servants. I—I don't know how I—I shall be a-able to t-tell Rob, Emmy. Or—or what he'll say when I d-do tell him. D-do you think he'll be angry?"

Emily recovered herself and managed a smile.

"No, Jamie, of course he won't. He would not expect you to give him your inheritance, in any case. Even if it had been a vast sum, he would not expect that."

"He would, Emmy," her brother asserted wretchedly. "Rob would."

"Papa provided for him."

"But not—n-not what he considered adequately."

Moved by his evident distress on their elder brother's account, Emily—for the first time in her life—permitted herself to offer an adverse criticism of him. "Rob," she stated firmly, "got what he deserved."

"How can you say that?" Jamie challenged indignantly. "That fellow Raven, the innkeeper, brought false charges against him out of malice. And it wasn't even malice against Rob—it was Papa he wanted to hurt."

Emily shook her head. "No, Jamie," she countered pityingly. "The charges weren't false. Rob told me the whole story. And," she added, "Simon heard the end of it from an old man called Parson Crickley, who sought him out after—after Papa refused to see him. I was supposed to tell him, but I didn't."

"What happened?" Jamie demanded suspiciously. "What did Parson Crickley say happened?"

"The girl that Rob was accused of—of having raped,

Rebecca Raven, drowned herself when Rob's ship sailed without her. She—'' Emily took a breath and forced herself to go on. "She was on her way out to join him, and Parson Crickley went in the boat with her and her father, in order that he might wed them on board. Or—" She relented. "That was what he claimed, when he spoke to Simon. It's possible that Rob didn't know—Mr. Raven may have made a last attempt to force him to wed the poor girl.''

"I'd swear Rob did not know,'' Jamie insisted, but Emily saw he was less convinced of their brother's innocence than he had been a few moments before. And, please God, she prayed silently, he need no longer feel any qualms concerning his inheritance, for Rob *had* been provided for. It was Jamie and she and their two small sisters for whom their father had not made adequate provisions. The house was large, its furnishings of some value, and it stood in extensive grounds, but there was still a mortgage on it of some hundreds of pounds, she knew. Even if it were sold immediately and well, she doubted whether the proceeds, when shared between four of them, would amount to as much as the sum Rob had received when their father had peremptorily ordered him to accept exile in New South Wales. Certainly it would not amount to much more.

"I told Mr. Peake that he should put the house on the market,'' Jamie volunteered. "I'm afraid that will leave you to—to deal with the sale, Emmy. I'll have barely a week before I have to report on board the *Success*. But if I give you a power of attorney, Mr. Peake says that will be all that is required.''

"I can deal with the sale,'' Emily assured him. "I just hope that it will not take too long, Jamie, because Simon has to book his passage and—we want to be married. Not an elaborate ceremony, of course—only a quiet ceremony at Saint John's when the rector can arrange it.''

"I wish it could be arranged before I sail,'' Jamie said wistfully. "I should very much like to see you wed and—well, perhaps to give you away, Emmy.''

Their banns had been called, Emily reminded herself guiltily. The old admiral had been hovering close to death for several weeks, and Simon had persuaded her to antici- pate her freedom so that, if he should be instructed to sail at an earlier date than he presently expected, they might be secretly married before his departure, and—if she were unable to accompany him—at least she and her little sisters would be able to follow him later on.

She bent her head in an attempt to hide the blush that came into her cheeks and answered quietly, "I think it *could* be arranged, Jamie—if it's really what you want. I . . . there's no reason for delay now. Papa does not need me to nurse him anymore. He—well, he did not approve of Simon, I'm afraid, so I could not tell him of my intentions. But I always intended to marry Simon, you know."

"Good for you, Emmy!" her brother applauded, his smile returning. "I remember Rob once saying that Papa would never approve of any suitor you might have, so long as he needed you to keep house for him. Well, you've done your duty a hundred times over." His smile widened and he jumped eagerly to his feet. "Shall I go and have a word with the rector and with your intended? I could explain that my time is very short and beg their indulgence, could I not?"

Emily lifted her head, her face aglow. "Oh, Jamie, would you?"

"I'll be more than happy to," Jamie asserted. "In fact I'll go this minute."

His powers of persuasion were scarcely needed. The old rector agreed willingly to his suggestion, and Simon Yates embraced him gratefully when the wedding day was ar- ranged for three days hence.

The ceremony, as befitted a family in recent mourning, was as simple as Emily had wished, attended only by their immediate family and the household servants, and by Simon's parents, who journeyed from nearby Walkhampton to be present, accompanied by his two younger brothers.

Emily wore her mother's wedding gown, taking it carefully from the closet in which it had hung, wrapped in a linen sheet, for over thirty years. To her joy, the lovely gown was perfectly preserved and required little alteration, and she was happily aware that she was looking her best as she walked slowly up the aisle on Jamie's arm to take her place before the altar at her bridegroom's side.

Simon Yates, a fair-haired giant of a young man, standing over six foot five in his stockinged feet, turned his adoring blue-eyed gaze on her, and Emily felt her heart pounding like a wild thing in her breast as his big hand closed gently over hers. How, she asked herself, how could her father possibly have imagined that Simon was a fortune hunter, concerned only with what, until now, he had supposed would be her substantial inheritance? She had nothing, but Simon had told her that he was glad of it.

"If we are to take God's word to the heathen Maoris, my dearest," he had said, "it is meet and right that we should go among them with no more worldly goods than they possess. God will provide us with food and shelter, and we need no more than that."

"Dearly beloved, we are gathered together in the sight of God and in the face of this congregation," the old rector intoned, "to join this man and this woman in holy matrimony . . ."

Emily listened gravely, conscious of the solemnity of the occasion and the all-embracing compass of the vows she would shortly be called upon to make. Her heart's wild beat subsided; she looked up at the great stained-glass window facing her above the altar and made a vow of her own choosing, coupled with a prayer that came from the very depths of her being.

"I will always be true to this man, whom I am taking as my husband . . . please, dear Jesus, help me to follow him wherever he may go and, of Thy divine mercy, grant me the strength never to fail him."

Behind her in the dimly lit church, her little sister Biddy asked suddenly, in shrilly penetrating tones, "Oh, Bella,

Dr. Yates won't take our dearest Emmy away from us, will he?''

There were amused titters as Bella hastily denied any such prospect and whispered to the child to be silent. Simon's fingers tightened about Emily's hand in quick, understanding sympathy, and she found herself smiling up at him, no longer embarrassed but amused.

He made his vows in a clear, deep voice, and then old Rector Theobald, whom she had known since her childhood, turned to her.

"Emily Margaret Willoughby, wilt thou have this man to thy wedded husband, to live together after God's ordinance in the holy estate of matrimony? Wilt thou obey him and serve him, love, honor, and keep him, in sickness and in health, for richer or poorer, and, forsaking all other, keep thee only unto him, for as long as ye both shall live?''

Emily made her response with quiet conviction, but her hand trembled a little when Simon placed his ring on it, and she heard him repeating the beautiful, age-old words. "With this ring I thee wed, with my body I thee worship, and with all my worldly goods I thee endow. . . .''

And then the rector announced, "I now declare you man and wife. Those whom God hath joined together, let no man put asunder.''

Events moved with almost bewildering speed after that. Scarcely had they gone, with the two little girls, to wave Jamie's ship farewell, when Simon received instructions from the Church Missionary Society to embark, with his wife and family, on board the transport *Countess of Harcourt*, due to sail from Plymouth in six weeks' time.

The ship was large and seaworthy, Simon assured his bride, a fast sailer of over five hundred tons burden, commanded by an experienced master, Magnus Johnson, and carrying a surgeon-superintendent, Dr. Charles Linton—to whom he would act as assistant—in charge of her cargo of a hundred and eighty-four male convicts.

Although Emily was eager to begin her new life, there was still much to be done, and six weeks was all too short a time in which to arrange their departure. In Jamie's absence, she found herself making decisions on his behalf that caused her considerable heart-searching, but her new husband was a tower of strength to her, and Mr. Augustus Peake, the solicitor—although clearly a man disposed to act slowly and cautiously by nature—responded to the urgency of the situation and handled the business of her father's estate with commendable dispatch.

The horses and carriages were quickly disposed of to willing buyers, providing sufficient funds for such immediate needs as fares to Sydney for Bella and the two little girls, and pensions for the other servants and Hawkins, who had decided to remain in England. Emily bought clothing, laid in a store of material for future use, and selected furniture from the house to take with them, before the remainder was put up for sale by auction. This, too, was easily sold, but the house found no buyer at the price Mr. Peake deemed worthy of its size and position.

"You will have to leave the matter in my hands, Mrs. Yates," he told her glumly. "If and when I receive a suitable offer for the property, I will deal with it expeditiously and forward the proceeds, less my fee and commission, to your brother in Sydney. Alternatively, of course, you could put it up for auction and let it go to the highest bidder."

"Which do you advise, Mr. Peake?" Emily inquired anxiously. She had come to trust the white-haired little lawyer implicitly, but even so, for Rob's and Jamie's sake, to leave him in sole charge of their one remaining asset was, perhaps, presumptuous.

"The decision must be yours, my dear young lady," Augustus Peake answered primly. He hesitated, seemingly undecided whether to confide in her, and then, coming to what was evidently a somewhat painful conclusion, added regretfully, "One of the investments your late father, Sir

Francis, made on my advice did not turn out profitably. He put a considerable sum of money into a tin mine—the Hensbarrow Mining and Smelting Company, in Cornwall—which, most unhappily, was compelled to declare bankruptcy eighteen months ago. I am bound to tell you, Mrs. Yates, that the shares—which I still hold in your late father's portfolio—are now worthless. Indeed, that is one reason—apart from the losses Sir Francis himself sustained at the gaming tables—why your poor young brother's inheritance is so modest. For that reason, I—well, I should like very much to sell Murton Chase well. If you are willing to entrust the sale to me, I will do all in my power to ensure that the proceeds are the highest possible.''

Emily was silent, torn by conflicting thoughts. Her first impulse was to postpone a definite decision until after she had consulted Simon, but he had made the long journey to London for a final meeting with the Missionary Society council and could not be expected back until at least the end of the week. In his absence she must decide, for as Mr. Peake pointed out, if the sale were to be by open auction before her departure, then there was no time to be lost. It would have to be extensively advertised, and that, he told her, would take time. . . . She frowned, in an agony of indecision.

"Of course, my dear Mrs. Yates," the lawyer said, breaking the brief silence that had fallen between them, "it is possible to place a reserve price on the property and to instruct the auctioneers that it cannot be sold below that sum.''

"Suppose the reserve price isn't reached, Mr. Peake?'' Emily questioned. "What then?''

"Why, my dear,'' Mr. Peake answered, visibly brightening, "in that event, it would be withdrawn, and you could then leave me to find a suitable buyer, as I initially suggested.''

"And—and no harm would be done?''

"None at all. That is quite frequently the practice when a large property is offered for sale.''

"Yes, I see." Emily's frown lifted. It was the realization that Rob—rather than Jamie—might reproach her for failing to bring the proceeds of the house sale with her to Sydney that finally enabled her to make up her mind.

"Then please will you arrange for an auction, Mr. Peake," she managed composedly, "and settle the amount of the reserve price."

If the old man's feelings were hurt, he gave no visible sign of discomfiture and, once again, put matters in hand with celerity. The local press carried advertisements, and the auctioneers printed handbills, which were displayed all over Plymouth and the neighboring towns and villages; and attracted by these, a large crowd—composed more of spectators than of would-be purchasers—gathered in the premises of the auctioneers in Citadel Road, three weeks later.

Emily attended, entering the crowded room nervously on her husband's strong supporting arm. She had planned to take a seat at the back of the room, but old Mr. Peake, bustling officiously about, saw her and sent his clerk to escort Simon and her to seats he had reserved for them in the front row. Here, conscious that she was the object of a good deal of curiosity and much surreptitious whispering, she clung to Simon's hand and wished herself many miles away; but when the sale began, the pointing and whispering ceased, and interest became centered on the bidding.

This, beginning slowly, was skillfully orchestrated by the auctioneer, and as the bids grew larger, the rapidity with which each was offered and repeated steadily increased. Finally, when the reserve price was bid and passed, Emily was able to see that there were three main contenders involved.

One, a somberly dressed gentleman in morning coat and top hat, who made his bids by means of a barely perceptible nod of the head, dropped out when the reserve price was exceeded. Of the other two, one was evidently a clerk, bidding on behalf of a client and obviously well known to the auctioneer, who addressed him by the name of his firm. It was the third of the ill-assorted trio who caused Emily most surprise and, for no reason that she could readily have explained, some misgivings.

He was a big, black-bearded man, with a heavy paunch, dressed in homespun jacket and breeches of a shapeless cut, who smoked a foul-smelling briar pipe throughout the proceedings and raised its blunt stem when he wanted to attract the auctioneer's attention. Despite his appearance, he seemed to be well-off, capping each bid made by the other two, and when the top-hatted gentleman withdrew from contention, he continued to oppose the estate agent's clerk, his voice loud and challenging, as if in an attempt to browbeat him.

"At eight thousand six hundred and fifty guineas, sir," the auctioneer announced, addressing him questioningly. "The bid is against you, sir."

The bearded man's roar echoed from end to end of the packed auction room. "Nine thousand!" he yelled pugnaciously. "And be damned!"

The estate agent's clerk was not intimidated. A raised finger set the bidding off again, and Emily saw Mr. Peake rubbing his bony hands together with satisfaction when it rose to ten thousand. Simon, she saw, was looking puzzled, but her whispered question to him was unheard and went unanswered in the excited hubbub of voices.

"Ten thousand two hundred and fifty guineas I am bid," the auctioneer intoned. "Against Messrs. Petty and Lovell." There was a sudden silence. "I will take advances of fifty guineas," the young man offered persuasively, and the clerk's hand was lifted.

"Ten thousand three hundred—any advance on ten thousand three hundred, sir?"

Again he addressed the bearded stranger, who, after a momentary hesitation, inclined his bullet head. "Aye—and fifty."

The clerk bowed to his opponent, acknowledging defeat;

the auctioneer, his hammer poised, looked round the room. "Have you all done, gentlemen? Going—going—gone! Sold for ten thousand three hundred and fifty guineas to . . . be so good as to give me your name, sir?"

The big man stood up. "Aye, 'tis Daniel Raven o' the Crown an' Anchor, North Quay!" he thundered. His dark eyes, in his mottled red face, were bright with the light of triumph, his stance aggressive. His gaze, ranging about the crowd, lit on Emily, and he moved toward her, the crowd parting to permit him to pass. Reaching her seat, he stood towering over her, his lips twisted into a malicious smile.

"The mills o' God grind slowly," he informed her. "But they grind exceeding small—just you remember that, Miss Willoughby! An' you can tell that miserable murdering young swine o' a brother o' your'n that he'll never set foot in his home again, not as long as he lives! Goin' out to join him, ain't 'ee, in the penal colony o' New South Wales, you an' the sawbones?"

Wordlessly, Emily inclined her head in assent, the sheer venom of his outburst striking chill into her heart. Raven went on, ignoring Simon's attempts to silence him, "Well, I'd see as he bides there, if I were thee. But you tell him as Dan'l Raven's bought your pa's fine mansion—be sure an' tell 'im that, now, won't 'ee? An' you can say as the hush-money your Pa paid, after my poor young Becky drowned herself, say *that* money helped to pay for it!"

Simon managed, at last, to swing him bodily round and send him on his way, but Emily was shocked and trembling, the bitter, vengeful words ringing in her ears like a death knell.

She could still hear the echo of them when, two weeks later, she boarded the transport *Countess of Harcourt* for the long voyage to Australia, for Daniel Raven's parting thrust had been the cruelest of all.

"I put God's curse on thy brother, Miss Willoughby," he had flung at her across the crowded auction room, "as my Becky lay dying in my arms. He'll come to a bad end, that's what'll befall the sinful young rogue—you mark my words!''

And despite Simon's repeated assurance that God forgave sinners and did not permit mere humans to invoke his retribution, Emily's fears could not be laid to rest.

CHAPTER XVIII

Alice crouched alone in the big wooden bed, with its curtains drawn across, listening to the pounding of the surf on the rocks below the house. It was close on midnight, she knew, but Nathan had warned her that he would be late—the newly appointed commandant, Captain Donaldson, had arrived in the *Mermaid*, and her husband's attendance had been required, with that of the rest of the Norfolk Island prison staff, to receive their new commander.

She had been on the island for almost four months, Alice reflected, and despite her determination to accept its conditions without complaint, her fortitude had been tried to its limit. Not on her own account—the chaplain's house, though small, was sturdily built and comfortably furnished; she had two convict servants, adequate rations, and even a tiny garden, in which fruit trees flourished and vegetables grew prolifically. And she had Nathan's devoted love. . . .

Restless, she reached out and drew aside a bed curtain, the solitary candle on the nightstand nearly flickering out. If they had lived anywhere else—in Windsor, perhaps, with the Cartwrights, or even in the isolated country beyond the Blue Mountains or in one of the new settlements springing up in the recently discovered land to the west— anywhere but here, how happy she could have been!

But on Norfolk Island, to permit herself to be happy was . . . akin to betrayal, because on every hand there were human beings, God's creatures like herself, condemned to expiate, in abject misery and degradation, whatever crimes they had committed.

Captain Turton, the first commandant, who had initially rebuilt the prison settlement, was not an unduly harsh man, and he was not deliberately cruel, but, as Nathan had attempted to explain, he had precise orders as to how the convicts were to be treated and the discipline to which they must be subjected.

Their hours of work were long, and the labor was very hard, made the more so because all were compelled to work in fetters and leg-irons, save for the few who—too old and frail for outside work—were given positions as cooks and cleaners or officers' servants. All the prisoners slept and were fed in the stockade, their primitive dormitories being surrounded by a high log wall, the gate of which was always guarded. Alice had not been inside the stockade, but Nathan had described it to her, adding grimly that the prison barrack was being enlarged, in anticipation of an increase in the number of long-term convicts to be accommodated there. At present, there were twenty men to each division or ward, he had told her. At dusk, when the day's toil was over, they were given their rations of salt meat and uncooked maize meal, and if not too exhausted, they had to boil their meager portion of meat in one of two large boilers and fashion the meal into cakes, to be cooked in the ashes of the boiler fires.

That done—or left undone—they were locked into their wards for the night. There, in total darkness, they were left to sleep as best they could, in hammocks slung from the roof timbers, and with their leg-irons still on.

"They are treated more like animals than men," Nathan had said, with stark bitterness. "And the lash is ordered for the most trivial of offenses."

He held a short prayer meeting each morning, when the convicts mustered for work; and on Sundays—the only day in the week when the chain gangs did not go out to fell trees, build roads, or work on the land—he conducted an hour-long service, at which attendance was compulsory.

"I should fare better if I were taking Christianity to heathen savages," he had asserted, more than once. "These poor devils come and listen to me only because they would be flogged if they did not. But for all the good I do, for all my efforts to save their souls, I might as well be a thousand miles away!"

Nathan's sad disillusionment was beginning to affect her, too, Alice thought with regret. She had no official duties, but for her husband's sake she went voluntarily among the women and children and did what little she could to aid and sustain them. There were fewer than a dozen women on the island now, and fifteen or sixteen children. The women had been carefully chosen and were, for the most part, the wives of overseers or trusted convicts, but like her they were kept apart from the prison and its inmates and lived in small huts some distance from the stockade. Despite this, they were a stabilizing influence, the mere fact of their presence—and their attendance at the Sunday service—seeming to have a good effect on all but the most hard-bitten of the prisoners.

There was a strange, half-demented old man, whose name was Job Scaife and who, apparently, had remained by himself on the island after it had been evacuated in Governor Macquarie's time. She and Nathan had encountered him, Alice recalled, when they had paid a visit to the old cemetery soon after their arrival. Suspicious at first, for Captain Turton had attempted to place him under restraint, he had gradually come to trust them, and when Nathan had prevailed upon the commandant to leave the harmless old fellow at liberty, he had taken to visiting them, always bringing with him a gift of some sort, however small.

And he had talked—how he had talked! From his tales, she had learned much about the original prison settlement, and having heard of the brutalities of earlier commandants— and in particular of one Job always referred to as "Flogger" Foveaux—she had come to the conclusion that, by comparison, Captain Turton was by no means the worst of the succession of military officers entrusted with the administration of the island.

Yet the place still horrified her. The sight of men working for hour after endless hour on the "crank mill," grinding grain and subjected to an overseer's lash if they paused even for a moment, still shocked her deeply, as did the utter exhaustion of those in the chain gangs, when they were marched back to the stockade at the end of their day's labors. They were spent and cowed and filthy, stumbling along in their heavy leg-irons, the old and weak permitted but few concessions, the strong seemingly indifferent to their sufferings, and the overseers' whips wielded with indiscriminate cruelty if the pace flagged.

Unknown to Nathan, she had started to keep . . . not a diary, but a written account of the life here, adding some of Job Scaife's more credible stories to her own daily observations. Alice slipped from the bed and, holding the candle aloft, searched for and found her neatly penned record. She had as yet no idea of the use to which she might put it, but . . . Her teeth closed over her lower lip as she read the last entry she had made, after paying a visit with Nathan to the prison hospital.

The hospital is a long, low building with about twenty beds. It is built of stone and stands so close to the beach that the heavy surf makes it perpetually damp. Medical equipment is sadly deficient, and the orderlies, who are elderly convicts and untrained, give very little attention to the sick confided to their care.

Nathan took me with him because the patient he had to visit was a child, and I wept to see the state the poor young soul was in. His bed is close to those of the adult patients, whose language and behavior appeared coarse in the extreme. I was thankful that I had brought a few delicacies for him to eat and a pannikin of broth, as he seemed hungry. Nathan read to him from *Pilgrim's Progress,* and I think our visit cheered him. He . . .

The sound of footsteps, followed by the opening of the front door, signaled Nathan's belated return, and Alice returned her papers to their hiding place and went quickly back to bed. It was not that she was attempting to deceive her husband, she told herself, but rather that, being the scrupulous person that he was, Nathan might consider what she was doing a breach of his contract of employment . . . a view that the commandant might well share. Her place, it had been made very clear to her, was in her home, looking after her husband's creature comforts, and not, in any circumstances, concerning herself with the administration of the prison or the treatment of its inmates.

Nathan came into the bedroom, and one glance at his face sent Alice's heart plummeting. He looked angry and upset—and it took much to anger him, as she had learned.

"Oh, Nathan," she whispered anxiously. "Dearest Nathan, what has happened? What is wrong?"

He came slowly toward the bed, divesting himself of his jacket and collar before slumping down beside her, the very epitome of wretchedness.

"The new commandant, Captain Donaldson, has brought instructions from the Governor that all the women and children are to be removed from the island—they're to be sent back to Sydney in the *Mermaid*." His tone was harsh, grating on her taut nerves, and Alice stared at him, momentarily bereft of words.

"*All* the women?" she managed at last. "Does this mean that *I* must leave?"

"That's what it means, my love," Nathan answered bitterly. "Not even the commandant is to be permitted to have his wife here. Norfolk Island is to become a place of the harshest discipline, from which there is to be no hope of return by any convict who is sent here. All sentences are to be for life. And"—there was a catch in his voice— "in the Governor's words, this is to be 'a place of the direst punishment short of death.' "

"And you must stay?" Alice questioned, on the brink of despair at the vision his words conjured up. "Nathan, are you bound to stay here?"

Nathan reached for her, holding her fiercely to him, and

as he laid his face against hers, she felt the salt dampness of tears on his cheek. "I cannot leave with you, my dearest. But I shall request a transfer. Without you, without your love to sustain me, this island will be unendurable. I—even if it means that I must resign from the prison service, I'll not remain here without you."

Alice drew his cropped head down onto her breast and let him weep, listening abstractedly to his angry condemnation of the prison system as it was practiced on Norfolk Island.

"The good Lord knows it is bad enough now, the way the poor wretches are worked, the way they are starved and punished. But Vance Donaldson is a hard man, and he has an evil gleam in his eye—it lies within his power to make the conditions here worse than they already are! Alice, he told me—he told me to my face that so far as he was concerned, I could go. 'We'll need no chaplain here,' he said. 'Save to bury the dead. And I can give them that service.' "

Alice looked about the dark, shadowed room, her own eyes burning. This had been her first home, as Nathan's wife. Here, alone together, they had loved and known a measure of contentment when the rest of the cruel world had been shut out, and it had been possible, for a few brief hours, to forget what lay outside these stout four walls. They had dreamed here of the child they would have to bless their union, and she had prayed that she might conceive—had even hoped, during the past few weeks, that she was pregnant. They both wanted a child—the children of the convicts had brightened each day, their merry voices had offered hope and solace, a reason for living to the toiling work parties, just as their womenfolk had offered comfort to the suffering.

But now they were to be banished, and only the prison, with its guards and constables, would remain; there would be no hymn singing at the morning prayer service, if Captain Donaldson dispensed with his chaplain, and the crack of the overseers' whips would echo in the silence the children had left behind them.

Alice drew a sobbing breath, recalling the record she had kept, to which must now be added a fresh page, or perhaps even a fresh chapter. Nathan raised his head, studying her face with great intensity in the dim candlelight.

He said thickly, "It is all to be done very swiftly— within the next two or three days, Alice. Captain Turton warned the new commandant that the women will seek to oppose the order, and he simply shrugged and said that any who proved recalcitrant would be placed in arrest by his soldiers and carried on board the ship—'frog-marched,' as he termed it. Clearly, my love, you will be expected to set an example, I'm afraid. Donaldson said as much."

"And what is to become of me and of the other women when we return to Sydney?" Alice asked. "Or does not Captain Donaldson care, so long as he rids himself of our presence?"

"He assured me that provision would be made," Nathan answered wearily. "You will be allocated quarters and the women offered domestic employment. Most of them are free or emancipists, are they not?"

"They are as free as I am," Alice countered, with unaccustomed sarcasm. "And indeed—" She broke off, shocked by the pain in his eyes. This was not Nathan's fault or his doing, she thought, filled with contrition. And it would be he who must remain in this hellish place, until his resignation was accepted and his relief sent to the island—she, little as she wanted to be parted from him, was at least about to be released and sent back to civilization. She put her soft arms about his neck, and he kissed her hungrily.

"God in heaven, I shall miss you so," he whispered, his lips in her hair. "Oh, Alice, my darling wife, I love you! How can I exist without you?"

They made love with a despairing passion that was akin to pain, and for a long time after their emotions were spent, they lay clasped in each other's arms, reluctant to sleep, lest oblivion rob them of these last few precious hours together.

Next morning, when the new commandant's order for their departure was made known to the women, there was an outcry. The women were distraught, unable to understand the reason for the order, and they pleaded—all of them in tears and several on their knees—for it to be rescinded. Captain Vance Donaldson heard their pleas in stony-faced silence, and when they had exhausted all arguments, he told them brusquely that he was carrying out instructions from the Governor, which were not within his power to amend.

"His Excellency is acting in obedience to a Colonial Office decision," he added coldly. "Only the worst type of convicts, guilty of serious crimes, are to be confined here. Your men have brought their sentences and their punishment upon themselves, and they must take the consequences. Be thankful that their lives were spared from the hangman's noose! You have twenty-four hours to prepare to return to Sydney on board the *Mermaid*, and any who fail to board the ship will be taken out to her forcibly."

In vain, Nathan attempted to soften the awful blow; his efforts to gather them in prayer met with no response, and Alice was hard put to it to restrain her own heartbroken tears as she helped the women pack up their few possessions and load them onto barrows, to be wheeled down to the landing stage, where the *Mermaid*'s boats were waiting.

One woman, the mother of three little children, whose hut was a model of cleanliness and order and whose garden had long been the envy of the rest, refused point-blank to obey the disputed order. Taking her children with her, all of them scantily clad, she made her escape into the forest, vowing not to return until the *Mermaid* had sailed.

Captain Donaldson, ignoring his predecessor's advice and Nathan's offer to go in search of the fugitives, sent a party of soldiers after them and a party of convicts to dig up the neat little garden and cut down its fruit trees and

bushes. Betsy Goff was brought back next day in wrist
fetters, and old Job Scaife, with whom she had sought
sanctuary for her youngest child, was brought in with her
and summarily sentenced to a hundred lashes—from which
only Captain Turton's angry intervention saved him.

Finally, under armed guard, the women and children
were mustered and marched down the road past the prison
to the landing stage. There, under the new commandant's
supervision, they were required to answer to their names
before being bundled into the two oared boats that were to
take them through the narrow, surf-lashed opening in the
reef to where the government ship lay at anchor. Ironically,
Alice thought, this was the same ship that had brought her
here with Nathan, four months ago. She remembered the
kindness of the ship's commander, Lieutenant Broome,
but . . . standing with her hand in that of her husband,
trying valiantly not to weep, this was small enough
consolation.

Captain Turton, also controlling himself with visible
difficulty, gestured to her to precede him into the second
boat. Alice's head lifted; with Nathan's arm supporting
her, she stepped aboard, hearing his choked farewell as the
young midshipman in charge of the boat assisted her to
seat herself beside him in the sternsheets.

There were men watching from behind the barred win-
dows of the hospital, others listening but unable to see
from inside the lofty walls of the stockade; and the chain
gangs, too, however far away their allotted toil had taken
them, would be tensely aware that the moment for departure had come. Alice longed suddenly to give them some
sign, to hold out some hope for those without hope, who
were being left behind in their tortured exile. But, although the impulse to sing was hers, it was one of the
other women—Bridie O'Flyn, the wife of an Irishman
convicted for armed rebellion—who translated her impulse
into action.

The woman, past her youth now, still possessed a sweet,
pure voice, and as the first words of the old, defiant rebel

ballad issued suddenly from her lips, the rest took it up, the children with them.

> . . . I go, but with me bearing
> A heart still true to you.
>
> And still the day may brighten
> When those tears shall cease to flow,
> And the show'r of freedom lighten
> Those spirits drooping low.
>
> Then should the glad breeze blowing
> Send an echo 'cross the sea,
> My heart with transport glowing
> Shall bless the hand that made thee free!

The words were strange to Alice, but the tune was not, for she had heard Bridie O'Flyn singing it many times before as she went about her work. Alice sang now, her heart near to breaking, and as the boat pulled away and headed for the opening in the reef, a score of men's voices echoed the refrain from the shore.

Jessica had seen the *Mermaid* come to anchor in Sydney Cove, and she and her younger son, Johnny, were waiting at the open door when Justin and Red came up the narrow garden path from the quayside.

She and Justin greeted each other with warm affection, which the two boys aped, Red—proudly wearing his new cadet's uniform—ready, as always, to boast to his brother of what he had seen and done on the voyage, and Johnny disguising his envy by pretending not to believe his claim.

"We sighted a waterspout off Lord Howe Island," Red asserted.

"Go on—there are no waterspouts in that area. You're trying to make a fool of me," Johnny countered.

"No, I'm not, honestly. It *was* a waterspout. And Dad put a boat ashore, and we caught some giant turtles—the biggest I've ever seen."

"I suppose you'll tell me next that you ate them?"

Red threw back his head and roared with laughter. "Dumbcluck, the cook made 'em into soup! We landed some at Norfolk Island, but—"

"Be off with you," Jessica chided. "I want to talk to your father, and I can't hear myself speak with all your chatter." As the two boys obediently left them together, she linked her arm in Justin's, and they went indoors, Jessica moving a trifle clumsily with the weight of her coming child.

"God willing, I shall be with you when this one is born," Justin said, eyeing her gravely.

"That will be a miracle," Jessica retorted with mock reproach.

"The *Mermaid* is overdue for caulking, and I want her careened, so that the job can be done properly. If she is, that will give us two or three weeks, at least, Jessie. Time enough for the new arrival to make his entry, surely?"

"Her entry," Jessica corrected. "I want no more sons with the sea in their blood—I want a little daughter, Justin, before you take Johnny away from me."

"Has Johnny said he wants to come to sea?"

"Oh, Justin, can you not see that he's eating his heart out?" The reproach was real this time, and Jessica did not attempt to hide it. "He keeps telling me that you took Red with you when he was nine. And Johnny will be nine in less than three months!"

"Then let us hope that your wish for a daughter is granted," Justin said defensively. He closed the door behind him and held out his arms to her, a smile playing about his lips. "Don't hold it against me if it turns out to be a boy, though, will you?"

"I expect I shall," Jessica answered, but she went into his arms, and he kissed her with lingering tenderness. "I have missed you sorely, wife."

"And I have missed you, Justin." She hesitated and then asked, with an abrupt change of tone, "If your ship has to be careened, that means a long voyage is in prospect, does it not? Where are they sending you next?''

Justin sighed. He had never been able to pull the wool over his wife's eyes, and, he thought glumly, it was useless to try. "There is a prospect of establishing a new settlement in Raffles Bay, on the northern coast,'' he admitted. "The Admiralty is sending a King's ship out— the frigate *Success*, under Captain James Stirling. I've been warned that I may have to accompany her or even go ahead of her to take men and stores to Captain Campbell on Melville Island. Nothing is settled as yet, but I am required to prepare my ship against the possibility that she'll be needed.''

"I see.'' Jessica's tone was more resigned than angry. She moved away from him and, crossing to the sideboard, poured him a glass of brandy and brought it to him unasked. Justin grinned, and raised the glass to her. "The sun's not over the yardarm, my love. What are we drinking to?''

Jessica's good humor overcame her momentary resentment. "Why, to your brother William,'' she told him. "And his bride.''

"His *bride*? Is Will married, for the Lord's sake?'' Justin's astonishment was mirrored in his face. "Whom has he married, the young dog? Not Dorothea Dawson?''

"Oh, yes. They eloped to Windsor two weeks ago, and the Reverend Robert Cartwright married them. Abigail and Timothy were at the wedding.'' Jessica smiled. "Once they had overcome their surprise, I gathered from Abigail that they both gave the match their warm approval.''

"And where are they now?'' Justin asked. "Will and Dodie, I mean?''

"On their way to Van Diemen's Land—to Launceston.'' Jessica's smile widened. "You just missed them by twenty-four hours, I'm afraid. They sailed on board a whaler called the *Esmeralda*, with Will's best ewes from Ulva. Your sister Rachel and George De Lancey gave a reception for them, before they left Sydney. Everyone was there, including the Governor and Mrs. Darling.''

"And Julia?"

"Yes, even Julia, though with a bad grace."

Justin held up his glass. "Then I'll drink to William and his bride, most gladly. May they enjoy long life and happiness!"

Jessica echoed his toast. "God grant they may! William is a fine young man, Justin, and Dodie's a darling."

They exchanged other items of news, and over luncheon Justin started to talk of his brief call at Norfolk Island. "We gave passage to the new commandant, Captain Donaldson, and brought all the women and children back here, to Sydney, in accordance with the Governor's instructions. It was—Jessie, it was a very moving occasion. The poor women did not want to leave." He described the parting in unhappy detail. "Poor old Turton was absolutely furious over how the whole matter was handled, but there was little he could do. He talked quite a lot on the passage back. He doesn't think very highly of his successor, I can tell you—and neither do I. Norfolk Island was no bed of roses under his command, but under Donaldson I fear it's liable to become a hell on earth. The poor devils who were respited will wish they hadn't been. And Donaldson displayed no pity toward the women. One ran away into the bush with her children, Turton said, and he had her brought back in irons. The chaplain—a decent young fellow named Cox—apparently received short shrift when he tried to intervene. And his wife had to leave with the rest."

"Mr. Cox's wife?" Jessica questioned.

"Yes. They had been married only a few months. The wife—Alice Cox—came out in the *Mary Anne*."

"As a convict, Justin?"

Justin nodded. "She was assigned to Lucy Van Buren and ran away. It was quite a romantic story. She apparently escaped with the help of that little half-caste boy, Claus, who's said to be Van Buren's son, and was trying to get to Upwey, to enlist Abigail's aid. She and young Cox met on the road."

"I do not blame her for running away from the Van Burens' household," Jessica put in thoughtfully. "And after what happened to those unfortunate settlers—" She did not complete her sentence, but Justin again nodded in agreement.

"Grave suspicion surrounds Van Buren on their account," he said. "The Governor respited the escapers who were charged with their murder, which was, to say the least, somewhat unusual. We brought four of them to Norfolk Island this passage. The fifth, a onetime highwayman named Vincent, was sent to Moreton Bay, I believe."

"Do *you* think they murdered those two poor young men? Did you talk to them?"

"Yes, and they denied it. But—" Justin shrugged. "As you know, I was at sea when they were tried, so I did not hear the evidence against them. But they were found guilty, were they not? And I missed seeing Rick, so I don't know his views on the affair—he gave evidence, didn't he?"

"Yes, he did. But I did not see him either," Jessica said. "He stayed only for the two days of the trial and then went back to Pengallon, so all I know is what was published in the *Gazette*. But there is a great deal of talk, Justin. There always is in Sydney, of course, only this time it's—well, as far as Major Van Buren is concerned, it's not very pleasant. They say that George De Lancey—who was on the bench at the escapers' trial—made a personal appeal to the Governor to have their death sentences commuted. I'm not sure whether or not that's true. Officially, it's never been admitted, and George and Rachel have gone to Newcastle to inspect land in the Hunter River district—they've been away for the past month or more. It doesn't reflect very well on the Van Burens, because there is talk about Lucy as well. She—" The belated return of her two young sons caused Jessica to break off in order to issue a mild reproof. "Red, Johnny— you both know at what hour we take our meal. Where have you been, for goodness' sake?"

The two boys exchanged anxious glances, and finally it

was Red who answered her. "Mam, we're sorry. We had business to attend to." He gave his mother a disarming smile and took his place at the table, motioning to his brother to follow his example. "I'm famished! It will be great to sample your cooking again, after being at sea. The *Mermaid*'s cook is getting past it, isn't he, Dad? He—"

"Red," his mother accused sternly. "You are trying to hide something—I know that look of old! What have the two of you been up to?"

"Nothing, Mam," Red protested. He helped himself lavishly to the dish in front of him, affecting not to hear her question.

"I'm waiting," Jessica warned.

Justin said crisply, "Out with it, lad. There are no secrets here, you know that."

Red flushed. "Well, all right, sir. We met Claus—you know, Claus Karimon, from the Van Burens'—and he told us that Major Van Buren is sailing for Batavia tomorrow in the *Dorcas*. He's taking Claus with him and says he's going to leave him there. He—"

Johnny interrupted, his young voice shrill with indignation, "He wants to leave Claus there *forever* and never let him come back! And Claus wants to stay here—this is his home now, you see. We—that is, Red and me decided to help him. We had to, Dad—you would've, if he'd asked you, wouldn't you?"

Thus appealed to, Justin decided that he would probably have done so; he had a weakness for the little dark-faced lad, who had displayed so much courage when the *Flinders* had been driven onto the treacherous rocks of Cape Hawke. But in his role as a responsible, law-abiding naval officer and a father to boot, he could not admit to such a weakness, and meeting Jessica's gaze, he said, aping her sternness, "How did you help him? For the Lord's sake, did you incite him to disobey his—that is, Major Van Buren?"

"We hid him, sir," Red confessed. "And we promised we'd keep him hidden until after the *Dorcas* sails. And

that's what we intend to do. Claus and the Van Burens'
houseman, Saleh, are Javanese.''

"I know that, boy—what difference does it make?''

"Under Dutch law, no Javanese can be enslaved,'' Red
asserted, with conviction. "Saleh is a well-educated man,
and he told Claus about the law. But they are treated like
slaves, all the Van Burens' servants are—they are beaten,
and they aren't paid. Claus is treated worse than any of
them, and yet he is Major Van Buren's son. He told us he
was, Dad, and he wouldn't lie.''

The poor little devil had told him the same, Justin
recalled, and then had begged him to forget the claim
because his swine of a father refused to acknowledge their
relationship.

"Why does Major Van Buren want to take him back to
Java, Red?'' he asked.

Red shrugged helplessly. "I don't know. I don't think
he knows. Or if he does, he didn't tell us, did he, Johnny?''

Johnny shook his small, dark head. "No. But he told
me a while ago that Major Van Buren did not trust him to
keep quiet about something—he didn't say what it was.
Only that he *could* be trusted.''

Justin frowned. In the light of the recent trial of Nicholas Vincent and his gang of bushrangers—and, yes, also in
the light of George De Lancey's evident doubts as to their
guilt—Josef Van Buren might have a very strong reason
for ridding himself of his half-caste son, he thought uneasily.
The boy had been with him when the duel took place . . .
could he, perhaps, have seen more than anyone suspected
and kept quiet about it, from a sense of loyalty? A much
misguided sense of loyalty, it now seemed.

"Where have you hidden Claus?'' Justin demanded, his
tone stern. "Devil take it, Red,'' he added, addressing his
elder son, "this is a serious matter! You did not take him
out to the ship, did you? Because if you did, you'll not sail
with me again.''

Red looked startled, but his denial was swift.

"No, sir, I wouldn't do that.''

"Well, then? Speak up, boy—I have to know."

Again his sons exchanged worried glances, and Johnny said, with a flash of defiance, "Dad, we gave Claus our word that we wouldn't tell. We can't break our word, can we—even for you?"

Justin glared at him. He was about to retort angrily when Jessica intervened, a restraining hand on his arm. "The boys cannot break a promise, Justin. But don't worry. I believe I know where they have taken Claus."

Both boys were silent, but their eyes were on her face, mutely pleading, and she smiled at them reassuringly. "Eat your food," she bade them. "If it rests with me, Major Van Buren will sail without Claus tomorrow morning. And you can leave me to talk the matter over with your father."

Justin curbed his momentary anger, conscious that, in any event, his sympathies were with Claus rather than with the arrogant Dutchman who had fathered him.

It was not until he saw the *Dorcas* haul up her anchor and set her dingy canvas at noon next day that he returned to the subject.

"Van Buren's gone, my love," he reminded Jessica gently. "So now it is quite safe to tell me where those two rapscallions of ours saw fit to conceal young Claus. Because you know, do you not?"

Jessica gave him her warm, endearing smile.

"Dear Justin, he's here, of course—in our shed, hidden beneath the spare suit of the *Flinders'* canvas you still keep there. I guessed that was where the boys had taken him when I saw Red slipping bread and cheese into his pocket and Johnny helping himself to twice as much as he normally eats. And"—her smile widened—"they had no time to take him anywhere else, so it was not hard to guess what they had done. Please, dearest, don't be angry with them, will you?"

Justin laughed. "Lord, no, of course I won't! The young devils fooled me. But you're not proposing to keep the boy in the shed indefinitely, I trust?"

Jessica shook her head. "Certainly not—he will be with us for lunch."

"And after that? Will you send him back to Lucy Van Buren?"

"I ought to, I suppose. But Claus tells me he wants to go to Mrs. Cox—the chaplain's wife you evacuated from Norfolk Island." Jessica's smile faded. "I made inquiries, and I understand she has been allocated one of those small, broken-down houses in Church Street—temporarily, until her husband returns. She will be coming ashore with the other women later today, will she not?"

"That is the arrangement," Justin confirmed. "I shall have to go out to the ship to supervise their landing."

"Then will you mention Claus's wish, perhaps, when you see Mrs. Cox?" Jessica suggested persuasively.

"I'll mention it," Justin promised. "And I'm pretty sure that she will be delighted at the idea. Alice Cox is very young, you know, and rather shy, but she talked of Claus several times during our passage. She also talked, with considerable feeling, of conditions on Norfolk Island." He frowned, recalling one of his conversations with the chaplain's pretty young wife, when she had unburdened herself to him one evening on the *Mermaid*'s deck. What she had said had been in confidence, but . . . it would go no further if he told Jessica about it, and the girl's revelations had worried him.

"She kept some sort of diary, she told me—a record of the prison settlement as she had seen it, with the addition of what the old man, Job Scaife, had imparted to her. You remember, don't you, that we found him on the island when we made the initial survey, and he told us he had hidden out there, after the evacuation in 'fourteen?"

"Yes, I remember." Jessica's voice was concerned, even anxious. "Justin, what does she intend to do with her diary? She would not be so—so foolhardy as to offer it for publication, would she?"

"Who would publish it here?" Justin countered.

"Mr. Wentworth might, in his new paper, the *Australian*.

It's—'' Jessica sought for the right words to describe the journal's purpose, her dark brows knit in a thoughtful frown. "I suppose you could say that it is dangerously liberal. I'm afraid Mr. Wentworth is asking for trouble. Some of the views he has expressed are said to have angered the Governor, Justin. You haven't read it, but—well, I think you would consider it too outspoken for Sydney, although you would probably agree with some of its aims.''

"I must read it," Justin said. "William Charles is a brave fellow, and he's no respecter of persons—he never was. I like him very much, Jessie—and never more than when he revealed himself as the author of that famous pipe against Colonel Molle!"

He laughed softly, recalling the sensation the younger Wentworth's wickedly satirical doggerel had created, but Jessica, he saw, continued to regard him anxiously, unable to share his amusement. He captured her hand and carried it to his lips, his laughter swiftly dying.

"Do not worry your head on my account, my love," he said soberly. "While I hold the King's commission, I cannot speak my mind or hold liberal views . . . and my mother and father were emancipists, as everyone knows. But I admire Wentworth's courage, and—strictly between ourselves, Jessica India, I was far from taken by the new commandant of Norfolk Island. I suspect he's something of a monster—and so, come to that, is Logan, the fellow who has been appointed to command at Moreton Bay. The Governor has chosen badly in both cases. The severity of the punishment meted out to capital respites and incorrigibles is one thing, but to go beyond severity can never be justified. And to deprive a man of hope is—oh, for God's sake, it is to destroy him! Perhaps Alice Cox's diary *ought* to be published—if William Charles has the stomach for a fight with this Governor. I think I will mention it to him.''

"No," Jessica pleaded. "Don't, Justin, please. She was a convict, and she would suffer—Mr. Wentworth could not protect her. Leave it, I beg you—just tell her about little Claus. And—have you forgotten that Murdo is still at Moreton Bay?''

"But surely he applied to be relieved months ago?''

"His request was refused.'' Jessica freed her hand from his clasp and went to the door. "I will tell the boys that they may bring Claus out of hiding. I imagine he must be hungry, poor little fellow. And—'' She hesitated, turning in the doorway to look back at him. "Why not bring Alice Cox here for a meal? I should like to meet her.''

"So that you can persuade her to suppress her diary, my love?'' Justin quipped.

"No,'' Jessica denied, reddening. "So that I may read it, if she will permit me to do so . . . and then decide what advice I ought to offer her.''

The door closed behind her, and Justin heard her voice raised, summoning the boys. A little later, Claus came shyly into the room, to bow and stammer his thanks.

CHAPTER XIX

Murdo lay naked on his trestle bed, racked alike by fever and his own conscience. He had been absent from duty for over a week, aware that his illness would be unlikely to afford the excuse for his absence for very much longer.

Captain Patrick Logan, commandant of the prison settlement at Moreton Bay, was a hard taskmaster, even to the troops under his command. To the wretched convicts, he was the devil incarnate, wielding his power over them with calculated cruelty. In common with everyone else, Murdo hated the tall, drawling captain, with his long, pale face and cold eyes; but to his second-in-command, Logan was always punctiliously correct, offering no opportunity for protest and turning a deaf ear to even the most carefully worded appeals for leniency.

He had applied twice to be relieved, Murdo reflected wearily. Even under the comparatively lax rule of Captain Bishop, he had been miserably unhappy here; yet for no reason that he could understand, his applications had been refused. This might, of course, be the result of his having elected to remain in the colony; had he not transferred from the 40th, he would, like Bishop, have left Sydney with the regiment. But as things were . . . He dragged himself with difficulty from his rumpled bed, cursing his weak, debilitated state, and went to lean against the open window in the hope that the faint breeze might cool him.

Outside on the hard-packed, sandy surface of the prison exercise yard, half a dozen soldiers, in their tight-fitting scarlet tunics, were engaged in setting up the floggers' triangles, in preparation for the now inevitable early morning punishment parade. Murdo glimpsed the limping, ungainly figure of the crippled convict known as Old Bumble, whom Captain Logan had appointed as his official flogger—a post that entitled the vicious old man to special rations and the payment of eightpence a day. Bumble was hated almost as much as the commandant, for he brought an obscene artistry to his work, boasting that any man whose back he had marked would be marked for life—and in hell after that.

God grant it may not be Nick today, Murdo prayed aloud, without any real hope that his prayer would be answered. Since arriving at Moreton Bay, Nick Vincent had been singled out for Logan's special venom—partly, Murdo could only suppose, because Nick had the accent and manner of a gentleman, and partly on account of the crime for which he had been convicted.

"The unutterable swine murdered two King's officers," Logan had announced, after studying the papers that had accompanied the prisoner. "He should have hanged—and, the devil take him, I'll make him wish he had been, if it's the last thing I do!"

Murdo let his aching head fall onto his outstretched hands. The most appalling shock he had ever experienced had come when Nick had stumbled ashore from the whaler *Clarence*—pressed into service as a convict transport, in order to deliver the latest batch of seventy bushrangers and capital respites from Sydney's jail and Newcastle's abandoned coal mines.

Nick had been heavily ironed, one of a long line of fettered men, bearded and blinking in the strong sunlight, and at first . . . Murdo cursed under his breath, still angry at the fate that had brought them together again. As he had stood at Patrick Logan's back on the landing jetty, he had not recognized the man to whom he owed so much.

Murdo vividly recalled the scene, hearing in memory the commandant's harsh voice uttering the veiled threats

with which he made a practice of greeting the felons newly
committed to his charge. Seated on the huge, eighteen-
hand black stallion he had brought with him from John
Macarthur's stud, Logan had singled Nick out even then
because his clothes, though shabby, had been well cut, and
because he had held up his head defiantly in response to
the threats. The lash of Logan's hunting crop had curled
out—Logan was adept in its use—and Nick's face had
borne its mark in blood.

Recognition had dawned then: Murdo had known dismay and mounting panic, but Nick's gaze had passed over
him without a sign of awareness that they had ever met
before, and for a little while panic had subsided and he had
supposed that his gold-laced officer's tunic had been sufficient disguise. It had been seven years—over seven years—
since they had last seen each other, in the Alton Arms
tavern at Buck's Oak in far-off England. Nick had brought
him there, after having freed him from the prison wagon
that had been taking him to a convict transport at Portsmouth—and then had handed him over to the recruiting
sergeants, and Murdo had found himself at Waterloo, in
the ranks of the 92nd Highlanders.

To that shrewd move of Nick's he owed his freedom
and—yes, devil take it—all that he now had and was!
Murdo groaned, his tormenting conscience once again re-
proaching him. Nick *had* recognized him, of course; but
with the quick thinking that had always characterized him,
he had waited until they were alone and safe from prying
eyes to disclose the fact.

Even then, Nick had made no attempt to blackmail him.
He had uttered no threats—Nick Vincent was a gentleman,
and for all he had made his living as a highwayman in
England, and had sought to follow the same profession in
the land of his exile, he had his standards, and he adhered
to them without fear or favor.

"They've split us up, Murdo," he had said ruefully.
"The other lads have been sent to someplace called Norfolk Island. But Joss Gifford's still in Sydney, and he's

virtually free—they gave him a ticket-of-leave and a job as coachman to Captain Piper. And Piper's the port naval officer, in case you didn't know it—which means that Joss is able to make contact with some of the ship's masters.''

He had paused then, Murdo recalled, to permit the significance of those words to sink in . . . and inevitably, they had. Nick was planning to escape. Gifford had been left with money and instructions to bribe the master of a whaler, a man named Harry Morgan, to bring his vessel to an agreed rendezvous on the coast and wait there, until Nick could join him.

"I can run," Nick had gone on quietly. "I can run from one of the timber-felling parties without your help, Murdo— and that's what I'd planned to do. But with your help, it will be a deal less risky, will it not? I didn't know you were here—Lord, I had the surprise of my life when I saw you standing there in your King's red coat! And an officer to boot, lad—you've done well for yourself, haven't you? And I'm glad for your sake, truly glad, though I don't envy you your job. Working under a bloody tyrant like Logan can't be easy.''

Murdo's mouth tightened at the memory of those words. Nick had not been long in Moreton Bay when he had uttered them, and he had not known then how foul and monstrous a tyrant Logan was, or conceived of the power he wielded. But he knew now, poor Nick—by heaven, he knew! And he had regretted the time lapse he had permitted Gifford and the whaler skipper, Morgan, before they put his escape plan into operation.

"We're giving it three months, Murdo," Nick had told him. "I reckon I can stand anything for three months. Harry Morgan came to visit me in Sydney Jail before I was shipped out, and he made that part of the bargain. He's dead scared of being caught, you see. But three months will pass, will they not? I have to be sure I can make it to the rendezvous without any slip-up. But with your help, boy, there'll be no slip-up, will there? Your secret's safe with me—I'd never give you away, rest assured of that.

But you owe me, Murdo—call it a debt of honor, if you like. I'm depending on you to pay it.''

And of course he would, Murdo told himself grimly; he had to, because it was a debt he owed—and because, in the role for which Nick had cast him, all those years ago at Buck's Oak, he had become an officer and a gentleman, to whom such a debt *was* a matter of honor. But he was afraid. His attack of fever was genuine enough, but fear had caused him to prolong it, and . . . He licked at his dry, peeling lips and felt the sweat break out anew, on brow and body, coursing chillingly down his spine.

The three months were up. Morgan would be at anchor this very week in the secluded bay they had chosen, if he had kept to his bargain. And it would not be too soon for Nick Vincent. He had said that he could stand anything for three months, but he had made that assertion without any notion of what Captain Patrick Logan was capable of doing to him, in the interests, as the commandant put it, of ''breaking the rogue's spirit.''

Even Nick's stubborn courage had not been proof against Logan's heartless, studied cruelty, and the defiance he had shown initially had won him no concessions. He had been flogged by the vicious Bumble, then compelled to work in an iron neck collar in addition to his chains; he had had the word *felon* stamped on his shirt—which singled him out for the overseers' abuse—and he had suffered two periods of solitary confinement on starvation rations, in a befouled wooden cage of Logan's devising.

He was a broken man, reduced to skin and bone, and only the hope of his planned escape had sustained him. He . . . Murdo saw the prisoners due for that morning's punishment being herded into the yard and drawn up, in a straggling line, in front of the triangles. Bumble, an obscene figure, with his wide, muscular shoulders and short, withered legs, stood dipping the lashes of his whip into a can of water to make them more pliable, and beside him, Logan's convict gardener, Gilligan, and a Negro named Pugh—both rivals for his pay and position—grinned at each other as they took their own whips from their cloth cases.

An anxious search of the faces in the line of prisoners revealed that Nick was not among them, and Murdo breathed his relief. Tonight, then, as they had arranged, he would have to secure Nick's release and smuggle in to him the loaded pistol he had promised to provide. Bile rose in his throat as he saw Patrick Logan ride into the exercise yard, and gulping it down, Murdo turned away and flung himself back onto his bed. But even with a pillow held tightly over his ears, he knew that he could not avoid hearing the slash of Bumble's cat-o'-nine-tails and the agonized cries of his victims.

As if from a long way away, the voice of the head jailer reached him, calling out the names of the prisoners to be flogged and the number of lashes each man was to receive.

"Alfred Dickens—for insolence, sir, three hundred lashes. John Cowley, for leaving his work to go to the creek for a drink, two hundred lashes, sir. Elijah Bray, attempting to escape, sir, five hundred lashes on your authority, sir . . ."

Five hundred lashes meant almost certain death, Murdo thought grimly. There was a surgeon present, as the law demanded, but young Martin Tyler was too much in awe of the commandant to intervene and order the punishment halted. Logan showed no mercy to any poor wretch caught trying to run, and if the flogger sought to lay on his lash with what the commandant held to be lack of zeal, he would demand that the two men change places. Bumble, of course, seldom if ever displayed a lack of zeal, and he would not in Bray's case, for Bray had once been an overseer and— There was a loud knocking on the door of his room, and Murdo sat up, startled.

His sergeant, a gray-haired veteran of Montevideo and the Peninsular campaign named Rolfe, came in with evident reluctance. He was a good man, and, Murdo was aware, he found his present posting far removed from his liking, although he was too well disciplined to admit to it openly.

"Sir—the commandant's compliments, Mr. Dean, and I'm to ascertain whether your health will permit your attendance in the orderly room, after the punishment parade is dismissed."

Murdo drew the sheet round him and moved to the edge of the bed. He was probably still running a temperature, he thought, but in any other circumstances he would have made an effort to return to duty. Remaining here was . . . well, it was partly cowardice, he knew, based on his faint hope that if he were officially off duty due to sickness, he would not be suspected by Logan of aiding the escape of one of the prisoners.

He glanced uneasily at Sergeant Rolfe's bony, expressionless face and sighed. "Be so good as to tell Captain Logan that I will attend him after the parade, Sergeant."

"Yes, sir, I'll tell him." Rolfe, unbidden, picked up Murdo's discarded shirt and held it out to him. "I'll send your servant to assist you to dress, sir."

Murdo repeated his sigh. But there was no escape; if he did not wait on the commandant in the orderly room, Logan would almost certainly come to his quarters. His servant brought him water; he shaved and donned his uniform, swearing irritably as he buttoned the tight, suffocating collar and felt the sweat pouring off his face and neck.

From the exercise yard outside, he heard the sickening, expected sounds and Logan's voice, raised reprovingly against one of the floggers.

"You damned idle rogue! Lay it on with a will, d'you hear me? The fellow's back is barely marked! Do your duty, man, or I'll find one who will!"

But at last it was over. The wretched convicts were cut down from the triangles and, barely able to stand upright, had their chains reaffixed and were herded back to join the working parties now being mustered outside the stockade. Elijah Bray hung limp from the ropes attaching him to the triangle, and when they cut him down, he was dead. The military guard assembled, and the fettered prisoners obeyed the shouted commands and shuffled off, their chains dragging in the choking dust. None of them dared look back at the limp body still lying at the foot of the triangles.

Murdo braced himself, took a hurried gulp from the bottle of brandy he kept in his room, and donned his cap. The two sentries pacing in front of the orderly room halted and came to attention at his approach—Logan, he thought scornfully, lived in fear of an attack and, unless he was mounted, never stirred without his armed escort, even within the confines of the military quarters. And inside his orderly room, his clerks were also armed. . . .

The commandant was seated behind his table of roughly hewn wood, his tunic unbuttoned and his stock untied, his normally pale face red from his recent exertions. He did not acknowledge Murdo's salute and kept him standing at attention while he selected a cigar from a box at his elbow and lit it. Then, from behind a thick blue cloud of his own creation, he drawled unpleasantly, "It's been brought to my notice that you have asked to be relieved, Mr. Dean."

Murdo met his gaze squarely. "That is so, sir."

"Twice, in fact?"

"Yes, sir. I have been here since this prison was built, and—"

Patrick Logan gestured with the end of his cigar to the medal pinned to his subordinate's tunic. "Ha! One of our heroes of Waterloo, and you can't stomach this place! You are a damned weakling, Dean, d'you know that? You don't keep proper discipline—you're lax with the men you are supposed to command, and your attitude to those scum who are sent here for punishment is—God's blood, man, it's reprehensible! They'd soon get the upper hand if *you* were left in command."

"They are men, sir," Murdo defended. "I don't hold with treating them like animals."

"You don't approve of my methods, then? You consider I'm too hard a taskmaster?"

The cold, light eyes were on his face, glinting dangerously. They were not the eyes of a sane man, Murdo thought; Logan was insane—he had to be. During the past few months, the power he wielded had corrupted him, sent him across and beyond the borderline between madness and sanity.

He let his own gaze slide away, avoiding the older man's. "Since you ask me, sir—then the answer is yes," he managed thickly. "In the main colony, the maximum number of lashes a convict can receive is limited to fifty. But you order two and three hundred, even five hundred for quite trivial offenses. I most certainly do not approve of that, sir."

Captain Logan's face was suffused with angry color. He half rose from his chair, a small pulse at the angle of his jaw beating furiously, and Murdo stepped back hurriedly, fearing that the commandant was about to strike him. "You asked for my opinion, sir," he began, "and I—"

"You insolent young swine!" Logan thundered. "Do you not know that every miserable convict sent here is sent because he is deemed incorrigible? They are the scum of the earth, unworthy to live in a civilized society—they are thieves and predators, murderers and rapists and filthy sodomites! My responsibility, my task, is to break their spirits, not to reform them and send them back—none of them will *ever* go back, don't you understand? They are here for life, for lifelong punishment, on the Governor's orders. . . ."

He ranted on, spittle gathering at the corners of his mouth as he spat out the chilling words, and Murdo listened in appalled silence, too shocked to attempt to reply to the bitter tirade.

Finally, controlling himself with a visible effort, Logan resumed his seat. His eyes lost their blazing light, becoming dulled and opaque, and he said, quite quietly, "I have decided to approve your application for relief, Mr. Dean. You are too lily-livered to be of the slightest use to me here. I need a lieutenant who is made of sterner stuff, and for that reason I intend to return you to the regiment in Sydney by the next vessel that calls here. You may go."

Dazedly, Murdo drew himself up and saluted, relief flooding over him. Tonight he would aid Nick to make his escape, and—perhaps within the next week or so—he, too, could leave this hellish place.

"Thank you, sir," he stammered and found himself wondering whether the new Governor—martinet though he was reputed to be—had actually issued such orders as those the commandant had outlined.

Or had Captain Logan, in his growing madness, put his own crazed interpretation on them?

He was at the door of the small, dark office when the commandant called to him to wait.

"That blasted gentleman of the road, the murderer Nicholas Vincent," he bawled, with a return to his earlier hectoring manner. "I caught the miserable ruffian in a serious breach of discipline yesterday evening, when I rode out to inspect the timber-felling parties. He'd sneaked off, contrary to my standing orders, to refresh himself at the river, and he displayed dumb insolence when I reprimanded him for it. He's serving a week's solitary confinement, and after that I intend to give him a flogging he won't forget. Three hundred lashes, Mr. Dean! I'll break the swine's spirit, by God I will!"

Murdo gave him no answer, but his sorely tried spirits lifted. That Nick should be in solitary confinement was, his mind registered, an unexpected stroke of luck. The wooden cage in which he would be enduring his week-long sentence was one of several, each placed at a distance from the others and out of sight and sound of the main stockade, so as to ensure its isolation. Because the cages had been built of stout timber and were chained and padlocked to preclude any attempt at escape, they were left unguarded at night, visited only at dusk and dawn by the jailer in charge of them. The keys to the padlocks were kept in the guardroom, and Murdo anticipated no difficulty in purloining them.

Indeed, he reflected, with growing optimism, it would be a good deal less risky to organize Nick's escape from his solitary prison than had he been locked up in the main stockade. Then, inevitably, he would have had to take the chance of being observed when he made contact with him, and Nick would probably have had to use the smuggled pistol to make good his escape from his working party, in daylight, with the danger of immediate pursuit. As it was, the infernal tyrant Logan had played into their hands! Murdo found himself smiling. If he obtained the keys when the guard changed and momentary confusion reigned, then he could release Nick while it was dark, give him food and the loaded pistol, and he would have the whole night in which to make his way to the rendezvous with the whaler. And even if its master were delayed, Nick should be safe enough, hiding there, since he would have food and a weapon with which to defend himself, should that be necessary.

And . . . Murdo was conscious of elation. He would have paid his debt of honor, and when the next transport called, he could leave with a clear conscience, on that account, at least. It might even be possible to bring the attention of Patrick Logan's commanding officer—or the Governor himself—to the appalling cruelty currently being practiced by a man who had apparently gone out of his mind. They would have to believe him; if he made a detailed report, they . . . Sergeant Rolfe approached him across the sun-baked parade ground.

"Sergeant—I am returning to duty," Murdo said, his voice flat. "And I intend to inspect the guard this evening. See that the guard commander is warned, if you please."

Rolfe eyed him sympathetically as he acknowledged the order, clearly supposing that the commandant had put an end to his sick leave.

The rest of the hot, airless day passed swiftly. Murdo made himself as conspicuous as he could, and when Captain Logan had ridden off to make his late afternoon inspection of the working parties, he set about making his own final preparations. The food he obtained from the mess steward was dry and unappetizing but had the advan-

tage of being easily carried in a knapsack. To his own
uneaten lunch of cold salt pork he added bread and ship's
biscuit, a half bottle of rum, and a pouch of tobacco. He
filled a water bottle, cleaned and loaded the pistol, and
wrapped powder and ball in an oilskin covering to protect
them from dampness, should Nick be compelled to take to
the river. Then he paid his visit to the guardroom, and as
he had expected, it was a simple matter to filch the key to
Nick's cell.

Finally, he took a seemingly casual stroll past the wooden
cages and, finding Nick in the most distant of them,
contrived to deliver his warning, together with the pistol
and the key.

"Wait till dark," he whispered. "I'll give you a whistle
when the coast is clear, and I'll be waiting for you at the
edge of those trees there, fifty yards behind you. Bring the
key—I'll have to put it back in the guardhouse to cover my
tracks. And I'll have water and provisions for you and an
unmarked shirt."

Nick's hoarse voice called on God to bless him, and
Murdo retraced his steps to the mess, still maintaining his
casual pose but with his heart thudding and his whole body
drenched in perspiration.

Captain Logan returned and, eschewing the mess, went
straight to his own house, to Murdo's intense relief. Dinner was served, with only Surgeon Tyler and the quartermaster present, and Murdo had to make a considerable
effort to choke down the ill-cooked food that was set in
front of him, while keeping up a desultory conversation
with his two companions.

But at long last the meal was over. Making the excuse
that his fever still persisted, he went back to his own
quarters, leaving the other two to their usual night of
heavy drinking. All was quiet when, burdened by the
knapsack and the rolled shirt, he emerged warily into the
darkness to take up his position on the edge of the trees.
His soft whistle brought no immediate response, and he
was about to repeat it nervously when he heard the sound

of footsteps, and a few moments later Nick's emaciated form, in filthy, ragged clothing, slumped down beside him, breathing heavily.

"Did you bring the key?" Murdo demanded. In the faint moonlight, Nick looked as white as death, his eyes dark pools sunk into his bony face, his lips grotesquely swollen from lack of water. But he was smiling as he held out the key, the old, reckless courage once again in evidence, now that the dream of escape had become reality. Murdo helped him to don the shirt he had brought, giving urgent, whispered instructions as to the route he must take to the rendezvous with the whaler.

"Do not put any trust in the blackfellows, unless you've no choice, Nick," he warned. "Logan rewards them if they bring in escapers. But if you're desperate or Morgan's whaler is delayed, use the rum or even your pistol to bribe them, and ask them to take you to a man named Mullalong. He helped some castaways we found here a few years ago, and they said he was good to them. Remember their names—Pamphlet and Finnigan—it might help."

Nick inspected the contents of the knapsack and slung it over his shoulder.

"How do I find the blackfellows?" he asked.

"They'll find you," Murdo answered gravely. "If you let them. But stick to the route I've given you, and you should be safe—there'll be no pursuit until daylight, so get as far away from here as you can. Logan uses dogs. If you hear them, get to the river as fast as you know how. I'll try to keep them off your trail."

Nick nodded his shaven head. His hand rested briefly in gratitude on Murdo's shoulder, and then he was gone, the trees swallowing him up. Murdo crept cautiously back to the cage. There was no way in which he could cover his tracks without suspicion falling on someone, he knew, but complicity would be hard to prove if he locked the slatted door again and returned the key to the guardroom—Logan could hardly arrest the whole guard, and the worst he could charge them with would be negligence. But he was

close to the limit of his fever-depleted strength by the time
he had deposited the key and regained his own room, and
he gulped down what remained in his bottle of brandy in
an attempt to subdue his jangling nerves. He had not
expected to sleep, but weakness and exhaustion brought
him welcome oblivion, and the sun had risen when Sergeant Rolfe shook him into wakefulness.

"There's bin an escape, sir," the gray-haired sergeant
told him ruefully. "That poor devil the cap'n has a grudge
against—Vincent. Broke out o' solitary somehow, he did,
an' the orders are he's to be brought back, dead or alive.
Cap'n Logan sent his compliments, sir, and you're to take
command o' the search party."

"Now, Sergeant?" Murdo managed, licking at lips that
had gone suddenly stiff and dry.

"Now, sir," Rolfe confirmed. "I have the men mustered,
sir, an' I've issued twenty rounds a man. When you're
ready, Mr. Dean, sir—" Helpfully, he picked up Murdo's
breeches and offered them to him. "I've a weapon ready
for you. A musket, sir—a pistol wouldn't be much use in
them woods. And," he added with conscious cynicism, "I
reckon we'll be doing Vincent a service if we bring him in
dead, don't you, Mr. Dean?"

Murdo nodded wordlessly. Still bemused by sleep, he
struggled into his uniform, making an effort to collect his
thoughts.

"Is the commandant joining the search?" he asked,
aware, as he buttoned his tunic, that his hands were
trembling visibly.

The sergeant shrugged. "I don't doubt but he will, sir.
At the present moment, though, the cap'n's questioning
the guard about the key o' the solitary confinement cage.
Seemingly he thinks it must have been taken in the night,
'cause the lock wasn't forced. But I wouldn't know anything about that, would you, sir?"

"No." Murdo avoided the older man's gaze and, forcing himself to move briskly, went to the door. Rolfe might
suspect him of having had a hand in Nick Vincent's escape,

but even if he did, he would not speak of it—he was loyal, and his dislike of Captain Logan matched his own, for all he never aired it openly.

The men lined up outside came to attention, and slinging the musket the sergeant had provided for him, Murdo led them off to commence the search. All were on foot—Logan possessed the only horse in the settlement—and the pace, brisk at first, soon slackened when they entered the closely growing timber by which the prison buildings were surrounded. The work parties were already out; their overseers, questioned, professed ignorance of any escaper or indeed of anything untoward, and the soldiers went on, fanning out so as to cover as much ground as possible.

Murdo, at pains to avoid the route he had advised Nick to follow, led them with every appearance of confidence, permitting them to rest at regular intervals and making frequent pauses to consult with Rolfe. The sergeant offered no criticism of the manner in which the search was being conducted, and, his gaunt face devoid of expression, he offered no suggestions of his own . . . yet, Murdo felt increasingly sure, Rolfe was too old a campaigner not to realize that he was being led on a wild-goose chase.

By noon, when he halted them to eat their haversack rations, his hopes had risen considerably. Nick had had the longest start it was possible to give him—he must, surely, have made good his escape and be well on his way to the rendezvous with Morgan's whaler by this time. And he was armed—the aborigines would not attempt to tackle an armed and determined fugitive, although they might follow him at a discreet distance, waiting for him to tire. And Nick was weak from the near-starvation diet and the heavy toil; he would tire easily, so that perhaps it was premature to hope that he had yet managed to get safely away. . . . Murdo smothered a sigh and offered his flask of rum to his sergeant.

"Thank you kindly, sir—" Rolfe began, then broke off, listening intently, the flask only halfway to his lips. "The cap'n, sir—he's over yonder. I can hear them dogs o' his baying.''

Murdo's straining ears caught the sound an instant later, and his spirits plummeted as he gauged the direction whence it was coming. Whether by chance or intention, Logan was following the route he had chosen for Nick, and his infernal hunting dogs, judging by their purposeful baying, must have struck the trail. There was time, however—Nick should have covered that ground during the night, and there was a creek nearby, which, if he had had his wits about him, he would have waded across in order to obscure his scent.

''If you're wanting to join the commandant, sir,'' Rolfe volunteered unexpectedly, ''you can leave me to carry on our search when the lads have eaten.''

Murdo studied his face, but it was as expressionless as before. Perhaps, he thought, it might be a wise precaution if he sought out Logan with the object of delaying him, if nothing else. Nick might have tired or, worse, have lost his way in the trackless timber. It had been a dark night, and such moonlight as there was would not have penetrated the close-growing foliage of the screening trees.

He nodded to Rolfe, not trusting himself to speak, and, grasping his musket, set off at a shambling run, guided by the excited yelping of the dogs, which seemed to be coming nearer. The thick undergrowth impeded his passage, slowing him down to little more than walking pace, but he went on doggedly, using the butt of his musket to protect his face from overhanging branches and trailing vines. Game broke cover in front of him, disturbed by the dogs' baying and his own noisy progress; half a score of small brown wallabies hopped from his path in agitated procession, and from a nearby creek a wedge of wild ducks rose skyward with an almost metallic clatter as they sought safety above the treetops.

Emerging at last into a clearing, Murdo saw that one of the prison chain gangs was at work there, chopping the branches from a giant cedar they had just felled. Logan, his dogs now silent, had pulled up beside them, presumably with the intention of inquiring whether they had seen any sign of the fugitive. Murdo halted behind the screening trees to regain his breath and heard the commandant's drawling voice, raised above the crack of the busy axes.

"All right, stop work! My hounds have lost the escaper's trail—but they were hot on it only a few minutes ago. He's here, is he not, the infernal scoundrel? If any of you have tried to hide him, I'll have the whole bunch of you flogged till your backbones are bared! Speak up now—where is the rogue?"

To Murdo's numb dismay, one of the convicts lifted his manacled hands and pointed to the creek, flowing sluggishly some thirty or forty yards beyond the fallen tree.

"He's down there, Your Honor—in the water. But the bastard's spent, he can't run no more—the dogs'll catch him easy!"

It could not be Nick, Murdo told himself. Nick had had the whole night and part of the day to distance himself from here. He had food and water and a pistol—for God's sake, he must have reached the rendezvous by now! Perhaps there was another escaper, a man from the working party who had attempted to run or . . . He froze, sick with despair, as he saw Nick rise from the creek and try ineffectually to claw his way up the steep, muddy bank on its far side.

But as the convict who had betrayed him had claimed, Nick was too spent, too weak and debilitated, to go on. He managed to ascend the bank at his second attempt, but it was too late. Logan had seen him and, putting spurs to his horse, drew his saber and resumed the pursuit, scattering the men of the chain gang as he put the big stallion at the tree and, clearing it effortlessly, went thundering down the slight slope, the dogs after him.

"View hulloo—tallyho!" he yelled exultantly, at the pitch of his lungs. "Yoi up and over, my beauties! The rogue's a dead man now!"

Nick halted and half turned to face him, but the ground

was treacherous and he stumbled, the pistol he had been holding jerked from his grasp. Defenseless and alone, he managed somehow to stand upright, facing certain death but refusing to run from it . . . and Murdo could remain an onlooker no longer.

Nick had been his boyhood hero, his leader in the old days on the High Toby, and the debt he owed—the debt of honor—had to be paid, whatever the cost to himself. He dropped to one knee and, raising the musket to his shoulder, took aim at the horse as, in a cascade of splashing water, the animal emerged from the creek and started to ascend the bank.

Logan's saber flashed in the sunlight. He brought the blade down on Nick Vincent's bare head in the same instant that Murdo fired. The range was long for accuracy, but the great black horse presented a massive target and it came crashing down, flinging its rider over its head as it fell.

Logan lay there motionless and evidently stunned, for he made no move to rise. Then, as if it had dawned on them suddenly that the hated tyrant was at their mercy, a concerted howl went up from the hitherto silent convicts.

Murdo heard a man screech, "Do for the bloody sod, boys! Come on, let's put an end to 'im!"

His cry was taken up by others in a vengeful, savage chorus. "Aye—let's kill 'im afore 'e kills us!"

"Send the bloodthirsty devil to hell, where 'e belongs!"

"Do fer 'im—*do* fer 'im! We shan't never get a chance like this again!"

"The sojers won't stop us, will you, lads? Don't the swine treat you nigh as badly as he treats us?"

Not a soldier moved, and the overseers uttered no protest. Gaining confidence from this, the convicts surged across the shallow creek, still linked by their leg-irons, dragging the fearful and the reluctant with them and screaming their hatred as they ran.

Logan heard them. He made a feeble attempt to rise and then slumped back into the mud, whimpering in pain and mouthing threats that were drowned by the shouts of the mob.

Aware that he was powerless to stop them, Murdo watched in horror as they hurled themselves upon the prostrate, scarlet-coated form on the far bank of the creek. Axes, crowbars, torn-off branches of trees, and even Logan's own saber were being used as weapons, and those who could not reach the helpless commandant fell, with almost equal savagery, upon his horse and the snarling dogs.

No man could live under so brutal an assault, and it was soon over, neither the overseers nor the guard making any move to intervene until the men of the chain gang started to stumble back through the muddy water of the creek.

Murdo stepped unsteadily from the trees that had sheltered him, but Sergeant Rolfe, coming suddenly from behind, moved quickly to bar his way. He took the still-smoking musket from Murdo's nerveless grasp, glanced at his white, shocked face, and said briefly, "It's best if you don't say nothin', Mr. Dean. An' better still, sir, if you don't remember what you just seen, ain't it, now? Beggin' your leave, sir . . ."

He lifted the musket and brought its butt hard down on Murdo's forehead, catching him deftly as his knees buckled under him and his senses left him. . . .

When he recovered consciousness, it was to find himself in his own bed, with Sergeant Rolfe gently swabbing his bruised and throbbing head.

"For the Lord's sake, Rolfe," Murdo protested as memory painfully returned, "what's happened? Is—oh, devil take it, man, what am I doing here? Is the commandant really dead?"

Rolfe's lined face betrayed neither regret nor guilt. He nodded and said in a matter-of-fact tone, "Yes, sir—him and the escaper Vincent. We buried them both out in the woods."

"You buried them *there*?"

The sergeant coughed apologetically. "They weren't in

no state to permit us to do nothin' else, sir. Them dogs and the horse, you see—'' He resumed his careful swabbing. ''This is a real nasty bruise you've got here, Mr. Dean. By rights the surgeon ought to have seen it, but Mr. Tyler . . . well, sir, not to put too fine a point on it, Mr. Tyler was drunk. He wasn't fit to attend to his duties—none of 'em, sir. Maybe that was what they call a blessing in disguise.''

His meaning slowly sank in. Young Surgeon Tyler had not seen the commandant's body, and now it was doubtful if he ever would—and the climate would do the rest.

Rolfe set down his bowl. ''You're the senior officer here now, sir—you're the acting commandant. You don't need me to remind you that it will be your duty to make out a report on the cap'n's death, do you, sir?''

''Oh, God!'' Murdo stared at him. He could not think coherently with his head throbbing unmercifully and his mouth so dry that he could hardly speak. Thoughtfully, the old sergeant filled a beaker with water and held it to his lips. He drank thirstily and lay back, his thoughts in turmoil. ''What the devil can I say, Sergeant Rolfe?''

''Well, sir,'' Rolfe suggested quietly, ''it'd be true to say as the commandant fell from his horse when he was chasin' an escaped convict, would it not, sir? If you state that in your report, no one will be the wiser, and we'll all be in the clear, I fancy. The way he fell, he must have broken his neck, Mr. Dean—stands to reason. Or perhaps, sir, some blackfellows saw 'im lyin' there helpless and finished 'im off.''

''Yes but—'' In spite of the water, Murdo's mouth was still dry. He swallowed hard. ''Rolfe, I—''

''Now, don't you go upsettin' yourself, sir,'' Sergeant Rolfe urged kindly, his gaze fixed on the freshly polished toes of his boots. ''There's not a soul except me knows as it was your musket ball that brought down the commandant's big bastard of a horse. An' I'm a man as keeps his own counsel, Mr. Dean—you know that. What my officers do is no business of mine an' never has been, in twenty-seven years' service. I'm lookin' forward to me pension now, sir, when I can get away from here.''

Murdo struggled into a sitting position.

"I hope to heaven we can both get away from here, Sergeant," he said faintly. "And—I shall write a report on the lines you—er—you've suggested.''

Rolfe beamed at him. "Very good, sir," he acknowledged. He added, his smile fading, "I took the liberty of orderin' Old Bumble a hundred lashes, on your authority, sir. I reckon he's only gettin' what's been comin' to him for quite a while, don't you, sir?" He came stiffly to attention. "Him an' the cap'n both, if the truth were known. I'll leave you to get some sleep now, Mr. Dean.''

He stumped out, closing the door behind him, and Murdo let his aching head fall back on the pillow. He felt no qualms of conscience, only a deep sadness on Nick's account and an overwhelming weariness.

"Please God," he prayed aloud, "let me be relieved of my duty here, or I shall wish myself in hell with Logan!''

It was almost six weeks before his prayer was answered and Justin Broome's *Mermaid* brought his relief and another forty capital respites, who came stumbling ashore, heavily chained, to begin their long, punitive exile.

They looked about them apprehensively, clearly having heard stories of the horrors awaiting them in their new prison. But only Murdo and some of the old hands saw, in memory, the cold-eyed officer on the great black horse who had once stood on the quayside, watching the new arrivals disembark . . . and the memory was already fading, even for them.

When Justin came ashore to announce, with pardonable pride, that Jessica had given birth to a daughter—whom they had named Jenny, after her grandmother—and that his promotion to the rank of commander had been gazetted, Murdo was able to smile with his old warmth.

"I'm delighted," he said. "On both counts, Justin. But I have to admit that I'm even more delighted to be taking passage to Sydney with you. As long as I live, I never want to see this place again!''

"It's been bad?" Justin eyed him gravely. "Yes, I can see that it has. But I hope and believe that conditions may soon improve, Murdo—both here and on Norfolk Island. A new journal called the *Australian* has been started by William Charles Wentworth and others, and it's taking up the cudgels for reform in no uncertain fashion. It ran a letter under the pen name Alcestis, which was written by one of the women who were recently expelled from Kingston by order of His Excellency Governor Darling.''

Justin paused, his mouth tightening. "The Alcestis letter gave chapter and verse, and it has caused the most almighty furor in Sydney, incensing the Governor and the officers of the Fifty-seventh. But at least it's had some effect—Donaldson has been replaced as commandant for Norfolk Island, and your commandant, Logan, if he had lived, would have been recalled. A captain of the Seventeenth by the name of Clunie is to be appointed in his stead, as soon as he arrives in the colony. Poor little Alcestis, though, is under fire from all sides, and there is much speculation as to her real identity.''

"Do you know it?" Murdo asked curiously.

"Indeed I do," Justin answered, with a wry smile. "She is a friend of Jessica's and is at present a guest in our house. She's an ex-convict, emancipated by marriage, which makes her very vulnerable. For that reason I cannot divulge her name, even to you, Murdo.''

"What if I were to join my voice to hers? What if *I* were to write a letter to the *Australian* also?" Murdo's tone was harsh. "I could reveal plenty about what is being perpetrated here, by heaven I could!''

"I will introduce you to Alcestis," Justin promised uneasily. "But it would be on your head. Joining Wentworth's crusade could cost you your commission, Murdo.''

"To hell with that," Murdo retorted. "It would be cheap at the price!" And, he thought defiantly, it would be a price he would be more than willing to pay.

CHAPTER XX

Governor Darling was angry. It was a cold, sternly controlled anger, but his wife, seated opposite him at the long, highly polished mahogany table at which they had met to break their fast, sensed his annoyance and sought, in her quiet, charming way, to put him in a better humor.

Her endeavors met with scant response. The Governor sat hunched in his chair, replying gruffly to her conversational sallies and picking distastefully at the food in front of him. Disappointed, Mrs. Darling glanced across the table at her husband's new military secretary, inviting his support.

She liked the thirty-year-old captain who had replaced Major Ovens. Charles Sturt was exceptionally well educated and intelligent; he had entered enthusiastically into the social life of the colony, and from the first had expressed a wish to take part in the exploratory expeditions aimed at opening still more virgin land for settlement. He had served in Canada, France, and Ireland and had a repertoire of witty and amusing stories that, normally, appealed to her serious husband, but . . . The Governor's wife glanced uneasily across the table. This morning, it seemed, nothing would distract him from his glum and wrathful thoughts.

"Damme!" he burst out suddenly. "There must be some way of curbing that infernal fellow Wentworth's campaign against me! First it was the letter he published in his miserable rag of a newspaper, purporting to be written by some convict's wife calling herself—what was it? 'Alcestis' or some such, so that she could not be taxed with it. She held *me* responsible for the supposedly harsh treatment of the felons on Norfolk Island. But now, devil take the man, he's produced another so-called witness, this time to alleged atrocities at Moreton Bay! And this busybody is also careful to call himself by some classical pseudonym! 'Eumen' something or other.''

"Eumenides, sir," Charles Sturt supplied. "The three avenging spirits, supposed to be dedicated to the punishment of those offending against the basic laws of society, if my memory serves me aright. Typical of young Wentworth, of course—he's a classical scholar."

The Governor glared at him, suspecting levity, and Mrs. Darling said hastily, "Mrs. Van Buren—whom I must admit I rather dislike—was insisting very loudly at the Dawsons' garden party that she knew who Alcestis was. I could not make up my mind whether or not to believe her . . . her claim was so preposterous."

"Who did she suppose it was?" her husband demanded.

"The wife of the chaplain at Norfolk Island," Mrs. Darling answered innocently. "Mrs. Van Buren told everyone who would listen that the young woman *was* a convict! And that she had absconded from her employment and from the Female Factory in order to marry the chaplain . . . I think she said his name was Fox or Cox. At all events, Ralph dear, she announced her intention of revealing the girl's identity in a letter to Mr. Wentworth's newspaper."

"Then I hope she does," the Governor said irritably. "And I hope Wentworth will have the integrity to publish it, if it's true. Though I take leave to doubt whether he will—he's too busy conducting a campaign of vilification against me. But he has a responsibility to tell the truth—don't you agree, Charles?"

Thus appealed to, Charles Sturt inclined his head. "Yes, indeed, sir, and I'm sure he realizes it. I mean, sir, if he's campaigning for a free press, he—"

"The people," Darling interrupted, an edge to his voice, "are taught by their newspapers to talk about the rights of Englishmen and the free and democratic institutions of the mother country. But it must surely be evident to the meanest intelligence that although this is an English colony, it is a *penal* colony. There is no similarity whatsoever in its constitution to that of England—but Wentworth appears unable to recognize that. You cannot have a democracy or fully representative government when one half of the community is deprived of citizen rights—and correctly—since it is criminal or was orginally so. And that is not solely *my* view—it is the view held also by the Colonial Office."

Sturt met Mrs. Darling's gaze and lowered his own. "Quite so, sir," he murmured soothingly.

But the Governor refused to be placated.

"I have reformed the public service," he went on aggrievedly. "Every department now functions efficiently, where before there was overstaffing, muddle, and the most outrageous waste of public money. But Wentworth and Waddell continue to demand a larger council, with, I can only suppose, the object of curtailing my authority and preventing me from instituting reforms. They want trial by jury, and Justice Forbes backs them up! But, damme, it's impractical, unless emancipated felons are to be permitted to serve as jurors and bring in verdicts when their own kind are brought to trial! Do they really want that, for heaven's sweet sake?"

Mrs. Darling rose and went to the window. In an attempt to introduce a change of topic, she said brightly, "Ralph dear, is that the regimental band I hear? They seem to be playing a very somber air—is there some special parade today?"

Charles Sturt murmured something she did not catch, and, to her dismay, her husband got to his feet so precipitately that he knocked over the chair in which he had been seated.

"Yes," he confirmed, tight-lipped. "There is, my dear. I am putting a stop to a practice that undermines military discipline. This morning two private soldiers of the Fifty-seventh, Sudds and Thompson, are to be drummed out of the regiment and sent to a road gang for seven years. I am determined to make an example of them, and my general order to that effect will be read at the parade, so that it is clearly understood by all present.'' He sighed impatiently when his wife stared back at him in frank bewilderment.

Sturt said tactfully, ''You see, Mrs. Darling, the Fifty-seventh will go on to India from here, and a great many soldiers are reluctant to leave the colony. They've formed attachments and want to become settlers. Hitherto—by what I can only call an abuse of the law—they have obtained dishonorable discharges by committing some form of larceny, for which they have been charged and, if found guilty, sentenced to transportation. Not, you understand, to hard labor. Transportation has meant that they simply stay here and—''

Governor Darling cut him short. ''Yes, yes,'' he rasped. ''There's no need to go into all that, Charles. What it amounts to, my dear, is that the rogues, having signed on for life, are deliberately breaking their terms of enlistment . . . and the regiment is short of men. Lockyer's much concerned on that score, as you may imagine—and so am I. So I'm putting a stop to it, as I told you. Well?'' His cold gaze went to the face of his military secretary. ''We had better go and see the sentence carried out, had we not? At least I'm well within my rights in this matter, since it's a question of military administration. Wentworth can hardly fulminate on that score, can he?''

''I scarcely think he can, sir,'' Charles Sturt assured him. He took a folded copy of a newssheet from his pocket and offered it to Mrs. Darling. ''A copy of the *Australian,* ma'am. You probably haven't ever seen it, for heaven knows it's a scurrilous rag, but in case you should wish to, here it is.'' He bowed courteously and followed the Governor from the room.

Left alone, Mrs. Darling returned to her seat at the table. She spread the two sheets of newsprint in front of her, smoothing out the folds in the crumpled paper. The leader was first to catch her eye, and she perused it meticulously.

Contrary to her husband's belief, Mr. Wentworth was not, it seemed, campaigning for democracy. Rather, he asserted that his guiding political aim was "the foundation of a self-governing British state in Australia, based on the British constitution." A constitution that, he declared, "recognizes all forms of personal and class distinction compatible with individual freedom and popular rights." Whereas democracy he "disclaimed and detested because it is based on a false theory—that of human equality."

To her surprise, Mrs. Darling learned that the liberal Mr. Wentworth visualized his self-governing state as one ruled by an Australian upper class, corresponding to the British landed gentry. He also appeared to uphold the system of deporting shiploads of criminals from the mother country to Australia, in order that "they might be utilized as assigned servants and laborers," to the eventual benefit of their adopted country and their own reformation.

Her curiosity now fully aroused, the Governor's wife read on. Part of the "address of welcome" with which her husband had been presented on his arrival in Sydney was quoted, and she read, with growing amazement:

> Your Excellency may rest fully assured that a Legislature, founded on the same basis as the Legislature of the American Colonies, can alone make us a happy and contented people . . . and any compromising measures on this head, which by possibility may hereafter be adopted by His Majesty's Ministers, will only serve to increase and perpetuate beyond remedy those internal dissensions, which unfortunately have disturbed our Community ever since the arrival and departure of the late Commissioner of Enquiry, Mr. Bigge . . .

The quotation continued, somewhat obscurely so far as Mrs. Darling was concerned:

There exists . . . in the Territory a race of men, already arrived at an adult state who, scattered in the distant and silent woods of their Country—unknown, unheard of as a political body—are yet destined to be the Fathers of the succeeding generation and the inheritors of our Lands.

The patronage of Office they have always disregarded . . . but Grants of Land, which they consider their own, as it were by natural inheritance, they have seen of late years lavishly bestowed upon Strangers without the capability of improving it . . .

Was this, Mrs. Darling wondered, a plea for the rights of the emancipated members of the community—those who, in Governor Macquarie's day, had earned their pardons and, restored to the rank in society each had previously occupied, had been granted land by their benevolent patron? Or . . . She reread the last paragraph. Was it an attempt to decry Governor Brisbane's policy of making large grants to wealthy adventurers fresh from England? Men of the type of the two unfortunates murdered by bushrangers in the wild country beyond the Blue Mountains . . . certainly they had been given thousands of acres of virgin land, and, in all probability, neither of them had possessed the capability of improving it.

In the distance, the sound of a dismal drumbeat was wafted through the open window, and Mrs. Darling stiffened, her attention momentarily distracted from the pages of the *Australian*. She understood and, indeed, concurred with her husband's decision to take action against the rogues of serving soldiers who, lacking in both loyalty and regimental pride, had committed criminal acts in order to be discharged from the army. It was right that such men should be punished, but . . . was the punishment he had ordered too severe?

Her husband was an upright and honorable man, a courageous officer, who had served his country with distinction in peace and war—and already he had proved himself an admirable administrator, in Mauritius and now here. But he expected a great deal from the men he commanded, and his standards were set high—too high, perhaps, for an army the great Duke of Wellington had described as . . . what was the word he had used?

Infamous—yes, that was it. The Governor's wife rose again and walked restlessly to the window. On the 57th's parade ground the two condemned soldiers would hear their sentences read, and then, to the roll of the drums, each man would be stripped of his uniform and, in convict garb, have iron fetters hammered onto his wrists and ankles before being marched off, first to the jail and then to join one of the chain gangs to labor on the roads.

She shivered, conscious of a nagging fear. In this place—in this penal colony—such sentences were commonplace. Surely even the crusading Mr. Wentworth could find in it no just reason to launch a fresh attack on the colony's Governor and commander in chief?

A servant entered and started silently to clear the table. Mrs. Darling permitted him to do so, and then, having asked him to bring her fresh tea, she sat down once more to resume her reading of the newspaper. She was, she reminded herself, the daughter and the sister—as well as the wife—of distinguished military officers, and she would not allow a man of William Charles Wentworth's caliber to upset or intimidate her.

Pulling the second sheet of newsprint toward her, she started to read the letter signed Alcestis. It had been discussed at the Dawsons' garden party a few days ago; she had listened to the discussion and, indeed, had taken part in it, but until now she had not seen the offending letter nor—in the light of the other guests' reaction to it—had she deemed it either desirable or necessary to do so. All the ladies had expressed disapproval, and many had been openly disgusted; and when Mrs. Van Buren had claimed to know the identity of the writer, virtually all of them had joined in her condemnation of the absconding convict.

Only Mrs. Dawson had sounded a dissenting note, but then Abigail Dawson was . . . The Governor's wife sought

an apt word to describe her hostess. Not *liberal*—that was
becoming an ugly word in her eyes now, since it was
frequently applied to the proprietor of the *Australian*. Kindly
disposed, trusting—a lady in the truest sense, who saw
good in everyone but, in that respect, was perhaps a trifle
unworldly. Her toleration of her ill-mannered stepdaughter
was praiseworthy but foolish. She . . . The manservant
returned with the tea tray she had requested, and Mrs.
Darling poured herself a cup, reluctant, now that it came
to the point, to read Alcestis's letter.

If, as Lucy Van Buren had asserted, this Alcestis was
now the wife of a chaplain in the employ of the government prison service, then the girl was disloyal, for her
action could have serious consequences for her husband.

The men sentenced to imprisonment on Norfolk Island
face a living death . . .

The words, stark in their simplicity, seemed suddenly to
leap out from the printed page, and almost against her
will, the Governor's wife read on.

The letter occupied three full columns and was in the
form of a diary, each entry briefly describing day-to-day
happenings on the island, but telling of such suffering and
deprivation that—perhaps because of its brevity and the
fact that the diarist was not well educated—the effect was
to carry conviction.

The enforced departure of the women and children was
described in terms one of the children might have used,
and to Mrs. Darling it was the more poignant on that
account, dispelling all idea that the editor of the *Australian*
might have put his own pen to work on it.

The women had gone willingly, giving up their freedom to
live in sight of the prison. By being there, they gave hope
to all the men. They tended gardens with flowers and fruit
trees in them, but when we stood on the deck of the ship
that was taking us away, we saw through our tears that the
gardens were being plowed up, the fruit trees cut down.

We sang, the children with us, to try to give comfort to those we were leaving behind, but they knew, as we did, that they would never see their wives and little ones again.

They are bad men, deserving of punishment for the evil things they have done, I cannot deny that. But to rob them of hope, even should they reform, is that not cruelty?

Is that what His Excellency the Governor means by punishment short of death? On Norfolk Island, it is a living death . . .

Mrs. Darling was deeply moved. She thrust the newssheet from her, finding the print blurred by the tears that started to her eyes. She was a regular and devout churchgoer, having a strong faith in her God and in Christian teaching, and she did not have to remind herself that the Lord Jesus Christ had, on innumerable occasions, according to his Gospel, enjoined repentant sinners to come to him for forgiveness.

If Alcestis had told the truth, then the Governor—the husband she loved and to whom she had always given her unswerving loyalty—was offering no chance of forgiveness to the felons he had consigned to Norfolk Island. True, they were bad men, as Alcestis had conceded—men condemned to death for the crimes they had committed since their arrival in the colony. Ralph had shown them mercy by commuting their sentences to life imprisonment, but— She felt her throat tighten. He had saved them from the hangman's noose only to condemn them to what Alcestis's letter called a living death, and by ordering the removal of the women and children, he had deprived desperate men of the last civilizing influence they had known.

And . . . surely it had not been on *his* instructions that the women's gardens, their fruit trees had been destroyed? The new commandant, Captain Donaldson, had perhaps been overzealous. Her husband was never vindictive; he was stern but he was always just, and in setting out the terms of imprisonment for what were called "capital respites" on Norfolk Island and at Moreton Bay, he was simply carrying out the policy of the Colonial Office in regard to them.

Only—had not another correspondent of Mr. Wentworth's *Australian* newspaper written of atrocities committed also at Moreton Bay? Her hand unsteady, Mrs. Darling poured herself a second cup of tea. The somber drumming had ceased now, her mind registered; the two soldiers who had offended against military law had been discharged from their regiment with ignominy and would be commencing their punishment. A punishment that, she reminded herself, a little while ago she had decided was severe but richly deserved. She sipped at the lukewarm tea, her thoughts in turmoil, torn between the conscience-stricken desire to seek out and question the woman who had called herself Alcestis and the fear—yes, the fear—that if she were to do so, she would be guilty of disloyalty to her husband.

A knock sounded on the door. To the manservant who entered, the Governor's wife turned a controlled but tear-stained face.

"Yes, MacCarthy?"

"A lady has called, asking to see you, ma'am. A Mrs. Van Buren."

Lucy Van Buren was the very last person she wanted, at this moment, to see, but . . . Mrs. Darling dabbed at her reddened eyes and, having composed herself, answered quietly, "Very well. Show Mrs. Van Buren in, if you please. And take my tray."

The dining room was not where she normally received callers, but at this early hour, it was probably as good a place as any for what should, if possible, be a brief interview. . . .

Lucy Van Buren came in a few moments later. She looked thin and ill, Mrs. Darling thought, studying her as they shook hands. Nonetheless, she was a good-looking woman, with her deep-set dark eyes and beautifully coiffed hair, and she was dressed in the height of current fashion, in a perfectly cut gown of deep-blue Indian silk, set off by lace at neck and wrists.

To put her at ease, Mrs. Darling expressed admiration of the gown and its material and was mildly surprised when the visitor exclaimed indignantly, "This was one of the gowns the convict girl Fairweather made when she was assigned to me, Mrs. Darling! She was not of good character, but she was very skilled with her needle, so you may imagine I was greatly put out when she absconded."

"Yes, you must have been," the Governor's wife agreed politely. "Good needlewomen are hard to come by in this town, as I know to my cost." She waited and then asked uncertainly, "Is it on—" She had almost said Alcestis, but stopped herself in time. "Is it on this girl's account that you have come to see me, Mrs. Van Buren?"

"Yes, indeed it is. You know, of course, that she was the writer of that biased and untruthful account of the conditions on Norfolk Island, calling herself Alcestis?" There was a harsh edge to Lucy Van Buren's voice, and Mrs. Darling recoiled from it.

"So you said, at the garden party the other day," she answered noncommittally. "But have you proof of it? Has the young woman admitted that she wrote the letter?"

"Her husband has. Mr. Cox was recalled from his post at the settlement and returned on board the *Amity* a few days ago. At my suggestion, Mr. Marsden—the Reverend Samuel Marsden, our principal chaplain—questioned him concerning the matter, and he admitted everything. I have been given to understand," Mrs. Van Buren added spitefully, "that Mr. Marsden—quite rightly, in my view—demanded his resignation from the prison chaplains' service. Clearly he is unsuited for such service, Mrs. Darling, since his views on the treatment of the base felons on Norfolk Island are similar to hers."

"I see." Mrs. Darling's tone was flat. The Reverend Samuel Marsden was not one of the colony's officials for whom she felt any warmth. On the occasions when he had come from Parramatta to preach at Sydney's Saint Philip's Church, she had endured his harshly accented, hectoring sermons with anything but enjoyment, and his oft-reiterated threats of hellfire and damnation, leveled at the ungodly, had struck her as being in bad taste when addressed to a congregation that had included the Governor and his staff.

And Marsden was, she had been told, not only one of the colony's longest-serving officials but also one of its wealthiest landowners, whose purebred sheep rivaled in number and value those of the Macarthurs.

She made a sound of concern and repeated her low-voiced "I see" without seeing whatever point Mrs. Van Buren was attempting to make. Unbidden, the last few lines of the Alcestis letter came into her mind. *To rob them of hope, even should they reform, is that not cruelty?* The chaplain's wife had written those words referring to the base felons of whom Lucy Van Buren had lately spoken with such searing contempt, and the colony's principal chaplain was, it appeared, only too ready to deprive the poor wretches of spiritual guidance, so that they might more swiftly meet with the retribution merited by the ungodly.

Mr. Marsden's reaction was, Mrs. Darling reflected sadly, typical of the so-called elitist faction—the respectable members of the colony's society, who had not come out to Sydney in chains, on board a convict vessel. He had demanded the resignation from the chaplains' service of Alcestis's husband, for no better reason than that the unfortunate young cleric had dared to uphold his wife's views. His wife's *Christian* views and—Mrs. Darling drew in her breath sharply—and her own, for had not Christ said, *Joy shall be in heaven over one sinner that repenteth, more than over ninety and nine just persons which need no repentance?* And— She moved restlessly. *He that is without sin among you cast the first stone. . . .*

"I passed the parade ground on my way here," Mrs. Van Buren was saying. "And I saw them drumming out those two soldiers. His Excellency was there and . . ."

Mrs. Darling scarcely heard her. "Why did you come, Mrs. Van Buren?" she asked, with an indignation that surprised even herself. "For precisely what reason did you wish to see me?"

Lucy Van Buren looked at her in hurt surprise. She made to rise and then sat down again, as if determined to yield no ground.

"I came to bring you proof of the identity of the *Australian*'s insolent letter writer, Mrs. Darling," she asserted. "I sensed, when we met at my sister Abigail's last week, that you doubted my claim that Alcestis was my assigned maidservant and thus of no account. I had thought that it would relieve your mind."

"Relieve my mind?"

"Why, yes. The letter was an attack on your husband's administration, which must be of concern to you, surely? And now I hear there's another—a somewhat similar one, relating to the Moreton Bay penal settlement. But I expect—" Evidently conscious that her welcome had worn thin, Mrs. Van Buren rose gracefully to her feet, and her tone was chilly as she went on, "I expect it will prove to have been written by some other malcontent, actuated by malice, as, it seems, is the proprietor of that unpleasant journal in which it is given prominence. I give you good day, Mrs. Darling, and thank you for receiving me."

She moved toward the door, and then, as the Governor's wife tugged on the bell rope to summon MacCarthy, she added, with more warmth, "Perhaps when my husband returns from his trading mission we may have the pleasure of entertaining you and His Excellency to dinner."

She swept out, and from the window, Mrs. Darling watched her enter her waiting carriage, attended by a small, dark-skinned boy who spread a rug over her knees and received a slap for his pains.

The Van Burens, Mrs. Darling recalled, employed a staff of Javanese servants who, if rumor were to be believed, were virtually slaves—and the boy was seemingly one of them, for he accepted the slap without complaint and jumped onto the box beside the coachman as the carriage moved off. Small wonder, then, that the girl who called

herself Alcestis had absconded from such a household . . .
it was to be hoped that her marriage to the young chaplain
would save her from having to return to Lucy Van Buren's
service.

Although, of course, her unfortunate young husband
was now without gainful employment. A slight frown
creasing her brow, Mrs. Darling turned from the window
and, gathering up her skirts, made her way upstairs to her
own sitting room on the second floor. She was an ex-
officio member of the board of governors of the Church
Schools Corporation, she reminded herself, and the board
was always seeking educationally qualified teachers for its
score or so of widely scattered Crown schools. Archdeacon Scott, who chaired the board, had made this point at a
recent meeting of the governors, bewailing the fact that the
new parochial school at Windsor had over forty pupils and
only the Reverend Robert Cartwright—who was shortly to
retire—available to instruct them.

So that perhaps . . . Mrs. Darling's frown vanished as
she seated herself at her bureau and searched for quill and
paper. Her husband, she thought, would prefer that Alcestis
should not remain in Sydney, in view of the furor her letter
had created. She wrote swiftly, addressing her note to the
archdeacon and offering the suggestion that Mr. Cox, a
young man in Holy Orders lately returned from Norfolk
Island, might fill the vacancy at the church school in
Windsor.

The note signed and sealed, she rang for her maid and
asked her to see that it was delivered at once.

There would be time enough for her to make the acquaintance of the young Coxes, she decided—perhaps when
she accompanied her husband on one of his regular tours
she might call on them. And it would not in the least
matter if neither of them was to know to whom they were
indebted for Mr. Cox's appointment to the new parochial
school at Windsor . . . indeed, it would be better if they
did not.

The clatter of horses' hooves on the gravel of the drive

was followed, a few minutes afterward, by the sound of her husband's voice, raised in anger. Dutifully, Mrs. Darling closed her bureau and hurried downstairs to receive him.

"The devil take it, Major Lockyer!" she heard him say furiously. "You say this damned Frenchman—what's his name? D'Urville has been at anchor in King George Sound with three ships—three frigates—for the past four or five weeks? What's the fellow up to, for the Lord's sake?"

"I think, sir," the 57th's acting commanding officer answered firmly, "you had better authorize me to find out. I can take the *Amity,* sir, and the *Fly* and a company of my men. And perhaps you could spare Charles Sturt."

"Take whatever you think the situation requires," Mrs. Darling heard her husband say.

She hesitated and then went to his side, linking her arm in his. He gave her a kiss on the cheek and said wearily, "It's been a trying day, my dear. A damned trying day! But I've done what I had to do."

CHAPTER XXI

Claus ran, as had become his habit, to the King's Wharf as soon as Saleh gave him permission to absent himself from the house in Bridge Street.

Each day since returning to the Van Buren household after his brief escape, he had made a careful inspection of the ships at anchor in Sydney Cove. There had been much coming and going of late and much firing of ceremonial salutes. Claus had watched the Government sloops *Amity, Fly,* and *Dragon* take troops and convicts on board and depart for an unknown destination. Not long afterward, in common with an excited crowd of sightseers who had gathered at every vantage point, he had witnessed the arrival of a fine ship of the line, flying a long blue pennant from her main masthead, and accompanied by two other King's ships.

Red Broome had told him that she was the *Warspite* of seventy-four guns, lately engaged in a war in a place he had never heard of—Burma—where her commodore, Sir James Brisbane—brother of the former Governor—had been naval commander in chief. The accompanying vessels, both frigates, he had named as the *Volage* and the *Success,* adding, with understandable relish, that the *Success* was under orders to sail for Melville Island and that his father would probably go there with her, because of his knowledge of the area. . . .

Claus came breathlessly to a halt, and, a hand shading his eyes from the strong sunlight, he searched the anchorage anxiously. The King's ships were all there, as was Commander Broome's graceful cutter *Mermaid*, but there was no sign of Major Van Buren's trading brig *Dorcas*, and the boy breathed a sigh of relief.

It was now over three months since the *Dorcas* had departed for the Dutch East Indies, Claus reminded himself—and ten days since Alice and her man of God, Mr. Cox, had left Sydney for Windsor, so that Mr. Cox could take up his new appointment as teacher at the church school.

Alice had invited him, very warmly, to go with them, but . . . Claus sat dejectedly at the edge of the wharf. Much as he had wanted to go, he knew that he could not desert his father and his father's wife—unless, that was to say, there should be another attempt to send him back to Timor. Then and only then would he run away as, in panic, he had done before; but surely by this time his father must know that he had not wavered in his loyalty and had not spoken to a soul of the terrible secret he and Dickon shared. Dickon could not, and— Claus jumped up, startled at the sound of gunfire.

A third frigate was approaching the anchorage, under forecourse and topsails, and she was flying the same ensign as the vessel that he and his father had encountered off Norfolk Island in the ill-fated *Flinders* . . . the *French* ensign! Her signal gun was firing a salute to the British admiral's flag, and the pilot cutter, with the port naval officer on board, was escorting her in, so that clearly she had not come with hostile intent. The *Warspite* acknowledged the salute, the new arrival took in sail, and Claus felt the tension drain out of him as he watched the Frenchman bring-to and heard the clank of her cable as she let go her bower anchor.

A familiar voice hailed him by name, and he saw Red and Johnny Broome, followed by two unfamiliar young midshipmen, coming toward him from the quay. A boat from one of the warships was pulling away, having, Claus realized, brought the two midshipmen ashore—presumably in order to meet the Broomes. Pleased, he hurried to join

them, and Red offered, grinning, "No *Dorcas* yet, Claus
. . . and I'll bet a pound to a penny you're in no hurry to
set eyes on her."

Claus stiffened, as he always did when there was an
implied slight on his father, but Red's friendly grin robbed
his words of any intention of giving offense. He introduced his two companions.

"Midshipman Tom Keppel and Midshipman Jamie Willoughby of His Majesty's ship *Success* . . . and this is a
good friend of ours, Claus Karimon."

Both midshipmen shook hands politely. They were a
little older than Red, as nearly as Claus could judge,
Keppel sturdy and broad-shouldered, with keen blue eyes,
and Willoughby tall and dark and a trifle hesitant in manner.
For a moment, the name Willoughby sounded familiar and
Claus wondered where he had heard it before, but all three
young officers were staring excitedly at the newly arrived
French frigate, and Johnny Broome said, in a faintly resent-
ful aside, "All they're interested in is the Frenchman,
Claus—goodness knows why!"

His elder brother turned on him reproachfully.

"Of course we're interested in her, dumbcluck! She's
the one who's been up to no good in King George Sound
and Western Port—one of the ships Major Lockyer's gone
in search of."

"There are said to be three of them," Midshipman
Keppel said. "She is the *Astrolabe*, commanded by Capitaine
Jules Dumont d'Urville. Our Captain Stirling spoke her off
Van Diemen's Land, but she was alone then."

Claus shook his head as memory stirred. "I think she is
not the *Astrolabe*, *Mijnheer* Keppel," he said diffidently.
"I have seen her before, and I remember her figurehead. It
is of a conch shell, shaped like a trumpet, you see? She is
the *Coquille*, which means seashell, I think."

"That is not what she told Captain Stirling." Keppel
eyed the younger boy curiously. "Where did you see the
Coquille, if I may ask—and when?"

Claus flushed under his scrutiny. "I saw her off Norfolk

Island—oh, it is now nearly four years ago.'' His English had improved considerably since that time, but suddenly nervous and fearing that he might have said too much, he lapsed into his old, heavily accented speech. ''You forgive, please—it is very long time. Maybe I make mistake.''

''Maybe you did, Claus,'' the midshipman answered, without rancor. ''Four years *is* a long time, is it not? Though Captain Stirling did say that French ships have been making what they are pleased to call voyages of exploration round this coast for a good deal more than four years. *He* says we must found more settlements to keep them out and maintain our sovereignty over the whole continent, or the French will contest it. In fact, when we go north in the *Success*, it will be for the purpose of examining possible sites for settlement in that region. There's Melville Island, of course, which is our ultimate destination, but Captain Stirling believes very strongly that the vicinity of a river on the western coast, the Swan, would be more advantageous, because it would be on the trade routes to India and the Dutch Indies. It's something to do with the prevailing winds, isn't it, Jamie? You're our navigation expert.''

Thus appealed to, Jamie Willoughby launched into a dissertation on the prevailing westerly winds in the higher latitudes of the Indian Ocean, which would carry vessels to the Australian shore and there unite with the southeast trades, assuring a fast passage to ports in the northern Indian Ocean and beyond.

''If there was a port in the vicinity of the Swan River, trading vessels from Europe would save six weeks, Captain Stirling has calculated, since there would be no necessity for them to call here, at Port Jackson. He's immensely keen on the notion, and he's hoping to convince Governor Darling of its feasibility.''

It was all beyond Claus, but Red was clearly excited by the prospect, plying both the *Success*'s midshipmen with eager questions and bandying the names of some of the early Dutch explorers with those of Matthew Flinders and his own father, whose observations he quoted with pride. Keppel and Willoughby were impressed, but Johnny's attention wandered, and he glanced at Claus in mute question. Claus nodded and they slipped away, their departure unremarked by the other three.

"Now that he's been made a mid, Red never talks or thinks of anything else but ships and the navy," Johnny complained when they were out of earshot. "I'm beginning to have second thoughts about going to sea. I mean, if I joined the *Mermaid*, Red would never give me any peace, would he? He'd be my senior officer as well as my elder brother, and that would be more than I could endure."

Claus eyed him thoughtfully. "What *would* you do then, Johnny?"

Johnny shrugged his thin, bony shoulders. "I don't know. Maybe I'd do some exploring. Or study law—I rather fancy becoming an advocate." He struck a pose, an impish smile playing about his lips. "My client pleads not guilty, Your Honor, and I am able to show that he could not have committed the crime he's charged with, because . . . oh, well, I'd think of some reason why he couldn't. And Mam would be pleased if I stayed at school." His smile widened. "I might even make her believe that I've got more brains than Red. She was pretty upset when he quit school, you know."

"I never went to school," Claus confessed, a trifle sadly. "But if my—if *Mijnheer* Van Buren returns and says again that I must be sent back to Coupang, then perhaps I would go to the school where Alice's Mr. Cox is to teach. Alice was telling me 'come should it be needful,' and I would do so."

"You like Alice, don't you, Claus?"

"Oh, yes—I love Alice. She is very good woman, Johnny. Good like my mother."

"I liked her too, while she was staying with us," Johnny agreed. "And she was brave to write that letter to the *Australian*." His brow furrowed. "You know, I might become a newspaperman, serve my apprenticeship with

Mr. Wentworth. I'd probably have to start by delivering papers or working in the print shop, but it would be interesting. Newspapers like the *Australian* can do good, Mam says.''

"Can they?'' Claus questioned dubiously.

" 'Course they can,'' Johnny assured him. "Look at that soldier—the one the Governor sent to jail, after ordering him drummed out of the regiment. His name was Sudds, and he died a week later, in the jail. The *Australian* had a big article about it, and so did the *Monitor,* and they both accused the Governor of being too severe. Mr. Wentworth even claimed he ought to be impeached.''

"What's that, Johnny—impeached?'' Claus wanted to know.

Johnny shrugged. "I'm not quite sure. But they'd hang him if he was found guilty, I know that.''

"Hang the *Governor*?'' Claus stared at him with dropping jaw, his eyes wide with astonishment. "But the Governor is . . . Johnny, is he not what is called a viceroy? Does he not represent the King of England?''

"Yes, he does,'' Johnny conceded, a trifle doubtful now of his facts. "I suppose Mr. Wentworth was just trying to shock his readers. But I know he printed some sort of pamphlet entitled 'The Impeachment,' because Dad had one and was talking about it to my uncle Murdo. Only I didn't listen very hard, because I hadn't thought of becoming a newspaperman then.'' He gestured to where his brother and the two midshipmen from the *Success* were still standing in earnest conversation and observed unnecessarily, "They're still jawing away. If Red doesn't stop soon, he'll make Mr. Willoughby late for his appointment with the Governor.''

"He has an appointment to see the Governor?'' Claus echoed, once again puzzled.

"Why yes—to break the news to him about his brother being killed. We were told not to say a word . . . Red was to meet him and take him to Government House.'' He talked on, but Claus did not take in what he was saying.

Of course, he thought, suddenly afraid—that was why the name Willoughby had seemed familiar! Mr. Robert Willoughby—the tall young gentleman who had been the *minnaar*, the lover of *Mevrouw* Van Buren, he who had stayed with her throughout the night and who . . . who had died in the woods near the *boerder*, the farm of Mr. Tempest, where he and Dickon . . . Claus felt his blood run cold. The Midshipman Willoughby was brother to that Willoughby, Claus now realized, but fool that he was, he had not—what was it called, in English? He had not put two and two together, had not had the wit to realize who the new arrival was. And he could not face him again, could not talk to him. . . . Claus grasped Johnny's arm, interrupting him without apology.

"I must go, Johnny. I have stayed too long. *Mevrouw*—Mrs. Van Buren will be angry."

Johnny looked disappointed, but Claus did not wait for him to argue. He took to his heels and ran in panic-stricken flight, giving a wide berth to Red and his two companions and barely pausing to touch his cap to Mrs. Broome, who was in her small waterfront garden with the girl baby who had recently arrived as an addition to the family.

"Dickon is back in Sydney, Claus," Mrs. Broome called after him, but her unexpected announcement only added to Claus's panic. He managed somehow to croak an acknowledgment and ran on blindly, coming to a halt only when Saleh met him at the door of the kitchen and, grasping him by the shoulders, swung him around.

"Why do you run, little *lip-lap*?" he demanded sternly in his own tongue. "Is it that our master is returned?"

Claus shook his head and then, unable to stem his tears, broke out into a torrent of weeping.

Saleh held him in strong brown arms and let him weep. After a while, when the torrent had passed, he said gently, "Do not fear, little one. You are safe with us here—we will protect you; and if we cannot, then nothing is more simple . . . we will send you to Alice in Windsor."

Claus gulped and made a brave effort to compose himself. "I do not fear for my safety, Saleh," he stammered at last. "It is rather that I do not know what I should do—that is, what it is *right* to do. *Mijnheer* Willoughby's brother is here—he is called Jamie, and he is a midshipman on board the King's ship *Success*. He goes now to His Excellency the Governor to be told of the death of his brother. He does not know that *Mijnheer* Willoughby is dead, and neither does he know in what manner, and—" The boy's voice broke. "Saleh, he does not know at whose hands his brother died."

Saleh regarded him with narrowed eyes.

"But *you* know, Claus?" he suggested shrewdly. "You were there?"

"Yes," Claus confirmed. "I and Dickon O'Shea—he who cannot talk. And Dickon is back here now, in Sydney. With his mother, *Mevrouw* Dawson, I think."

Saleh was silent for so long that Claus began to wonder whether he had understood his quandary or, indeed, whether, for all his wisdom, the majordomo could help to solve it.

"Saleh," he began miserably, "it was my father who—that is, he—" But even now he could not bring himself to utter the damning accusation. "I cannot betray my father, Saleh. I cannot tell what I saw."

Saleh sat down and drew the boy to him. "What did you see, little one? You can tell Saleh."

And, Claus realized, it would be a relief, a great lightening of the burden he had borne for so long, if he told Saleh the whole horrifying story. It would not be betrayal, for did not Saleh also serve his father? Was he not also loyal?

Hesitantly at first, and then with more conviction, he embarked on his narrative. "Dickon and I ran away when they set off to fight with their pistols. That is, my father and *Mijnheer* Willoughby. We were afraid, we did not know what would happen. We heard the pistol shots, and we watched them go back to *Mijnheer* Tempest's house, and we saw that my father had been shot in his arm. They talked angrily, all of them—*Mijnheer* Daniels was seeking to keep the peace, but my father would not listen to him."

"But he was wounded in the duel?" Saleh intervened, frowning. "He was shot in the arm by *Mijnheer* Willoughby?"

The boy nodded. "Yes. But his wound was bound up, and he mounted onto his horse. He would ride to Bathurst to the hospital, he said. I wanted to go with him to help, but Dickon held me back and I was afraid, because he was greatly angered, so I did as Dickon wanted. We stayed among the trees and followed him, but he did not go toward the town of Bathurst, Saleh. He turned back in the way we had come, and we saw him dismount from his horse and leave it tied to a tree. On foot, he went on and hid himself behind some rocks, and he had his hunting musket with him, the one he is using to hunt for kangaroos. We stayed watching, and Dickon made a picture of him, with the black stuff he uses. We were laughing, thinking only that it was odd that my father should hide in the rocks and not go to the hospital, as he had said. And then . . ." Claus's voice broke with a sob. "Oh, Saleh, then it was terrible!"

"Go on," Saleh prompted. It was evident from the gleam of anger in his eyes that he had guessed what was to come, and his arm tightened about Claus's thin shoulders. "Tell me the rest, little one."

Claus shuddered but went on. "They came, riding on their horses, talking together—*Mijnheer* Willoughby and *Mijnheer* Daniels. They saw nothing. Dickon seized my arm and dragged me away—not far; there was no time. We heard the shots, and we knew from where they came, and we heard a man cry out. Then we heard my father go crashing through the woods and a little later saw him on his horse, galloping away. We waited, for we were both much afraid and did not know what we should do. Then Dickon went back to where we had hidden before, and I went also. From there we could see the two English men, and they lay very still, so that we knew they must be killed dead.''

"You did not go to them?" Saleh questioned.

Claus shook his head. "We were afraid. I feared that my father might come back and kill us, too. And Dickon wanted to draw another picture. He cannot talk, you see, and he made the picture so that it would be proof of what we had seen. But before he had finished it, the bad men came—the men who had escaped from the place that is called Emu Ford, I think. They had muskets and only three horses, although there were five of them. . . .''

Claus paused, seeing again in memory the scene he was trying to describe. The men had looked dangerous; they had been bearded and unkempt, wearing rough clothes, and two of them had been barefoot. They had argued among themselves in loud, angry voices. One of them, who had been dressed as a gentleman, had tried to persuade his companions to leave the poor dead men alone, but they had shouted him down, and one of the shoeless ones had dragged *Mijnheer* Daniels's boots off. . . .

"They stripped the two dead ones of their clothing and took their horses and pistols. Dickon and I—we were frightened in case they might see us, and so we ran away. I—'' Claus hesitated, looking up into Saleh's face anxiously. "I was alarmed for my father. I thought—oh, Saleh, *Mijnheer* Van Buren *is* my father, even if he will not permit me to say that I am his son. Dickon had the pictures he had made, but who, I asked him, would believe him if he were to show them? I made him promise that he would not show them to anyone. Let the bad men take the blame—that was what I said to him. They were escapers, convicts—they would be caught soon and punished, perhaps hanged, just for escaping. And that was so, that was what happened, was it not?''

"Yes," Saleh agreed uneasily. "That was what happened—but they were not hanged. They were sent to Norfolk Island." He sighed, regarding him now, Claus saw, with deeply troubled eyes, and his conscience again began to torment him.

"Did I do wrong to keep silent for my father's sake, Saleh?"

"I do not know," Saleh confessed. "In your place, I do not know what I should have done, little one." He sighed once more, more deeply than before, and then asked quietly, "Does *Mijnheer* Van Buren know that you and your friend saw what he did?"

"He has never spoken of it to me. But I think perhaps he may have guessed. Why else," Claus added, with bitterness, "should he have said that I must go back to Coupang? I had done nothing to anger him."

"True, Claus. I myself had wondered what his reasons could have been."

"And now," Claus whispered miserably, "*Mijnheer* Willoughby's brother is here, and he will be told that *Mijnheer* Willoughby is dead. And Dickon has come to Sydney. All the time since it happened Dickon has been at the farm of *Mijnheer* Tempest, and I think he has kept silent only because he promised me he would. But perhaps now he will not continue to be silent."

Saleh's smooth brown face grew thoughtful. "Permit me time to consider this matter, little one," he said, after an appreciable pause. "I do not, in all truth, know what advice to give you. My first idea is that you should go without delay to Alice and her man of God, before *Mijnheer* Van Buren returns. But—" He frowned. "It might be an act of greater prudence were you to tell all you have told me to *Mevrouw* Van Buren before you go away from this house."

Claus stared up at him, stricken. "Tell *her*? Tell the wife of my father? Saleh, I cannot!"

"You cannot be sure that Dickon will keep silent," Saleh reminded him. "Or prevent him from showing his pictures—perhaps to this young brother of *Mijnheer* Willoughby, or to *Mijnheer* Dawson. Come—" He took the shrinking Claus firmly by the arm. "Let us go now to

Mevrouw Van Buren and tell her what must be told. She will know what to do."

Governor Darling received Midshipman Willoughby in his wife's presence and in her sitting room at Government House. As considerately as he could, he broke the news to him; but the bare facts, delivered in his clipped military voice and seemingly without compassion, left Jamie trembling with shock, every vestige of color drained from his cheeks.

Mrs. Darling frowned at her husband and made to put an arm round the boy's trembling, blue-clad shoulders, but mindful of the dignity that went with his naval rank, Jamie contrived to elude the well-intentioned gesture. He drew himself up, a hand on the dirk at his side, and said in a controlled voice, "It is a—a blow to me, Your Excellency. I had been greatly looking forward to seeing my brother. We—that is my sister Emily and I—had planned a—a family reunion. She, too, is on her way to Sydney, sir."

"Alone?" Mrs. Darling questioned in some alarm.

Jamie shook his head, his composure returning.

"No, ma'am, with her husband. After our father's death, Emily married a surgeon named Yates, and we put the house up for sale, with the intention of coming out to the colony to join . . . so that we could all be together, you see. Dr. Yates is to be employed by the Church Missionary Society in New Zealand eventually, and he and Emily are bringing our two younger sisters with them. They were to follow soon after I sailed on board the *Success*, ma'am."

"Do you know in which ship, Mr. Willoughby?" the Governor asked.

"No, sir, I don't. We sailed on January the twenty-fifth, and Simon and Emily were hoping to obtain passages in a transport soon after that, sir. I had to leave the sale of the house in my sister's hands. I wrote to Rob—to my brother, sir—to tell him all this, but he—I don't suppose my letter ever reached him if he—that is . . ." He broke off, having again to fight for composure. "I'm sorry, sir. I still can't quite take in the fact that he—that Rob was murdered, sir.''

Embarrassed, Governor Darling passed a hand through his thinning hair. ''I'm afraid there's no doubt that he was, Mr. Willoughby. He and his companion, Mr. Henry Daniels, were set upon and robbed by a gang of what are called bushrangers here—escaped convicts. The miscreants were apprehended and brought to justice, and if it is of any comfort to you, all are serving life sentences in the prison settlement on Norfolk Island at the present time. Your poor brother's death did not go unavenged.''

''No, sir.'' Jamie's lips were stiff, his throat aching. If only Rob had lived just a little longer, he thought wretchedly—long enough, at all events, to know that his brother did not intend to take a penny of what their father had willed to him! But as it was, poor Rob had not even been aware that his whole family were on their way out here to join him. . . . He gulped down the cup of tea Mrs. Darling had insisted on pouring out for him and again braced himself.

''Where was my brother killed, sir? In this town, in Sydney?''

''We do not permit escaped convicts to roam the streets of Sydney Town under arms, Mr. Willoughby,'' the Governor retorted coldly. ''Your brother and Mr. Daniels had been allocated land grants in the country beyond the Blue Mountains, some miles distant from the Bathurst settlement. They had gone there in order to make arrangements for buildings to be erected and stock driven up.'' He explained the situation of the grants in careful detail, ignoring Mrs. Darling's attempt to catch his eye. Nevertheless, he brought his description to an abrupt end, leaving Jamie with the impression that, for some reason, he had not revealed as much as he had initially intended. ''Both unfortunate young men are buried in the cemetery at Bathurst, and headstones have been placed on the graves. Er—your father was an admiral, was he not? Admiral Sir Francis Willoughby?''

"Yes, sir," Jamie confirmed, wishing that he could bring the interview to an end.

"He was a baronet?" the Governor suggested.

Suddenly bereft of words, Jamie could only stare at him. For God's sake, he told himself, the title should have gone to Rob, who was—had been—the elder son. But now . . . Governor Darling put it into words for him.

"Then you inherit the title, do you not? You are—ah—Midshipman Sir James Willoughby?"

"I . . ." Jamie swallowed the lump that had risen to his throat. The title would not even be on poor Rob's tombstone in the Bathurst cemetery, he thought regretfully, because his death had taken place before their father's. Rob had deserved better than that, he . . . oh, the devil take it! Rob had not deserved to be murdered. "Sir, I—"

Mrs. Darling came to his rescue. "Mr. Willoughby—James, all this has been a terrible ordeal for you, I'm afraid. I expect you would like to be alone for a little while. You are welcome to stay here or—did one of your shipmates come with you?"

"Tom Keppel did, ma'am," Jamie managed. "He'll be waiting for me. And a mid—I mean a midshipman named Broome, from the *Mermaid*, brought us here. I—er—it's very kind of you, Mrs. Darling, but perhaps I'd better go."

"I hope we shall see you again before your ship leaves Sydney," Mrs. Darling said kindly. "Your Captain Stirling is dining with us tomorrow evening. And I expect we shall be under the obligation to extend official hospitality to the newly arrived French captain, since he is here on what he is pleased to call a mission of goodwill." She met the Governor's reproving gaze and smiled. "Oh, come, Ralph my dear—James is a naval officer. He knows what the visit implies."

"I'll take him back to his friends," Governor Darling offered crisply. He grasped Jamie's arm and, cutting short the boy's stammered attempts to bid farewell to Mrs.

Darling, propelled him down the graceful, curving staircase to the ground floor.

Tom Keppel and Red Broome were waiting in the hall, talking to an officer in military scarlet whom Tom introduced as Major Dumaresq. Together, the three midshipmen took their leave, and as they walked slowly down the tree-shaded drive to the gates of Government House, Tom said awkwardly, "I'm deuced sorry to hear about your brother, Jamie. It must be a nasty shock, when you'd been looking forward to seeing him here."

"He was murdered—Rob was murdered," Jamie answered angrily. "By some damned rogues of convicts. He and a friend who was with him, near some place called Bathurst."

"Yes," Tom said. "Major Dumaresq told me. But they caught the men who murdered him, didn't they?"

"So it seems. But the Governor did not tell me much. I . . ." There was a sick feeling in the pit of Jamie's stomach. "Not the whole story. I'm not sure that I want to hear it, except . . . oh, perhaps I owe it to Rob. He's buried in the cemetery at Bathurst, the Governor said."

Red Broome fell into step beside him. "My grandmother is buried there too," he volunteered. "And if you *do* want to hear the whole story of your brother's death, Willoughby, the man who can tell you is Mr. Rick Tempest. He was a lieutenant in the navy and came out here to settle after the American war. It was on his land, about twelve miles from Bathurst on the Macquarie River, that your brother's body was found."

Jamie turned to regard him uncertainly. "How shall I find him? Shall I have to go to Bathurst to talk to him? Because we shall be sailing soon, as you know. I may not be granted leave."

"No." Broome smiled. "As it happens, he's in Sydney—he's come here for his wife's confinement, my mother told me. You will find him at that house over there—the two-story house with the big garden, overlooking the cove. See it?" He pointed. "His sister lives there—Mrs. Timothy Dawson. Give it a day or so; they've only just arrived. Then I can take you there and introduce you. That is, of course, if you do want to ask questions.''

Jamie hesitated. Did he really want to know any more, he wondered, or was it best to leave matters as they were? Knowing would not restore Rob to life, and the men who had killed him had been caught and punished, the Governor had said. He remembered the last occasion when he had seen Rob, remembered, with a pang, what their father had accused him of, what he had done, and the old man's biting, contemptuous words.

You have brought disgrace on our family name, the admiral had flung at his elder son. *Four generations of Willoughbys have been your predecessors in the King's service. You have had the example of a long line of brave men . . . and I named you Robert Horatio believing that you would, in your turn, do honor to one of England's greatest admirals. But you have caused me bitterly to regret having done so. . . .*

Perhaps, Jamie thought, perhaps, by the manner of his death, poor Rob had proved their father wrong—perhaps, in dying, he had redeemed himself.

"There was a duel," Red Broome went on quietly. "Your brother fought a duel with a Dutchman named Van Buren a few hours before he was killed by the escapers. I know that because it came out at the trial and I heard my parents talking about it, though I don't know any details.''

It was a warning, Jamie thought. His head came up and he stiffened.

"I do want to ask questions, Red," he asserted. "And to know the truth. I should be obliged if you would introduce me to Mr. Tempest.''

He saw Tom Keppel's eyes widen and grasped his arm. "What is it, Tom?''

His fellow midshipman was gesturing to the *Warspite*, at anchor in the cove.

"The commodore's pendant, Jamie—it's being hauled

down! And look . . . Captain Stirling's putting off in his gig! Something grave must have happened."

Two hours later, on board H.M.S. *Success*, Captain Stirling addressed the assembled ship's company.

"It is with deep regret that I have to inform you that the commodore, Sir James Brisbane, died this morning of a fever contracted during the recent campaign in Burma. The funeral will take place in the Sydney Town churchyard on Wednesday at noon, and the commodore will be buried with full military honors." He issued precise instructions and went on, "In consequence, our sailing will be delayed, but no shore leave will be granted until after the funeral. Captain the Honorable Richard Dundas is promoted to command of His Majesty's ship *Warspite*, Lieutenant Young is to command His Majesty's ship *Volage*, and Lieutenant Belcher is to transfer from the *Volage* to this ship, with the rank of third lieutenant. That is all. You may dismiss the ship's company, Mr. Young."

Below, in the midshipmen's berth, Jamie was thoughtful. He had never seen Sir James Brisbane, who had been confined to his cabin by illness since the *Warspite*'s arrival in Port Jackson, so that he felt no personal grief. But, he thought, their postponed sailing would give him time to find out the truth about poor Rob's death and might even allow him to visit his brother's last resting place.

He owed Rob that, he told himself. It was the least he could do.

CHAPTER XXII

Lucy Van Buren listened to Claus's story in stone-faced silence.

The boy was frightened, and fear caused him to hesitate and search vainly for words, so that his narrative was punctuated by lengthy pauses and, at times, by tears. Lucy was too shocked to speak, and it was Saleh who prompted and encouraged him, demanding sternly that he tell the truth but holding his thin little body in gentle, kindly arms in an effort to overcome the boy's conscience-stricken reluctance to betray the man who had fathered him.

For all the tight rein she kept on her emotions, Lucy was torn between grief and anger, her silence and her seeming calm a mask for heartbreak. She had loved Robert Willoughby, deeply and passionately, and had mourned his death with agonized regret, but it had never occurred to her that her husband could have been responsible for it. Yet Claus's stammered words carried conviction, and instinctively she sensed that the despised little *lip-lap* was, indeed, telling her the truth.

The duel had been intended as deception, she told herself, or perhaps Jos had meant to kill his rival when they faced each other with their loaded pistols across a few feet of trodden turf. That he had failed to do so had not lessened his determination to rid himself of his rival—it might even have increased it. Jos, like most of his countrymen, prided himself on being a man of honor . . . he might take his pleasure with convict prostitutes and women like Leah, but his wife could be permitted no such freedom. The knowledge that poor, dead Robert had been her lover must have driven him beyond the bounds of prudence. . . . Lucy drew an aching breath as Claus hesitantly described how he and Dickon had watched his father take up his position behind the rocks and, despite his injured arm, prepare his ambush.

It was a measure of her frozen state of shock that, although Claus had twice referred to Jos Van Buren as his father, she had not reproved him for it, and, emboldened, the boy talked on, telling her now of the pictures Dickon had drawn with his sketch pad and charcoal.

"He is here, *mevrouw;* Dickon is here in Sydney after this long time," Claus warned.

Dickon had come with Rick and Katie, Lucy remembered —Abigail had told her that she was expecting them, so that Katie might give birth under proper medical supervision. Dickon would almost certainly have brought his sketches with him, as proof of what he and Claus had seen . . . if she needed proof of her husband's infamy, it would probably be there for the asking. She stirred uneasily. She did not require proof on her own account; she knew that what Claus was telling her was the stark truth, for it was in character—it was what Jos would have done. And he would not have thought twice about letting the convict escapers take the blame—rather he would have counted himself fortunate that such convenient scapegoats had happened on the scene.

But what—God in heaven, what should she do, armed with her new awareness? What *could* she do? Lucy's small hands clasped each other nervously in her lap.

Hatred was the strongest emotion she felt now—hatred and the desire to avenge herself for the pain Jos had caused her by robbing her so ruthlessly of her lover. But to make a formal accusation, to demand her husband's arrest and trial, would result in an appalling scandal, in which she, too, would inevitably be caught up.

With sickening certainty, Lucy thought of what the

clacking tongues of Sydney would make of it. Whatever punishment was meted out to Jos, her reputation would be torn to shreds. Society would ostracize her, and those she had once scorned for their lack of breeding would take a malicious delight in passing her by in the street, cutting her, refusing her invitations, and issuing none of their own.

Life would be unbearable—the scandal far more damaging than it would have been had she agreed to leave Jos and run away with poor Robert. And she had shrunk from that. Robert had pleaded with her, but she had refused, for all she loved him so passionately. She had been afraid, she—

There was a soft knock on the door, and Leah sidled in, her brown face wearing an insolent smile. Saleh reproved her sharply, but she ignored him and announced spitefully, as if sensing the consternation her news would cause, "The master has returned—Amos, the *koetsier*, has seen his ship come to anchor. Soon he will be here, *mevrouw*. Is it your wish that I prepare his room for him?"

Claus emitted a strangled cry and would have taken flight had it not been for Saleh's restraining hands on his shoulder. Lucy eyed him scornfully.

"Keep the boy here, Saleh," she ordered. "Out of sight until he is needed. And tell Amos to bring the carriage round at once. I shall go to my sister, to Mrs. Dawson's. Let Leah greet her master, since she is so eager to do so."

A cold anger filled her. It was typical of Jos Van Buren, she thought resentfully, to time his return so inappropriately. But it would be an hour or so before he came ashore; there were customs formalities to be dealt with and the required medical inspection of his crew. Suddenly resolute, Lucy rose to her feet, but the emotional shock she had suffered had taken its toll. She had a vision of Robert's body—his fine, strong body, from which she had derived so much pleasure—lying bloody and naked in the dark confines of the gully where Jos had lain in treacherous wait, with murder in his heart and a loaded musket to his shoulder, and a sob escaped her. The room whirled round, and she had to steady herself with a hand on the back of her chair.

Saleh watched her anxiously, and when the carriage drew up outside, he helped her to descend the steps from the front door and had virtually to lift her into its cushioned interior.

"You will see the young *Mijnheer* Dickon?" he asked, solicitously draping a rug over her knees. "And the pictures he has made?"

"Yes." Lucy drew herself up stiffly. "Yes, I shall ask to see them, Saleh."

The pictures should suffice, she thought; if she showed them to Jos, taxed him with them, he would be compelled to admit his guilt and . . . Her mouth tightened. She would be rid of the husband she hated, for surely Jos would not dare to remain in Sydney with the threat of disclosure hanging over him? He had his ship; he could go back whence he had come, to his own people in Coupang or Batavia, and there need be no scandal. And no vengeance either, if he were permitted to escape.

Unless . . . Lucy's resolution hardened. Perhaps she could shame him into making reparation in the only way possible for the man of honor he had once been. Perhaps . . . Saleh took a small, oilskin-wrapped package from the concealment of his white jacket and laid it on her knee.

"A very long time ago, *mevrouw*," he said softly, "this package was brought from *Mijnheer* Broome's ship. The master took it from you. It was in his room, and I—*mevrouw*, I do not know its significance; it has, I think, papers inside, but I cannot read. I remember only that my master was angered because it was given into your hands."

She remembered the incident also, Lucy thought, startled. It seemed ages ago, after Jos had been wrecked in the small trading vessel he had chartered—the *Flinders*—and Justin Broome had rescued him. The package had been inadvertently left on board the ship, and Jessica Broome had brought it to her. Jos had been beside himself with rage, and . . . what had he said? He had demanded to

know if she had read the papers the package contained,
because . . . Oh, good heavens! Had he not told her that
they could hang him? Was that not why the incident had
remained in her memory and, it seemed, also in Saleh's?
His anger and his words that, at the time, she had not
taken seriously . . .

The carriage moved slowly down the cobbled street,
and, her fingers trembling in their haste, Lucy tore open the
package. To her dismay, she saw that the papers were
written in French, of which she had but scant knowledge.
There were two letters and a map—or chart, she was not
sure which—with what appeared to be navigational refer-
ences marked on it and the outline of what she could only
guess was part of the Australian coast. At its foot, in faded
ink, badly affected by seawater, she was able to decipher a
few words.

Corvette La Coquille . . . Capitaine Louis Duperrey,
followed by a date that she could not make out. But quite
clearly marked as *Isle de Norfolk* on the chart was a small
cross in red ink. She had time only to glance at the letters,
but in one she found the names of two more ships—*Thétis*
and *Espérance*—and what, she decided, after a vain attempt to translate the text, appeared to be an illegible date,
using the French calendar.

The most significant discovery, however, was of a folded
square of vellum, little affected by the seawater in which it
had been immersed. This, too, was written in French, in
ornate, flowing characters, and as its meaning slowly became clear to her, Lucy was gripped by a cold, unforgiving
anger that had its roots in bitter disillusion. The document
was a commission, made out to ''Jozef Hendrik Van
Buren,'' in the rank of lieutenant in the army of the
Emperor of France, and it was dated seventeen years
previously—prior to the British invasion and capture of
Java.

Small wonder that Jos had been anxious lest the package
fall into the wrong hands, she thought. Dear heaven, even
though his commission dated back to the reign of Napoleon,

the fact that he had held it would have made him the object of suspicion in Sydney! Suspicion and worse . . . She looked again at the chart with its revealing, red-inked cross, and found herself wondering whether her husband had used his trading voyages as a cloak for other than trading purposes. Was it possible that he had met the French ships at some prearranged rendezvous, in order to supply them with up-to-date charts of Australian waters or . . . The carriage came to a halt, and Lucy thrust the papers into her reticule and, gathering her skirts about her, prepared to alight.

Abigail met her at the door, looking at once pleased and surprised at her unexpected arrival.

"Lucy my dear!" Her greeting was warm, as it always was, and she kissed Lucy affectionately before leading her into the house. "What brings you here? Have you heard the news and come to join us in celebration?"

"In celebration?" Lucy regarded her blankly. "What are you celebrating?"

"Why, the birth of a healthy boy child to Katie and Rick, less than an hour ago," Abigail told her, her face wreathed in a smile. "Is that not cause for celebration, after all those two have endured? Rick is scarcely able to contain himself, and—"

Lucy cut her short. "I'm pleased, for their sake," she answered, without enthusiasm. "Naturally—it is what they wanted, is it not? But I—it is Dickon I want to see, Abby. And it is very urgent. Jos has returned, and I . . . it's most important that I talk with Dickon at once. And alone, if possible."

"Alone?" It was Abigail's turn to express incomprehension. "Well, of course, if it's urgent, but—will you be able to understand him? Or make him understand what you want of him?"

She probably would not, Lucy thought; Dickon could lip-read, but his efforts to talk were unintelligible to all save his mother and his immediate family. "Perhaps," she requested, restraining her impatience, "you would tell him that I wish to see the sketches he made of Major Van Buren at Pengallon when—when poor Robert Willoughby and his friend were murdered.''

"Dickon made sketches?" Abigail echoed. Her smile faded, and she added reproachfully, "Oh, Lucy, I don't think he did. He never told me he had.''

"But you haven't seen him for months," Lucy pointed out. "He's been at Pengallon, surely? And he was there when—when Robert and Henry Daniels were killed. And when Jos fought the duel with Robert.''

"Yes, that is so," Abigail conceded. Her joy in the birth of their brother's child had faded as swiftly as her smile, and she spoke coldly; but to Lucy's relief, she did as she had been requested. "I'll ask Dickon—he's upstairs. Would you like to wait in the dining room? Rick is with Katie, and Tim and Julia are in the drawing room—I presume you won't want to see them yet?"

"Not yet," Lucy confirmed, tight-lipped. "You will understand why when you—that is, when Dickon shows you his sketches.''

But Dickon, to her annoyance, while admitting that he had the sketches, refused to show them, even to his mother. "He says he promised Claus that he would never show them to anyone," Abigail reported. "Lucy, for heaven's sake, what is this all about? I really do not begin to understand.''

"I will send for Claus," Lucy answered. "Amos can bring him here." Making a visible effort to control her irritation, she went out to give the necessary order to the coachman and returned to the dining room, to find Abigail standing by the window overlooking the cove.

"Your husband is on his way ashore, Lucy," she said, without turning round. "That is his ship, is it not—the *Dorcas*, at anchor off the naval office?"

"Yes, the *Dorcas* is his ship. I told you that he had returned." Lucy made no move to join her at her vantage point, and Abigail turned reproachfully to face her.

"Should you not be at home to receive him?"

"If I could avoid it," Lucy burst out, her control strained suddenly to the breaking point, "I would never enter my home again when he was there! But I . . . Abby, I have to see him once more, and please God, it will be for the last time. Josef Van Buren is . . . God in heaven, he is a murderer and worse! No bushrangers killed Robert Willoughby—Josef killed him. I loved Robert, Abby, I truly loved him. We were lovers, Robert and I, and my husband lay in wait for him and murdered him. He murdered poor Henry Daniels, too, simply because he was there. He . . ." Lucy was sobbing wildly, and Abigail went to her, putting her arms about her in helpless pity.

"Lucy, what are you saying? It can't be true—the escapers were tried and condemned; they were guilty. Josef couldn't have killed those two poor young men. He was wounded in the duel. Who has told you such a tale? Even if Robert Willoughby was your lover, I cannot believe that Josef would—would *murder* him. Shall I call Rick? He was there when it happened, and—"

"Dickon was there," Lucy sobbed brokenly. "And Claus. They saw what happened, Abby, and Claus told me that Dickon drew what he saw. That is why I—why I want his sketches. I shall confront Jos with them. I shall compel him to leave Sydney. It's not only that he is a—a murderer; he is also in league with the French. He—" She held up her reticule, fighting for control, and ended bitterly, "The proof is here, the proof of his treachery, Abby. He held a commission in the French Emperor's army."

Abigail sighed in bewilderment. "Let me call Rick, Lucy. If it's true—I mean, if it is necessary to confront Josef, would not Rick be the best person to do it? He is a man, and—"

"No." Lucy shook her head. "I don't want Rick to know—or anyone but you, Abby. Please, you must promise me that you will not talk of it. I can deal with Jos. I married him, and I can end the marriage . . . I *will* end it, for I feel nothing save hatred for him now. Nothing but loathing, I— Promise me, please, Abby. Rick must not know, or Tim either. The scandal, if it were to get out, would finish me.''

''Yes, but—''

''Please, Abby. We *must* keep it to ourselves! Dickon and Claus will not talk . . . they have kept silent for almost a year.''

Reluctantly, Abigail gave her promise. The carriage drew up outside, and Lucy bit back her tears and went to meet Claus. The boy was trembling and more frightened than ever, but he ran obediently upstairs to Dickon's room, and the two emerged ten minutes later, Dickon with the sketches in his hand.

They were crude, Lucy saw, made in charcoal on a small pad, but Dickon had evidently touched them up with pen and ink, and he had a true artistic talent. The man, crouching behind a screen of rocks with a hunting rifle cradled in his arms, was unmistakenly Jos Van Buren— and there was a bandage about one shoulder, showing beneath his shirt. Below, half hidden by the overhanging branches of a massive gum tree, two horsemen were outlined—unrecognizable, but . . . Lucy began to sob as she studied the second sketch.

The two prone figures depicted in it were poignantly recognizable, for against the dark shading that Dickon had used, a shaft of sunlight appeared to illuminate Robert's face—his dead face, upturned as if, even as he died, he were seeking his killer in order to accuse him. Henry Daniels lay beside him, slumped face down, the hat he had been wearing fallen from his head and his arms outstretched in front of him. Both men, in Dickon's drawing, were fully clothed. . . .

With shaking hands, Lucy opened her reticule and thrust the sketches into it. ''Robert's brother—Claus says he is here, that he is a midshipman in one of the King's ships. He must not know, Abby.''

''No,'' Abigail conceded unhappily. ''He'll learn nothing from me—I gave you my word. But I truly think that Rick should be told, Lucy. He—''

Lucy shook her head. "Least of all Rick. Has Katie not given him the son he wanted so much? Let him enjoy his happiness. This is not his affair—it is mine, and I . . . Don't worry, Abby, I beg you. I know what I must do."

She refused the glass of brandy Abigail offered and, leaving Claus with Dickon, bade her sister a restrained farewell and climbed, unassisted, into the waiting carriage, affecting not to hear when Rick called to her from the half-open door. Abby would have to explain her precipitate departure as best she could, she . . . Lucy opened her reticule and looked again at the sketches, her resolution hardening as Amos whipped up his horses and the carriage gathered speed.

Jos had returned, Saleh told her apprehensively when she reached the house. He was in his room and had called for shaving water and brandy, and Leah was with him. Lucy acknowledged this information with a brusque inclination of the head, but she scarcely heard what he had said. A strange calm enveloped her, and her tears were gone, leaving her at once bereft of both fear and pity. She flung open the door of her husband's room and dismissed Leah with a single contemptuous word. Waiting only until the girl had left them, she confronted Jos with the first of Dickon's sketches, and as he gazed at it stupidly, his mouth agape, she made her accusation in a clear, cold voice that defied him to deny it.

"You killed him, did you not? You killed Robert Willoughby! And poor young Daniels, too . . . look, here is the proof!" The second sketch was thrust across the table at which he was seated. "You were seen, Jos! Everything you did was seen!"

For a moment, Jos was taken aback by the sheer unexpectedness of her accusation, but then, recovering himself, he challenged angrily, "And if I did? It was what the young swine deserved, as God's my witness! You are my wife, and Willoughby made love to you, did he not, when my back was turned? I am no cuckold, I . . ." He looked again at the smudged charcoal drawings. "These are no proof! Who made them?"

"Dickon O'Shea. He was there, with Claus. They watched you—they saw what you did, and they told me," Lucy flung at him. "They are proof enough, Jos."

"You are a fool, woman! Who will believe the ravings of an idiot boy, who can neither hear nor speak? So he draws pictures—who is to say that he did not draw these from his imagination long afterward? In any event"—he was sneering at her now, Lucy saw, a defiant smile curving his lips—"those scurvy escapers were tried and convicted of the crime. I am safe; it is over and done with. You will only be wasting your breath if you seek to accuse me."

"Not if Claus supports Dickon's story," Lucy reminded him.

"He would not! Claus is my son, as you well know. He is loyal. He loves and respects me."

"If I ask him to, he will. He has no love for you, Jos—only fear."

"That is not so," Jos blustered, but with less conviction.

"Why did you try to take him back to Timor with you? If you believed him loyal, if you trusted him, surely that was not necessary? It was fear that you might insist on sending him back that loosened his tongue. He told me everything, Jos, and it was he who obtained these sketches from Dickon." Lucy's tone was scornful, and it stung Jos to anger. He cursed her furiously, but she ignored his attempt to intimidate her. "There is only one honorable action you can take, don't you understand? You cannot stay here—Sydney will no longer tolerate your presence when it is known what you have done."

"Or yours, if you make it public! The devil take you, woman—you are my wife! My unfaithful wife . . ." Jos tried to rob her of the sketches, but Lucy backed away, holding them out of his reach. He had been drinking, she realized as he lurched after her unsteadily and she caught the whiff of spirits on his breath. On a table by the window there was a heavy pistol that he must have laid there when he had first come into the room.

Years ago, in Coupang, she recalled, Jos had taught her how to use a pistol, and keeping the width of the table between them, she picked up the weapon.

"Careful!" Jos roared at her. "It is loaded. Give it to me—God's blood, what do you think you are doing?" He staggered up to the table, grabbing the pistol from her and, swaying dangerously, leveling it at her. "I could kill you," he threatened hoarsely. "As I killed your lover—it would not take much to make me!"

Suddenly, Lucy lost all fear of him. "Then they would certainly hang you, for you would have no escapers on whom to pin the guilt," she asserted disdainfully. "A Dutch officer and gentleman—would you bring so great a shame on yourself? You are disliked and mistrusted here, for it is known that you met the French ships—the ships that are not supposed to exist! I have proof of that also. I have your French commission, Jozef Hendrik Van Buren . . . lieutenant in the army of the French Emperor." She heard a groan escape him and, with contempt, saw him lower the pistol.

"You would not reveal that . . . Lucy, you are my wife! You . . . God in heaven, what can I do?"

Lucy faced him. "You have a choice, Jos. There is your ship—you can make your escape. Or there is the pistol you are holding. I do not care which you resort to, but I will keep your secrets—all of them—if you use the pistol."

She turned and walked away, her back toward him, a vision of Robert's face floating before her. As her hand went to close the door behind her, a shot echoed dully from the room she had left, and she clung, half fainting, to the doorjamb, the courage she had found now ebbing out of her and leaving her limp and afraid. But it was justice, she told herself, a life for a life, and by the time Saleh and Leah came running, she had recovered some of her lost composure. Leah's high-pitched, terrified shriek and Saleh's shocked gasp warned her of what she would be called upon to face if she returned to her husband's room, but Lucy summoned the last remnants of her flagging resolution and, with every appearance of calm, followed the two servants.

Jos was slumped over the table, a hideous wound in his forehead and the pistol lying close to his right hand. She swiftly averted her gaze, and Saleh, who had been bending over the crumpled form, straightened up and told her, in a voice that was devoid of expression, "The master is dead, *mevrouw*. It would seem that he has shot himself."

"It was an accident," Lucy said, making a determined effort to maintain her rigid self-control. "The master was cleaning the pistol, and it must have gone off. Send for Dr. Bowman, Saleh, and—" In sudden fury, she turned on the sobbing Leah. "And rid me of that woman at once!"

Saleh obeyed her. He took Leah roughly by the shoulders and propelled her unceremoniously from the room. That done, he gave Lucy a respectful salaam and said quietly, "I will send Amos for the doctor, *mevrouw*. Do not upset yourself, I pray you. Without doubt, it was an accident. I can bear witness to that, should it be required of me."

Their eyes met—Saleh's dark and inscrutable, Lucy's wide and lackluster—and then, with a long, pent-up sigh, Lucy's head came up and she walked from the room in front of him, her reticule in her hand.

In her own room, with meticulous care, she tore Dickon's sketches and the contents of the oilskin-wrapped package into small, unrecognizable shreds and then dropped to her knees among them.

"May God give you rest, Robert," she whispered, "and extend His mercy to me!"

CHAPTER XXIII

On January 17, 1827, His Majesty's ship *Success* sailed from Sydney to begin her mission. After a stormy, ten-day passage southward, during which her tender was so badly damaged that she was compelled to put back, the frigate dropped anchor in the Derwent River, off Hobart Town, Van Diemen's Land.

Jamie Willoughby, unlike the majority of the ship's company, had been glad to leave Sydney. True, the hospitality offered by all the town's inhabitants had been generous and warm. The Governor and Mrs. Darling had given a splendid ball at Government House, which had been attended by the officers of the French ship *Astrolabe*, as well as those from the British squadron, and there had been numerous invitations to dinners, receptions, and picnics. With his fellow midshipmen, Jamie had dutifully accepted them, but . . . He paused in his measured pacing of the anchored frigate's deck. Rob's death and, to a lesser extent, the death and funeral of Commodore Brisbane had left him sadly at odds with both his shipmates and himself, and even his friend Tom Keppel had reproached him for his lack of enthusiasm.

"Make the most of what Sydney offers, Jamie," Tom had urged. "Once we sail, it'll be all work and no play, you know—and it will probably be quite dangerous, if the local natives prove hostile. Trying to find out how your brother died won't bring him back, will it?"

And of course it would not, Jamie reflected resignedly.

All the same, he had wanted to learn more, yet . . . those whom he had taken the trouble to question had proved curiously reticent and evasive.

Red Broome had introduced him to Mr. Richard Tempest, and Tempest had been very kind and hospitable, but he, too, had suffered a recent bereavement, of which, for some reason, he had not seemed anxious to talk.

Jamie frowned as he continued his pacing. All he had managed to elicit from Mr. Tempest was the fact that the dead man—a Dutchman by the name of Van Buren—had been the one with whom Rob had fought his duel, and that the man's death had been the result of an accident, when he had been cleaning a pistol. Mr. Tempest had not seemed particularly sorry about the accident, for all that it had left one of his sisters a widow. Indeed, Jamie thought, looking back on the occasion, he had been left with the distinct impression that Tempest had been more relieved than regretful and that there had been no love lost between him and Van Buren. Tempest had not seemed to have approved of poor Rob, either, and in his account of the duel had been more than a little censorious, reserving what pity he had expressed for Rob's friend and second, Mr. Henry Daniels—also a victim of the bushrangers' attack.

Jamie stared blindly ahead, the beauty of his surroundings lost on him as he wrestled with his problem. Tom had gone ashore with Lieutenant Barrett-Lennard and some of the other officers to shoot quail; they were to dine afterward with the Lieutenant Governor, Colonel Arthur, and he had been invited to go with them, but . . . He stopped his pacing and stood at the rail. He had been unable to raise any enthusiasm for the proposed shoot, still less for yet another formal Government House dinner. Standing a harbor watch was usually tedious and uneventful, but at least, he told himself, it permitted him time to think over what little information he had managed to obtain concerning his brother's short sojourn in the colony and his unhappy death.

His encounters with other members of the Tempest and

Dawson families had done virtually nothing to enlighten him. He had not met Mr. Tempest's wife, who had recently given birth to a baby son; and Mrs. Abigail Dawson, Tempest's elder sister, had been kind but uninformative, confining herself to expressions of sympathy. But her stepdaughter, a waspish young woman named Julia, had gone to the other extreme, throwing out hints that he had found disturbing.

With scant regard for his feelings, she had described Rob as "one of the upstart adventurers the previous Governor inflicted on us . . . whose sole aim was to make money out of the large land grants they were given."

"I always disliked Major Van Buren intensely, Mr. Willoughby," Julia had told him. "And I cannot imagine why my aunt Lucy ever married him. He was uncouth and ill-mannered, and he frequently drank to excess. Nevertheless, your brother set out to deceive him, and had he perished at Major Van Buren's hands when they fought their duel, I believe most people would have said that it was no more than he deserved. We do not want settlers of his type here. I'm sorry that he was murdered, of course, but . . ." She had talked at length, condemning the late Major Van Buren at one moment and railing against poor Rob the next. Yet nothing she had said had served to explain what had happened, nor did she offer any reason for the two men having fought a duel only a short time before Rob's death.

Unless . . . Jamie frowned, reluctant to think ill of his brother yet compelled to wonder whether, perhaps, Julia's spiteful tirade had been intended to suggest that Rob had been having a love affair with Major Van Buren's wife. If she were good-looking and younger than her husband, it was possible that Rob might have been attracted to her. He had in the past been something of a lady's man, Jamie was compelled to concede, all too easily attracted and taken in by the opposite sex. The wretched girl Becky Raven had been the cause of poor Rob's downfall, the reason why their father had disinherited him and sent him out here to Australia . . . and to his death.

The dreadful scene with the old admiral was still a vivid memory, never to be erased from his mind, but, thinking of it afterward . . . Jamie felt tears sting his eyes. Rob had been condemned virtually unheard by their father, and yet the whole miserable affair of his impending arrest and the charges against him could easily have been fabricated by Daniel Raven, the girl's father. Raven, Rob had told him, had long harbored a grudge against the admiral, and ruining his elder son could well have been an act of revenge aimed not at Rob himself but at their father.

Listlessly, he crossed the deck to look out across the blue, sun-dappled water to the distant town. Hobart had grown out of all recognition, one of the older hands had told him, and where once there had been only a few irregularly situated huts and cottages of flimsy construction and a small whaling station, there were now well-built brick houses, a fine government house, water mills, and a substantial pier for the whalers in Sullivan's Cove.

Lieutenant Belcher, who was the duty watchkeeper, came to join him, sketch pad in hand. Peter Belcher was a skilled artist and an expert botanist, and as he deftly plied his pencil, he pointed out and identified some of the buildings.

"The military barracks, do you see—over to our left? And the jail—no settlement is complete without its jail. Not that they house the really bad convicts there. Those poor wretches are sent to Macquarie Harbor or Maria Island, mostly for the term of their natural lives. There's talk of removing them to an even more remote spot, though—between Cape Pillar and Cape Raoul, in what's called Stewart's Harbor. Remember sighting Cape Pillar, youngster? All lofty cliffs and basaltic columns, resembling massed chimney stacks or crumbling ruins of the Tower of Pisa?"

Jamie nodded, his interest kindled. "Yes, I do, sir. It's a pretty desolate spot."

"That it is." Belcher sketched busily, his cap pulled down to shade his eyes from the strong sunlight. "But good enough for escapers and bushrangers, I suppose. Though they say that Governor Arthur has been making strenuous efforts to put a stop to the depredations of the bushrangers and has most of 'em under lock and key now. They had their heyday under a previous Governor—a onetime major of marines, who came out here with the First Fleet and was known as Mad Tom. A profligate fellow, by all accounts, whose death was unlamented." He gestured with his pencil. "The new Anglican church of Saint David—the hospital, d'you see, and that imposing building is the customs house. They do a thriving trade here, I'm told."

"Do they, sir?" Jamie was surprised. "I thought Hobart was mainly a whaling station."

"Not at all, young Willoughby," Belcher corrected. "I spent yesterday evening listening to Colonel Arthur extolling its merits. The population—including convicts, of course—is at present close on five thousand. Apart from the local trade with Port Jackson, Hobart imports British manufactured goods and European wines, in exchange for exports of wool, sealskins, hides, and whale oil. Since the ending of the East India Company's monopoly, the colony is building up trade with China and India, the Cape, and even Brazil. Our esteemed captain was greatly encouraged by the Governor's account. If our survey of the Swan River comes up to expectation, Captain Stirling visualizes a similar settlement there, which will have the immense advantage of being very much nearer to the established trade routes than either Hobart or Sydney. You know his theory, don't you?"

"Yes, sir," Jamie confirmed. "His prevailing-winds theory. I was trying to explain it to some of the people I met in Sydney."

"Well, I hope you made a good job of your explanation." Neatly finishing off his sketch, Lieutenant Belcher offered it for inspection and then, rolling it up, began on a second.

"You ought to take a run ashore, Willoughby, instead of skulking on board the ship, you know. The hospitality may not be as civilized as it was in Sydney Town, but the people are extremely friendly and eager to make us welcome. And," he added, with a smile, "Governor Arthur's daughters are exceptionally pretty. So pretty, in fact, that I'm tempted to quit the Royal Navy and become a settler . . . though I might delay a decision until we see what prospects the Swan River area is likely to offer." His smile widened. "What about you? Have you thought of doing something of the kind?"

Until that moment, he had not, Jamie reflected. Rob had made no will—poor Rob, he had not expected that his life would end so soon and obviously had not seen the necessity to bequeath his land and stock to anyone. Jamie knew that both could now be his; the Governor had told him as much, but . . . He glanced up uncertainly into Peter Belcher's smiling face, wondering whether or not to take his last remark seriously.

Emily and her husband were coming out to Australia—they were probably well on their way by now—and he had decided to leave the matter of Rob's property in abeyance, until such time as he could ascertain their wishes. Simon Yates was committed to the Mission Society's settlement in New Zealand, and as he was coming out under their auspices, he could not stay in Sydney beyond the agreed period of probation—unless, that was to say, he repaid the cost of his passage. But at least both he and Emmy would almost certainly be there when the *Success* returned to Port Jackson, and the final decision could be made then. Rob's sheep, Mrs. Dawson had assured him, were being kept on one of her husband's farms, and he need have no anxiety on that account. . . .

"I don't know, sir," he said, since Lieutenant Belcher appeared to expect an answer. "I haven't made up my mind. I like being at sea, and I'm looking forward to exploring the Swan River."

"So am I," Belcher confessed. "We'd both be wise to

give it time, eh? But you want to go ashore, youngster. Brooding over your brother's death won't do any good, will it? He was killed, and the rogues who killed him have been tried and punished—you've got to try to put it out of your mind. I've watched you ever since we left Port Jackson, and I've seen what you're enduring.'' He laid a hand on Jamie's shoulder. ''I tell you what—if you don't want to enter the social scene, how about coming with me tomorrow? I've arranged with the owner of one of the newspapers here—a delightful fellow named Damien Hayes—to take me on a two-day trip into the interior, so that I can learn something about the island's flora and fauna. You could assist me to collect specimens and make yourself generally useful . . . and I'd welcome your company.''

Jamie felt suddenly as if a great weight had been lifted from his spirit. Lieutenant Belcher was right—brooding over Rob's death did no good at all, and an exploratory trip into the interior held a strong appeal for him.

''Thank you, sir,'' he answered gratefully. ''I'd like to come with you very much.''

The trip exceeded all his expectations. With so limited a time at their disposal, it was not possible to travel far, but Mr. Damien Hayes, aware of what Lieutenant Belcher wanted to see, proved an admirable and very knowledgeable guide. They crossed the Derwent by ferry and proceeded on foot up a thickly wooded hill, from whose summit a magnificent view of the surrounding country all but took Jamie's breath away. Below, the Derwent River sparkled in the sunlight, its banks gay with the golden-yellow mimosa that was everywhere growing in profusion.

Peter Belcher was in his element as he and the owner of the Hobart *Chronicle* traded Latin names for ferns and orchids and, with awesome ease, identified the birds they disturbed as they moved among the trees.

''A fire-tailed finch, young Willoughby—see it? And that's *Myzantha garrula*, the so-called soldier bird or noisy miner.''

They camped that night by a pleasant rivulet under the stars, the two older men talking almost until dawn, while Jamie slept, no longer disturbed by the nightmare visions of Rob's dead face that had haunted him for so long. Next morning they set off, heading westward and plunging deeper into the forest, with Mr. Hayes identifying the different varieties of eucalyptus and pine trees, blackwood and tea trees, and Lieutenant Belcher again busy with his sketch pad.

They met no aborigines, and Hayes said, sadness in his voice, that virtually all had been driven away or slaughtered by the settlers during the past decade.

"They are primitive people—they do not fish and have no canoes—and initially they were well-disposed to us, even though we invaded their country and robbed them of their hunting grounds. But they stole stock, and the settlers went after them with muskets, killing men, women, and children indiscriminately. Governor Davey did nothing to halt the slaughter; Governor Sorrell endeavored to and met with concerted opposition; and it's been left to our present Governor to introduce sterner measures. Three years ago he issued a general government order declaring that the aborigines were to be protected and that killing any of them was to be a capital offense, but . . ." Hayes shrugged in a gesture of helplessness. "It goes on, and the blacks are seldom seen in these parts now. They hide where they can, but our settlements are growing and spreading out, and very soon they'll have nowhere to hide. And, of course, when they are attacked, they retaliate, and if they come across a white man on his own, they murder him."

As Rob had been murdered, Jamie thought wretchedly— only Rob's murderers had been white men, not the dispossessed blacks of whom Mr. Hayes had spoken so movingly. There might have been some excuse for them, and . . . He felt Lieutenant Belcher's hand on his shoulder.

"Look, young Willoughby—" he urged, "a fine example of *Cystoptens fragilis*—brittle bladder fern to you, and close to your left hand. Pick it for me, will you please, and add it to the others in your knapsack?"

Jamie obeyed him, grateful for the distraction.

At noon they halted to brew tea and eat a frugal meal of bread and cold meat, and Damien Hayes said regretfully, "We shall have to head back, alas, if you two gentlemen are not to overstay your leave. But it has been a most pleasant break for me—I spend too much of my life in my office these days. The Hobart press, including the *Gazette*, is engaged in a trial of strength with Governor Arthur, which is keeping both Mr. Bent of the *Gazette* and me on our toes. It is not, I hasten to add, as acrimonious a contest as that being waged by Mr. Wentworth and the *Australian* in Sydney, but we, too, have our anonymous letter writers. Ours calls himself Colonist, while those addressing Mr. Wentworth appear to prefer classical pen names." He smiled. "However, I think we are all campaigning for the same aims—freedom of the press, of course, and representation of the people in government and the judiciary."

Peter Belcher rose to his feet. "Mr. Willoughby and I, thanks be to heaven," he retorted, laughing, "are under military discipline and are thus spared from such contests. I wish you luck, all the same, Mr. Hayes. Having met your Lieutenant Governor, I think you may need it. Shall we make tracks?"

The journey back to Hobart, by a more direct route than they had taken initially, occupied only four hours. They boarded the ferry, and from its deck Jamie observed that a big convict transport had entered the anchorage in their absence. Belcher's glass enabled him to identify her as the *Countess of Harcourt*, and he said, lowering the glass, "Who knows . . . your family may be on board, Willoughby. They were leaving soon after us, were they not?"

Jamie's heart leaped. It was possible, he knew—Emmy had assured him that she and Simon and their two small sisters would take the first available passage after the sale of Murton Chase was completed, but . . . He answered noncommittally, afraid to set too much store by what, at best, was only a possibility.

Damien Hayes accompanied them to the *Success*'s duty boat and there took leave of them. Cutting short Belcher's thanks, he offered kindly, "If you would like to give me the name of the family party you are expecting, Mr. Willoughby, I can make inquiries for you. Would it be Willoughby?"

"No—Yates, sir. My sister is married to Dr. Simon Yates. I—I'd be very grateful indeed, Mr. Hayes, if you could find out for me whether they are on board."

"I will indeed." Hayes shook Jamie's hand, smiling down at him. "I'm invited to dine on board your ship this evening, as it happens . . . as the guest of a very old friend of mine, who is sailing with you in, I understand, the capacity of volunteer."

"You mean Commander Broome?" Peter Belcher questioned, surprised.

"That I do, Mr. Belcher. Justin Broome and I have known each other ever since I came out to Sydney fifteen years ago. His brother has settled here now, near Launceston . . . he came last year, bringing a bride with him and some purebred merinos. Commander Broome has not, alas, been able to visit them in Launceston in the limited time at his disposal, but"—Damien Hayes smiled—"he has entrusted me with a letter and numerous messages, which I shall deliver as soon as I can."

He bowed and stood back, and the boat put off for the short pull to where the *Success* lay at anchor. With the aid of Lieutenant Belcher's telescope, Jamie vainly searched the decks of the *Countess of Harcourt* in the hope that he might catch a glimpse of his sisters or Simon Yates, but her decks were deserted, save for the men on watch, and he was despondent when he boarded his own ship in Belcher's wake.

It had been too much to hope, he told himself—too great a coincidence—and their reunion, when it took place, would have to be three to four months hence, when the *Success* returned from the Swan River.

Commander Broome, Jamie noticed, was on deck when he and Belcher halted to give the traditional salute; recognizing Jamie, he called him over.

"A happy surprise for you, I fancy, Mr. Willoughby," he said. "You have two visitors from the *Countess of Harcourt* waiting to greet you. In Captain Stirling's absence ashore, I took the liberty of offering them hospitality, which they elected to take in the midshipmen's berth. Dr. and Mrs. Yates are eager to see you, and your messmates have done their best to entertain them, pending your return. And," he added kindly, lowering his voice, "I told them of your brother's death, Jamie, in the hope of sparing you."

"Thank you, sir." Jamie could scarcely contain himself. "Thank you very much indeed, I—"

"Hey, have a care with my specimens," Lieutenant Belcher admonished him. He grasped the knapsack Jamie had been carrying and then, grinning, slapped him on the back as the boy relinquished it. "Cut along, then, youngster—and I'm deuced pleased for you!"

Jamie obediently hurried off, his heart thudding. In the cramped messroom, surrounded by his fellow midshipmen, Emily was seated, her tall, smiling husband beside her. They both rose when Jamie entered, and Emily came to meet him, holding out her arms to him in eager welcome. She looked tanned and well, and could hardly restrain tears of happiness as they clung together and he bent to kiss her, overjoyed by the sight of her.

"Oh, Jamie dearest, what a wonderful stroke of luck to find you here! I could scarcely believe my eyes when we came into the anchorage and saw your ship was here."

Led by Tom Keppel, the other midshipmen made their exit, leaving them alone, and Simon Yates came to wring Jamie's hand. "Your two little sisters are anxiously waiting to see you," he said. "We're hoping that you will dine with us. Commander Broome says you're sailing tomorrow, and in your captain's absence he's given you leave until midnight.''

"Then I'll be delighted," Jamie assured him. "You heard—that is, Commander Broome told you about poor Rob?''

"Yes," Emily confirmed, her smile fading. "He told us, Jamie. What can I say? I'm deeply sorry, of course— and particularly sorry that we weren't with you in Sydney when you learned of Rob's death. It must have been distressing for you.'' Her arms closed about him, and Jamie made no attempt to evade her embrace.

"I wish he could have known that I'd no intention of robbing him of his inheritance," he managed huskily. "I keep thinking of the last time we saw him, Emmy. When Papa—'' He could not go on, and Simon Yates offered consolingly, "Perhaps he does know, wherever he is, Jamie.''

"Perhaps," Jamie conceded. "But at least we'll be together. We're coming back to Sydney, you know, sometime in April, if all goes well with our survey. You will still be there, won't you? I mean, they won't send you to New Zealand before then, will they?''

Emily exchanged a swift glance with her husband, and Simon sighed.

"It is in God's hands," he answered gravely. "But it may be a long while before we are able to go to New Zealand, Jamie. The principal chaplain here, the Reverend William Bedford, told me that the Maori tribes are waging war on each other, and in consequence some of the mission stations have had to be abandoned. The Methodist mission at Kerikiri was attacked, and even the Reverend Samuel Marsden's station at Whangaroa is suffering grave hardship. They cannot grow sufficient food to support themselves, and most of the stock they brought with them has died or was stolen by the Maoris. Apparently a chief by the name of Hongi got his hands on a supply of muskets and is bent on subjugating the whole of the North Island, slaughtering all who dare to oppose him.''

He looked again at Emily and shrugged resignedly. "I still want to go, of course, but clearly it would be madness to expose your sisters to such risks. In the meantime, Mr. Bedford has asked me to stay here, on a temporary basis, and he has assured me that this can be arranged with the agreement of the Church Missionary Society."

"Would you stay here?" Jamie asked. "In Hobart?"

Simon Yates shook his head. "No, not here. It seems that the settlement at Richmond, on the Coal River, lacks a surgeon and a resident chaplain, and I'm to act in both capacities, as physician and lay preacher. I understand, however, that my principal task will be to reconcile the white settlers with the native blacks, who are at present waging war on one another in savage and bloody fashion." He explained the location of Richmond and added wryly, "Who knows, perhaps I may bring Christianity to both black and white, if I set my mind to it, eh, Jamie? At least it may give me useful experience before I try to tackle the Maoris . . . and Chief Hongi. Commander Broome was telling me that he met Hongi a few years ago, when he was in Whangaroa in a King's ship with Mr. Marsden. From what he said, Hongi sounds like a pretty formidable character."

"I'd hoped you were going to Sydney," Jamie said uneasily. "There's the question of Rob's land and stock, and—"

"They are yours, Jamie," Simon Yates put in, his tone brooking no argument. "You are the heir. Emmy and I need nothing, do we, Emmy my love? And we have the purchase price of your late father's house to make over to you, when the draft arrives from the attorney, Mr. Peake, in due course."

"Yes, but I—" Jamie began.

Emily cut him short. Linking her arm in his, she said gently, "We can talk of these matters over dinner, can we not? You may wish to make financial provision for Charlotte and Biddy later on, but . . . it was Papa's wish that *you* were to inherit his estate, Jamie. And it's not a large one, although the house was sold very well."

"Who bought it?" Jamie asked, mildly curious, and was surprised to see his sister again exchange a guarded look with her husband.

"Daniel Raven bought it," she said at last, and Jamie sensed the hurt in her voice. "It was his final act of revenge against Rob and Papa. But it no longer matters, does it? Poor Rob is dead, and we are starting a new life, in a new country. He cannot touch us here, Jamie. So please God, it will all turn out for the best."

"Amen to that," Simon offered cheerfully. "Commander Broome promised us a boat to take us across to the *Harcourt* . . . and the master keeps a fine table. We'll celebrate our reunion, shall we, before our ways part once again? You and I and your sisters . . . almost a complete family. And the good name of the Willoughbys is in your keeping now, as your father wanted it to be. I don't think he was a bad judge, Jamie."

Jamie reddened, but his step was light as he led the way to the deck of the *Success*. Looking back afterward, he was to recall that it was then—staring across the anchorage at Hobart Town as he waited for the boat to be called away—that he made up his mind to stay in Australia and finish what Rob had begun.

CHAPTER XXIV

Abigail's note had arrived three days ago:

> We are giving a farewell dinner for Katie and Rick, before they leave for Pengallon, and also to celebrate Julia's engagement to Major Dermot Macintyre of the East India Company's Bengal Engineers. I do hope, dear Lucy, that we may have the pleasure of your company on Friday evening at eight P.M.

She had accepted, Lucy reflected, but as she dressed, assisted by the sullen Leah, she wished that she had devised some excuse for refusal. Abby's dinner parties were usually well organized and the food excellent, but . . . Lucy's small, delicate mouth curved into a pout as she inspected herself critically in her dressing-table mirror. They were invariably very dull, with Timothy Dawson talking endlessly about sheep and other agricultural matters to anyone who would listen, Julia recounting whatever spiteful gossip she had lately picked up, and Abby—always the conscientious hostess—trying vainly to introduce changes of topic. Rick and Katie, it was true, enlivened the conversation a little, but since the birth of their son, they, too, had become boring, since they could speak of little else; and as for Julia's new beau . . . Lucy's pout turned into a frown of contempt.

It was, of course, the wretched girl's last chance—she was well past marriageable age, and none of the 57th's subalterns had spared her a glance; and Dermot Macintyre was a small, dried-up Scotsman, with thinning ginger hair and a pedantic manner. Furthermore, he was a widower, with a young family, and if the Sydney gossipmongers were to be believed, he had come to the colony for the specific purpose of finding a suitable female to take back with him to India, in the capacity of stepmother rather than wife.

Leah clumsily twisted a strand of hair into the teeth of the comb she was using, and Lucy wheeled around and slapped her across the cheek.

"Have a care, you stupid woman! Use the brush, can you not?"

Leah emitted a rebellious whimper, but she picked up the brush, plying it so vigorously that, losing patience, Lucy wrested it from her and finished her coiffure unaided.

"Fetch my cloak," she demanded, taking the towel from her shoulders and throwing it to the floor, so that Leah had to kneel in order to pick it up. "Goodness knows, Alice Fairweather had her faults, but at least she was not clumsy or stupid! I shall tell Saleh to beat you, since it's no more than you deserve. Now go and tell Larkin to bring the carriage round at once."

Amos, the excellent coachman she had employed since her return to Sydney, had served his sentence and engaged himself as farm foreman to a wealthy settler, and his replacement, Samuel Larkin, was, Lucy reflected irritably, a very poor substitute. He was admittedly good with horses, but he was rough and uncouth, his attitude frequently insolent, and his honesty questionable. He would have to go, or be relegated to the work of a groom, she had decided, as soon as she could prevail upon the assignment board to find a more suitable replacement. The trouble was, of course, that singularly few skilled coachmen committed crimes that rendered them liable to deportation.

Leah brought the cloak and draped it carefully round her mistress's shoulders. She stood with downcast eyes, making no attempt to obey the order Lucy had given her, but clearly trying to pluck up the courage to voice a request.

"Well?" Lucy snapped. "What is it? I am late—I've no time to waste, Leah."

Leah looked up to meet her gaze. "If you please, *mevrouw*," she answered in her careful Dutch, "I am wanting to wed. I—"

"*You* want to wed? What man would consider taking you to wife?" Lucy's voice was scornful, but Leah stood her ground. Her slapped cheek was swelling, and her dark eyes held fear when Lucy raised her hand again.

"Please, *mevrouw*, do not strike me. I mean no harm, and I am not wanting to leave your service."

Lucy lowered her hand. The girl had done her little injury, she was forced to concede—rather it had been convenient that Jos Van Buren had used her, since it had kept him from her own bed and from claiming marital rights that had long since become repugnant to her. She relented and asked, in a more placatory tone, "Who is the man you would wed? It is not Saleh, is it?"

"Oh, no, *mevrouw*, certainly not."

"Then who? A convict?"

"Yes," Leah admitted. "The new man, *mevrouw*. Samuel Larkin."

"That rogue! You would be a fool if you were to wed such a villain, Leah. For your sake I could not permit it."

"*Mevrouw*, I am with child," Leah whispered wretchedly. "And *Mijnheer* Van Buren is dead. He would have provided for me had he lived. The child is his."

Lucy stared at her aghast. Another by-blow of Jos's, she thought indignantly, another miserable little *lip-lap*, like Claus, that he had fathered. But . . . the girl might talk. Or Larkin, perhaps. She inclined her head reluctantly.

"Very well, I am willing to give my consent. But Larkin is a rogue, Leah. Do you know for what crime he was transported?"

"Oh, thank you, *mevrouw*!" Leah exclaimed eagerly. "He told me that his crime was that he abducted the daughter of his employer, that is all . . . and he did so because the child's mother paid him for it. She was wanting to leave her husband, you see, but he would not allow her to take the little girl with her. That is not a wicked crime, is it, *mevrouw*?''

Perhaps it was not, Lucy thought cynically, but according to his record, the kidnapping was not Larkin's sole misdemeanor. He had also robbed his employer and offered him physical violence, and his sentence had been for fourteen years.

"Does he know that you are pregnant?" she asked.

Leah nodded happily. "Yes, *mevrouw*. Larkin has children in England, whom he had to leave behind. But he has no wife—his wife is dead. And he—*mevrouw*, he loves me."

Which might or might not be true, but . . . it was at least a satisfactory solution to any problem Leah's pregnancy might pose. They could be sent to the farm at Portland Place as soon as they were married, Lucy told herself, and she would demand that the assignment commissioners find her both a new coachman and a maid. On the mantelshelf, the ornate Swiss clock Jos had given her years ago chimed the hour . . . she would be late, and Abigail's dinners were always punctual.

"Go," she ordered impatiently. "And tell Larkin to bring my carriage to the door."

The dinner party, as she had expected, proved dull, save for the fact that George De Lancey was present, having come from Newcastle for a meeting of the Governor's council, to which both he and Timothy Dawson had been nominated. The council now consisted of twelve members, representing the church, the judiciary, the landowners, and the merchants; and although its business was conducted in strict secrecy, Lucy, by dint of listening surreptitiously to remarks the two men exchanged, was able to piece together some of the results of its proceedings.

The Governor, it seemed, had been exonerated by his advisers of any guilt in the Sudds and Thompson affair, despite the agitation that William Wentworth and Edward Hall had stirred up by means of their respective newspapers, the *Australian* and the *Monitor*.

"Dr. Bowman let the poor Governor down," George said, his voice prudently lowered as he replied to a question from Major Macintyre. "Private Sudds was admittedly taken to the jail in an iron collar—no one disputes that. He and his fellow, Thompson, were sentenced to a chain gang and to the collars, as are many other secondary offenders. But the unfortunate Sudds was seriously ill with a kidney infection *before* his trial, and it was that which caused his death . . . a fact that the chief surgeon has failed to make public. None of this clamor in the press would have arisen if he had; Wentworth would not have had a leg to stand on!"

"In my view, Judge," Macintyre asserted pedantically, "the Governor had every right, every justification for acting as he did in the matter. Military discipline has to be enforced. . . ."

He continued at some length, and Lucy listened with waning interest, but she pricked up her ears again when she heard Timothy say, "For all that, Major, Wentworth and his supporters are demanding His Excellency's impeachment. They want an inquiry by a select committee in the British House of Commons and are insisting openly that Mr. Joseph Hume has agreed to bring the matter to the attention of the House, by means of a question to the Colonial Secretary."

"And what's General Darling doing about it, sir?" Macintyre resembled an aggressive little terrier, Lucy thought, and she suppressed a smile at the sight of his bristling indignation. Julia, she told herself with satisfaction, would meet her match when she became the major's wife, for clearly Dermot Macintyre was a man who would permit the expression of no views that did not reflect his own. And the girl was already unusually subdued, addressing her betrothed submissively and confining her remarks to softly spoken echoes of his opinions.

"Well?" the Scotsman persisted. "Surely to heaven His Excellency isn't going to take such infernal insolence lying down?"

To Lucy's surprise, it was her brother, Rick, who answered the question. "What can he do, Major? Wentworth has formed a so-called patriotic association to campaign for the Governor's impeachment and recall—and he's enlisted some powerful support, both here and in London. Hume, Lytton Bulwer, and Buller in the Commons; and here the merchants are all for him, and the emancipists, of course, and Dr. Bland—"

"That damnable troublemaker!" Macintyre exclaimed. "Plague take it, Tempest, William Bland killed a man in a duel in Bombay, when he was serving as a naval surgeon's mate! He was *transported* to this colony, with a seven-year sentence hanging over his head, and your previous Governor, the late General Macquarie, foolishly gave him a free pardon. What store can be set by him?"

Rick shrugged. His gaze went to Katie, who was seated beside him, and in response to her warning headshake, he smiled and lapsed into silence. There was a new bond of affection between them, Lucy realized, and she echoed her brother's smile, struck by the change in both of them since the birth of their son.

Abigail's well-trained servants came to remove plates and serve the main course, and as Timothy rose to carve the ample joint they had brought in, Abigail herself adroitly turned the conversation into less controversial channels by inviting George De Lancey to tell her about his move to the Hunter Valley.

"Do you regret it?" she inquired.

"Indeed we don't," George assured her. "We are most happily settled. We, too, have a son, a little older than yours, Katie, whose name is William. And our house at Adamstown—just outside Newcastle—was completed three months ago. Rachel loves it—we have two thousand acres of excellent land, and she's following in her mother's footsteps and breeding horses, as well as growing vines and tobacco and running a small beef herd.''

"You are a farmer, then?" Major Macintyre put in, in some bewilderment.

George shook his head, looking amused. "No, my wife is the farmer. I am a member of the judiciary. This means that I'm unable to spend as much time on the farm as I should like to—I'm on the Newcastle bench and also on circuit, and, of course, Major, I have to come to Sydney periodically to attend meetings of the Legislative Council." He turned back to Abigail and went on quietly, "We're both glad we pulled up our roots. Now that the majority of long-term convicts have been transferred to Norfolk Island, the Hunter Valley is attracting new settlers, and Newcastle has become a very pleasant town indeed. Mining continues, and, believe it or not, we are now exporting coal to the Dutch East Indies, as well as to Sydney, and the port is expanding rapidly."

"Nevertheless it is quite a small town, is it not?" Major Macintyre suggested, his tone disparaging.

"It is growing, sir," George returned mildly. "And it is exceptionally well laid out, thanks to the foresight and vision of Captain Wallis of the Forty-sixth, the previous commandant. He built a splendid church and began the building of a breakwater, which will enlarge the harbor considerably when it is completed. A remarkable man, James Wallis—it was a pity he wasn't persuaded to stay on after the regiment left for India. I confess I'm less enamored of his successor, Major Morisset, but we're shortly to lose him—he's been appointed commandant of Norfolk Island. That is to say if he can get the Governor's permission to take his wife with him. As you may know, women are forbidden on Norfolk Island—there was much correspondence on that subject in Mr. Wentworth's newspaper, after the prisoners' wives were evacuated."

The letter Alice Fairweather had written, Lucy thought resentfully—the letter that had started William Wentworth's campaign against the Governor. . . . She said acidly, "A great deal of unnecessary fuss was made about that, Major Macintyre—and by a miserable convict girl who absconded from my employ.''

"Is that so, Mrs. Van Buren?" Dermot Macintyre turned his gaze on her with renewed interest, eyebrows raised.

"Yes, it is," Lucy returned. "After all, Norfolk Island was reopened for the purpose of ridding the colony of the worst felons—the capital respites and the absconders and bushrangers, those who commit crimes after their arrival here. Governor Brisbane made it clear that no convict sent to Norfolk Island should ever be permitted to return to the mainland. And our present Governor went further, did he not, Mr. De Lancey?''

"He did, Mrs. Van Buren."

George offered no more, and Lucy flushed with annoyance. She turned back to Major Macintyre and went on, "Governor Darling announced that the Norfolk Island settlement was to be a place of the extremest punishment, short only of death. The withdrawal of the women was, in my view and that of most of the respectable inhabitants of the colony, amply justified. But of course, with such dangerous radicals as Mr. Wentworth and Dr. Waddell and now this Mr. Hall publishing newspapers, in order to express their so-called liberal opinions, a mountain has been made from a molehill. And the poor Governor's position is made the more difficult in consequence. Do you know that members at a dinner of the Turf Club publicly insulted him?''

"Good God!" Macintyre exclaimed, shocked. "Did they indeed? That is appalling." He laid a hand on Julia's arm and added sanctimoniously, "Well, my dear, I promise you'll not find such behavior in India, where there is a proper respect for authority. I'd no idea under what conditions respectable people had to live out here, but . . . the basic problem, I suppose, is that those who were deported as felons are permitted to return to society once they have served their sentences—I mean, of course, those I hear referred to as emancipists. But, unhappily, the leopard does not change his spots, does he?''

There was a moment's constrained silence, and then Timothy, returning to the table, observed with quiet conviction, ''I am no radical, sir, and I believe I can claim to be a respectable member of the community. But—'' He paused, looking from Macintyre to Lucy. ''The emancipist farmers and merchants are the backbone of this colony, and so are their descendants. Their hard work and dedication have made it what it now is, and speaking personally, I support their claim for citizen rights and a new constitution. I back Mr. Wentworth's campaign in that respect, although I do not hold with the attacks on the Governor.''

''I should think not, sir,'' Macintyre put in, pink with indignation. ''Damme, the Governor is His Majesty's representative! It's treasonable to attack him or question his authority.''

Timothy shrugged. ''Every Governor we have ever had has been subjected to criticism and verbal attack—or worse. And the best Governor of all—the late Governor Macquarie, sir—was no exception. I supported his emancipist policy at the time he instituted it, and I still believe it was the right policy for this colony. General Macquarie held that, when a convicted felon had earned his freedom by—and I quote, sir—by servitude, pardon, or emancipation, he should thenceforth be considered on an equal footing with everyone else in the colony, according to his character and rank in life—''

Lucy lost patience. Ignoring Abigail's pleading glance, she said with icy disdain, ''Yes—and in Governor Macquarie's day, Major Macintyre, an invitation to dine at Government House almost invariably meant that one was seated next to an emancipated forger on one side and an Irish traitor on the other—or, worse still, a common thief! I can even recall an occasion when Their Excellencies saw fit to entertain the debased men of a chain gang, who had been employed to make repairs to Government House!''

Julia chimed in, ''Aunt Lucy's quite right—I can remem-

ber my poor mother going to call on Mrs. Macquarie and
finding the Government House garden filled to overflow-
ing with rough, uncouth convicts, drinking beer and listening to a military band!''

Her remark earned her a nod of approval from her
betrothed, but before he could engage in further discussion,
Abigail intervened.

''We are here this evening to bid good-bye to Katie and
Rick and their beautiful little son,'' she said firmly. ''As
well as to celebrate Julia's forthcoming marriage. Let us
leave criticism of government policies to a more appropriate time. Pray fill your glasses and let us drink to the
happiness and future prosperity of all four—or perhaps I
should say all five, if we include young Edmund Tempest
in our toast.''

Tim Dawson came instantly to his wife's support. He
rose, lifting his glass, and proposed the toast; and until the
ladies left to take coffee in the drawing room, the conversation became more frivolous and personal and, to Lucy's
mind, of singularly little interest.

Twice she attempted to stir the party from its com-
placency—once by suggesting that the new secretary of
the colony, Alexander McLeay, was far from being a
worthy successor to Major Goulburn, and then by deplor-
ing the manner in which the people of Sydney had lavished
hospitality on the French commander, Dumont d'Urville,
and his officers during their stay—but no one disputed her
claims. She was in a mood of some irritation when Abigail
caught her eye and they left the gentlemen to their port and
cigars, and her ill temper was in no wise lessened when
Katie brought her eight-week-old son from his nursery,
and even Julia went into ecstasies over his chubby perfection.

She had never had a child, Lucy thought with bitterness,
regretting the fact—and not for the first time. Perhaps she
would have been happier had she given birth to a son, as
Katie had . . . and as her sister, Abigail, had—although a
child like Dickon would have been unendurable. Or, indeed,
a child fathered by Jos Van Buren. She shivered, thinking

of Claus and of the child Leah was now carrying in her womb. God had at least spared her that. But Robert's child—ah, she would gladly have borne poor Robert Willoughby a child!

When the gentlemen came in, Katie and Rick went together to restore their son to his cot and Kate Lamerton's ministrations, and, to Lucy's surprise, George De Lancey sought her out. He drew her aside and said, in a carefully lowered voice, "Mrs. Van Buren, I left a package for you at your house. I left it on my way here, as I was not aware that we should both be guests of the Dawsons this evening. And—" His expression hardened. "I was not aware of your husband's death, I regret to say, until I came back to Sydney yesterday."

He expressed no sympathy, and Lucy responded coldly, "My husband's death was an accident, Judge, as perhaps you will have heard."

"Yes," he confirmed flatly. "I was informed of the coroner's verdict, Mrs. Van Buren. And I am acting on instructions your husband left with the package—instructions that require me to deliver it to you in the event of his death. The package is sealed, but I understand it contains a copy of his will and—"

"His *will*!" Lucy exclaimed incredulously. "I did not—oh, for goodness' sake, why should he leave a will? I am his wife—his widow—and as such surely I must inherit his—his estate? He had no other legal heir." George De Lancey was silent, and, in sudden fear, she grasped his arm. "Mr. De Lancey, did you draw up his will?"

George De Lancey shook his head. "No, that was done by a lawyer in Batavia, and it is in the Dutch language, which I shall have to have translated. From a covering letter, however, I understand that your late husband appointed me his executor." He paused, eyeing her searchingly, and then went on, "Both the will and the package were deposited with my clerk at my old chambers in Macquarie Street. I apologize for the delay in informing you, but my clerk, supposing it to be a personal matter, simply put the envelope containing them into the safe, pending my return to Sydney. That was remiss of him, but . . . I can only ask your indulgence.''

Lucy drew in her breath sharply, her brain racing as her fears grew. It would be like Jos, she thought resentfully, just like him. He . . . Recovering herself, she asked uncertainly, ''For how long were these documents—the envelope in your safe?''

''From what my clerk told me, Mrs. Van Buren,'' De Lancey replied, ''it would seem that your late husband left the envelope when he came ashore on the day of the—er—the accident that deprived him of his life. My clerk did not, of course, open it.''

''And the will—do you know its—its provisions?'' Lucy faltered.

''No. As I mentioned, it is in Dutch. The instructions to me were contained in a brief covering letter, in English. I should suppose,'' George De Lancey added, continuing to subject her to a cool scrutiny, ''that the package I delivered to your house will make the provisions of the will clear to you. You speak Dutch, do you not? Can you also read it?''

Lucy stiffened. ''Not well,'' she admitted. ''I . . .'' There was evidently no more to be learned from this dry-as-dust lawyer. She thanked him without warmth and did not offer to aid in the translation of the will. Presumably he would find a translator to enable him to fulfill his function as executor, but until he did, she could count on a little leeway.

Lucy took her leave of Abigail and Timothy, bade a cursory farewell to Rick and his wife, and, ignoring Julia, shook hands with Major Macintyre. A few minutes later, she was on her way back to her own house.

Saleh met her at the front door, the package on a salver, from which she snatched it impatiently, waving aside his explanation.

''I saw Mr. De Lancey at my sister's. Bring brandy and

some sweetmeats to my room. And then you may retire, Saleh. And I shall not want Leah to attend me.''

His dark brows rose, but, good servant that he was, Saleh did as she had bidden him, set a tray on her bedside table, bowed silently, and withdrew. Lucy poured herself a glass of brandy, and not troubling to do more than remove her dress, she clambered onto the wide, four-poster bed and, propped on its pillows, tore open the package Jos had left for her.

The copy of her late husband's will was the first to come to light; it was, as George De Lancey had said, written in Dutch, and so, also, were two other documents folded inside it. She put them aside for perusal later, for there was a letter, addressed to her and written in her own language. With fingers that trembled a little, for all her efforts to control her fears, Lucy spread it out on the counterpane and moved the oil lamp nearer, the memory of the shock she had sustained when reading the contents of Jos's other papers still vividly in her mind.

The letter was vindictive and wounding—intentionally wounding, she thought bitterly as she read it.

You are no longer a wife to me. Your wanton infidelity with Robert Willoughby has finally opened my deluded eyes to what manner of woman you have become. And you are childless.

But I have a son, to whose existence I have been, at your behest, oblivious—worse, I have, because of you and your social pretensions, denied him the right to claim that he is my son. And I came close to doing my son an irreparable wrong by planning to send him away from Sydney—an action I now deeply regret, since I am aware that he has been loyal to me, and I have, by calling that loyalty into question, almost certainly forfeited it.

In my last will and testament, a copy of which you will find enclosed with this letter, I intend to make reparation to my son Claus Van Buren. To him, I am leaving my trading vessels and all the profits I have earned from them, deposited in my name in the Bank of New South Wales.

Also the house in Bridge Street, which is in my name—your countrymen refused to permit me to own land in the colony, but you will find that the house purchase was conducted legally by myself, before the late Governor proscribed me because of my nationality.

I shall be dead when you read these words, in what circumstances I know not. But you will read them and know, at last, the contempt in which I hold you.

The attached certificates—my marriage certificate and the birth certificate of my son—are copies, like my will; the originals are in the hands of Justice George De Lancey, whom I have appointed my executor, knowing him to be an upright and honorable gentleman. Despite certain differences between us in the past, I am confident that he will carry out my wishes.

I have charged him also to make provision for all the servants I brought with me from Java, and in particular to deal generously with the maidservant, Leah Hopal, in recognition of her devoted service to me—a service you, in your arrogance, would not perform.

Lucy flung the letter from her with a strangled cry. So Jos had sought to take his revenge, she told herself, sick with impotent anger. From the grave in Sydney's burial ground, his dead hand had reached out to deprive her of virtually everything that was hers—her beautiful house, her *home*, the ships bought with the proceeds of her jewels, and the considerable sum of money he had amassed from his trading and deposited in the colony's principal bank.

Only a few days before, the master of the *Dorcas*—believing her to be the vessel's owner—had come to her for permission to carry out the contract Jos had made, to ship a cargo of coal from Newcastle to Batavia. She had given him permission, but . . . Lucy's heart leaped. He had not yet sailed, he . . . Her lips tightened into a firm, hard line.

The despised little *lip-lap*, the frightened little fool Claus, was now to claim his birthright, because, at last, his father had acknowledged him. She could not let that happen, she would not, while she had the means to prevent it. And if she moved swiftly and secretly, the means were there, to her hand . . . the same means Jos had contemplated, when he had doubted the wretched boy's loyalty and feared that he might reveal what he had witnessed, all those months ago, on Rick's farm beyond the Blue Mountains.

And Claus *had* revealed it—he had, in the end, betrayed his father out of fear. Fear that he would be sent back to Coupang . . . Lucy smiled mirthlessly. Well, he should go back to Coupang. Once he was there, even the upright and honorable Judge De Lancey would be hard put to it to carry out Jos Van Buren's wishes, as expressed in his will, and ensure that his despised native-born son should inherit that to which *she* had prior claim. Claus should vanish long before George De Lancey had found a Dutch-speaker to translate the will . . . or the boy's birth certificate.

Lucy spent an almost sleepless night, first composing a written order for the master of the *Dorcas* and then herself struggling with the intricacies of the Dutch language, in order to learn the exact terms of the will. When the new day dawned, she had made her plans, recalling, with a certain satisfaction, what Leah had told her of the offense for which her new convict coachman had been deported.

To Saleh, when he brought her morning tray of chocolate, she presented a smiling face.

"Where is Claus, Saleh?" she asked as he drew the window shades back.

He turned in surprise. "He is going about his morning duties, as usual, *mevrouw*. Do you want him?"

Lucy shook her head. "No, not yet. But see to it that he does not leave the house. Later, I wish him to go with Larkin to deliver a note to the captain of the *Dorcas*. And I will see Larkin in half an hour, when I am dressed." She sipped appreciatively at her chocolate, and added, continuing to smile, "I have given Leah my permission to wed Larkin. And when they are wed, I intend to send them to work on my farm at Portland Place." That farm, at least, was hers, she thought, and her smile widened.

Saleh bowed. It was evident that he suspected nothing,

and when Larkin presented himself, Lucy gave him his instructions, adding the promise that, provided he carried them out to her satisfaction, he should take Leah to wife and they would be given work and a cottage at Portland Place.

"You understand, Larkin, I am carrying out my late husband's wishes in regard to Claus. It was Major Van Buren's intention that the boy should return to his own people, where he will be much happier than he is here. It will be your responsibility to see that he remains on board the *Dorcas* and that the master gets under way as soon as possible after receiving my note."

"Yes, ma'am," Larkin acknowledged woodenly. His dark eyes held a gleam of understanding; he was no fool, Lucy decided, and she could afford to take no risks with him.

"Should you fail to do as I have bidden you," she told him brusquely, "or if there is any trouble with the boy, you will be discharged from my employ, and I shall recommend that you are sent to a road gang. Then, of course, there can be no question of marriage to Leah or anyone else. That's clear, is it not?"

"Yes, ma'am," Larkin assured her, the gleam fading swiftly from his eyes. "I'll do just like you said, ma'am."

"And keep a still tongue in your head," Lucy warned. "I want no servants' chatter. And the boy must be told nothing."

Larkin knuckled his forehead and backed from the room.

A few minutes later, watching from her bedroom window, Lucy saw him leave the house, with Claus skipping excitedly at his side. They boarded one of the oared boats that plied for hire, and she saw it put off and row across to where the *Dorcas* lay at anchor. With the aid of her late husband's glass, she watched the two contrasting figures climb up to the brig's entryport, and knew some minutes of acute anxiety when both vanished from sight.

Then relief flooded over her. Larkin's short, stocky figure descended alone to the waiting boat, and he was still only halfway across the anchorage when the crew of the *Dorcas* came crowding onto her deck. A dozen of them swarmed aloft; the dingy topsails were set, and her anchor came up. There was little wind, but, expertly handled by her master, the brig got slowly under way and headed across the harbor as her crew loosed more sail. . . .

It was late into the afternoon when Saleh came to tell her that Claus had not returned.

"I suppose," Lucy answered, with well-simulated indifference, "that the boy has run away again. Probably to Alice Fairweather. Or perhaps he has gone with Dickon O'Shea to my brother's farm over the mountains. He is a foolish boy, Saleh, and a great coward, you know, whose fears are usually without foundation. I expect he will come back when it suits him. What does Larkin say of his disappearance?"

"He says nothing, *mevrouw*," Saleh admitted. "Save that Claus left him, after they had been out to the ship *Dorcas*. He does not know where he went then."

Larkin had done precisely as she had ordered, Lucy reflected, pleased. "Send Larkin to me," she commanded. "And Leah also. I shall make arrangements for their marriage and their removal to Portland Place."

Saleh hesitated, as if wanting to say more, but finally deciding against it, he bowed obediently and left her alone.

CHAPTER XXV

The *Dorcas* lay at anchor under the shadow cast by the dark bulk of Nobby's Island, as if attempting to merge into the background, so that her continued presence should pass unnoticed. She had entered the Hunter River just before dusk two nights ago and had spent the day loading a cargo of coal destined for Batavia, according to her master, a shifty-eyed individual named Meesman.

Murdo watched her, frowning. Since his transfer to the military garrison at Newcastle, he had been given command of the port authority guard. It was not a particularly onerous assignment, since most of the capital respite and long-term convicts had been removed to Norfolk Island, and there were now few attempts at escape.

The men working in the mines sometimes ran, for the conditions in which they were compelled to toil were both unpleasant and dangerous; and even the more fortunate souls who worked on the Stockton Peninsula, burning shells to make lime, also occasionally tried to sign on with ships whose overseas destinations offered a chance of freedom. And, Murdo was well aware, masters whose ships were short of hands were ready enough to take them, without asking questions, and readier still to smuggle absconders on board when offered a bribe to do so.

According to his sergeant—a Veteran Corps noncommissioned officer who had served in Newcastle for several years—Meesman was among the worst offenders in this respect, although he had only once been caught, and then

had contrived to bluff the magistrates into releasing him
with a fine, when brought to trial a year or so ago.

"Owned by a Dutch gentleman, the *Dorcas* is, sir,"
Sergeant Lee had said disgustedly as they watched her
come into her berth at the coal jetty below the commandant's
walled garden. "A Major Van Buren or some name like
that. 'Twas he got her slippery rogue of a master off the
hook an' paid his fine. The court took his word that it were
all a mistake, though we nabbed the scoundrel red-handed
with three escapers hidin' below. He'll bear havin' an eye
kept on him, Mr. Dean—he hadn't a full complement
when we inspected the ship this morning. Chances are
he'll hang about in the hope o' grabbin' a couple of men."

Lee was a good NCO, who did his job well, and he had
volunteered to keep the *Dorcas* under observation. He was
there now, Murdo realized as he descended to the jetty,
but like the ship herself, the sergeant was keeping to the
shadows, only the glow from his pipe betraying his presence.
He did not move when Murdo came to a halt beside him,
but said, in a tone of gruff approval. "Good o' you to
come, sir. But so far there's nothin' doing."

"I dined with Major Morisset, and it's only a stone's
throw from his house, so I thought I'd see how you were
doing, Sergeant." Murdo stifled a yawn. The commandant
had been very hospitable, plying him with food and wine,
and in the fresh night air, drowsiness threatened to overcome him.

He had not wanted to come to Newcastle; exploratory
expeditions were being planned in Sydney, and he had
hoped he might be included in one of them, on the strength
of his experience with William Lawson and the Cunninghams and his own exploration of the Brisbane River with
Major Lockyer, and later alone. But . . . the *Success* had
gone on her expedition to the Swan River, and the only
officer from the colony that she had taken with her was
Justin Broome. Alexander Hume, too, was rumored to be
preparing an attempt to trace the course of the lower
Macquarie River—familiar territory to him, Murdo reflected,

with some bitterness—but as yet no suggestion had been made that he should join this or any other party.

Newcastle was a backwater, in many ways; too far from the center of things for his liking, although it had its compensations—not least the opening up of the Hunter Valley to free settlement and the new settlers' unofficial but vigorous attempts to establish road and river communications with the Hawkesbury settlements and Sydney. And there was George De Lancey, who had taken a land grant not far from the town. . . . Murdo smiled. He had always liked and admired the man, ever since they had come out to the colony together on the same ship. And lately, both De Lancey and his pretty young wife had admitted him to their friendship, and even issued an open invitation to him to visit their fine new house in Adamstown whenever he felt inclined.

And Newcastle itself was growing, its prosperity based on timber cutting, as well as coal mining. It was well laid out, with close on a hundred residential houses and convicts' cottages, a courthouse, a well-built stone hospital, a handsome church, and the inevitable jail. His own quarters were more than passably comfortable, and he had recently installed a convict girl to keep house for him and attend to his creature comforts. She was young and unlettered, but on the whole she did most creditably. Certainly his circumstances now were infinitely better than they had been at Moreton Bay; but for all that, he yearned for more purpose to his life and . . . yes, more excitement, the thrill of discovering new country.

He yawned again, and Sergeant Lee said in an almost apologetic whisper, "Not a sign o' movement on her deck, sir. Yet I'd take me oath that rogue Meesman's up to somethin'. He could've sailed this afternoon, if he'd wanted to—and he didn't. *And* he's dropped his hook pretty close to Nobby's. If he'd meant to let his crew have a run ashore, I don't reckon as he'd have done that, sir, do you?"

"I don't suppose he would," Murdo agreed. He was

wearying of his self-imposed vigil and was about to move on when the sergeant asked curiously if he liked being stationed in Newcastle.

"You must have read my thoughts, Sergeant! I was standing here wondering just that," he admitted. "But why do you ask?"

"Well, sir, Sergeant Rolfe, who was with you at the Moreton Bay settlement, he's by way of bein' a friend o' mine. Served together in the Peninsula, we did, as young lads—" Instinctively, Murdo stiffened, fearing that Rolfe might have talked out of turn, but the older man's next words swiftly reassured him. "I seen him, when I was in Sydney for a spot o' leave, an' he was singin' your praises, Mr. Dean."

"I'm glad of that, Sergeant. But—"

"We both of us served under Captain Logan, sir," Lee said, and his tone, rather than his words, conveyed his meaning. "Killed by blackfellows, wasn't he?"

"That was the supposition," Murdo confirmed cautiously. "Nothing was ever proved, except that his horse fell and injured him, when he was leading the search for an escaper."

"Aye, that was what Rolfe told me. He said as there was some letter published in a newspaper in Sydney about conditions in Moreton Bay. You'll have read it, I don't doubt, sir."

"Yes, I read it." Murdo was wide awake now, all desire for sleep having evaporated. Bluntly, he repeated his earlier question, "Why do you ask, Sergeant?"

Sergeant Lee tapped out his pipe and cast another long, searching gaze at the *Dorcas*'s dark outline before replying. Then he said evasively, "No partic'lar reason, Mr. Dean. 'Cept it occurred to me that if you'd found your feet here, so to speak, you might think o' transferring to the Veteran Corps. I have, an' Rolfe's considerin' it . . . and the terms for an officer are good. A thousand-acre grant, sir, with the choice o' a site, convict labor, and a fair allowance in seed an' stock. I took five hundred acres when I signed on with the corps—near Lake Macquarie it is, and prime land at that, with plenty o' good timber for buildings. You could do a lot worse, sir—an' if you was to stay here, you might get the commandant's appointment, when the major goes to Norfolk Island.''

Murdo looked at him in surprise. Major Morisset, over dinner, had been adamant—he had no intention of accepting the Norfolk Island appointment, unless the Governor rescinded his ban on women and permitted him to take his wife and his two small children with him. Having met his lovely young wife, Murdo could well understand. ''I don't think the major will go,'' he said. ''He's determined not to leave his family, and I don't blame him. In his place, I'd feel the same. Women are a civilizing influence in settlements like Norfolk Island and Moreton Bay, and—''

''Aye,'' Sergeant Lee put in shrewdly, '' 'twas what that letter in the newspaper was on about, wasn't it, sir? An' the other one—the one they say was written by the chaplain's wife when the women was removed from Norfolk Island. There's—'' He broke off, muttering an oath under his breath, and pointed in the direction of Nobby's Island. ''Look, sir—a boat's put off from the *Dorcas*!''

He was right, Murdo saw . . . and it was a boat with muffled oars, only just discernible in the faint light of the cloud-obscured moon.

''What the devil are they aiming to do, Sergeant?'' he exclaimed. ''The mine's abandoned, isn't it?''

''Aye, sir,'' Lee asserted. ''These past five or six years. But the old workings are there, mostly collapsed. Could be some absconders are hiding there, waiting for Meesman to pick them up once it's dark. If so, he's kept 'em waiting.''

''Absconders would have had to swim across,'' Murdo reminded him. ''In fetters.''

'' 'Tis no distance, sir, for a strong swimmer. An' good-conduct prisoners aren't fettered. Most of the miners aren't, they—'' Sergeant Lee swore again. ''The boat's landed half a dozen men on Nobby's—look, sir!''

''Yes, I see them. Better call out the guard boat,

Sergeant," Murdo decided. "We'll go and find out what's happening."

The guard boat, with six armed soldiers at the oars, covered the distance to the island in less than ten minutes, its approach hidden from anyone on the *Dorcas*'s deck by the partially built breakwater. Murdo was the first to step ashore, and he looked about him in some bewilderment, seeing the oared boat that had brought the seamen from the brig, but no sign whatsoever of the men themselves.

"They're in the old mine, sir," Sergeant Lee told him as he clambered breathlessly up the grass-covered slope to Murdo's side. "But it'll be contraband, not escapers, I'll wager! Meesman will have struck a bargain with some o' the convicts, an' now he's hidin' the stuff—rotgut rum, likely—for 'em to pick up when they think no one's lookin'. We'll need to be tricky, sir, an' catch the villains in the act, or they'll claim as 'tweren't them that put it there. There's no law says they can't land on Nobby's, seein' the mine's abandoned." A soldier came with a lantern, and taking it from him, Lee led the way to the boarded-up entrance to the mine.

Murdo followed him, stumbling over a pile of rotting timber that he had not seen in the semidarkness. Inside the mine it was dank and very cold. Several passageways, cut through the solid rock, led off the sharply sloping entrance; two at least, Murdo saw by the flickering light of Sergeant Lee's lantern, had fallen in and were impassable, and one appeared to end in a sheer drop just beyond the smashed remainder of what had probably been a lowering cage for the mine workers.

Lee halted, holding up a hand for silence. From a passage to their right came the faint but unmistakable sound of shuffling, as if heavy objects were being dragged across the rough-hewn surface, and the old sergeant exclaimed triumphantly, "Like I said, Mr. Dean, they're hidin' rotgut liquor! We've got the scurvy rogues." He gestured to two of his men to follow him, signing to the others to stand guard over the entrance. "There may be another way out—some o' these passages connect—but we'll see 'em if they try to make a run for their boat. Stay here, will you, sir, and keep your eyes skinned?''

He was off down the right-hand passageway without waiting for Murdo's reply, two of the soldiers at his heels. Thankful to escape from the cold and noisome confines of the old mine, Murdo returned to the entrance, drawing great gulps of fresh air into his lungs. In the old days, he recalled, convicts sentenced to work in the mine had been kept in its depths for six days a week, eating and sleeping below ground when their toil was over, and permitted to come to the surface only on Sundays, for divine service. He shivered, acutely aware of what the poor wretches must have endured, their lives and limbs constantly at risk from falling rock due to inadequate shoring, or the collapse of the coal pillars used initially as roof supports when mining had begun on Nobby's. The new mine, Major Morisset had told him, was deeper—over a hundred feet in depth— but it was a great deal safer, and the thirty-odd convicts employed to work it were underground only for the duration of their shifts.

Poor devils, he thought, looking down at the anchored *Dorcas*—if they wanted to drown their sorrows in rotgut liquor, who could blame them? But the law had to be enforced, and masters like Meesman punished for breaking it. He—

"Look out, sir!" one of the soldiers shouted. "They're making a run for their boat!"

He raised his musket to his shoulder, but Murdo bade him hold his fire. "Halt! Stay where you are!" he yelled at the running seamen, who had emerged from the far side of the squat mound that was the summit of Nobby's Island. Evidently, as Sergeant Lee had warned, there was another way out of the mine, and the rum smugglers had taken it. "Halt!" he ordered again. "Or we'll open fire!" To the man with him, he ordered briskly, "Off with you to their boat. Shoot if they try to board it."

The seamen—six of them—taken by surprise, came to a

halt. They offered no resistance and, indeed, were unarmed, Murdo found when he descended to confront them. Only one—the master, he supposed, though his face was blackened and unrecognizable—attempted bluster, and his defiance abruptly ceased when Sergeant Lee and his men emerged from the mine with evidence of their clandestine activities in the shape of half a dozen liquor kegs retrieved from their hiding place.

"Put them in arrest, Sergeant," Murdo ordered. "We'll search the ship and leave a guard on board. And—" The master started to voice a protest that was more alarmed than angry, but when Murdo ignored it, the man resorted to a sullen assertion that there was nothing on board the *Dorcas* deserving of attention.

"Take me to the jail, if you must," he growled. "But my ship's another matter. You've no right to search her."

"We have every right, Captain Meesman," Murdo returned curtly. "Your ship will be detained, pending a magistrates' hearing. Load them into the boats, Sergeant Lee, and we'll go across to the *Dorcas* right away."

The *Dorcas*, when the guard boat came alongside, was under the command of her mate, a dark-faced Javanese, who met Murdo on deck with the assurance, delivered in broken English, that she was carrying only the cargo of coal she had loaded the previous day.

"No more liquor, *Mijnheer Luitenant* . . . nozzings. No need for search ship." Meeting the gaze of his captain, when Sergeant Lee hustled him on board, the mate showed such obvious signs of dismay that Murdo became convinced they were attempting to cover up some other breach of the colony's laws. Brusquely he ordered a thorough search to be carried out.

"Lead it yourself, Sergeant—and look in every nook and cranny. Shift the coal, if you have to. I'm sure they are hiding something—an absconder or two at least."

To his astonishment, however, the terrified boy the old sergeant carried on deck was the sole result of the search. The boy was gagged, his legs and arms tightly bound with rope, and his clothing filthy. He was so weak that when his limbs were freed and the cruel gag removed, he could neither stand nor speak, and Sergeant Lee said pityingly, "We found the poor little devil in the after hold, sir, half buried under the coal. God knows who he is or what he was doin' there, but at a guess I'd say they was abductin' him. They certainly wasn't wantin' him to be found. I reckon he'd have died if he'd been kept tied up like this much longer."

Murdo took out his hip flask and, going down on his knees beside the prostrate boy, held it to his lips. "Who is he, Captain Meesman?" he demanded angrily. "And why were you treating him in such a fashion?"

"He's a stowaway," Meesman answered, avoiding Murdo's eye. "We teach him a lesson, that's all."

He refused to say more, and finally losing patience with him, Murdo ordered him taken ashore, with the five arrested sailors, and lodged in the jail.

"The mate can stay on board, but the ship is to be held under guard. I'll report what's happened to the commandant first thing tomorrow. And as for this unfortunate little stowaway—" Murdo replaced the cap on his flask and stood up. "Until we know who he is, there's not much we can do. Load him into the guard boat, Sergeant. I'll take him to my quarters for the night. Maybe he'll be able to talk when he's eaten and had a good night's sleep. But I don't think he was a stowaway—more likely he was abducted for some reason."

The boy talked next morning, but, although tearfully grateful for his rescue from the *Dorcas*'s coal bunker and for the ample breakfast Murdo's convict housekeeper cooked for him, he revealed very little about himself. He was a half-caste—that, at any rate, had become clear when the coal dust had been washed from his face—and the name he gave, Claus Karimon, suggested that his nationality was the same as that of the master of the *Dorcas,* Meesman. But he would bring no charges against the Eurasian; all

Murdo's attempts at persuasion met with a polite but adamant refusal.

"Is all a mistake, *mijnheer*. I ran away, then I change my mind and wish to stay, and the *kapitein* is angry and tie me up."

"Did you stow away—did you go on board without the master's knowledge, Claus?" Murdo asked.

The boy shook his head. "No, I not do that. Please, *mijnheer*, there is mail ship that goes to River Hawkesbury, is there not? I have no money, but if I work for you, *mijnheer*, perhaps you will give me money for fare? I am wanting to go to Alice Cox and her husband, who is Reverend Cox—I am wanting to go to their school in Windsor Town. I stay there with Mrs. Alice Cox and not again run away. . . ."

The mention of the name Alice Cox—Alice Fairweather—temporarily distracted Murdo's attention from what the boy was saying. Even now he felt a stab of regret as he recalled how deeply he had been affected by her courage and beauty, when first she had arrived in Sydney on the convict transport. And later, after his return from Moreton Bay, when Justin had introduced them, he had barely been able to hide his feelings. Of course he had been surprised to discover it was she who had written the Alcestis letter—surprised and, yes, disappointed to learn that she was now Mrs. Nathan Cox. But she seemed happy, married to an admirable young clergyman, and it was no use dwelling on lost opportunities. Murdo looked down at the thin little half-caste and abandoned his interrogation.

The boy's desired destination seemed, on the face of it, the best place for him. Alice—Mrs. Cox—could no doubt be relied upon to care for him, and if he would not give evidence against Meesman or accuse him of abduction, there was no point in detaining him. It chanced that the Hawkesbury mail packet was due to sail on her fortnightly passage upriver that day, and Murdo saw the boy on board after making his report to Major Morisett, who concurred with his decision.

"You will have enough evidence to convict that scoundrel Meesman without calling the boy, I agree. And he would probably complicate matters, if he's unwilling to bring charges. Besides, he's a Javanese half-caste, is he not, and little more than a child? The court would be unlikely to give his evidence much credence, in any event— let him go, Dean. Meesman will get ten years, even if he tries to claim he's Dutch—his vessel is Sydney registered, and his crew are mostly convicts or ticket-of-leave men. You did well to catch the rogues."

It was not until a week later, when George De Lancey returned from Sydney, that Murdo solved the mystery of Claus Karimon's identity.

"He is the late Major Josef Van Buren's son," De Lancey told him, when the court adjourned for lunch. "And his heir. Ironically, that means, under the terms of his father's will—which I have just had translated—that Claus is the legitimate owner of the *Dorcas,* as well as of the Van Buren residence in Sydney and another vessel."

"Which was why he was abducted?" Murdo suggested.

"I think there is no doubt of that," De Lancey confirmed gravely.

"But who was responsible? Surely not Meesman, on his own?"

"No—I imagine he was well paid for doing it. And he probably was not averse to undertaking the task—he's a dyed-in-the-wool rogue. He would have succeeded in it, too, if he hadn't let his avariciousness get the better of him and waited to sell his liquor here. Ships aren't usually searched in this port, are they?"

Murdo shook his head. "Only if they invite suspicion, Judge." He hesitated, his curiosity now aroused, and George De Lancey answered his unvoiced question.

"This is strictly between ourselves, Michael. But . . . the person who paid Meesman had good reason for it, and although I am the executor of Van Buren's will, I do not anticipate that, in law, I shall ever be able to prove who that person was."

"Not prove it!" Murdo echoed indignantly. "But for the Lord's sake, sir, if you know who it was, then surely it can be proved?"

"I am reasonably certain I know who it was, my dear fellow. However—" De Lancey's tone was dry. "I also know the boy Claus, who *could* provide proof but who is most unlikely to do so. He refused to bring any charges against Meesman, did he not, on your own admission? Well, his reason for refusing was simple—*he* knows who paid to have him kidnapped, but he has no intention of bringing the guilty party to justice. And Meesman will not talk, since he is not being charged with kidnapping."

"But why should the boy protect the guilty party?" Murdo persisted, far from satisfied with De Lancey's dry legal explanation.

"Because he's loyal, Michael. He has no vice in him, and I was a witness to his courage, when he and his father were wrecked off Cape Hawke in Justin Broome's *Flinders*." De Lancey smiled at the memory, and then his smile faded. "All his life, the poor little devil has been treated as a servant in the Van Buren household—his father never acknowledged him. Until now, that's to say. But Claus does not know about the will."

"You're going to tell him, surely?"

"Of course. I shall send my clerk to Windsor by the next mail boat, to acquaint the lad with his good fortune— that is my duty as executor. What he does will be up to him. But in the meanwhile, he will be safe enough with the Reverend and Mrs. Cox, I imagine." De Lancey rose and reached for his wig. "We're due back in court, Michael. And if the jury of your fellow officers bring in the expected verdict, then I shall take satisfaction in sentencing Meesman and his crew of rogues to hard labor. The *Dorcas* will have to be impounded, but her release can be effected when Claus Van Buren claims her, as, in due course, he will be entitled to." He moved to the door. "Ready?"

Murdo prepared to follow him. It was, he supposed, the only possible outcome in the circumstances, but . . . His mouth hardened in a frown as he recalled the state in which the frightened boy had been found in the *Dorcas*'s filthy hold, the gag in his mouth and the cruel ropes biting into his flesh.

As far as he himself was concerned, he had no knowledge of the Van Burens, and he had spent too little time in Sydney to be conversant with the town's current gossip. He knew Abigail Dawson, of course—knew and liked her and her family, but . . . there was also a sister, a sister who had been supposed lost at sea off Timor but who had survived and returned as . . . yes, returned as the wife of Major Josef Van Buren.

"Is there not—" he asked, halting by the door into the courtroom, "Judge De Lancey, is there not a widow, a Mrs. Van Buren?"

"Yes," De Lancey answered readily. "There is indeed, Michael—the boy's stepmother, Lucy Van Buren." He laid a hand on Murdo's scarlet-clad shoulder and said quietly, "What the law can do is strictly limited, in a matter of this kind. But as the late Josef Van Buren's executor, I shall endeavor to ensure that justice is done to all who are concerned—not least to his widow, I assure you. Now—" He gestured to the door. "Let us go—we have work to do."

In obedience to the court usher's summons, the lawyers and the military jury rose, the accused were jerked to their feet by their jailers, and De Lancey took his place on the bench, gravely responding to the bows that greeted him.

Murdo, who had given his evidence before the recess, found a seat and waited for Sergeant Lee to be sworn. Outside it was raining heavily, and thunder rumbled in the distance; a vivid flash of lightning lit the shadowed courtroom, and the usher went hurriedly to close the window above the bench.

"You are John Francis Lee, serving in the New South Wales Veteran Corps in the rank of sergeant?" the prosecuting attorney began. He took the sergeant briskly through his evidence, Lee replying woodenly to the questions.

When, however, they reached the account of the arrest of Meesman and his landing party and the subsequent search of the ship, honest indignation got the better of the veteran sergeant.

"We found no contraband liquor on board—no, sir. But we found a young lad in the hold, Your Honor. Trussed up like a chicken, he were, an' nigh to breathing his last. . . ." His description was graphic and openly accusing, and as it continued, there was a hurried and low-voiced altercation between Meesman and his counsel. The young defense lawyer rose to his feet.

"Your Honor, I must take exception to this line of questioning. Captain Meesman has not been charged with any offense against this boy, and neither has any member of his ship's company. I have, sir, a letter from the widow of the ship's owner, Mrs. Van Buren, delivered to the captain prior to his sailing from Port Jackson. The letter gives him instructions concerning the boy, who is named as Claus Karimon. I beg Your Honor's indulgence and permission to read it to the court, since it clears Captain Meesman of any suspicion of having abducted him."

George De Lancey gave permission, his expression unchanged, and Murdo listened intently, straining his ears to hear above the claps of thunder overhead and the splashing of heavy rain on the courthouse roof. The letter was brief and, he realized, appeared to clear its writer of complicity, even more effectively than it cleared the master of the *Dorcas* of a kidnapping charge. And the boy was no stowaway.

Mrs. Van Buren had instructed Meesman that the boy, Claus Karimon, was to be given passage in the *Dorcas* to Coupang, *"there to be repatriated at his own request and in accordance with the wishes of his late father."* There was no suggestion of coercion, no instructions that the boy was to be held under restraint, but the letter ended: *"He is, as you know, a high-spirited and mischievous boy and should not be permitted to interfere with the smooth running of your ship or to give orders to your crew."*

"He was larking about, sir," Meesman said from the dock, his tone aggrieved. "Making a racket on deck. I had him tied up and put in the hold, but I swear, sir—Your Honor—and my men'll swear that he had not been down there above an hour. We'd have let him go free, as soon as we finished our business ashore. I said he stowed away 'cause I was scared, sir, and—"

"Address your remarks to me through counsel, Captain Meesman," George De Lancey ordered sternly. To the prosecuting counsel, he said formally, "Since the Crown has made no charge against the accused in relation to the boy, and he has made none, be so good as to confine Sergeant Lee's evidence to the charges they are facing, Mr. Ridley. Proceed, if you please."

The barrister bowed, and an hour later the hearing came to a close. The military jury took only twenty minutes for their deliberations, before finding the accused guilty on all the charges brought against them.

Outside, the storm continued unabated, with vivid flashes of lightning illuminating the leaden sky. Murdo shivered as he listened to the sentences being pronounced. What manner of woman, he wondered, was Mrs. Lucy Van Buren to act as she had toward an innocent boy of perhaps fourteen?

An avaricious one, certainly; a woman lacking a conscience and devoid of moral scruples, it seemed—and as unlike her sister Abigail as it was possible for a woman to be.

But the news that reached him, when he went to report to the commandant on the outcome of the trial, put all other thoughts from his mind.

"I have received orders in the mail from Sydney concerning you, Mr. Dean," Major Morisset told him. He permitted himself a wintry smile. "I fancy they will please you. You are to proceed to Sydney at once to join an exploratory expedition led by Mr. Hume and the Governor's military secretary, Captain Sturt. I understand that your orders come at the behest of Mr. Hume—you've served under his leadership before, I suppose?''

"Yes, sir, I have," Murdo confirmed eagerly. He was soaked to the skin, and the thunder was still rumbling in the distance, but that was of no account. He left the commandant's office and plunged again into the rain-wet darkness, his heart singing. The Veteran Corps and its land grant could wait, he told himself happily, and Judge De Lancey could be relied upon to deal with the boy Claus and the woman who had sought to rob him of his inheritance. For him stretched the allure of the unknown, and it was irresistible. . . .

CHAPTER XXVI

The storm, growing in violence, broke over Sydney and Parramatta in the late afternoon.

Lucy Van Buren had left in her carriage when Sydney was still bathed in warm autumn sunshine and only a few heavy black clouds in the northern sky hinted at what was to come. The carriage, with its pair of speedy, high-stepping hackneys, had traveled almost ten miles along the turnpike road to Parramatta when, with scarcely any warning, the storm clouds burst.

To the accompaniment of vivid flashes of lightning and reverberating claps of thunder, rain fell in a torrent, flooding the road ahead and drenching Samuel Larkin and his wife, Leah, who were seated together on the box.

They had been wed the previous day, and Leah was wearing the best dress she owned and was bedecked in various small pieces of finery given to her by her fellow servants. Across her shoulders was draped a colorful embroidered shawl from Saleh, but Leah realized to her chagrin that, for all its beauty, the garment was too light and flimsy to withstand the assault of the driving rain. She cried out in dismay, and Samuel Larkin pulled up the horses in the shelter of a clump of trees. Both animals were frightened and restive, and he held them still with difficulty.

"Get down, lass," he bade his shivering bride, "and ask madam to let you ride inside with her. You can't stay outside in this."

"*Mevrouw* will not permit me to ride with her, Samuel," Leah objected.

"Ask her," Larkin growled. "Go on, do as I say. I don't want you catching your death of cold when we're only just wed."

His words were drowned by the crashing thunder, but the push he gave her made his meaning clear. With trepidation, Leah slid down from her seat; her head bent low beneath the dripping shawl, she stumbled back to the door of the carriage and, after two attempts, managed to open it.

"Well?" Within the carriage it was warm and dry, but in spite of this, Leah saw only that her mistress was angry, and instinctively she recoiled.

"If you please, *mevrouw*," she stammered nervously. "I—I mean Samuel—"

Mrs. Van Buren cut her short. "Why has he stopped?" she demanded. "We are quite close to Portland Place—it will take us perhaps half an hour to reach shelter. Tell Larkin to drive on."

"Y-yes, *mevrouw*. But he sent me to ask that I might ride inside the carriage with you. It is very bad outside, and I am very wet. And also cold, *mevrouw*."

Lucy Van Buren regarded her with distaste.

"Certainly not," she returned, in a tone that brooked no argument. "I cannot have you in here in such a state . . . you will damage the seat cushions. Go back to your husband and bid him drive on."

Leah knew better than to protest. She closed the carriage door and splashed back to the front of the vehicle, her thinly clad feet now as wet and sodden as her body.

"Samuel, she say no. You are to drive on," she called up to him wretchedly. Larkin swore.

"The poxy bitch! Well, we'll see about that, by God we will! I'm not drivin' anywhere, not until you're out of the wet. Whoa, there, you sons o' Satan—hold still!" he yelled at the horses, and, the reins looped over his arm, he jumped down angrily from the box. In his haste he landed awkwardly, falling against the hindquarters of one of the horses and grabbing its traces to save himself from the muddy road.

The spirited creature, already alarmed by the noise of the storm and the hissing lightning, took fright. It reared up, jerking the reins from Larkin's grasp, and before he could recover his wits, both animals were off, whinnying their terror as they hurtled down the flooded road, the carriage careering from side to side in their wake as they gathered speed.

"Oh, Gawd!" Larkin exclaimed hoarsely. He started to run, knowing that there was little hope of catching his fleeing charges but compelled, in spite of it, to try. Leah followed him, sobbing.

Inside the carriage, Lucy was flung from her seat and hurled this way and that as the cumbersome vehicle lurched sickeningly over the ruts in the road. Suddenly, horrifyingly, a memory was dredged up from the limbo of the past—a memory that, for years, she had sought to erase from her mind. She had been very young, a girl of barely seventeen, and Henrietta Dawson—Timothy's first wife—had accused her of wantonness and, as punishment, had elected to take her to her sister's farm on the Hawkesbury and to an exile she had dreaded.

They had been in Henrietta's carriage on that occasion, and the horses had bolted, just as they were bolting now, and . . . Icy fingers of fear clutched at Lucy's heart as she relived the terrible moment when the carriage had turned over. Henrietta had been crushed, pinned down beneath the shattered floorboards of the wrecked equipage, and horribly injured. And the unfortunate woman had screamed— she had screamed and screamed and gone on screaming. She . . .

Beyond Lucy's vision, a great, gnarled tree branch was struck by lightning. Already hollow and rotten, it crashed down onto the road, blocking it completely. The runaway carriage horses saw and heard it fall, but they were too close and galloping too fast to be able to stop in time. Both made a gallant attempt to leap over the obstacle, but with their harness and the shaft of the carriage holding them back, they stumbled and fell on the far side of the branch. The carriage itself hit the branch and turned over, and Lucy was flung with appalling force against the splintered wood and smashed glass of what had once been the left side door.

Once again she heard the agonized screams that went on and on and did not stop. She had silenced them, all those years ago, by thrusting a seat cushion into Henrietta's face and holding it there, but now— Desperately, Lucy sought to free herself. Her strength ebbed away; the ghastly, unpalatable memory faded and was gone; and as she sank into merciful unconsciousness, she knew that the screams she had heard had been not Henrietta's but her own.

Larkin was still fifty yards from the wrecked carriage when a flash of lightning illuminated the scene with hideous clarity. He halted, breathing hard and shocked into immobility, and then, forcing his leaden limbs to obey him, he stumbled on, muttering obscenities under his breath.

This would be the end for him, he thought—for him and Leah both, if their mistress was still alive. She would never forgive either of them—he would be sent to one of the chain gangs, Leah to the Female Factory. For the accident had been his fault; he would be blamed for letting the blasted horses go, and a convict accused of anything of the kind had no defense, as he knew only too well.

He reached the overturned carriage, and a glance sufficed to show him that both his horses had been killed. Poor brutes, they had had no chance, with the carriage a deadweight, dragging them down as they had jumped. Unmanly tears filled his eyes as he looked down at them. Barney and Betsy they had been called, and in the short time that he had looked after them, he had come to love them. But . . . he would have to climb into the carriage, he knew. He would have to see what fate had befallen Mrs. Van Buren. Larkin waited, his heart thudding, and then, to his intense relief, the dripping figure of Leah appeared, stumbling toward him, breathless and sobbing wildly.

"Pull yourself together, lass," he urged. "And go see what's happened to Mrs. Van Buren."

"*I* should do that? Oh, no, Samuel, I cannot!" Leah's English was poor, and her teeth were chattering so violently that Larkin was hard put to it to understand her. But her headshake was clear enough, and he took her by the shoulders, dislodging the sodden shawl.

"You're a woman—'twouldn't be proper for me. In you go—come on, I'll lift you. She must be a goner—I can't hear her hollering out."

Another thunderclap drowned his words, but ignoring his wife's feeble objections, Larkin managed to open the door atop the overturned vehicle, and seizing Leah in his muscular arms, he lifted her bodily into the interior of the wrecked carriage.

She was gone for what seemed to him a long time, and though he listened intently, he could hear no sound of voices. At last his wife's pale, shocked face appeared in the window aperture, and she signed to him to open the door and help her out. He did so, and holding her, his fingers biting into the flesh of her thin, bare arms, he demanded to know what she had found.

"She's dead, ain't she? Mrs. Van Buren's dead?"

"Now she is," Leah managed. "But—"

"What d'you mean, girl? Weren't she dead when you got to her?"

"No. Dying, yes—but first she speak to me. Claus, she say—the boy Claus—"

"Well, what of 'im?" Larkin shook her. "Tell me what she said, for pity's sake!"

Leah clung to him, sobs racking her, and, relenting, he took her into his arms and spoke more gently. "There now, lass, calm yourself. Just tell me what she said about Claus."

Leah looked up at him with anxious, tear-filled eyes.

"*Mevrouw* said bring Claus back to Sydney. Her last wish, she say—she did wrong to him. He must not go to Timor."

"Well, he's on his way now," Larkin asserted grimly. "It's a mite too late to bring the poor little devil back." He shrugged resignedly. "I seen to that, on *her* orders. There weren't nothin' about it in the note she give me for the master o' the *Dorcas*. *I* was to tell him, when I took the boy on board, that there'd be an 'andsome reward awaitin' when he come back from Coupang without the boy. The late Major Van Buren's wish, she said it was, that Claus was to go back there; but me and Cap'n Meesman, we had to drag him down to the hold an' tie him up. He didn't want to go, poor young wretch. Why—" But the shivering girl in his arms was not listening, and he broke off, swearing under his breath. "That's what it cost me to wed you, lass," he told her softly and held out his hand, spinning her round to face away from the wrecked carriage and its tragic burden.

"Come along," he bade her. "We'll have to walk to Parramatta and report what's happened. We'd best keep quiet about Claus. It's done now, and the one who done it can't talk, can she?"

Leah glanced back at the carriage and then, still sobbing, took his hand.

Alice looked down at Claus's small, dark head, an affectionate smile on her lips. He was, she thought proudly, the most willing and certainly the most diligent of Nathan's pupils, and he was making commendable progress with the curriculum of the junior class.

"He wants to learn," Nathan had said of him. "So many of them don't—they come to school only because their parents compel them to. Claus comes with enthusiasm."

It was almost three weeks since the boy had appeared at the door of the schoolhouse, unheralded and with only the clothes he stood up in, with a plea that he might stay and no explanation whatsoever as to how he had come to leave Sydney. Alice knew that he had arrived in the Hawkesbury mail ship from—of all places—Newcastle and the Hunter River, and that an officer had paid his fare, but . . . apart from singing the praises of Lieutenant Dean, who had apparently befriended him, he had told her nothing.

"Better I do not," he had said gravely. "It might make much trouble. I am here, and I go to your school. I work for you and your man of God, dear Alice, and never go from here for very long time. All right?"

"But of course it is all right," she had assured him warmly. "I invited you, did I not? And Nathan will be as happy to have you as I am. After all, we should never have met if it hadn't been for you, should we?"

True to his promise, Claus had worked. Alice had her hands full now, and, to her joy, she was pregnant, the arrival of her firstborn expected in two months' time. The Cartwrights had left Windsor and gone to Liverpool, to a fine new church and a better-paid living, and until a new rector was appointed, Nathan conducted services in the parish, in addition to running the church school. To help him, Alice had started to teach elementary subjects to the younger children and lately had organized sewing and millinery classes for some of the older girls.

It was a full life and a busy one, but both she and Nathan were ideally happy, the unpleasant memory of their brief sojourn on Norfolk Island at last beginning to fade, if it could never be entirely forgotten. She had written no more letters to the *Australian*—the Church Schools Corporation's board of governors had left her in no doubt of the consequences were she to do so, and in the interests of Nathan's future in the colony, she had bowed to their wishes. Rumor had it, in any case, that the newly appointed commandant of the Norfolk Island penal settlement was insisting on taking his wife and family with him to the island, and that, Alice had decided, might, God willing, lead to the return of the prisoners' wives in the not too distant future.

"What are you writing, Claus?" she asked, mildly curious. "Is it an exercise for the class?" He was so absorbed in his task that he did not hear her, and she had to repeat the question.

"No." He shook his head. "I write a letter to Saleh. He cannot read English, but perhaps he will find someone to read it for him."

"Is that to tell him you are here?"

"That is so." Claus added a few more words, with painstaking care, and then passed his letter to her. "See, Alice—it is the first letter I ever write in my life."

The wording was simple, the letters large but neatly formed, and the little boy flushed with pleasure when Alice praised its clarity.

"I am making progress?"

"Indeed you are, Claus. Wonderful progress!"

He held out his hand for the sheet of ruled school paper and folded it before giving it back to her. "Please to send it by the next mail to Sydney. I can pay the cost. I earned one shilling for chopping logs for *Mevrouw*—I mean Mrs. Carter and the head constable."

Alice accepted letter and money. Claus, she already knew from experience, had his pride; he took nothing without paying, in any way he could, and had almost certainly delayed the writing of his letter to Saleh until he had earned the cost of mailing it.

"I would have written to Saleh as soon as you arrived here, had you allowed me to, Claus," she reproached him gently. "But you said that no one must be told where you were."

"Yes. Yes, I know." He looked ashamed. "But I feared—that is, I thought that *Mevrouw* Van Buren might find out and take me away from you. I thought best to wait till she think I am far from Sydney and then tell Saleh. Saleh is very good man, you know. I trust him always."

So Mrs. Van Buren *had* been responsible for his mysterious arrival in Newcastle, Alice thought, studying the boy's small, intelligent face with concern. She remembered the

previous attempt, made by Major Van Buren, to send
Claus to Timor. He had run away then, but surely Mrs.
Van Buren had not sought to follow her husband's example?
What possible reason could she have had? Her husband
was dead, and there were odd rumors as to the manner of
his death, but Claus had said nothing of that, either, and
she had hesitated to ask questions. No doubt, in his own
good time, he would tell her; now, since he evidently
wished to keep his own counsel, it might be wisest to
probe no deeper.

Claus sprang to his feet, beaming at her. "I go to make
tea. Soon Mr. Cox coming back from school and thirsty,
like always, from so much talking. You stay, do mending
if you wish, but rest a little, not? I am here, like elder son,
to take care of you."

Alice echoed his smile and did not raise any objection.
It had been a long day, and she was tired, the child in her
womb growing heavier. She pulled her mending basket
toward her but did not open it, hearing footsteps outside
and the sound of voices.

"I think Nathan has brought a guest," she called after
Claus's retreating back. "Make a big pot of tea, will you
please? And we could have some of my walnut cake."

"I see to it, do not worry," Claus promised. He skipped
happily away, and Nathan came in, accompanied by a tall,
dark-haired young man whose sober dress suggested that
he followed a clerkly calling. He was a stranger, Alice
realized, and she rose in some confusion, smoothing her
crumpled skirt.

Nathan planted a kiss on her cheek and gestured to the
newcomer. "This is Mr. Rodney Akeroyd, my love, clerk
to His Honor Judge De Lancey . . . my wife, sir. Mr.
Akeroyd has just come in with the mail carrier, from
Newcastle, and he desires to see Claus, for whom he has
some quite remarkable news. But let us sit down, shall
we?"

Akeroyd bowed courteously and took the chair Nathan
had indicated. "I am here on behalf of Justice De Lancey,

Mrs. Cox. As you are probably aware, the boy Claus Van
Buren——'' Alice's eyes widened in surprise at his use of
the surname, but Rodney Akeroyd appeared to notice nothing amiss, and he went on, ''Claus Van Buren was found
on board a vessel bound for Batavia, which called at
Newcastle to take on a cargo of coal. He had seemingly
been held under somewhat brutal restraint, in the ship's
hold, from which he was released and restored to liberty
by the officer commanding the port authority military
guard—a Lieutenant Dean, ma'am. As I understand it, Mr.
Dean then sent him here to you, at his own specific
request?''

''Yes,'' Alice confirmed. ''Claus came here. I—that is
we——'' She glanced at Nathan, who smilingly nodded.
''We had told him that there would be a home for him
with us if ever he needed it. I suppose—I mean, after what
he suffered on board that trading vessel, he decided to
come to us. We didn't know——'' Again she glanced uncertainly at her husband. ''Claus never said a word about his
ordeal to us. But did the ship's master . . . I don't know
the legal term for it——''

''Abduct him, Mrs. Cox?'' the judge's clerk supplied.
''That was what was generally believed, but the master,
whose name is Meesman, cleared himself of suspicion
when he and his crew were brought before Justice De
Lancey. Meesman had a letter of authority from the ship's
owner, you see, stating that the boy was returning to the
Dutch Indies in accordance with his own and his late
father's wishes.''

Mrs. Van Buren, Alice thought, suddenly sickened. *She*
would be the owner of the ship, following Major Van
Buren's death, and undoubtedly she had—for whatever
reason—attempted to rid herself of Claus.

Dimly she heard the clerk add, ''Meesman was found
guilty on a number of other charges and was sentenced to
ten years' hard labor. But——'' He cleared his throat, and
reaching into a small valise he carried, drew out some
papers. ''The reason I have been sent here, Mrs. Cox,

is—as I informed your husband—to acquaint Claus with some extremely good news. He—"

Claus himself came into the room, bearing a tray of tea things, and Akeroyd broke off. The boy set down his tray, looking anxiously to Alice for approval, and having received a reassuring nod, he was about to slip away when Nathan gently bade him wait.

"This gentleman has come to speak with you, Claus. His name is Mr. Rodney Akeroyd, and he is clerk to Judge De Lancey. He has brought you good news. Sit down, lad, and hear what he has to say."

Claus hesitated, his eyes wide with alarm at the mention of a judge's name, and then he went instinctively to Alice to seat himself, cross-legged, at her feet.

"This," the judge's clerk said, holding up a sheaf of papers, "is a translation of the last will and testament of the late Major Van Buren. He appointed Justice De Lancey his executor, and His Honor had the translation made from the original, which was in the Dutch language, prepared, signed, and witnessed in Batavia. The original document was delivered to my keeping in the judge's chambers in Sydney just prior to Major Van Buren's—er—unhappy demise."

"Come to the point, Mr. Akeroyd," Nathan advised. "This is all a mite beyond the boy's comprehension."

"I am bound to give him an explanation, Reverend sir," Akeroyd defended aggrievedly. "However—" He turned to Claus. "In his will, young sir, Major Van Buren acknowledges his relationship to you. He has supplied copies of his marriage lines and your birth certificate, and he stated in his will that you are his legitimate son and his heir."

"But I—" Claus stared at him, openmouthed and visibly bewildered. "I do not deserve, I . . ."

"Hear what Mr. Akeroyd has to tell you, Claus," Alice advised. She slipped from her chair and knelt beside him, taking him in her arms, feeling him tremble. "Your father is only trying to put right the wrong he did you."

"Indeed, that is so," Akeroyd confirmed. "Permit me to read from the will." He paused, peering at his sheaf of papers, and then read out solemnly, " 'In this, my last will and testament, I wish to make reparation to my son Claus—known as Karimon, which was his mother's name—for having, throughout his life, denied him the right to claim me as his father. It is my wish that he should henceforth take the name of Van Buren and bear it always. To Claus Van Buren, therefore, I bequeath everything of which I die possessed, which shall include my trading vessels and the profits I have earned from them, deposited in my name in the Bank of New South Wales. Also the house in Bridge Street, in the township of Sydney, New South Wales, my nautical instruments, my weapons and my wearing apparel—' "

Claus emitted a strangled cry, and Rodney Akeroyd eyed him reproachfully.

"You will be very rich, my young sir," he pointed out. "And I should be happy were I in your shoes, as would many others, I fancy. Ah—there is more, if you will permit me to continue." His gaze returned to the paper in his hand. "Your father makes a request, and he charges his executor to ensure that it is carried out equitably. He says, and I quote: 'I ask my son to make provision for the household servants I brought with me from Java, in particular for the majordomo, Ibnu Saleh, and that he deal generously with the maidservant, Leah Hopal, in recognition of her devoted service to me.' " Again he cleared his throat, then continued. "As executor, young sir, His Honor Justice De Lancey has instructed me to tell you that he will give you all the necessary advice and assistance you may require in carrying out the late Major Van Buren's wishes regarding his servants."

Claus managed a nervous smile, and Alice's arms tightened about him. Nathan, sensing the strain the boy was under, crossed to the neglected tray and started to pour out tea. "I think we can all do with this," he said. "A cup for you, Mr. Akeroyd? And some of my wife's walnut cake—I can assure you, it is excellent.''

"Thank you, sir, that will be most welcome. But—'' The conscientious young clerk again delved into his valise. "There is just one other matter. This letter, Master Van Buren, was attached to your father's will. It is addressed to you, and as you will observe, the seal is unbroken. No doubt you will wish to read it in private. I will wait until you have done so, and then, having ascertained your wishes in regard to your inheritance, I will return to Newcastle by the mail packet and inform Justice De Lancey. His Honor will be in Sydney in two weeks' time, and he has instructed me to request that you meet him there for consultation.''

Claus took the letter and turned bewildered eyes to Alice's face. He looked stricken, and supposing this to be because they both knew that he had not yet progressed sufficiently far with his reading lessons to be able to decipher the letter, she put in quickly, "We will go to your room, Claus, and you may read your letter there.''

She held out both hands to him, and the boy assisted her to her feet. When they were alone and the door closed behind them, Claus's control deserted him, and he started to sob. They were heartbroken sobs, Alice realized, his grief adult in its intensity, and she sat on the edge of his bed, not knowing how to console him. That he was deeply troubled was evident; he had no joy in his unexpected good fortune—rather, it seemed, he regretted the news that Judge De Lancey's messenger had brought him.

After a while, his tears ceased and he sat up, regarding her shamefacedly. "Alice, I cannot take that which my—my father has willed to me. His ships—the house, money that is in the bank. The house—it is the house of my father's wife; I would not take it from her . . . I *could* not! She think I do—that is why she try to send me back to Coupang in the *Dorcas* . . . because she afraid that I rob her. And my father . . . oh, Alice, I betrayed my father! I did not keep silent; I told what he had done—I told *her, Mevrouw*

Van Buren. And he die—he take his life because of what I tell her.''

Under Alice's gentle prompting, the whole unhappy story came out, in garbled words, punctuated by the boy's bitter weeping. She was shocked and appalled, both by the events he related and by the effect these had had on the boy himself. When, at last, he came to the end of his revelations, a torrent of sobs overwhelmed him, and still unable to find words, Alice could only hold his small, trembling body in her arms in a vain attempt to comfort him.

Nathan, she thought despairingly, Nathan would know, so much better than she, what counsel to offer, what advice to give, and she was on the point of calling him when she remembered the as-yet-unread letter.

"Claus dear," she offered diffidently, "shall we read the letter your father left for you? Shall we read it together?"

He shivered. "My father hate me," he whispered brokenly. "Always he hate me, and *Mevrouw* Van Buren also. Both of them try to send me away, back to Coupang."

"Perhaps, in his heart, he loved you, Claus," Alice suggested, but—recalling the manner in which Major Van Buren had treated his son—she spoke without conviction, and the little boy looked up at her sadly.

"You know he did not, Alice. No one love me—only you. And Saleh, of course, and my mother. No one else."

"Nathan does."

"He man of God, love everyone," Claus pointed out unanswerably. "My letter, if you please. I take it."

Defeated, Alice gave him back the letter. "Don't you want me to read it to you?"

Claus shook his head. "I keep it, Alice. When I can read it myself, then is time to learn what my father said. Please, let us go now to tell Mr. Akeroyd that I do not want anything my father willed to me. Let *Mevrouw* Van Buren have all, save only what should be given to Saleh and Leah. I stay here with you and Reverend Nathan—

learn reading lessons, learn to speak like you. I happy here with you, Alice.''

Alice could not dissuade him, and when they rejoined Nathan and Mr. Akeroyd, the boy remained adamant, despite the clerk's reasoned arguments and his attempts to invoke legal precedents. He took his leave at last, in order to catch the mail packet, having extracted the reluctant promise from Nathan that he would arrange for Claus to go to Sydney to see and talk the matter over with Judge De Lancey.

In the following days, things continued much as they had before, with Claus applying himself assiduously to his school lessons, working about the house and garden and in the township during his free time, but obstinately refusing to talk of his father's will or to prepare himself for the promised journey to Sydney. Alice felt only compassion for him, aware of the tension under which he was laboring, but as Nathan reminded her, compassion was not enough.

''He must go to Sydney, my love—we both know we should not keep him here. Judge De Lancey will advise him—we cannot.''

It was true, Alice recognized, yet she was reluctant to force the boy, against his will, to go. Mrs. Van Buren was in Sydney, and . . . She dared not put her fears into words.

''Then I will go with him,'' she ventured. ''He cannot go alone, and you cannot leave the school.''

''The journey will be too much for you, in your condition, my dearest,'' Nathan continued. ''If necessary, I will close the school for a week and accompany him. As you say, he cannot go alone.''

With that she had to be satisfied. But then, ten days after the visit of Judge De Lancey's clerk, Saleh appeared, driving a hired curricle. He told them of Mrs. Van Buren's death, making the announcement without emotion, but Claus, when he heard it, stood stiff and rigid, every vestige of color draining from his cheeks.

"She is *dead*? The wife of my father is dead?" he echoed, seemingly unable to believe it.

Saleh gravely described the accident. "Leah was at her side as she breathed her last," he ended. "And her last words were of you, little *lip-lap*. The wife of your father said that you must be brought back to Sydney. 'He must not go to Timor' was what she told Leah. I find out you are here, not in Timor, when your letter come."

It was, Alice thought as she watched him, as if an unbearable weight had been lifted from Claus's thin shoulders. His face lit up, and his dark eyes lost the haunted look that had filled them for so long.

"Then I go back to Sydney," he said. "I go with Saleh, and I talk with Judge De Lancey concerning my father's will. My father will me his house and his ships, Saleh, and also money for you and Leah."

Saleh betrayed no surprise. He took the boy's hand and bore it to his forehead.

"I make salaam to my new master," he offered solemnly. "And I will take him back to his house."

When the time came, early next morning, to make her farewells, Alice did so with a light heart. Claus was in good hands, she knew, and the big, unhappy house in Bridge Street would no longer be a place that either of them need fear to enter.

"I will return to the Reverend Nathan's school," Claus promised, his thin young arms entwined about her neck as he reached up to hug her. "And then I read my father's letter. Perhaps it will say that he did not hate me so much as I fear. Perhaps he tell me he not sad that I am his son, and perhaps one day I can forget that I betray him."

"I only know," Alice whispered, feeling her eyes fill with tears, "that if I have a son, Claus, I hope he will be like you."

She stood, with Nathan's arm about her, to watch the curricle drive away, and heard her husband say softly, "I echo your hope, my dearest. If God should bless us with a son, I, too, pray he will be like that boy."

"And if it should be a daughter?" Alice asked, gently teasing.

Nathan laughed. "Why then, my sweet wife, I pray that her resemblance will be to you!"

CHAPTER XXVII

Justin stood on the lee side of the quarterdeck as H.M.S. *Success* nosed her way slowly into the Sydney Cove anchorage. The cove, he saw, held no ship wearing the French flag, and beside him, Major Edmund Lockyer emitted an undisguised sigh of satisfaction.

"The *Astrolabe* seems to have taken herself off, eh, Commander? I feared we might find her still here, not to mention her consorts. They'd vanished into thin air, of course, when I reached King George Sound, but I still had to go through the formality of claiming the land in the King's name . . . just in case. I don't trust the infernal French, never have."

"It's evident that the home government doesn't either," Justin responded. He put his glass to his eye, focusing it on his own small, white-painted waterfront cottage, and his feeling of well-being increased when he was able to make out Jessica's slim figure, waving from the garden.

It was three months since the *Success* had sailed on her exploratory expedition to the Swan River, on Australia's western coast, and he was glad to be home. Major Lockyer, who had been engaged in the arduous task of founding a new settlement, which he had named Frederick's Town, had been away six weeks longer. The *Success* had picked him up from King George Sound on the return passage, but he had spent most of his time in his cabin, trying to shake off the ill effects of a fever. Until now, Justin had scarcely spoken to him.

Following the direction of Justin's gaze, Lockyer smiled. "Your family?" he suggested. "Eager to greet you?"

"My wife, Major, my daughter, and—yes, my younger son." Justin lowered his glass, smiling too. "It's good to be back."

"This is your home, is it not? You were born here?"

"I was, sir, yes. My sons call themselves Australians, and with some pride, but I used to be called a currency kid when I was their age. It was something of a stigma then."

"But hardly one now, eh? You're a commander in the Royal Navy, and Captain Stirling says you served under Matthew Flinders in the *Investigator*. As a boy, presumably?"

Justin nodded, and the major went on thoughtfully, "Flinders surveyed the King George Sound, I believe, and noted that it was a superb harbor. Do you agree, Commander?"

"I do indeed. It is easy of access, landlocked, and more than adequately protected from all winds."

"Which," Lockyer put in shrewdly, "for all our revered Captain Stirling's enthusiasm, no anchorage in the vicinity of the Swan River can offer . . . that's so, is it not?"

But Justin was not to be drawn into criticizing his superior, and he grunted noncommittally. He did not, in fact, entirely share James Stirling's enthusiasm for the Swan River as site for a new settlement, for just the reason Lockyer had advanced. There were several possible anchorages for large vessels in the vicinity of the river, but all had disadvantages. The two nearest were unprotected from northwesterly winds; the best—named on the chart as Cockburn Sound—was some distance from the river; and entry to the river itself was rendered impractical and even hazardous by the presence of numerous reefs and sandbanks, and by a bar across its mouth.

Stirling had crossed the bar in his gig and later with two

boats, in order to explore the upper reaches of the Swan, and he maintained that the bar could be removed without difficulty, to give access to what, he was convinced, could become a harbor second to none.

Justin had accompanied the main party of explorers, spending ten days in an extensive examination of the country inland. His companions had been the botanist Lieutenant Belcher and young Jamie Willoughby, whose enthusiasm came close to matching that of their commander, but—as Major Lockyer had sensed—his own reaction had been tempered with caution. Perhaps as a seaman, he reflected, he had been more concerned with the danger to shipping a northwesterly gale might pose.

As if reading his thoughts, Lockyer observed, gesturing to the tall figure of the frigate's commander as the bower anchor splashed down into the blue, shimmering waters of the cove, "Whatever Stirling says, whatever extravagant claims he makes for his infernal Swan, there is no finer harbor in the world than this one. And Cook missed it! Well, I didn't miss the possibilities of King George Sound, and I'm quite sure Captain d'Urville didn't either."

He probably had not, Justin thought, although during the *Astrolabe*'s stay in Sydney, neither her urbane and courteous commander nor any of her officers had mentioned their lengthy visit to the site of the new British settlement . . . a matter of weeks prior to the arrival there of Major Lockyer and his detachment of troops and convicts.

"King George Sound is ideally situated as a port for whalers and sealers," Lockyer went on, his tone a trifle sour. He went into detail, and added emphatically, "And it's strategically placed to guard the southerly sea route for British ships plying to Hobart and Port Jackson, as you don't need me to tell you. I just hope to heaven I can convince the Governor that Frederick's Town must be given priority over Captain Stirling's nebulous plans for the Swan River. It's a thousand pities that I was unable to have Charles Sturt with me, as I wanted—Charles has His

Excellency's ear, and he's a damned persuasive talker. But perhaps I can send him there, before he goes off on the expedition he's so infernally keen on, with that fellow Hume. Unless he's already gone, of course.''

The topmen of the watch, their task of furling sail completed, came swarming back on deck, momentarily interrupting the conversation. Justin made to excuse himself, but Major Lockyer grasped his arm firmly and led him aside.

"Look," he said aggrievedly. "They're lowering the captain's gig. Stirling's going ashore—he wants to get in first with the Governor, I don't doubt."

"It is a courtesy, Major," Justin suggested mildly. "I can ask the officer of the watch to call away a boat for you, if you wish."

"I'm not ready yet," Lockyer retorted. "That infernal fever laid me so low I haven't got all my kit together."

"If you need assistance, sir, I'm sure—" Justin began, but his companion shook his head.

"No, there will be time enough. The assistance I need is, not to put too fine a point on it, Broome, yours. Your support, when I present my case to the Governor. You can give me that, can't you?" Reluctant to commit himself, Justin hesitated, and Lockyer asked unexpectedly, "What sort of fellow is Stirling? You've spent the past three months in his company, and I've not said more than two words to him. What's your opinion of him, eh?"

Faced with so direct a question, Justin was taken aback. He liked James Stirling very much, as a man, and there was no denying that he was a most competent sea officer. Now only thirty-six, Stirling had attained post rank nine years before and, as a young officer, had served in both the French and American wars. However, his obsession with the plan to found a settlement on the Swan River was, to Justin's mind, somewhat puzzling. Stirling had arrived with a plan already drawn up, and, within a week of the *Success*'s appearance in Sydney Cove, had persuaded the

Governor to authorize him to postpone the mission on which the Admiralty had sent him—which was the removal of the Melville Island settlement in the north to a more suitable location—and, instead, to permit him three months' grace, in order to make a survey of the Swan.

True, the wet season was not the best time to take a sailing ship into northern waters, but even so . . . Justin eyed his questioner uneasily, and Major Lockyer urged, a distinct edge to his voice, "I want the truth, Commander. It won't go any further, I give you my word."

"Well, Captain Stirling is a first-rate officer, and he is well liked and respected by his entire ship's company," Justin offered. "Indeed, sir, he's a most likable fellow, and—"

"Spare me your platitudes, damme!" Lockyer interrupted irritably. "I want to know *why* he's so infernally set on founding a settlement on the Swan. It's all to do with trade with India, isn't it?"

"That is Captain Stirling's main argument," Justin conceded. "And it is a sound argument. He calculates that vessels sailing to India could reach Madras in three weeks and be back at the Swan in a month. Java would be within ten days' sailing, and the Cape under six weeks. The prevailing winds, you see, sir, make such times possible. Furthermore, Captain Stirling believes that the convict transports, which almost always sail north after unloading their people here in Sydney or at Hobart, might well take the Indian Ocean eastern passage, pick up cargoes at the Swan, and then continue on to China. They are under charter to the East India Company, as you know, and they sail with their holds virtually empty to pick up tea cargoes in Canton."

"Ha!" Lockyer exclaimed. He thumped his hand down on the rail in front of him, casting a resentful glance at the assembled side-party, which was standing by, preparatory to piping their captain into his boat. "So that's it, is it! The East India Company—I should have guessed. Stirling's father-in-law—Mangles, James Mangles—is a director of the honorable company. Dammit, Broome, that's the answer—it *has* to be. Stirling has an interest in the Indian trade. He probably visualizes the Swan River as a second Singapore, with himself as Lieutenant Governor.''

"I don't believe—" Justin began, but the older man cut him short. He was smiling, his temper completely restored.

"Well, he's still got to go to Melville Island, hasn't he? That gives me time, by heaven! And I shall use it—I'm not going to stand by and do nothing and let Stirling use his influence with the East India Company nabobs to have Frederick's Town abandoned.''

He said no more about invoking Justin's support but stumped across to the after hatch, presumably to return to his cabin. Justin watched him go with some relief. He hoped that he could avoid controversy; he had accompanied the *Success* on her mission solely on account of his knowledge of the coastal waters to the west, and in all probability, his opinion would not be asked. James Stirling had Peter Belcher and the Sydney botanist Charles Fraser to call upon should any questions concerning the fertility of the soil arise, and the sailing master of the *Success*, an experienced officer, had worked unremittingly on his survey and charting of the available anchorages throughout their ten-day stay at the river mouth.

Perhaps Stirling's interest, so far as the East India Company was concerned, was, as Lockyer had suggested, a trifle suspect, but even if it were so, Justin decided, it was no affair of his. He had done what had been required of him, and after an absence of three months, he was anxious to return to the bosom of his family and to his own command. At his request, Lieutenant Barrett-Lennard, the officer of the watch, called a boat away for him, and he was rowed ashore.

In the garden, Jessica was waiting for him, with Red and Johnny, and the new baby—wonderously grown—in her arms.

"Oh, Justin!" she exclaimed eagerly. "It is so good to see you again." She lifted her face for his kiss, and with his arm about her slender waist, they went into the house together, Red leading the way and Johnny, forgetful of his dignity, clinging to his free hand.

They lingered long over their meal, exchanging news. Red demanded an account of the Swan River expedition, and Justin described it as graphically as he could, both boys hanging on his words.

"We ascended the river in two boats, eighteen of us. At the mouth, there were just barren downs and sandy beaches, but as we progressed farther upstream, the banks became very picturesque, bordered by lofty trees and bright green shrubs. Unfortunately we were frequently driven aground on mudflats, and one night, after dragging our boats for almost two miles, unable to find a channel, we had to bed down in them, too done in to continue."

"Did you meet any natives?" Red asked.

"Indeed we did. And they were the reverse of friendly, following us along on either bank, shouting and threatening us with their spears. However, they became less hostile when we threw them a swan we had shot, and eventually we were able to persuade them to accept a few gifts of clothing, which they appeared to find desirable. . . ." He talked on, both boys asking excited questions, and Jessica listening with interest.

"Would you want to settle there, Dad?" Johnny asked, when he came to the end of his recital.

Justin shook his head. "No, I don't think so. But it's good country, once one leaves the coastal area—well watered, with wooded hills and fine grassland, and an equable climate. Captain Stirling intends to go back, and several of the *Success*'s officers and men expressed a willingness to go with him." He smiled. "As earnest of their return, they left some livestock on an island at the mouth of the river—a cow, two ewes in lamb, and three goats, confident that they'll thrive and multiply in the interim. And they probably will—the island, which we called Garden Island, was well supplied with meadow grass and water. Here—'' He opened his valise. "These will give you an idea of what the country is like. Peter Belcher and the ship's surgeon, Dr. Clause, made sketches, and they gave me one or two, as souvenirs. And this is a chart I made of the anchorage in Cockburn Sound.''

Both boys pored over the sketches with growing interest.

''Dad,'' Johnny said, pointing to one of Dr. Clause's watercolors, ''he's painted the swans black. *Were* they black? I thought swans were white.''

''They were black,'' Justin confirmed. ''The river takes its name from them because they appear to be peculiar to the region. The first European to ascend the river was a Dutch captain, Willem de Vlamingh, about a hundred and thirty years ago, and he charted it as the River of the Black Swans. That was shortened to *Zwaan Rivier*. There are a great many Dutch names on the charts on the west and, of course, on the north coast of Australia. Portuguese and French, too, come to that, but mostly Dutch—a whole host of Dutch ships from Batavia explored the coastal regions during the last century, and Abel Tasman, of course, discovered Van Diemen's Land.''

''But they didn't stay,'' Red commented. ''Why not?''

''No,'' Justin answered, thinking of Major Lockyer. ''They didn't recognize Australia's possibilities, Red.''

And the British, he reflected wryly, had deemed it fit only for a penal colony. James Stirling, at least, saw it differently.

He passed the sketches to Jessica and questioned Red about his doings in the *Mermaid*.

''We took Captain Clunie and twenty capital respites to Moreton Bay, sir, and called at Newcastle on our return passage. Uncle Murdo came back to Sydney with us—he's joining a new exploratory party with Mr. Hume and Captain Sturt. I—'' He broke off, reddening.

''What is it, lad?'' Justin prompted.

He glanced across the table at Jessica, and she said, a glint of amusement in her eyes, "Like his father, I'm afraid, Red has the wanderlust. He was disappointed at not going with you to the Swan, and now he's got it into his head that he would like to join Murdo's expedition—that's so, isn't it, Red?"

Red's color deepened. "It's not that I don't like being at sea, Father. But—well, that is—"

"Carrying capital respites to Moreton Bay hardly fills the bill for you—is that what you're trying to tell me?"

The boy nodded, and Justin gave him an understanding smile. "How would you fancy joining a King's ship, son?"

"A *King's* ship, sir? You—you don't mean the *Success*? She'll be going north, won't she—to Melville Island?"

"Yes, she will—and I do mean the *Success*." Justin's smile widened. "I'm reasonably sure that it could be arranged. Captain Stirling is losing a mid—young James Willoughby has decided to quit the service and stay here. He wants to take over his brother's grant eventually, but he's very young and has no experience of farming. I promised him that I would ask Tim Dawson to have him at Upwey for a year or so, to serve his apprenticeship. Or perhaps Rick might be willing to take him on—Pengallon is near the Willoughby land. But the lad wants to stay in Sydney until his sisters and brother-in-law arrive. The brother-in-law is a doctor, whose eventual destination is New Zealand, but he's doing a temporary assignment in Van Diemen's Land and won't be here for a few weeks. In the meantime—" He paused, eyeing Jessica expectantly.

She sighed. "You offered Mr. Willoughby a home with us?"

"Only if Red takes his place as one of Captain Stirling's mids, my love. And I don't know—"

But Red's eyes were shining. "Sir, I'd jump at the chance! A King's ship and a cruise to Melville Island—the Barrier Reef and Endeavour Strait, the Gulf of Carpentaria!

They're places I've dreamed about, places you went to with Captain Flinders. I'd give my right hand to go.''

"Then I shall use all my powers of persuasion on Captain Stirling," Justin promised. "But—" Again his gaze was on Jessica's face, and it was to her he spoke, rather than to his son. "You would have to stay with the *Success*, Red. She'll be returning to England after she completes her mission and relieves the Melville Island garrison. And when she pays off, you would be dependent on Captain Stirling's patronage to help you find another ship. It could be any ship, on a three- or four-year commission, bound anywhere in the world."

Jessica drew in her breath sharply but said nothing, and Justin turned back to Red. "You had better take a little time to think about it, son. Because it will mean making your future career in the King's navy. You could be away for a long while."

"I don't need time, sir," Red began and then hesitated, his cheeks flushed. "So long as Mam is willing for me to go, I—it's what I've always wanted, only I never thought I'd be given the chance. It would be a—a wonderful chance, if Captain Stirling will accept me."

"Well?" Justin prompted. "What do you say, Jessie my love? Are you willing for him to go?"

Jessica looked from her husband to her son, her small, pale face devoid of expression, but Justin knew what it cost her to give her consent. She gave it, with neither hesitation nor reproach.

"It is your life, Red, your future—you must decide. If it is what you truly want, I will not stand in your way."

Red jumped to his feet and crossed to her side to hug her. He was just twelve years old, Justin thought, with a pang. He was so well grown and sturdy that he looked older, but . . . he was still only a boy, and they were allowing him to decide on his whole future. Perhaps it would have been wiser to wait before putting the proposition to him. Perhaps . . .

Red said, with complete conviction, "It truly is what I want, Mam, I—thanks. I'll come back, you know. You can depend on that—I'll *always* come back." He grinned. "I'm an Australian, aren't I?"

"Yes," his mother agreed, her voice tremulous. "You are an Australian, Red."

"Johnny—" Red grabbed his brother by the shoulders, hauling him from his chair. "Come on—you've finished, haven't you? Let's see if we can get a boat out to the *Success* and call on Willoughby and Keppel in the mids' berth, shall we?"

Johnny, nothing loath, went with him. Left alone, Jessica started to pile up the used crockery, but Justin shook his head at her and set her burden down.

"Not now, my love. Come and sit by the fire and tell me what's been going on in my absence. I've been away for three long months, you know."

"Yes," she echoed, with a hint of asperity. "And I've missed you for three long months. I ought to be accustomed to it by now, I know—but I'm not. And now I must face up to missing Red for . . . oh, God, Justin, for how long will it be? A year—two years, three?"

"I don't know," Justin was forced to admit. He took her into his arms and kissed her hungrily. "I've missed you, too, the Lord knows. I love you, Jessie—dear God, I love you! And the more for giving Red his chance, believe me. Because it is a fine chance—he'll be commissioned into the Royal Navy, in the fullness of time, and one day he may command his own King's ship. That could never happen if he stays here in the colonial service."

"No," she conceded. "I realize that."

Justin took her hand and led her to the two armchairs drawn up in front of the fire. They were both silent for a little while, and then, hearing the baby cry, Jessica excused herself and went to attend to her. When she returned, she was smiling, and she bent to kiss Justin's bent head before resuming her seat. As if by mutual but unspoken agreement, the subject of Red was excluded, and she talked of other matters.

"There are strong rumors that Governor Darling will shortly be recalled. In the last three months, Justin, he has added immeasurably to his unpopularity. The free press continues to attack him, and he has tried unsuccessfully to censor papers like the *Australian*. Chief Justice Forbes opposed him on every count, and lately he has resorted to bringing legal actions for slander and libel against individuals. He sued Mr. Edward Hall of the *Monitor* for seditious libel and not only caused him to be heavily fined, but deprived him of the right to lease land and employ convict servants! And he wants all newspapers to be licensed. Mr. Wentworth sold his share in the *Australian* to his partner, Dr. Waddell, and he has appeared as advocate for the defense in almost every case the Governor has brought—as well as campaigning for trial by nonmilitary juries."

"You have become quite the partisan, my dearest," Justin observed indulgently.

Jessica reddened. "Yes, perhaps I have. I certainly support Mr. Wentworth, and so do a great many others who believe that we should have representative government and a free press. It is time to reform, Justin. The people here are ready for it."

"Are they?" Justin questioned doubtfully.

"Yes, they are. But Governor Darling won't have it, and there's no denying that he is deserving of criticism on that account. He is too severe, too autocratic, and he won't tolerate anybody who dares to speak against him, even if what they say is true." Jessica sighed. "Murdo was exceptionally fortunate, you know," she went on gravely, "that Mr. Wentworth refused to reveal that he was the writer of that letter he published in the *Australian* about conditions in the Moreton Bay prison."

Justin sat up, frowning. "How so, Jessie?"

"Because he might well have shared the fate of Captain

Robison, of the Veteran Corps. *He* spoke up about the treatment of those two soldiers, Sudds and Thompson . . . you remember, the Governor had them drummed out of the regiment and sentenced to hard labor.''

"Yes, I remember. Sudds died in jail. What happened to Captain Robison?''

"Governor Darling had him tried by court-martial and cashiered. He is still being held in arrest, Justin—and he has a wife and family to support. Murdo, thank heaven, has gone with a party led by Mr. Hume to explore one of the rivers beyond the Blue Mountains. The Macquarie, I think. He was here for a few days, and I was thankful to see him depart for Bathurst with the advance party. But . . .'' Jessica's expression relaxed. "I haven't told you one of the best things that have happened whilst you've been away.''

"No,'' Justin confirmed, with mock severity. "All I have heard so far has been a tirade against the Governor. Tell me about this good thing, will you not? To whom did it happen?''

"To the boy Claus—Master Claus Van Buren, as he is in future to be known.'' Jessica paused, to let her words sink in.

"Van Buren?'' Justin's face registered his astonishment. "What on earth happened, Jess?''

"You remember, of course, his father's death,'' Jessica continued. "Well, Lucy Van Buren is also dead. She was on her way to Parramatta during a very bad storm, and her carriage horses bolted and crashed into a fallen tree.''

Justin felt no regret on Lucy Van Buren's account; he felt still less when informed that she, too, had attempted to follow her late husband's example and send the boy back to the Dutch Indies.

"Murdo told me about it,'' Jessica went on. "By a lucky chance, the master of the *Dorcas* was arrested, and they found poor little Claus tied up in the hold. . . .'' She enlarged on the story and added, "The good—the wonderful part is that Major Van Buren must have relented. He

left a will, admitting that Claus was his legitimate son by
his first wife and making him his heir. He inherits
everything, Justin—the house, Major Van Buren's ships,
and a considerable sum of money! Of course, there's a
spate of gossip and speculation—every tongue in Sydney
has been wagging about it. The elitists are horrified at the
thought of a little half-caste boy becoming so rich. But I'm
delighted. Most of all, I think, I'm glad for Claus's sake
that his father acknowledged him. That will mean so much
to him."

More, perhaps, than even Jessica realized, Justin thought,
as memory stirred and he remembered the boy's frightened
words when first he had been brought on board the *Elizabeth*,
badly burned by the distress rocket he had been attempting
to fire from the half-submerged *Flinders*.

Oh, please, sir, he had begged, when addressed as
Master Van Buren, *do not call me by that name. I am
known by my mother's name—which is—was Karimon.*

"And what does Claus intend to do with his newfound
wealth?" Justin asked. "Has he said?"

"He told Johnny that he wanted to build a fine new
school for Mr. Cox, in which"—Jessica was smiling—"he
himself proposes to enroll, and he's invited Johnny to join
him. He was with the Coxes—with Alice and her husband—in Windsor, it seems, when the news of his inheritance reached him. But he's here in Sydney now, and I
understand that he will give a party for all his friends at the
Bridge Street house before he goes back to make his home
with Nathan and Alice. And look, Justin dear—" Jessica
rose and took a small piece of pasteboard from the
mantelshelf. "We are invited . . . all of us, including little
Jenny. It will be quite an occasion, I think, so I hope that
you will be free to escort me there."

The invitation was handwritten, in painstaking and somewhat uneven capitals, and Justin felt an odd tightening of
his throat as he read it. In the Van Buren's day, neither he
nor Jessica would have been deemed worthy of inclusion

on the guest list, but now . . . He restored the card to its proud place on the mantel and, turning, drew his wife into his arms.

"You are right, my sweet wife—that *was* one of the best things that happened in my absence. And I shall make a point of being free so as to escort you to Bridge Street. Now I must tear myself away and go out to the *Mermaid* for a couple of hours. You'll be here when I come back, won't you?"

"I shall be here," Jessica told him softly. "I shall always be here, waiting for you to come back—you and Red—for as long as I live."

Afterword

The discovery of gold in the Bathurst area of New South
Wales in the mid-nineteenth century marked a turning
point in Australia's history. Small quantities of alluvial
gold had been found and reported before that time, but
successive Governors, from Macquarie to Gipps, fearing
the effect of such a discovery on the largely convict
population, had suppressed the reports and discouraged
further searches.

These momentous years will be the background for *The
Gold Seekers,* Volume Seven in The Australians series.
Readers who have followed the adventures, lives, and
loves of the fictional characters in perhaps two or three, or
even all six, of the books in the series, will miss them, as I
shall myself. But they have played their part in the foundation of Australia; it is now their descendants who will take
the stage—Justin and Jessica Broome's sons and their
daughter, Jenny; Rick and Katie Tempest's children, and
those of George and Rachel De Lancey; the lonely little
boy Claus Van Buren, now grown to manhood; Jamie
Willoughby and his sisters; Dickon O'Shea and Alice Cox.

Australia will have grown by 1850, with new states and
capital cities following in the wake of New South Wales
and Sydney . . . Perth, Western Australia, the fulfillment
of Captain Stirling's dream; Melbourne—originally named
Bearbrass—in the state of Victoria; Adelaide, South Australia, which resulted from the dream of a man sent to
Newgate Prison for eloping with an heiress, and who
worked out a theory for successful colonization without
ever seeing Australia.

The transportation of convicts to New South Wales will have ceased since 1840; Perth and Adelaide were built without their labor, and even Van Diemen's Land—renamed Tasmania in 1853—eventually called a halt to this method of clearing British jails of their felons, but was left with almost seventy thousand even then.

Courageous explorers such as Charles Sturt, George Grey (who was later to govern New Zealand), the brothers Hamilton, John Hume and the two Cunninghams, George Macleay, T. L. Mitchell, Edward Eyre, and Count de Strzelecki have followed in the footsteps of Oxley, Meehan, Throsby, and Hovell, finding vast pastures and long rivers, new lakes and hostile, waterless deserts. Settlers, "squatters" with their ever-increasing demands for more land for their flocks and herds, overlanders, with meat on the hoof to sell to new communities, have in turn followed the explorers and the pioneers. Convicts—many transported for trivial offenses—have toiled, unnamed and now forgotten, to build roads and homes and farmsteads, to guard the sheep and shear them, and muster and drive the cattle herds through trackless country to wherever their destination might be.

It has taken the efforts of all these, as well as those of soldiers and seamen, lawyers and judges, merchants, traders, shipbuilders, chaplains, and surgeons—and of their womenfolk—to build Australia. Now the lure of gold, the dream of riches there for the taking, will influence, in some way, every living soul among them, with the exception of the native people they have displaced. . . .

William Stuart Long
November 1983